a good girl
comes undone

a good girl
comes undone

polly williams

phere

SPHERE

First published in Great Britain in 2008 by Sphere

A CIP catalogue record for this book
is available from the British Library.

ISBN 978 1 84744 069 3

Typeset in Sabon by M Rules
Printed and bound in Great Britain by
Clays Ltd, St Ives plc

Sphere
An imprint of
Little, Brown Book Group
100 Victoria Embankment
London EC4Y 0DY

An Hachette Livre UK Company

www.littlebrown.co.uk

For my boys

Acknowledgements

A special thank you to my agent Lizzy Kremer and my editor
Jo Dickinson, also Duncan Spilling, Tamsin Kitson, Helen
Gibbs, Tamsyn Berryman and everyone at Little, Brown who
have worked so very hard on all my books. I really couldn't
have finished this novel without the support of my family and
friends since I went and had a baby in the middle of writing
it, so thank you mum, Mel and the Queen's Park posse, especially Willie Birrell for making Fridays so much fun on so
little sleep. Thanks to Abi Fry for the medical stuff (any inac-
curacies are mine), Tammy Perry for helping me through Title
Torment, and Cheryl Konteh for being there back then and
making me laugh about it now. Finally, big thank you to my
husband Ben Chase – I couldn't done it without you.

One

A mild Monday morning in September. Happily, it doesn't feel like the kind of day when anything much is going to happen, not from where I am sitting, collapsed as I am in the comforting leather scoop of a hairdresser's chair. Then, at 11.06 a.m., I get the call. I leap up from the chair, tugging at the overall's tie belt with clumsy fingers as the confused stylist reluctantly uncoils a section of my hair from the barrel brush. I apologise profusely, explaining that yes, it *is* my day off, but I've been called back to the office. I can't risk my career for a blow-dry, sorry. Outside the cloakroom I pull on my coat with one hand and use the other to call my younger sister Georgia and cancel lunch.

'Boring,' says Georgia. There is loud music in the background. 'Your office is like a bloody gulag. Can't you just say you didn't pick up the message or something? Or better still, can't you just say no, just once? Go on, Annie. I dare you.'

'I've got to go in,' I say, cradling the phone uncomfortably under my chin as I stand at the reception desk, punching my pin number into the credit card machine. 'I would much rather have lunch with you, believe me. It's been ages. Is everything OK?'

'Everything is amazing. Totally amazing. I just wanted to run through wedding stuff, that's all. Never mind. I'll just have to do what I do best and carry on shopping,' Georgia says, in deliberate self-parody. Georgia is shopping for honeymoon lingerie in Selfridges. She can do this on a Monday because she doesn't work. 'Love you,' she says. And the line goes dead.

On George Street I fling a hand up at the stampeding traffic to hail a cab. My coat flaps open, exposing clothes that I threw on this morning with the cover-up of a hairdresser's overall in mind. My apple-green pillow-sized handbag pulls one side of my body pavement-wards so that I have the gait of a woman perilously askew, as if a little nudge might send me off balance. I get into the taxi with a loud exhalation.

'Bad day, love?' the driver asks.

I smile and nod and catch sight of my nodding reflection in the window. Oh. Do I look like a woman who has just stepped out of the salon? No. I do not. The taxi window reflects a forehead as shiny as a patent pump and half-blown-out hair that has already regressed back to its natural state of Billy Connolly frizz. My left eyelid twitches. My jaw is locked. This is what happens when I get stressed. This is what happens when I am called into the magazine offices for some kind of crisis management, without the right shoes (I'm in ancient trainers) or mental preparation. The transformation of Annie Rafferty, eldest daughter of the Raffertys of Lower Dalton – 'sensible, hard-working, like a good shire horse', as my dad once memorably described me – to savvy, urbane glossy magazine journalist is not an effortless one.

Pressing my face closer to the window, I watch London stream past, a blur of feet, movement and urgency, a city that should have been somewhere else ten minutes ago. When we stop at the traffic lights, everything seems to freeze-frame. I text Nick: *Back to office. Sigh. xxx*

Nicholas Angus Rupert Colt, age thirty-six, hotel PR. My lovely boyfriend. I left him this morning in a bit of a state at the breakfast table, trussed up in a suit and talking about how he was mourning the loss of his self-respect. Nick, bless him, is having a career crisis. He has a lot of these. Over Marmite toast, I did my best to provide wise counsel about his PR job, reassuring him that a job is just a means to an end – grateful he didn't press me as to what end exactly – and that it really doesn't define you as a person.

'How can you of all people say that?' he said, swiping the last piece of toast off my plate and giving me a Marmitey kiss on the lips. 'It don't wash, babe.'

I guess he has a point. Three years ago, after a long stint working on the no-frills features pages of a tabloid newspaper magazine, I got the job I'd always wanted, on a monthly. No matter that it was features editor of *Glo*, an understaffed mid-market glossy with cascading sales figures. No matter that my editor, Pippa Woodside, told me that she appointed me because I reeked of hard work. And Pippa was right: I've worked hard, very hard, to prove myself: long days, weekends, phone calls from LA in the middle of the night, an endless stream of editorial ideas spewing out of me like a long document rolling out of a fax machine. And the slog has paid off. A few weeks ago I got promoted to deputy editor, a move which has put me firmly on track to the apex of the masthead.

As my responsibilities have grown, the job has burrowed itself into my subconscious, implanted itself in my DNA. I find it tricky to pass a newsagent without rearranging the shelves, hustling *Glo* to the prime selling pitch. I wake up in the night panicking about flat plans. I regularly dream in cover lines, so that the most surreal, delicate dreams, even the erotic and nightmarish, assume a kind of jingoistic quality, floating through my head like advertising flags dragged across the sky by small planes. Sometimes I think up free gift ideas during sex.

So, yes, I guess my job does kind of define me. But, as Nick likes to point out, my job does not always make me happy. I explain that happiness isn't the point. It's not, is it? Happiness comes inexplicably and unexpectedly when you're busy doing other things, like organising tins of chickpeas in the kitchen cupboard according to their descending sell-by dates, or striding along a London street, wind in the hair, rushing between appointments, and for no reason at all you get that elated feeling in the chest, exactly where the heart is and you prickle with aliveness. I think I am far more scared of being bored than I am of working hard, which is possibly why I have suitcases beneath my eyes. The thing is, I am still officially on trial period and therefore have to prove myself worthy of the deputy editor role on a daily basis. So yes, I may be near the top of the masthead, but it feels like it's swinging perilously in a mounting gale. Pippa can turn around in a few months and say, 'Do you really feel this is working out, Annie?' Subtext: 'It's not working out. You're rubbish. Move over.'

This scenario is terrifying for many reasons – the shame, obviously, a lifetime's ambition shattered around my feet, etc. – but also because the day after my promotion, flushed with my salary hike, Nick and I pulled out of buying a two-bedroom flat in Harlesden and snapped up the house we really wanted instead, the much more expensive three-bedroom cottage in Kensal Rise with the lovely leaf-green door.

We moved in last month, feeling childishly grown-up, marvelling at how wonderful it felt to have a house with stairs, bullish about paying the fat mortgage on our new appreciating asset.

It's noon now. I'm tipping the cabbie. I'm smiling hello to Jacqui behind the reception desk and swiping through the barriers, up, up, up in the juddering lift. I'm walking across the Starbucks-stained carpet tiles. I am at my desk. Now, for the crisis. Bring it on!

Seven hours later, I slam down the phone, muttering, 'Make it stop!' I try to work out how to launder the facts of their grubbiest bits before relaying them to Pippa. This is difficult, very difficult. Despite spending most of the afternoon with my ear soldered to the telephone, I have not managed to negotiate a cover star for our December issue. We did have one booked – a young up-and-coming actress – but recent glowing reviews means she's now up, and consequently she's dumped us for a more prestigious magazine. Our cover, which must go to the printers pretty soon, remains alarmingly empty, like an unpopular abdicated throne.

Most people have gone home now. The office is very quiet, melancholy, like an empty shop out of hours. I gaze out of the two enormous tinted windows – a perk: the more senior you are, the more window you get – which are at right angles to my kidney-shaped grey plastic desk. At eight floors up it's a good view. The snake of the Thames. Waterloo Bridge. The Royal Festival Hall. And, my favourite, the London Eye, which turns so slowly it always strikes me as a rather good symbol of life's important stuff – faces, relationships – that changes imperceptibly but surely by the moment. Good days, up here, I feel on top of the world. On bad days, like today, I feel more like a specimen in a grubby glass box, breathing in

5

the air-conditioned cocktail of other people's autumn viruses. (I suspect that they emanate from the great unwashed working at Quad-Bike Digest on the third floor.) The moon is already visible, white, cut like a fingernail. It is late. It is time to admit defeat and wrap the day.

I knock on Pippa's door. No response. Pushing it slightly ajar, I see the HQ is empty. It is a square space about the size of two large walk-in wardrobes, with sparkling floor-to-ceiling windows on one side, framing London like a postcard, opaque glass walls on the other. The back wall is stamped with black-and—white photographs of cover stars. Pippa's desk is large and glacier-white. Her high-backed black leather ergonomic chair dominates one side of it. On the other side of the desk is a small low-backed orange fabric chair, designed to foster feelings of inferiority and discomfort. The desk itself has a neat, ordered, end-of-the-day landscape: one Yellow Pages-sized diary; a square glass vase of antique-pink roses; a stack of invitations to parties and PR events; a photograph of Pippa's husband Martin, a man in his late fifties, Big In Telly, salt-and-pepper-haired, wearing jeans and an open-necked shirt in the freshly pressed way of a man who spends most of his life in a Kilgour suit.

One day that should be my name on this door, and if not this door, another door. That's always been the plan. I bite my lip. It tastes coppery, like a two-pence piece. A ceiling vent shudders a refrigerated wind down upon my head. Shit. Where is Pippa?

'Hi, Annie,' says Belle, suddenly appearing at my side. Belle is Pippa's PA, a gentle twenty-two-year-old with a head of chestnut Klimt curls and the longest, thinnest legs. She walks with the uncertain gait of a newly born faun.

'Hi there. I'm looking for the boss,' I say.

'She's gone already, I'm afraid. Power Plate session,' Belle explains. 'Then she's got the hairdresser.' She winces apologetically. 'She said you'd understand.'

Yes, I understand. Pippa is successful because she delegates. Mostly to me. 'Shit.'

'She's back in tomorrow, late morning, after breakfast at the Wolseley,' says Belle. 'Shall I book you in?'

'Thanks, Belle.'

I return to my desk and swipe my life into my bag: Carmex lip salve, gnarled notebook, mobile, a bag of raw almonds, address book with G and H come loose and an assortment of biscuit crumbs squashed between its pages. I turn off the computer. But rather than shutting down the screen, which displays my email inbox, it freezes and flickers. The hard drive starts to hiss malevolently beneath my desk. Cursing the new IT system put into the offices at great expense and with much pedantry last month, I fiddle with the computer, hitting random buttons in vain.

As I smack the keys harder and harder, something balloons inside. A weird, foreign feeling locks in my throat, an exhausted, tearful heaviness. What on earth is *wrong* with me? Hormones. It must be hormones. Throwing myself back in the office chair, I swivel it around 180 degrees with my feet up like a petulant child, stopping to face the window. The traffic hoots. The London Eye turns. My stomach knots. Then, suddenly, a small fleet of starlings appear from nowhere, as if dislodged from the building itself, and arrow past the window, like uncaged office souls plunging to freedom.

For a moment, I allow myself to think the unthinkable. Is this it? Petty skirmishes with celebrity agents. The prospect of turning into Pippa. What if, after all my work, all my

7

grafting, I'd actually be a happier person doing something else? Isn't there something else at the heart of me, packed petals waiting to unfold, to flower?

Deep breath.

Eat half a Pret a Manger brownie.

I remind myself: I'm not trapped. I am not like my friend Vicky, who, still single, has no one to split the bills with, no one to cushion her should she ever fall, that she is unlikely ever to fall is beside the point. Knowing that Nick is the net beneath me is immensely reassuring. Together we are strong, more than the sum of our parts. If I wanted to change lanes, I could. Thank goodness for Nick. The panic subsides. My breathing eases. The computer finally shuts down, inexplicably, as if it's just got bored of being difficult. I slip out of the office. Outside, it is raining lightly. Kicking up the conkers scattered over the pavement like dropped chocolates, I make my way through the wet grey autumn evening, towards the comforts of home.

Back in Kensal Rise, Nick sits with his blue-socked feet up on the armchair, a beer in one hand, remote control in the other, channel-hopping to locate rugby scores. He's already changed out of his suit. Seeing me, he grins, takes his feet off the chair. He is a different shape to the man who left for his office in such a hurry this morning, his body longer, relaxed, like a cat flexing in the sun. Nick's sexiness – his tufty blond hair, the lazy curl of his wide smile, and his gentle eyes, hazel lined with calligrapher's black – brings a bubble of love to the surface. It is good, very good, to be home. I throw myself towards him and land on his knee, all ten stone of me hitting him with the force of an emergency food parcel drop. I wrap my arms around his neck and smatter his cheek with kisses.

'Ugh, you're soggy!' He laughs, pushing me away. 'Wasn't it meant to be your day off?'

'Yup.' I don't need to say any more. This has happened many times before. I recently had to cut short a romantic long weekend in Venice. I stand up, take off my damp coat and hang it on a peg in the hall.

Nick rises to his gangly six foot, all elbows and long sandy eyelashes. 'I've got something to tell you, Annie.'

'Really?' I say over my shoulder. 'Can we talk over supper? I need to eat, Nick, or I shall start gnawing the sofa. I'm thinking Lebanese. In fact, I've been fantasising about those fatayer pastry things all the way home. Or Indian. I could do Indian actually. To fatayer or to korma, now that is the question.'

Come here. Please. I want to tell you this first. It's important. I've made a decision.' Nick holds my hands and pulls me down next to him on the sofa. 'Do you remember we were talking this morning about me finding my . . .' he puts on an American accent, 'true vocation?'

I nod. We've had this conversation on and off for the whole three years we've been together. 'Yes, sweetheart.'

'Well. I've taken the first small step.'

'Great!' Fatayer. It's got to be Lebanese. I slap his knee. 'One small step for Nick, one huge step—'

'I'm taking a little sabbatical,' he interrupts.

'Oh? OK.' I sit up straight now, confused. A sabbatical? What a strange idea. 'I'm not with you.'

Nick grins. 'Well, it's a bit more than a sabbatical.'

'You're taking a break from the PR agency? When did you—'

'I've just taken voluntary redundancy, Annie.' He brings my right hand to his mouth and kisses it. 'I'm free!'

'Sorry?'

'I've taken voluntary redundancy!'

'You've *left* your job?' I ask, disbelieving.

'I have!' he says triumphantly. 'I have indeed.'

We stare at each other for a few bewildered moments.

'Why on earth . . .'

'It's all right, Annie. Don't worry. I've got an extra two months' salary.' He looks, more uncertain now. 'Tax free.'

'Two months?' I run my fingers through my hair. 'Is that all?'

'Yes.' Nick deflates, leaning forward, elbows on knees. 'Shit. Man, I thought you'd be pleased.'

I fiddle with the fingers on his left hand, bending them at the knuckles, stroking up their slim freckled length. Panic is lapping at my supportive intentions. 'Why didn't you mention it before?'

'I wanted to make this decision on my own. I needed to.' He pulls his hand away. 'It's my life and—'

'It's our mortgage. We've just bought a house.' This is not entirely accurate. Nick didn't have any money to put towards the deposit, whereas I'd managed to save thirty thousand pounds. It was his suggestion that the house be in my name only. He said, 'We're in it for the long haul so it doesn't matter.' And most of the time it doesn't matter. It makes sense: I wouldn't have bought the house without him because the mortgage is too big. He wouldn't have anywhere to live without me. We are symbiotic, interdependent, two creatures curled up in the same cosy nest, reliant on one another for our survival.

'Don't go into one. I'll get another job, Annie.'

I push into the pressure points on my temples. 'But you had a job, Nick.'

We glare at each other for a few moments as we both struggle to absorb our wildly opposed reactions to the same event. I can't believe he didn't tell me. If I was considering something like this, he would be the first person I would want to discuss it with. I feel cut out and hurt.

'Don't look at me like that, Annie. I hate that look. Man, you don't realise how lucky you are knowing what you want out of life.' Nick sighs. 'It was so impossible trying to get another job, the right job, when I was working at that soul-sucking vortex of a PR agency. I had no time, babe.'

'You had time to watch *Top Gear*.'

There is a silence, a blank blue sky filling with falling bombs of mutual resentment. I chew the inside of my cheek. Is it so terrible to wish the person you love could be a little less like themselves sometimes?

Nick shakes his head. 'You don't get anywhere in life without taking risks.' He speaks quietly, so I have to strain to hear him. His voice always becomes quieter and posher when he gets defensive, reclaiming the consonants he has shed since leaving public school. He reaches for my right hand and holds it tight. 'Have some faith in me. I feel like you have no faith in me.'

'That's not true.'

'Shhh.' He gets off the sofa, kneels on the floor and slips off my socks and shoes. He kisses the sole of my left foot. 'First a foot massage.' He kisses the sole of my right foot. 'Then I'll cook you supper.' He looks up, smiling. 'And you know what? While I look for another job, I am going to make you, my darling Annie, a most excellent wife.'

Two

'So how's the job-hunting going, sweetheart?' I ask carefully, as a boom of sunlight swings over the motorway and into our eyes.

Nick pulls down the sun visor, presses his foot on the accelerator and we roar faster down the A40, overtaking a juddering Tesco lorry. 'I've not started the actual hunting yet.' He glances at me. 'You know I said I wanted a bit of time to kick back and, like, think.'

'Of course,' I say, trying to be understanding. I've been trying to be understanding for three weeks now. 'I respect you for taking the plunge, I really do. But I do wonder . . .'

Nick grips the steering wheel harder, knuckles paling. 'Fuck, it's difficult,' he sighs. 'You know, one moment I want to make shitloads of money, become a property developer or something. The next I want to do something genuinely help-ful, become a fireman. Give something back. But most of the time . . .' he grins boyishly, 'I just want to DJ.'

The word DJ feels like a razor-edged twelve-inch record flung across the car and embedded in my stomach. The DJ-ing is a hobby that brings in the odd hundred quid here and there, if he is lucky. It is not a job. But I suspect that Nick, even at the age of thirty-six, still hopes he'll become the next Mark Ronson. Maybe he will. Maybe I should have more faith. 'OK.'

Nick frowns. 'What do you mean, OK? I hate your OK.'

'Nothing, Nick.'

'I know you disapprove, Annie. I know you think I should have it all sussed by now. But I never promised I would, and I haven't. Cut me some slack.'

'I didn't say anything!'

'You don't have to.' He presses his foot on the gas. 'I go against your Protestant work ethic. I'm a talking, walking, living embodiment of all your catastrophist fantasies.'

I smile, because there is a smidgen of truth in this.

Nick puts on a woman's high voice. 'The house will get repossessed! The house will burn down and we won't have insurance! All my alphabetically-arranged books will get muddled up! The sky is falling in!'

I whack him playfully on the side of the leg. 'Shut up, you!'

Nick hits the gas harder. I shoot him a glance and think how attractive he is when he drives, when he speeds. Part of me is turned on seeing him at the wheel, focused, in control.

After a few moments the car slows and turns off the motorway towards the A road that leads through the damp green Cotswold countryside to my parents' house. We park. Putting our differences aside, we interlace hands and walk across my parents' short gravel driveway and up the path to their front door. Having not visited for a few weeks, I am struck by how rundown the house looks. The flint-tiled roof is sinking in the middle. The blue paint on the front door is chipped, as is the paintwork around the upper mullioned windows. Ivy and Virginia creeper drape over the buttery

Cotswold stone walls and flare out along the ground like a skirt. The honeysuckle, gnarled and twiggy, is taking over the porch so I have to knock it back as I walk past and a shower of small insects falls into my hair. I ring the bell – one of those singsong ones from the eighties – and hear Mum amble down the hall with her tricky hip.

'Annie! Nick!' she exclaims, opening the front door. Her weatherbeaten face brightens at the sight of the pair of us, whom she always calls, just a little cringily, 'my accomplished daughter and her lovely Nick'.

'Sorry we're late,' I say. We are always late for my parents. It's not intentional. It just kind of happens.

'Oh, gosh, don't worry. Georgia's late too, of course. Wow, don't you two look glamorous!'

Although at work I am one of the least glamorous people in the office, at home it's as if I've just stepped off the red carpet. It doesn't take much to be glamorous in Lower Dalton. As we walk inside, the reassuring smell of home – cleaning products, digestive biscuits and peaty country dust – hits me. The hall leads to the kitchen, in fact the whole house seems to lead to the kitchen, its domestic drumbeat of boiling kettles and firing boilers. As long as I can remember it's always looked exactly the same: the walls are painted sunshine-yellow gloss, country-style pine units rims its edges, alongside a temperamental ivy-green Aga and an old oven that can be reliably counted on to overcook most meals. The cupboards are archaeological: I recently unearthed a congealed pot of Bovril with a sell-by date of April 1999. Grease-spattered family photos, Oxfam leaflets and local flyers for Indian restaurants flutter in the draughts that creep through the brickwork. Occasionally the leaflets loosen from their Blu-Tack and drop down on to the rectangular pine table, the centre of the room, where decades

14

of family mealtimes ferment in its grooves and dips. Dad, the grumpy beast answering to the name Arnold Rafferty when the mood takes him, sits at the far end of the table, bent over *The Cotswold Journal*, his familiar bald head a pink disc among rogue grey wisps. He looks up and his eyes light like rooms. Dad loves a visit.

'Hi, Dad,' I say, kissing him on his bristly cheek, as familiar as my own. He smells faintly of whisky.

'Cup of tea?' interjects Mum, as if scared of Dad speaking and boring us before she's had a chance to secure us firmly in the house with hospitality. She is the only person I know who offers tea before lunch.

'We brought some wine.' Nick hands over a tissue-wrapped bottle of red. It is from a garage, bought in a mad rush en route and, shamefully, not the kind of wine we'd take to a dinner party in London.

'Oooh.' Mum peels back the tissue carefully. 'Very posh. You shouldn't have. You do the honours, Arnold.'

Dad stands up. Has he shrunk? He looks shorter than I remember. He attacks the neck of the wine bottle with an ancient bottle-opener, pulls the cork out with a wild jerk of the elbow and looks up triumphantly at Nick, as if a small masculine ritual has been accomplished. Dad can be embarrassingly competitive.

Mum stands at the cabinet to pull out some dishwasher-smeared wine glasses, the small ones that seem to fit only a thimble of wine, not like the large bowls on stems Nick and I use in London. I admire her great figure. Unlike most of my friends' mothers she has not grown stodgy with age. When she's not cooking for all the family – an occasion that usually means seventies food, chilli con carne, pasta bake – she lives on a diet reminiscent of post-war rations – new potatoes,

15

unseasoned lamb chops, peas and cabbage from the garden –
and this has kept her remarkably lithe. (My father is not so
lithe; the pints of beer and decades of fried breakfasts in the
work canteen have puddled around his middle.) I only wish
Mum would realise she's gorgeous. If she was a lady of the
same age and figure living in Kensington, she'd probably be
wearing skinny jeans and a tailored blazer and look thirty-five
years old from behind. But Mum's A-line knee-length skirts,
neat little cardigans and floral blouses have remained more or
less the same for as long as I can remember. They are not a
young person's clothes. (Judging from the family albums,
Mum stopped being young – as in fashion-conscious and friv-
olous – at about the age of thirty.) After a glass of wine she
will sometimes joke, 'I am above fashion.' But what she really
means, I guess, is that fashion isn't relevant to a woman in her
sixties called Marjorie living in a small village in the
Cotswolds. Still, I admire the fact that she's unashamedly
much more interested in runner beans. And Dad, of course,
doesn't give two hoots what she wears. He loves her truly,
madly, deeply, whatever. We all love her whatever.

Mum pours the wine carefully and sits down with a
Sunday afternoon sigh. 'Well,' she says. 'Well.' She studies me
in that particularly hawk-like maternal way, assessing the
sheen on my hair, the clearness of my skin, looking for tell-
tale signs of urban decay. 'It's lovely to see you both. I know
how busy you get.'

'Don't be silly. This is a treat. We were gasping for fresh
air,' I reassure her. Unlike my more leisured sister, Georgia, I
don't visit as much as I should. Mum tries to understand and
puts this down to my job, as if I were running the country
rather than working on a floundering glossy magazine. I feel
bad about not visiting more.

16

'Fresh air. One thing you Londoners can't buy,' acknowledges Dad gruffly. He is suspicious of London, wary of its influence, as if we are living under the guardianship of a particularly irresponsible and spoiling aunt.

'How is the big city?' Mum is convinced that knife-happy teenagers, jihadis and crack cocaine exist on every London street corner. 'And your mortgage is manageable, is it? There's talk of interest rates going up, you know.'

Nick shifts awkwardly in his seat. 'Well . . .'

I strangle the stem of my wine glass with my index finger. I know that Nick is rearranging his thoughts to get it to sound OK. They'll find out sooner or later, so he has decided to come out with it. Just as his mouth opens, he is interrupted by the doorbell.

'That'll be your sister! Always so late.' Mum speeds to the door, tricky hip forgotten.

There is the sound of extravagant kissing and Georgia's unmistakable public school accent, developed without ever going to public school.

'Annie! Nick, gorgeous!' Georgia skits over and throws her arms around Nick, then me. 'At last we manage to actually meet up this century.'

I laugh, starting a little at quite how beautiful she is. Her looks are genuinely impressive. They always have been. When we were growing up, I almost felt a sense of sibling pride about her beauty, as if it rubbed off on me in some way. Because there was such discrepancy in our looks and she was younger than me, jealousy wasn't as much of an issue as it might perhaps have been, although as teenagers I did wish we could have shared a few more genes, obviously. But when we were little, little-girl little, strangers frequently stopped on the street to look at Georgia, just stop in their tracks and stare. I would stiffen when they reached out to touch her red curls, ready to snatch her back and fight them off. I was always protective of her, sensing even as a child that her beauty made her vulnerable, too easily the canvas on to which people projected their abstract dark desires. I remember thinking that if a baddie were to steal one of us away, they'd take her. I would be safe.

My sister has grown into her beauty gracefully, accepting it without shyness or awkwardness, and built her personality around it, as you can build an entire wardrobe around one exquisite coat. Her hair, possibly the first thing you might notice about her, is thick, wavy and the colour of rich gingerbread. Her eyes are uncommonly far apart and a warm syrupy brown. Her upper lip is slightly swollen, like it's been artfully banged. Put her in a shellsuit and she'd still look like she'd stepped off the pages of *Vogue*. Of course, Georgia doesn't wear shellsuits. Even the North Face puffa jacket she's wearing makes her look like a pretty child bundled up against the wind. (Puffa jackets make me look like a large piece of camping equipment come lose from its mooring.) Georgia shakes the coat off, and unwraps herself like a present to reveal a gamine navy A-line mini-dress, accessorised by slim bare legs and black ballet flats, a quilted gold-chained bag slung over one shoulder. She is the kind of woman all magazine editors desperately hope actually exists.

Mum strokes Georgia's arm, concerned. 'Darling, you look so thin.'

'Really?' Georgia grins. She's inherited Mum's neat, petite ectomorph, unlike me, who has to battle genetic sympathy with a 'big-boned' Scottish great-grandmother. Mum might think that Georgia looks too thin, but the truth is she looks fabulous, still curvy, just teeny, without an inch of surplus flesh, like a Hollywood actress. She collapses into a breathy heap on a kitchen chair, pulling her slim legs beneath her, flashing the gusset of pink knickers with the carelessness of a little girl in a playground. 'God,' she says. 'Olly sends huge apologies. He's completely devastated that he can't be here.'

Mum looks awkward, pours Georgia a glass of wine and puts a small earthenware bowl of green olives on the table. 'It's OK, dear. We understand.' She doesn't understand, nor does Dad. It is beyond them why a healthy thirty-five-year-old city banker poised to marry such a beautiful girl as Georgia is having 'a bit of a life crisis' and has chosen – no, paid – to spend a week in a mental health institution. My father can't square this with Olly's ability to earn vast sums of money: is he an alpha male or isn't he?

'He's back from Tranquillity tomorrow,' says Georgia, sipping her wine and wincing at its sour garage cheapness. 'I'm hoping a nice rest will have sorted his head out.'

Georgia makes Tranquillity sound like a health spa holiday. Being more from the 'pull yourself together school', like my father, I'm of the opinion that the people who really need treatment are walking the London streets talking to cans of Special Brew, rather than city bankers who are functional enough to holiday in Miami days before they check in.

'I read in the papers that that place costs thousands a week, or some such nonsense,' huffs Dad, pulling at his beard. He flashes an amused glance in my direction. I smile. We both know he is playing to the house.

'It does, yeah,' says Georgia casually, nibbling an olive. When it came to finances, she is no longer her father's daughter.

'Good grief!' exclaims Dad. 'Maybe I should open my own bleeding loony bin.'

'That really would be a case of the lunatics running the asylum,' I joke.

Mum clears her throat. 'Let's all hope Olly's feeling much more like his old self.' Uncomfortable with the conversation, unsure what she can usefully add, she walks across the undulating terracotta floor with a slightly lopsided gait and puts garden vegetables in the plastic stack steamer.

'So how's tricks, Nick?' asks Georgia. 'I'm feeling like a stranger to you two right now. Annie blew me out for lunch again last week. How is a girl meant to keep up?' Georgia bats her dark lashes. She flirts with Nick, always has done. She's flirted with all my boyfriends. It is just the way she relates to men. All of them fall a little bit in love with her. There's nothing I can do about it. Anyway, I figure if they want to be with a girl like Georgia, they wouldn't be with me.

'Well,' says Nick slowly. We exchange glances. We both know it is time. I brace myself.

Nick looks around the kitchen, avoiding Dad's eye. 'Actually,' he hesitates, scratching his stubble, 'I've taken voluntary redundancy to give myself a chance to find something more interesting.'

Georgia claps her hands. 'Bingo! I've got a new cinema matinee partner! Well done! Working's totally overrated.' Georgia gave up paddling around what she calls the shallows of the publishing industry two years ago, after getting engaged to Olly. Her income was not needed and they decided her time would be much better spent decorating the house and, more recently, helping the wedding organiser organise their wedding.

'George,' I say, plucking an olive out of her fingers and putting it in my mouth, 'if you try to turn Nick into a lunching lady, I'll have a tracking device attached to his ankle.'

Nick laughs awkwardly. 'I'm looking for other work. It's not a permanent state of affairs.'

'Shame,' says Georgia.

Out of the corner of my eye, I see Mum frozen with a sieved spoon raised in her hand, face loose with bewilderment. I want to turn around and reassure her, but fear this will undermine Nick.

'So you've finally got on the property ladder and you've chosen to become unemployed?' asks Dad. Unemployment and debt – even the smallest credit at the grocer – are things he's avoided all his life. He has worked and saved, saved and worked. Volunteering for unemployment is as incomprehensible to him as volunteering for a mental health institution.

'For the moment, Arnold,' says Nick, struggling to maintain a bright smile.

'Blimey. I didn't see that coming.' Dad shakes his paper out and unplugs a piece of food from his incisors with his tongue. 'Marj shouldn't be inviting you down here for Sunday lunch. I'm sure you want to be getting on with the job hunt.'

'There's plenty of time, Dad,' I say, loyally. Hell, I'll embellish. 'Nick's got a very good redundancy package.'

Georgia laughs. 'Yeah, he's got you, Annie!'

Nick scuffs his trainers against the table leg. I roll my eyes at Georgia in an exaggerated fashion so that she knows there's a line and she's crossed it. Georgia mouths 'sorry' to me from behind her hand, but is smiling mischievously and doesn't look very sorry at all. She is always cheekier, more alive somehow, more like my sister, without Olly in tow.

Dad looks sternly at Nick. 'The problem . . .' he drains his glass of wine, 'the problem, my son, is pensions. That's what you've got to keep in mind. You don't want a big gap in your pension contributions when you and Annie are my age.

21

You don't want to be working when you've got a dicky ticker.'

'Nope!' Nick cocks his head to one side and smiles deferentially. He understands Dad instinctively, his need to dominate, to play the silverback in his family of females. But he cannot imagine he'll ever have a dicky ticker. He's a DJ, after all. DJs don't get dicky tickers. DJs don't get old.

'As you know, your dad officially retires next week,' says Mum, banging some potato off the masher into the pan. 'Which is just as well. I thought he was going to carry on working until he dropped.'

Dad shrugs, but I can tell that secretly he is pleased that Mum has brought his hard work to our attention. 'Nothing falls into your lap,' he always tells me. (For some reason he never feels the urge to offer the same advice to Georgia. Beauty is its own currency, perhaps.)

'We're going to have a bit of fun with it, aren't we, Arnold?' says Mum. 'Do start, everyone, before it gets cold.'

'Well, I don't know about fun. But I'm looking forward to putting my feet up in the sun somewhere and getting out of this godforsaken country for the winter.' Dad pushes his glasses up his nose.

'I can see you on a Caribbean beach, Dad. Can't you, George?' I say. 'Pina colada. Handkerchief on your head, tapping along to "No Woman No Cry".'

Georgia puts her hands over her face. 'Don't! I've got visions of Dad on holiday. God, he's going to be such an embarrassing retiree.'

'Oh, I fully intend to be horribly embarrassing.' Dad grins. 'This smells bloody good, Marj.' He turns to Georgia. 'Olly's got his pension sorted, I suppose?'

Georgia and I lock feet under the table. For some reason

we start to get the giggles, as if we were teenagers. Visiting our parents always makes both of us regress about twenty years.

'Arnold,' says Mum. 'Money talk is so very dull at Sunday lunch.'

'Only because you make no effort to understand it,' says Dad, who has long been gatekeeper to the household finances. Mum, being a woman, understands other things. Like his daughters. And how to cook a good Sunday roast. 'Georgia?'

'Daddy.' (Georgia inexplicably started calling Dad 'Daddy' two years ago, which is kind of irritating.) 'It is different when you're earning as much as Olly.' She tosses flames of red hair off her face. 'He is probably going to retire next year. After our honeymoon.'

'Next year!' Dad clatters heavy cutlery to his plate. 'Gordon Bennett! He'll be thirty-six, won't he? Has the world gone stark raving mad?' He looks at me for collusion. I think he thinks I am the nearest he's got to a son sometimes. This may have something to do with the fact that I refused to wear dresses when I was a girl. I liked trousers and shorts and Dad's old boyhood train set. Whereas Georgia inhabited a pink planet orbited by sequins. These differences were tolerated by my mother and indulged by my father – 'Some girls will be boys,' he'd chuckle – until about the age of twelve, when they decided that if left to my own devices I might be in danger of turning into Martina Green on Birch Close, a lesbian who wore hand-knitted rainbow-striped jumpers. So Mum took me shopping at Laura Ashley. Understandably, my parents were confused but delighted when I moved from tabloid newspapers into women's magazines, and the fact that, after a long romantic drought, I met Nick soon after was put down to the more feminine career move.

'Olly's worked so hard, so very hard,' continues Georgia, as if salary is directly related to effort, which, sadly, in my experience it isn't. 'He's earned enough now, what with the boners—' Georgia crushes her hand to her mouth and can't meet my eye because she knows she'll explode if she does. She jokes about them being boners because Olly's always randy after landing one. 'I mean bonuses.'

'A man needs to work,' Dad mumbles through a mouthful of potato.

'Goodness,' says Mum, taking it all in. 'Goodness.' She takes a large swig of her wine. 'Well, you're a very lucky girl, Georgia. A very lucky girl indeed.'

Georgia smiles brightly. 'I know I am.' Her sugar-brown eyes flash with happiness. I feel a stab of tenderness for my younger sister. When she is conscious of her good fortune it is impossible to begrudge it. Some people have charmed lives, and Georgia is one of them, born not so much with a silver spoon in her mouth as a perfect open pout ready to accept one. 'But money really doesn't matter,' she sighs, pulling on a Brora cashmere cardigan that must have cost little short of £200. 'You know what? I'm just looking forward . . .' She pauses. 'And I know Annie, being scarily successful, will think I'm some kind of twenty-first-century anachronism . . .' she smiles apologetically at me, 'but I'm just looking forward to being a wife and having kids.'

Dad guffaws with approval.

Nick makes an annoying 'ahh' sound like this is the cutest thing he's heard all year.

Dig beneath the surface and is this what all men want really? A beautiful girl with uncomplicated desires mostly concerning handbags and babies, as opposed to a tricksy career-driven thirtysomething with attitude (Dad's words, not mine).

Mum, her pinked eyes betraying the effects of the wine, beams at the end of the table. She leans over and squeezes Dad's hand. 'A husband and kids made me very happy.'

I'm torn between finding this comment sweetly moving and, well, kind of irritating. Sometimes it's hard not to wonder what the slog has all been for – the good grades, the work experience, the career, all the things my parents both encouraged – if at a certain point they then turn around and tell me that the most satisfaction a woman can get from life comes from a husband and children.

'Nick, Annie. Have you . . .' Mum's voice drifts as she began to question her tact. But it's too late.

There is silence bar the sound of collective chewing on a particularly muscular organic fowl.

'Sorry, have I said the wrong thing?' asks Mum, making it all instantly more wrong.

'Marjorie . . .' Dad wipes his greasy fingers on an ironed 'Sunday lunch' napkin. He shoots Nick a sharp glance, as if Nick were a man taking advantage of his elder daughter, a daughter who, in his eyes, is getting on a bit and could do with taming with a wedding ring.

I stare at my plate. What neither of my parents realises is that me and Nick haven't discussed marriage, not properly. It isn't marked on life's wall chart in red pen. Only in the last few months, partly because of our respective ages – me thirty-four, Nick thirty-six – but mostly because of Georgia's imminent wedding, has the subject taken up residence in our bedroom at odd hours, squatting there watchfully during arguments or in tender pauses after lovemaking. I wonder what Nick thinks. I don't want to have to ask him. I'm not one of those women who kept a wedding file from the age of twenty-five, collecting ideas for flowers and napkin origami.

25

(Georgia did.) But I always assumed that at some point the issue would just resolve itself organically. Part of the rationale for buying our house was that it had three bedrooms, room for growth, in Nick's words. That, with or without rings, when we wanted to start a family, firstly Nick would be the father, and secondly he'd be in a position to support the family. Call me old-fashioned.

'Well, I know you are quite the modern woman, Annie,' compounds Mum. 'But . . .'

Dad coughs. His Adam's apple lifts then descends ominously. I fear something tactless is brewing in his vocal cords.

'Marj,' he says, 'Nick is hardly in a position to marry Annie right now when he's got no darn prospects!'

(I feared right.)

Nick bends forward over the table on his elbows, his shoulders narrowing. He is blushing. He never blushes. 'Arnold . . .'

'Annie deserves—' Dad just manages to stop himself.

Mum bats the words away with a serving spoon. 'Oh Arnold, please. Don't be so Victorian. Look, you're embarrassing them both.' She coughs. 'Now, anyone for seconds?'

Everyone declines. Our benign Sunday lunch has slammed against something awkward and immovable, like a swimmer gaily diving into too-shallow rocky waters. I feel an overwhelming urge to leave, to run from the crumbling old country house, from perfect Georgia and Nick's embarrassment and everyone's ideas about who I am and what I want, to run and run until I reach my office in central London, where I can tell myself that I don't mind about Nick's change of circumstances at all. I don't mind supporting him for a bit. This is the twenty first century. These things just don't matter.

Three

'I am celebrating, Maggie. I haven't so much lost a salary as gained a housekeeper!' I declare, draining my glass. 'That's my line and I'm sticking to it.'

'You do that.' Maggie laughs and leans back against the bar. 'Maybe you're right, anyhow. I certainly have no idea how I'd manage without Jake at home.'

'But we both know that you've got kids, Maggie. Nick's got a PlayStation.' I grin and raise an eyebrow. 'Comrade, do you think we have a problem here?'

'Did have a PlayStation, Annie. Did. Time for it to disappear for a while, perhaps?' Maggie ruffles her short black elfin crop and swivels to face the bar. The barman attends to her straight away: a notably tall, slim woman with flawless half-Indian olive skin and a strong nose, a woman with a centrifugal force field who doesn't even need to smile to make an impact. Maggie is everything I'll probably never be: chic, quietly confident and composed. She's a loyal friend, unimposing, non-hysterical. And she is very well dressed, always, which peps up our meetings, however everyday, with a certain life-enhancing glamour. Today she is dressed in her signature look: long, wide Katharine Hepburn-style pants, a wide belt, silk blouse, heels. She only wears trousers partly because she hates her calves but mostly because she is a trouser type of woman and has the best trouser bottom in town. 'Two more glasses of champagne. No, not the house. The Moët.' She turns to face me, eyes bright in her startling, angular face. 'Politeness dictates one more round and then I think we've done our duty. But where is Vicky?' She sighs. 'I don't know why we imagine Vicky is capable of being on time when all the evidence of the last ten years points to the contrary.'

'One minute. I'll check.' From the vantage point of a small step, I survey the crowded Greek Street bar. A blanket of heads bobs up and down, many long-forgotten faces from my past. We are all here as guests of Dave and Ig, television's new cult darlings, who are celebrating the recommissioning of their comedy show, *Hatch*, which airs late on Tuesday nights on Channel Four. My parents have known Dave's parents for years. His mother, Peggy, talks so much George and I call her 'The Wall of Sound'. Now that Dave is A Success Story, she's an unstoppable verbal juggernaut. When we were teenagers, both Peggy and my mother went to embarrassing lengths to get me and Dave to be friends. It didn't work. But a few years later, when we discovered we were both going to Edinburgh University and could interact without the watchful enthusiasm of our parents, we hung out a bit. Now he has lots of friends – hundreds listed on Facebook in fact – most of whom seem to be here tonight. As my old dorm-mate Greg Jefferson confides drunkenly, 'Just to remind ourselves that if Dave and Ig, who couldn't even get laid at uni, can fucking make it, there's hope for all of us.'

Seeing old faces from my student past – a handful of unre-
quited crushes, clusters of those super-confident glamorous
girls who used to talk over me in tutorials – is odd, very odd.
Back at college, I'd never have been able to predict how we
would all turn out. Too many of the once-sexy men are now
a little overweight and balding and working in jobs with titles
that I don't understand, such as 'director of marketing and e-
information resources'. The women are rather more fabulous,
in their prime. Holding court in the corner of the bar is
Samantha Keynes, once an art history graduate with a repu-
tation for dancing on tables blind drunk and flashing her
double-D assets, now deputy head at a posh prep school,
with a set of twins: Heather – is it Heather? – yes, Heather
Western, sans her student beer bloat, looking self-assured in
a neat trouser suit, works for a city law firm apparently.
Heading into the Ladies is Kay Smith, once a stalwart of the
drama department who used to write excruciating plays
about Polish garbage collectors, now a well-known financial
columnist, married to a Tory MP. Then there is my dear
friend Maggie, of course, owner of her own successful holistic eco-bath products company and mother of two boys; and,
well, me . . . no, I haven't done too badly.

When people ask, I underplay *Glo* – 'Oh, it's not that
glamorous really' – partly because it's so not *Vogue*, partly
because of my sensitivity to the job's fluffier overtones – I am
hardly decoding the human genome – but mostly because I
am aware that I don't fit people's preconceptions of a glossy
magazine journalist. I don't want people imagining that I
have delusions of glamour. I always feel a little like a tourist
in the magazine world, an outsider looking in, just as I do at
parties like this. Intruder syndrome, Nick says. I have always
loved magazines – their refusal to kowtow to the humdrum

of everyday life, the gluey smell of a new issue, their unashamed girliness, which somehow makes up for the lack of my own – but however hard I try, I'm not someone who looks like they care that much about a handbag. I am a magazine journalist trapped in a tabloid reporter's body.

'You know what you should do?' Maggie nudges me again. 'Draw up some kind of agreement, a domestic dossier, so that you and Nick both know where you stand. Set down the ground rules.'

I splutter into my champagne. 'What, like redundancy dishwasher duty? Hand-washing my Wolfords? I'm liking it, Maggie. Although I spot a flaw,' I say, only half-joking. 'Do we honestly think that Nick is capable of meeting my domestic standards?'

Maggie laughs, low and throaty. 'Of course not! You'll just have to be less perfectionist. Embrace the man-mop-slop.'

'I fear he doesn't even know where the mop is kept.'

Maggie crushes her hand to her mouth. 'Shit. You know what? Nor do I.'

Maggie is endearingly undomesticated. She perches on a bar stool, her bottom assertively claiming it from three other women who have been staring at it, longingly but passively. 'Still, you don't want to end up the one slapping out to work every morning while he rearranges his record collection at home.'

'I'm not paying the bills yet, Maggie. And he's got—'

'Two months' pay or something, you say.' She nods at me and smiles. 'There's nothing like doing nothing to ratchet up the bills.' Maggie scans the room before turning to me, hand over her mouth. 'Oh Lordy, isn't it Vicky Vick Vicks? It *is* Vicky Vick Vicks. Check out that outfit!'

Ploughing through the crowds like a powerful yacht

through rough seas, Victoria Vickerson approaches, her raspberry-pink cocktail sluicing in its glass. The cocktail is the same colour as her mouth. The first thing you notice about Vicky is always her mouth, partly because her voice is so boomingly loud, but also because her mouth is so large, the plump lips so animated and her smile so ready and gap-toothed. It's the kind of mouth men either find incredibly sexy or worryingly sensual. She used to do a trick with a cigarette, sticking it in the gap and smoking. Totally bonkers but super-smart, thirty-eight but with the energy of a seven-year-old, Vicky is a successful entertainment lawyer – a thwarted actress who ended up doing law – and normally she dresses like a successful entertainment lawyer.

But not this evening. Vicky is wearing a tight black jersey dress advertising an enormous glittery cleavage – it looks like her boobs have collided with a disco ball – and a pair of towering patent black platform heels that could have come from a sex shop. A leopard-print bra strap strays falls down over her strong fleshy shoulder. Her dark glossy hair is big, very big, blown up at the roots in the shape of a question mark.

'Love love love your new look, Vicky,' I say. 'If I were a man I'd be crawling towards you on my knees, leaving a trail of dribble.'

'Dare I ask, where is your dancing pole?' asks Maggie.

Vicky hoots loudly. 'On my birthday list, please. Hey, isn't it genius? Look at this.' She digs into her patent handbag and pulls out some scraps of paper: an old receipt, a scrawled-upon Tube ticket, a business card. She holds them up for inspection. 'That's three men's numbers, girls. I jest not, three! I've only been out since six p.m.!' She pushes her hair off her face. It doesn't move much on account of all the

31

product suspending it in a state of voluminous animation. 'Me and Jessie, she's around somewhere . . . Remember sweet Irish Jessie from my office?'

'Go on,' I laugh. Vicky's single antics are always a reliable source of amusing anecdotes. Being a boring old couple just can't compete.

'We're becoming legends in our own lifetimes. We've ditched the tailoring, dolled ourselves up. Less is so not more, let me tell you. And, this is key – are you listening, Annie? – we never mention our jobs. Honestly . . .' She moves closer. Her perfume is overpowering. 'The results are kind of cool. Men, poor darlings, aren't intimidated by us. They love it.' Vicky grabs a seat next to Maggie, swinging one leg over the other.

'I bet they do,' I say, laughing. 'I bet they limpet to your legs and beg you not to kick them off.'

'They do, darling! Although some of them like to be kicked, of course.' Vicky pulls at one of her fake eyelashes. 'Damn this thing,' she says, as it comes loose. She flicks the black curled lash on to the floor. 'Anyway, up to three weeks ago, when our little experiment started, the most exciting sexual encounter I'd had in months was being frisked at Heathrow. Seriously, I've had more sex in the last three weeks than in the last three years.' She grins her gap-toothed grin. 'Open-and-shut case.' Vicky hoots with laughter again. It's that kind of wonderful, infectious laugh that makes other people think, that woman's having a better time than me. And she usually is. 'Don't you shake your head at me, Annie Rafferty. Now, tell me honestly, do my eyelashes look lopsided?'

I study her face. 'Hmmm. A bit. I'd take a couple off the other eye to even it up a bit.'

'Will you do the honours?' she asks.

'Of course. Stay still . . .' I hold Vicky's face with one hand as I carefully pull a couple of fake eyelashes off her right eye, watched by a group of bemused men. 'Got it! There, that's better.' I flick the eyelashes on to the floor. 'Still, it's a weeny bit sad that men are such Neanderthals that you must pretend to be something you're not.'

'We all pretend to be people we're not.' Vicky winks. 'I mean, really, where's the fun otherwise?'

This gets me thinking. I've never pretended. Nick says he knew I was the one when I arrived late for the first dinner he'd ever cooked me because I was stuck on a conference call to LA, and that his heart leapt when I handed him a business card at the end of the evening. After three years spent trying to disentangle himself from his ex, the beautiful but needy Melinda Armstrong-Smith (Labrapoodle owner and trust-fund babe without a cause apart from him), he'd wanted an independent, strong, sensible woman.

'I'm not entirely convinced,' says Maggie. 'Are we skimping on the quality control here?'

'Oh, probably. Who cares?' Vicky slugs back her cocktail, leaving raspberry smudges on the glass. 'Listen, you got the diamond, Maggie. But as a fortysomething—'

'You're thirty-eight!' Maggie says.

'I'll be thirty-six again next year, if you don't mind. But I'm talking as a representative demographic here, so don't confuse matters. Yes, as a veteran of the dating jungle, I will tell you now that Jake is a rare gem indeed, rarer than a diamond worn on the left hand in my office.'

I can see Jake streak through Maggie's mind. For a fleeting second all her features soften sweetly.

Vicky nudges me. 'Isn't that your fella, Annie? He's prowling, hunting you down, honey.'

Nick? Surely not. I didn't think he'd bother to come. Nick's lanky, handsome frame lopes its way through the crowd, his big baggy hip-hop jeans slumping over the waistband of his boxer shorts.

I make my way through the crowd towards him, but before I can get to Nick, TV success story Ig, Dave's writing partner, stands in front of me and locks me into social interaction. He seems bigger – all stubble and jaw – and less nerdy than last time I saw him, which must have been at a barbecue in Shepherd's Bush sometime in the late nineties. 'How's tricks, Annie?'

'Great. Thanks. Well done, Ig. You and Dave have done brilliantly. I love *Hatch*. If I hadn't known David since he had braces and a Blue Peter badge collection, I would honestly be starstruck.'

Ig laughs. 'Hey, here, meet my mate Don. Don, Annie.' He steps aside to reveal a short man with heavy black eyebrows that almost meet. He is wearing a suit and looks more corporate than anyone else in the room. When he extends a hand, I notice that his wrist is covered in dark hairs, as if it's been dipped in hundreds of eyelashes. His handshake crushes my hand. 'Pleasure,' he says, his voice gruff, a smoker's voice, cockney at the edges. His eyes are dark and hold my gaze intensely for a few moments. Then he turns to greet a friend.

I stare at his broad back as I talk to Ig. '*Hatch* is so good,' I say. 'Too good really. I think you should go away and do something less good so that the rest of us don't get status anxiety.'

Ig grins, not looking in the least bored at receiving such praise despite the fact he must have received a similar blandishment from every person in the room. 'I hear you've not done too badly yourself, Annie. Got the magazine industry by the balls, eh?'

'Not exactly. One can but try.' Our mutual admiration has no obvious conversational continuum. There is a pause. I am about to fill the gap with a weak joke about being invited to the party in order to provide new material for the next series of *Hatch* when Nick appears. I kiss him on the lips.

Ig thumps him on the shoulder. 'All right, mate. You must be the other half.'

'Nick,' I say. 'This is Ig, works with my old mate David on *Hatch*.'

The dark, compelling man turns away from the crowd and rejoins our circle.

'And, er . . .' The man's name escapes me. Hopeless. I am the world's worst networker.

'Don,' he volunteers.

Nick looks at Don shyly. 'He is a genuine fan of *Hatch*. 'I think your show is hilarious. I love that moment when Lewis—'

Don holds his hand up and snorts gruffly. 'Nothing to do with me, mate.'

'Oh . . .' Nick hesitates, a little thrown. 'Sorry, I assumed you worked with David too.'

Ig raises his glass, swigs his beer back casually, eyeing Nick up for contact potential. 'So what do you do, Nick?'

There is a pause. Nick's eyes drop to the floor. He clears his throat.

'I was working in PR.' I know that Nick feels self-conscious telling people, especially celebrated creative people, that he is a hotel PR, as if it labels him a bit of a wanker somehow, which is ridiculous. He cares what other people think too much. But I guess he just wants to let people know it isn't the real him. 'I've just been made redundant.'

35

'Nice one,' says Don and laughs. It is not a particularly kind laugh.

Nick looks mortified.

I try to transmit invisible little love parcels to let him know that I think he has more untapped talent in his little finger than Ig or Dave have in their whole bodies. I squeeze his hand. But he pulls it away.

I glare at Don. It is all his fault somehow.

Ig scans the bar for other social opportunities. 'Let's catch up later, guys.'

As Don and Ig swagger into the crowd, I think, snobs, horrible snobs. Nick bends down so his mouth is close to my ear and I think he is about to kiss me. I lean towards him to reciprocate the kiss but it doesn't come. Instead he hisses in my ear, 'Your world is full of twats. Don't ever become like them.' Then he strides towards the bar, chest puffed, to reassert himself and buy a large round of drinks that he can't afford.

Four

'Magazines improve slowly but go wrong fast,' says Pippa Woodside, slipping her feet out of flat pumps and into heels under her desk. I am the only person in the magazine, apart from Belle, who gets to see Pippa's bare feet. When I got my first glimpse of Pippa's pump-stripped foot it was like hearing a feared teacher peeing in a toilet stall, the bunion-toes somehow proof of her human vulnerability. I'm not so surprised by them these days.

She starts to fan herself with the latest copy of *Glo*. 'Christ. Is it hot in here or is it just me?'

'Hot,' I say. It is not hot. It is actually cold, which is why there's been a cashmere outbreak in the office. But Pippa, the office has realised, is going through The Change. We're not sure if she realises it or whether she's in denial, but either way we're screwed if we don't pretend the Arctic air con is heating up faster than the world itself.

I notice a huge designer bag squatting beside her desk, half unwrapped from its tissue paper. It is rust red and tortoiseshell, covered in gold chains. It is a gift from an international designer. It is also pretty hideous. Since *Glo* started losing readers, Pippa's freebies have got noticeably worse. Whereas other editors receive the It bag of the season, Pippa receives the kind of bag that sells well in Moscow. Not that she's noticed.

'New bag?' I say.

'Isn't it darling? I'm going to give it to my housekeeper for Christmas. Only way to keep the staff.' Pippa's Brummie accent is undetectable today, which is a good thing. It only goes public when she's angry. She readjusts her toffee-highlighted hair with a shake of the fingers. She is the only woman in the office to have a 'do': an artfully moppy Nicky Clarke-style creation, reminiscent of newsreaders in the nineties. Most of the office either have long glossy tresses or neat bobs. But Pippa is older than us and likes to assert her authority and advertise her income with grooming and a high maintenance cut. A bit old school, she's an editor who made her name in the stodgier reaches of magazines, the cheap weeklies aimed at the older reader, which sell by the truckload. The hope was that she'd work her circulation magic at *Glo* too. Unfortunately, since she took over three and a half years ago the circulation has nose-dived. 'So you're off to meet the new editorial directive executive, are you, Annie?'

'He's got a very illustrious title, hasn't he?' I say mischievously, knowing his title will irritate.

'Hasn't he just?' Pippa stands up and reaches for her jacket, an expert bit of Jil Sander tailoring that gives the fifty-four-year-old the waist of someone twenty years younger. 'But who am I to dispute the wisdom of some male maverick barely out of nappies?'

I smile but make sure I don't laugh. Pippa associates enjoyment with laziness. Laugh too hard and you get given yet another assignment.

'I hear there was a ruckus between beauty and features. How very tedious. Fill me in.'

'Oh, it was nothing much.' Pippa doesn't like to hear about problems. Only solutions. It is my job to ensure that the power struggles play out before they reach her door. Half my job is crisis management. Of late I've been wondering if the biggest crisis is actually the fact that she's the editor. 'All sorted.'

But it's not sorted. Far from it. It all began about three o'clock yesterday. The stress of the still unfilled December cover had brought our minx of a features director Alexis out in livid facial eczema – the office was alerted to it by a rash of faux-concerned emails emanating from Alexis's closest enemy on the features desk – and this raised red skin on her otherwise perfect cheek set off a chain of cataclysmic events, much like how a tiny shift of subsidence might cause a large crack along a wall. Without asking, and thus wilfully ignoring Beauty Desk Etiquette, Alexis rifled through the beauty cupboard for a camouflaging foundation, preferably a really expensive one by Laura Mercier. Louise, the Fraxel-faced beauty director (lots of free treatments = perfect skin), enraged that her fiefdom had been thus invaded, strode up to my desk and, struggling to emote through her Botox, hotly demanded that I issue an office email reminding everyone about Beauty Cupboard Rules. I did and I probably shouldn't have. Alexis took it very personally, declared war with Louise and isn't talking to me, which is something of a relief. We're not the best of friends. Alexis hates any reminder that I, Annie Rafferty, the least fashionable and non-thinnest girl in the office (it shouldn't matter, but it does), won the job of deputy, not her fragrant self. Pippa anointed Alexis with the newly cooked-up title of features director as a consolation prize. But it hasn't consoled her. Not come close.

'Departments should be communicating, not squabbling,' says Pippa. She opens a desk drawer, pulls out a bottle of perfume, gives herself a squirt on her left wrist and briskly rubs her wrists together. 'I want to hear no more of it. Right! Let's brainstorm!' Pippa stands tall in black trousers and heels, thick gold bracelets thumping dully as they pile against each other on her wrist like ammunition. She runs her fingers through her hair. 'I'm thinking spas, Annie. I'm thinking about that spa supplement.' She cocks her head on one side. 'Let's step back from this for a moment, shall we? Do people still go to spas, do we think?'

'Our readers seem to like them.' We do a supplement every year for this very reason.

'I'm not so sure, Annie. Not so sure.' Pippa walks towards the vast plane of window. In the bright sunlight I notice a few frazzled white-blond moustache hairs sprinkled across her upper lip, like fine hairs on an old carrot, that she has obviously bleached. I try really hard not to look at them, but my eye is tugged towards them. When her mouth moves, the hairs move too. 'Let's throw everything in the air and think outside the box for a minute. Are we missing a trick here? Could spas be one of those things we imagine readers will like?'

Pippa has less in common with her readers than any editor I know. Whenever they turn up at reader events she's absolutely horrified. She likes to imagine that our readers are size eight PR consultants who live in Kensington rather than hard-working size sixteen secretaries living in the less fashionable areas of Northampton.

'I'll let you reflect on that, Annie.' Pippa checks her man-sized Cartier tank watch. 'I'm off to lunch. I should be back about three. Get that anti-ageing supplement proposal together for my return, please.'

'Of course, Pippa.' The anti-ageing supplement has put ten years on me. I'm not close to finishing it because the brief changes more often than Pippa's shoes. I walk back towards the main office, put my hand on the cool stainless steel of the door handle.

'And Annie . . .' Pippa looks stern. 'Only relay the good news.'

'Of course.' Good news means omission. So no, I won't mention the on-going fracas with one of London's most powerful agents, who has prevented all her A-list clients from working with the magazine in the future unless we promise covers for three of her D-list 'stars'. Given *Glo*'s ever-slipping status, she knows it's well worth a try. I won't mention that the fashion cupboard thief has struck again. We lost one Marni dress and one Luella handbag last month. A Matthew Williamson coat the month before. Nor will I mention that at every fashion and press award ceremony not only do we never win anything, we are always seated behind the widest pillar in the room. I won't mention the fact that the second subeditor has just handed her notice in. Or the poaching of the best beauty writer by a rival magazine. Nor that the fashion desk is near mutiny since the announcement of Pippa's latest cost-saving exercise: no more taxis. It doesn't help that Pippa's own personal driver is still very much in evidence. Pippa doesn't recognise that the fashion desk have the hardest job on the magazine. No one wants to lend us samples any more. They had to lunch Alexander McQueen's PR for a year before getting hold of just one dress to shoot. The dress was allowed to be in *Glo*'s grubby possession for all of forty-five minutes before being biked to *Harper's*. And the fashion desk have to contend with the humiliation of being shunted back a row at the fashion shows every season. Three years ago our most senior fashion staff were row B. Now it's row D, if they're lucky. 'Did you see the show?' I asked Lydia, the fashion editor, last week. 'No, sweetie,' she said drily. 'I saw the tops of the models' heads.'

I walk through the office, ducking demands from colleagues as if ducking paintballs, knowing that if I stop and get into a messy discussion I will definitely be late for my meeting. The lift judders up to the fifteenth floor. I am rarely invited this high, to the elite upper echelons. The building is a metaphor for corporate success: the upper-floor corridors are painted a different colour to that of the rest of the building, sponged a not entirely successful shade of burgundy, as opposed to the functional office grey, and accessorised with brass fittings, as opposed to the regulation nickel, and a deep-weave blue carpet, as opposed to grey carpet tiles. It is the look, Lydia says, of a four-star business hotel. Readjusting the waistband of my black wool trousers, I knock on the conference room door. Through the door's glass panes I can make out two figures, the featureless courgette shape of Tina Krum, our publisher, and the back of a stocky man with a mop of black hair. Tina looks up and, seeing me through the glass, smiles and beckons me in.

'Annie!' She walks across the office, bottom out, nose forward, head moving ever so slightly backwards and forwards like a peahen. She air-kisses me. 'You look great!'

'Thanks,' I say warmly. Compliments on one's physical appearance are the conventional means of greeting here. I have learned not to take it personally.

'Meet Don Wilberforce.' She clears her throat. 'Our new editorial directive executive.'

42

The man in the dark suit stands up and extends a hand. It is a large, olive-skinned hand. As soon as I shake it, I recognise the unmistakable gorilla grip of a handshake. The hairs like eyelashes. Oh my God. It is him. The rude man from the party, Ig's mate. The one who dissed Nick. Something inside prickles.

'I do believe we've already met, Annie.' He studies me for a few moments, then his short, square brow clears. He looks pleased with himself. 'Ah, yes. That was it. Ig's party, last Thursday. You were wearing a very nice pair of green heels.'

Was I? Indeed I was: old sample sale chunky-heeled Miu Mius. 'Excellent shoe recall. You're obviously a women's magazine natural.'

We stare at each other for a moment which feels weirdly drawn out, elastic. I'm not used to encountering men at work. There are a few in the building but most of them are either gay or so senior that they are not often spotted below the heights of the fifteenth floor.

Tina coughs loudly, as if to break our silent dialogue, and takes her jacket off the back of her chair. 'Well, we're all done here, I think, Don.'

Don turns to me. 'I suggest we get to know each other over a quick lunch.'

He touches Tina's elbow, in a way that is a little overfamiliar considering Tina is the publisher. He is cocksure of himself, this one. 'You will be joining us?'

'Booked already.' Tina looks gutted, as if this is the social diary clash of the month. 'But this has been a good meeting, Don. A very good meeting.' She beams. 'We're absolutely thrilled to have you on board.'

Outside the tall, stone-clad building, the sun is shining. The air is cool and clean. It has a new smell to it. It is the air of seasons in transition. A large lorry thunders towards the lozenge-shaped puddle adjacent to me on the road. Don, like a minder who spots an assassin before anyone else, pulls me back sharply, so that the spray just frills the edge of my coat. The lorry rattles past. I suck in my breath, surprised at the physicality of the encounter. Goodness. I find myself readjusting my coat rather primly, like an Edwardian lady might after an unexpected brush with a sweating working man. 'Thank you.'

Don throws a hand up at the two lanes of traffic. A black cab stops straight away. He holds the door for me as I clamber in rather inelegantly. 'Oh, treat to be in a taxi,' I say, not expecting him to get the office joke.

'Yes, I heard.' Don grins. 'I won't tell if you won't.'

We drive down the Strand, turning right towards Covent Garden. Something about Don unsettles me. Perhaps it is because he looks absurdly young for someone in such a senior position and yet carries himself with the charm and command of a man twice his age. The boundaries feel blurred. I am unsure how to play it.

At the entrance of the restaurant, stairs lead down to a noisy basement famous for its history of attracting actors and publishers and old, boozy London – an unusual restaurant choice for an exec perhaps. Don stands aside, gesturing me through as if I were a debutante with a three-foot-wide skirt. The waiter leads us to a table, pulls back a chair. I pick up the menu and stare at the list of dishes blankly.

After a few moments Don interrupts. 'Would you like me to recommend something?'

My instinctive answer is no. Then I think, well, why not? It strikes me that this is the first time for an age I've been out for lunch on my own with a man who isn't Nick. 'Thanks.'

'The duck. The lamb, both excellent. Unless you are a veggie, of course.' He looks at me approvingly. 'You look more like a carnivore to me.' He orders the meal, then cups his wide jaw in his hand and stares at me. It's unnerving. 'So I bet you're thinking, who is this tosser who's been brought in to meddle with the magazine?'

'Don't be silly,' I lie.

Don slumps back in his chair, stretching his arms out behind him. I can't help but notice the width of his chest. He seems almost as wide as he is tall, powerful, chunky, a human version of a Hummer. 'I better give you my USP, Annie. I'm overseeing the women's magazine division. At *Glo* I'll be working mostly with Pippa.' He studies me, eyes zigzagging across my face as he speaks. 'And I'll be spotting new opportunities in the market, helping the company reach its full potential.'

Ah. Just the usual corporate bollocks then. Pippa has nothing to be paranoid about.

'I hope to nudge things in a more profitable direction.' He smiles. 'I've heard good things about you, Annie. Don't look so startled. You are popular among your colleagues.'

'Ah. So they aren't just pretending,' I laugh.

'And you're still young. There's a lot you could achieve.'

'Really?' How exciting. My elation at this compliment brings out the klutz-mouth in me. 'You're not exactly ancient either.'

Don's eyes crease when he smiles. They are deep-set grey eyes; if he was a girl he'd have nowhere to put eye shadow. 'Ah, you speak what other minds think,' says Don. 'You will be useful to me.'

I crush my hand to my mouth. 'Sorry. I didn't mean . . .'

He pats the sides of his hair. 'Greying above the temples,

sadly. But yes, I'm kind of young, I suppose, compared to some of the fossils on the top floor.'

Fossils? Tina Krum would love that. I try not to smile.

'I've been in New York for the last few years,' Don continues. 'But I've been working in publishing since I was twenty.'

Ah, a wunderkind. Right. That makes sense.

He grins. His teeth are short and square. There seem to be too many of them. 'How do you know Ig, the jammy bastard?'

'Uni,' I say. 'You?'

'Oh, friend of a friend. Mike Lindeman? That big cheese at Channel Four? You know, fat guy, bald as an egg.'

I shake my head.

'Good. It's nice to meet a woman who hasn't slept with him.'

I'd anticipated a long, dry, interrogative lunch. This suddenly seems like it might be more fun.

'And that was your husband I met at the party?' He raises an eyebrow.

'Boyfriend.'

He glances at my hands. 'Aha, I see. No diamonds.' Is he flirting? He is flirting.

'Not yet, no.' I'm not sure why I say this, implying as it does that I am expecting diamonds at any moment, when, of course, I am not. I fix Don with what I hope is an impenetrable smile and fiddle with the starched napkin in my lap, uncomfortable with the conversation's sudden high dive into the complex waters of my relationship. (I note he isn't wearing a wedding ring either.)

The main courses arrive. Don eats hungrily, like an animal, noisily swallowing large chunks of rare meat, whipping at his

46

mouth with the napkin, totally without self-consciousness. After he has consumed his food, he sits back on his chair with a satisfied grunt. 'Pudding?'

I shouldn't. Not with Georgia's wedding coming up. I've got to pour myself into a bridesmaid's dress. More importantly, I need to get back to the office and get on with my work. 'No thanks.'

But Don bends back and barks at the hovering waiter, 'Two chocolate pots, please.'

But I don't want a chocolate pot. 'Don, I've got to get back to the office.'

He ruffles his dark hair with a large square hand. 'Oh, blame me.'

Who is this guy? Well, he is my superior, and the fact that he doesn't feel he has to act like it just underlines his power. I should keep my mouth shut. But something about him, something about his swagger, those thick fingers, something really riles. 'Actually, I've got piles of work,' I press on, determined to frustrate him. 'I don't want a chocolate pot.'

'You will. Just wait until they arrive.' He leans back in his chair, legs splayed, thighs like beams that the waiters have to manoeuvre themselves around.

'I don't.' He is beginning to piss me off now. Who the hell does he think he is? But bar walking out of the restaurant, which would probably be an over-reaction, I have little choice but to comply.

Don fixes me with amused, playful eyes. I glare back, wondering how a normal business lunch has descended into this strange mental dual. I can feel myself pumping up with adrenalin, like red ants under the skin. The noise of the restaurant – the scrape of chairs, the clatter of cutlery and the jazz-like rise and fall of the talking diners – seems to get louder and louder.

The floor feels hot, pushing against the soles of my feet. My head thumps. Then the chocolate pots arrive.

'Eat,' Don demands.

I hesitate. His order pisses me off as much as it thrills a small, unexpected part of me.

'Eat,' Don repeats, more sternly now.

I find myself obediently digging the shiny silver spoon into the dark goo and lifting it to my mouth, where it hovers uncertainly a few inches from my lips. Despite the warm chocolatey smell curling up into my nose like the anticipation of taste, I have to fight the urge to fling the spoon back down on the plate as if it were burning my fingers.

'Eat.'

With my eyes unable to leave Don's irritatingly triumphant face, the chocolate-filled spoon enters my mouth. Eating the pudding feels like some kind of surrender. For no explicable reason, it makes me want to cry.

Five

I can hear the music – Gnarls Barkley – blaring from the street. That'll be Nick's Bose sound system then. I can just imagine our poor new neighbours muttering behind the Ikea roller blinds, 'There goes the neighbourhood!' When I get in, there is the composty tang of grass in the air. Nick is sitting in the kitchen, nodding his head to the bass. He looks different. At first I'm unsure why. Then I realise. His hair is different, shaved above his ears like a rapper's and messed up on top, all Jamie Oliver faux-casual floppiness. Fuck. Nick has Crazy Hair.

'You have crazy hair.'

'What?'

'Turn the music down,' I shout. 'I said. 'You have crazy hair.'"

'Well, I like it.' He swigs from a bottle of Corona. 'It's sweetly liberating. I feel like it's two fingers up at . . . at . . . Well, you know what I mean.'

'But I loved your hair. I've always loved your hair.' I put on a stern voice. 'Tell me who did this to you?'

'I used your bikini-line strimmer.'

I start to giggle. 'Are you having a mid-life crisis, darling?'

Nick rolls his eyes. 'I'm not old enough to have a mid-life crisis, Annie! It's more of a personal ongoing state of emergency.'

This is just a little too true to be funny.

Later, restricting my sightline to below his eyebrows, I swallow a warm, herby mouthful of shepherd's pie, relishing the smooth cream of the potato, the subtly seasoned meat. Nick's cooking is a discovery, a whole new side to his personality revealed. In these last few weeks he has become diligent about following recipes, adventurous about trying new ones, tackling food in the opposite way he tackles his job-hunting. Unfortunately, cooking – mighty fine though it is – is proving to be the full extent of his wifery skills. The dishwasher remains a stranger to him. Last week he put my favourite grey cashmere sweater in the washing machine and it now fits a two-year-old. I'm trying to remain positive: the good thing is that as he couldn't be worse, he can only get better. 'This is just fantastic pie. You are clever, Nick. You know, I have absolutely no idea how I'd go about making a pie.'

'Face it, Annie. I'm not with you for your culinary flourish. You are many things but you aren't a cook. My darling, you even find carrot peelings troubling.'

'Ugh, those long, muddy, spooky orange things, you mean, those things that you peel directly on to the floor, or, perhaps, if you're feeling really creative, over my favourite boots?'

Nick laughs and flops back in his chair, swigs his beer. The candlelight casts his familiar lanky shadow puppet against the wall. 'So, what were you saying this morning? There's some new exec being brought in to whip the mag into shape?'

I am touched that Nick is trying to be attentive to my job. But I am aware that he feels he has to be, and that he is not that interested. And the truth is I'm not that interested in humouring his fake-interest either. I don't want to have to explain the intricacies of the magazine's politics, not when I've been wading about in them all day. And I don't want to think about the way Don made me eat that chocolate pot. 'Same old. What have you been doing with yourself?'

He shrugs. 'Spun a few tunes in preparation for tonight.'

I look at him blankly. Tonight? Shit, what's happening tonight?

'I'm playing down at the Arts Club for John's party, remember? No, obviously not. It's a very late slot. I guess you won't be coming then?'

'Knackered,' I say, shaking my head. I haven't been to one of Nick's gigs for months. I'm not a clubber, basically. The bass isn't in my bones, like it is in his. In this way we are an odd couple. I like to dance at weddings, girls' nights, that kind of thing, but I've never seen the attraction of swallowing dodgy pills, prescribed by a criminal, then grinding my jaw till dawn. I'd rather sleep. To be fair, Nick's jaw-grinding days are well over too. His passion has always been more about the music than anything else. He's one of life's hobby-ists.

'By the way, I also bought some paint for the front room, a nice mushroomy colour. I tried out a few tester pots, hence my painting clothes.' He holds up paint-splattered hands. 'And fingers.' He starts to laugh. 'Fuck. I look like your peas-ant boyfriend.'

A shudder of sexual tension holds us tight in eye contact. For a fleeting second a fantasy about Nick taking me in his paint-splattered work clothes tenses my thighs. It doesn't last.

51

Who am I kidding? Nick isn't a bit of rough. Nick is a nice middle-class ex-public school boy who has not yet found his calling. My personal theory is that it is the very privilege of his upbringing – his mother a screwy psychotherapist, his father a gloomy retired lawyer, who, thankfully, live far away in a vast vaulted medieval chateau in the south of France – that allows Nick to have his somewhat fluid attitudes towards work and money. That and the fact that his father put so much pressure on him to succeed – sending him to a hothouse prep school, then St Paul's – that he long ago lost any sense of what he really enjoyed. It's not his fault. And not a bad thing. The aggressive alpha male his father had tried to nurture became the soft, sensitive Labrador of a man that I fell in love with. But he can never measure up to his dad's expectations and this means there's a little chink in Nick's confidence, like the missing brick in the wall that weakens the whole structure. I've tried to fill this chink with love and reassurance but nothing seems to work, not permanently anyhow. So, no, I never expected Nick to become a city trader. Still, I guess I never expected him to be unemployed either.

Lovely blond lanky Nick. We met through work. I was trying to arrange a press trip for some capricious overhyped reality TV star and he was the hotel PR with whom I negotiated the freebies. He wasn't like other PRs I'd met. He was posh, a little bonkers and wore odd socks, one navy, one polka-dot grey. And he retained a wry sense of humour as he rattled through his PR pitch, his eyes laughing like we were both in on some kind of joke and he didn't believe a word of what he was saying. He didn't move like a PR either. He didn't move with a sense of purpose, but with a playful hesitant dawdle, as if ready to stop and examine anything that came across his path, butterfly, funny street sign, cloud formations. The very qualities I found so endearing, I'm now finding a bit frustrating. In my darker moments I do wonder if I've ever thought his personality through to its logical conclusion.

'You won't renege on your promise to go late-night sofa shopping, will you?' I ask Nick after supper, as he stuffs plates into an overcrowded dishwasher while I scrub the greasy pan. We have one ratty two-seater sofa that has to be covered with a wall hanging on account of its lurid green velour covering. It is about as comfortable to sit on as a thong.

He groans like a man in pain. 'God, really? Don't make me. I beg you. I was hoping to have a chill night in front of the PlayStation before the gig later tonight.'

'No chance!' I put my arms around his neck and kiss him. 'You promised.'

'I had my fingers crossed.'

'Nick!' I punch him lightly on the arm. 'It's me or the PlayStation. It goes or I do . . .'

He rubs his chin. 'That's a tough one.' He continues stacking the dishwasher, looks up at me and grins. 'Oh, go on then, if you insist.'

'Oh, and Nick darling . . .'

'Yeah?'

'Persil washing machine tablets don't work in the dishwasher.'

We park outside a vast furniture emporium, its glass frontage lit by coloured acrylic lamps that radiate out a welcoming shimmer to the rain-slick pavement. Inside, dozens of bulbs hang down from the ceiling, an upside-down forest of light. It's hot. Nick develops blooms of sweat beneath his armpits. This, combined with the mushroom-coloured paint in his blond hair and down his jeans, makes him look like he's just walked off a building site. We browse various upholstered seating arrangements, Nick passively following me around the shop, in increasingly sulky silence. I spot a sofa that speaks to me and throw myself at its squishy caramel cushions, legs kicking up in the air. 'Whee! I like this. It's like jumping into a doughnut.'

'Can I help you?' a brisk shop assistant asks me. She ignores Nick. I guess it's the clothes. Nick is not the kind of man that female shop assistants typically ignore. They normally flutter around him like moths.

'Just admiring this sofa.' I run my hands up and down the fabric, relishing its nubbles against my fingertips. 'Nick, do you like it?'

'Dunno.' Nick stares distractedly around the shop, moody. 'It's all right.'

'Do you think it might be The One?'

'Suppose.' Nick gazes upwards as if appealing to the light bulbs to beam him up and remove him from the sofa shopping experience.

This is what happens when you get settled into a relationship, I guess. In the early days Nick pretended he loved shopping with me. He even agreed to go to Ikea once. He's since admitted that he was humouring me. But at the beginning of our relationship he'd really do anything to make me happy.

'OK, male inability to connect with material object. What about this one?' I point to something sculpted, modern and lipstick red, a complete contrast, more to his taste.

Nick strokes the sofa's red arm. 'OK.'

'Curb your enthusiasm, Nick.' His passivity is suddenly

absolutely infuriating. 'You choose a sofa. I may as well be shopping on my own.'

'God, Annie. This is like being dragged around shops with my mother.'

'Don't compare me to your mother!'

'What's wrong with my mother?'

'Your mother is great. But I don't want to be cast as your mother,' I say more sharply this time. 'I am your girlfriend.'

The assistant smiles tightly and takes a polite detour out of our orbit. Suddenly Nick slumps down on a green sofa, elbows on his knees, his handsome golden-skinned face drawn in the bright lighting.

I squat down beside him. 'Nick, darling, are you OK? What's the matter?'

Nick looks up from beneath his tufty fringe, his eyes darkening. 'I can't buy anything. Not yet. Not until I've got another job. Don't you understand? I'm broke, Annie. I cannot afford to buy a new sofa, no, not even half a new sofa.' I ruffle Nick's hair, its golden strands gritty between my fingers, my sympathy for him undercut by a great wave of childish disappointment: it is like visiting a sweetie store and leaving without so much as a pear drop. Can I really face another month – no, months; apparently it takes an age for sofas to arrive – sitting on that springy monstrosity after a long day at work? The truth is I can afford a new sofa, on my own. Is there a written rule book that says the man has to pay half? If I were out of work, wouldn't Nick pay? Of course he would. And it is a beautiful sofa. A very beautiful sofa. It is a girl's sofa, with curves and hips and padding. It is also a sofa that Nick would possibly not choose were he paying half. I gaze at it longingly.

As I gaze, the shop seems to get brighter and brighter, as if someone is twisting up a light dimmer. 'Don't worry. I'm going to buy it on my own,' I say, walking off to organise payment. As we leave the shop, I become aware of something indefinable shifting in our relationship. Nick drives home preoccupied, as if there is a small, irrational part of him, a part that not even he understands, that will never, ever forgive me for buying that sofa on my own.

Six

'Come in, come in,' says Georgia excitably, as she opens the door to her Notting Hill mews house.

Nick and I hesitate because Nick has his hand in the back pocket of my jeans and it gets stuck as he tries to retrieve it. It's just a little thing, but it strikes me that his hand would never have got stuck in my pocket a few months ago. It's almost as if there's a new clunkiness to our partnership, a loss of intuitive physicality somehow. 'Fab dress, George,' I say, twisting slightly and freeing Nick's hand.

My sister is wearing a draped Grecian jersey dress in pale toffee-taupe, accessorised by bare, small, pretty feet. Unlike my own hammer-headed frighteners, Georgia has feet as daintily proportioned as a five-year-old's, despite a lifetime's passion for high heels. She looks down at her body approvingly, running her hands up and down the smooth contours of her hips. 'Olly bought it for me. And this . . .' She holds out her arm to display a gold charm bracelet.

'Stunning.'

'Now come in, shit, it's freezing out there!' She ushers us inside.

Georgia and Olly's candle-scented Notting Hill mews house is scarcely recognisable from the small dark cave it once was. Georgia has been overseeing an extensive modernisation project for the last two years, with the result that the ground floor is now a large knocked-through space. It would be cavernous and echoey were it not for her good eye and love of organic, expensive finishes: lumps of artfully gnarled wood for coffee tables, a large central hearth suspended from the ceiling, like a UFO coming in to land, logs piled up artfully in the corner. David Gray drones from the Bose sound system. I glance at Nick, knowing that he will notice the music and that we will laugh about it later, not unkindly but because it is gratifying to spot the small imperfections of taste in Olly and Georgia's otherwise pretty perfect existence. We sink into a downy covering of piled sheepskins on the vast modular sofa.

Nick whispers in a mock-Loyd Grossman accent, 'You know what this house says to me? We're loaded.'

I giggle and elbow him in the ribs. 'Shush.'

We sit in silence for a few moments, expectant of Olly's imminent clattering down the banister-less stairs. Georgia appears holding two large glasses of red wine. She calls up the stairs, 'Olly! Drinks, darling.'

I don't think I've ever said to Nick, 'Drinks, darling.' More like, 'Can you please stop leaving your bloody beer cans in the bathroom!'

Georgia starts to climb the stairs, her feet making soft pink shapes on the underside of the glass. 'One sec, folks. I'll go and get him.'

Eventually there are footsteps. Georgia leads Olly by the hand, as if he might be unwilling to make the journey on his own. He does not look like his normal clean cut self, the usual well-worked-out man in a bespoke suit. His hair is uncombed, sticking up at the corners of his long square skull and his receding hairline seems to have receded further. And he is wearing a pale blue pashmina, which is worrying somehow.

'Glad you could make it,' he says, not sounding like he is glad at all. He tugs on his pashmina, tightening it around his bulldog-thick neck.

'I really hope you're feeling better, Olly,' I attempt, feeling that I have to allude to his depression in some way. Is there some kind of etiquette required after a therapy sabbatical? Do I sound too cheery? I'm very fond of Olly but we're still on make-an-effort terms. Once he's actually locked into the Raffertys by marriage, I suspect we'll relax around each other a bit more. He'll be like the brother I never had. I look forward to teasing him about his pashmina.

Olly sits down next to Nick on the sofa, his body tightly controlled – legs crossed, hands knotted together. Georgia strokes his arm as if it were a kitten, stretching her long brown legs out on a zebraskin ottoman.

'Must be nice to be home!' Nick says too jauntily.

Olly sighs the sigh of the terminally misunderstood. 'The journey's not over yet.'

Nick and I exchange glances. Journey? Yikes. How bad can life be? A doting Georgia as wife-in-waiting. Imminent retirement with a not-so-small fortune. Mortgage-free deluxe pad in one of the world's most expensive patches of real estate.

'Glass of wine, Olly?' Georgia asks.

'Georgia!' Olly says witheringly. 'Don't . . .'

'Shit. Sorry.' Georgia crumples her fingers to her mouth. For a moment she looks like she might be about to cry. 'Doh! I'm so dozy. I just keep forgetting.'

Olly bends forward, elbows pot-holing his jeans. 'I am off the booze,' he explains, sounding like a man who really could do with a stiff drink.

Georgia stands up, smoothing her dress with fidgety fingers, and walks quickly into the kitchen. She cuts up bright green limes, the knife flashing beneath the halogen spots, which downlight hundreds of mysterious-looking gleaming kitchen implements that are rarely used. Lime cut, crushed and carbonated, she walks over and plants the fresh lime soda at the top of the dining table. 'Guys, come and sit down. It's almost feeding time.'

After the awkwardness of Olly's outburst, we move towards the table with a collective sense of relief, like swimmers discovering a warm current in cold water. Olly sits at the top of the table with his lime soda. Nick sits within foot-nudging distance of me. I take a sip of wine. Even my uneducated palate appreciates its richness, the warm blaze in my throat. 'We've been jealously admiring the house, Olly. It's looking fabulous.'

Olly snorts. 'Fuck, have the damn thing.'

Georgia giggles nervously, tongs her hair with her fingers. 'Can I tell them about our plans?'

Olly looks at her as if she exhausts him. 'Your plans.'

'What? You've bought the entire street and are going to knock through every single one of those houses to make a vast open-plan bathroom?' says Nick.

'Good idea. I like it. But no,' laughs Georgia. 'We need to move. A bigger house. Somewhere that would work better for kids.'

I can't help but wonder: apart from the fact that they don't yet have any children, how much square footage does a seven-pound baby actually need?

Olly upturns his hands in mock bewilderment. 'No, I don't get it either.'

Georgia bends over Olly, her hair falling over his face as she kisses him, creating a fringed private boudoir. 'You know we need more rooms, darling.' Olly pats her bottom, then digs his hand through the dress fabric into her knicker elastic, which he pulls and releases with a ping.

I look away politely. Nothing wrong with Olly's libido, then. Me and Nick haven't done it for a while. How long, a couple of months? Since he lost his job, to the day. It was that morning, before we had breakfast, sleepy and cosy, half awake. Then we rolled back to sleep again before the brutality of the alarm clock.

'Well, you won't have any problems selling this place,' says Nick, staring at the square glass vase rose display dominating the table.

Georgia looks up. 'Oh, we won't sell this place. Will we? I adore it.'

Olly slaps her bottom, harder this time so that it makes a Carry On slap sound. 'Yes, we'll keep it, Georgia. Anything to make you happy.'

'Oh, for God's sake.' Olly rolls his eyes. 'I promise. I fucking promise, OK?'

Ouch. I study the table arrangements, shocked at the rapid transition between the display of affection and Olly's unexpected bite. How dare he speak to my little sister like that?

We sit in silence. Georgia fidgets on her chair and glances at the vast clock that is projected as shadow on to a white wall. 'The folks are late, you know.'

'Impossible. They are constitutionally incapable of ever being late,' I say, pouring my second glass of wine. The wine really is very good indeed. 'They are compulsively early,

George. Throw Tube strikes or snowstorms at them, they'll still arrive ten minutes early. They're the punctual juggernauts of Lower Dalton.'

Olly smiles properly for the first time today. 'Ah, but maybe that's what they think one does in London now. You know, be late.' Sometimes I suspect Olly doesn't think our parents are quite good enough. Too provincial.

'Wait. Aha!' says Georgia, looking at the front door. 'I think that's them.'

'It's them!' I say, rushing to the window and peering through the sparkling glass.

Outside in the cobbled street stand Mum and Dad, Dad coughing, Mum rubbing at a blister on her left heel caused, I can see, by wearing her 'smart' courts that she rarely wears and hasn't broken in. 'I didn't hear the bell,' Mum is saying. 'I'm sure it didn't ring. Arnold, ring it again.'

'I keep telling you to get your hearing checked out,' Dad mutters. 'But if you insist . . .' He rings the bell again, mildly arthritic finger sticking on the button.

The door rattles as I fight with the intricate security system. As the door opens, Mum steps back, pushing up the carefully teased curl at the nape of her neck. I can hear Dad muttering something about Fort Knox. He and Mum still leave their back door open despite The Incident of last summer when the Simpsons in neighbouring Rose Cottage had their gnomes decapitated – it made headlines in the local newspaper. But Dad has deemed himself not a man to be cowed by hooligans (i.e. bored fourteen-year-olds wearing Primark hoodies).

'Gosh, I am so sorry we are late,' says Mum, in a fluster. 'Is the lunch ruined? I really can't bear the thought of the lunch being ruined. We got lost, dear. I know it sounds absolutely ridiculous. Arnold took the wrong turn off the . . . the . . . is it the Westway or something?' She looks sharply at Dad. 'Didn't you, Arnold?'

'They've changed the damn road signs again,' grumbles Dad. 'Bloody Ken Livingstone.'

'Mum, you are not in the least late, not by our standards, anyway,' I say, giving her a hug and smelling the reassuringly talcy smell of her floral perfume.

Dad stands in what was once the hall and his mouth drops open like a hatch. 'Good grief! What happened to all the walls?'

'We've finally finished knocking through, Daddy. We took the last one out a few weeks ago,' shouts Georgia from the dining table.

'Looks like it's been bombed.'

'Rubbish! It's like walking into the pages of an interiors magazine,' coos Mum.

'It's due to star in *Livingetc* next month,' I say.

'Gosh!' Mum flushes with pleasure. 'Hilary will never believe it. You two girls, I don't know how I managed to produce you.'

'Come and sit down.' I usher them to the dining room table. They sit down. Dad pulls up his freshly pressed trouser legs, Mum folds her skirt carefully beneath her so it doesn't crease. She smiles – a tight, strained smile – at Olly. Goodness. What does one say? Talking about Olly's affliction in such a convivial setting obviously makes her feel awkward. 'Are you feeling better, dear?'

Olly crunches into a waxy green olive. 'Much, thanks, Marjorie.'

Mum looks relieved not to have received a more complex answer and doesn't pursue the subject.

There is a moment of awkwardness at the table, broken by

the appearance of Georgia carrying hot plates from the kitchen area, each starring a neat foil parcel housing fennel-scented sea bass, which wraps her face in a veil of steam. I am impressed. When did Georgia learn to cook? When does anyone have time to learn to cook?

Dad stares at his fish in its foil in bewilderment, as if wondering at what angle and with which implement he must attack the parcel.

'Like this, dear,' says Mum, reading his hesitation. 'Just slip it open with a knife. Hilary and I had these last week at that fancy new restaurant in Moreton-in-Marsh.'

There is the sound of chewing. I am thinking how nice it is to see my parents in London, rather than in their comfort zone of Lower Dalton, when suddenly Dad clatters his cutlery to the table.

'Marjorie,' he says gravely. 'Are you going to tell them or shall I?'

Mum's smile – which is one of her occasion smiles, brought out for best like her favourite peach silk blouse or her shoes – flat-lines. 'Let's not ruin lunch.'

'What? Daddy?' says Georgia. 'We're all family here . . .' She gazes lovestruck at Olly. 'Or soon will be. Tell us. What is it?'

'Arnold,' hisses Mum. 'Not now.'

'I think I'll have to, Marj,' says Dad apologetically.

Mum covers her mouth with her hand, as if anticipating digestive gas.

'Dad?' A funny feeling unsettles my stomach.

Dad coughs. 'You may remember that last time we saw you, we mentioned we talked about our pension.' He looks from face to face around the table sternly. 'Well, I am sorry to say—'

Mum makes a funny yelp noise.

Dad takes a deep breath and continues. 'A large proportion of our money is not there.'

'Not there?' I am confused. 'What do you mean, not there?'

Dad drops his eyes to his plate. 'Well, there's less there than we expected, rather screwing up our retirement plans, as you can imagine.'

'Fuck,' I say.

'Oh, Daddy,' Georgia exclaims, hands to her mouth. 'Olly knows about these things. You'll be able to sort it out, won't you, Olly?'

Olly shrugs, catching the fringing of his pashmina in his sea bass. 'I can look into it certainly. But it's unlikely that—'

Mum's throat makes the yelp noise again. 'It's a disaster, a complete disaster.'

'So I'm afraid, if you're wondering what it means,' continues Dad, addressing me, knowing I am the daughter – 'the coper', he calls me – who won't get hysterical, 'it means—'

'The wedding. Oh shit, the wedding,' cries Georgia, speaking through the fingers that clam her mouth.

Olly interrupts and raises his hand. 'Arnold, please do not worry about the wedding. I want to pay for it.'

Too right. Georgia and Olly's wedding is being organised by a wedding planner only too keen to splash Olly's cash. A vast stately home hotel has been booked in Gloucestershire. Jazz bands and classical quartets have been arranged. A dress commissioned at great expense. It's sounding more and more like a cross between a royal nuptial and Elton John's White Tie and Tiara ball.

'Your wedding will go ahead fine, George.' Dad clears his throat. 'I'm afraid, girls, what this means is selling Hedgerows.'

'Hedgerows? No!' I sit back in my chair, hand over my mouth. My parents have lived at Hedgerows for thirty years. The house *is* my parents. The idea of them selling it is appalling. Poor Mum. Poor Dad. I blow out heavily and blink furiously to clear the tears. How can I help? What can I do?

'Never! Not the family house!' Georgia is pale. 'You can't! You can't possibly! I want my children to inherit that house one day.' Her voice gets higher and higher and then bursts into a tearful plug-glugging sound.

'There must be something we can do,' says Nick. 'This seems all so wrong.'

Dad glances at him dismissively. 'I don't think there's anything you, of all people, could do. You're unemployed, son.'

'Dad . . .' I say.

'Arnold!' Mum exclaims.

'Sorry. Sorry.' Dad's head sinks into his hands. I've never seen him look so old and defeated. It's horribly disturbing. 'I'm just at my wits' end. It feels like the sky has fallen in.'

Seven

'So Don poked you on sit-on-my-Facebook? Cheeky bugger.'
Maggie scoops the tea bags out of the mugs with a fork and
dumps them in a steaming heap next to the sink. She places the
mugs on her large oak kitchen table, sloshing hot tea over the
sides. 'Now what can I tell you about him? Cocky. Successful,
obviously. Working-class boy made good, well that's his story
anyhow. I met him about five years ago at my mate Holly's
party, must have been before he went to New York.'

I cradle my chin in my hands above the cup of tea, enjoying the mist of steam against my jaw. 'Ah, you're a useless
source of gossip, Maggie.'

'I know, sorry. Still, he's not someone that strikes me as a
particularly dark horse. What you see is what you get. Brawn
and swagger.' She looks up at me and grins. 'Sexy?'

'Pardon?' I splutter a mouthful of Earl Grey.

'Do you think he's sexy?'

'Maggie! Ugh, no! Asking the question means that *you*
do.'

Maggie studies me. 'In a rough kind of way, no? Face like
a handsome boxer.'

'He's fat.'

'You've been working in women's magazines too long!'

'No. Not my type.' But I keep thinking about it: the spoon hovering a few millimetres from my lips, his dark red mouth instructing me to eat, the slip of the warm chocolate down my throat, sharply followed by a billowing feeling of defeat as if I'd let myself down – no, make that womankind down – by obeying him.

'Hi, Annie!' Maggie's husband Jake opens the kitchen door. He is a pale, charismatic man with dancing eyes who always wears a chef's apron that he ties around his waist. He calls it his housewife uniform. Not that he makes the joke so often any more, not after four years looking after the children. He kisses me on the cheek. He smells of Play-Do.

'You've been missed. Have you been in hiding?' I ask.

Jake rakes his stubble with his fingers. 'I tend not to hang out at media parties these days,' he says drily, opening a cupboard. 'I find that Musical Monkey Magic fulfils most of my social cravings.'

Jake is a freelance journalist, not a particularly prolific or high-powered one. After they had their first child, swiftly followed by another, it made sense for him to look after the kids and for Maggie to earn the dough, considering her earning power was greater and her business was taking off. Besides, they'd reasoned at the time, Jake would be able to continue working at home. Except he hasn't, not really. Maggie's company has gone from strength to strength, taking away any financial incentive for Jake to work.

Jake pulls a packet of rice cakes out of the cupboard. 'Maggie, how many times . . .'

'What?'

'The tea bags. Do you have to dump the tea bags on the

side of the sink? It's disgusting. Why can't you just put them in the bin?' He picks them up with a sheet of kitchen roll and tosses them abruptly at the swing bin, where they splatter against the lid before falling into its depths. 'I'm sick of clearing up after you,' he mutters under his breath.

Maggie is not and never is going to be the kind of person who cares about a tea bag's final resting place.

'Sick of it,' mutters Jake.

I check my mobile for texts, to give Jake and Maggie the space to bicker. Maggie recently told me that the last few weeks have been difficult. Jake is being testy, apparently. Sometimes he suffers from terrible mood swings. Hormones, I quipped.

There is a loud bang as Frankie, Maggie and Jake's two-year-old, bashes open the kitchen door with his wooden trolley and waddles into the room, trailing plastic fruit and vegetables. 'Mama. Mama,' he whines, whacking my ankles as he takes the most direct route to Maggie under the table.

Maggie scoops him up and sinks her nose into his crown of dark curls. 'Hello, Bobo. It's almost your bedtime.'

'Not bedtime. Not yet,' pipes up a little voice by the door. Johnny, his four-year-old brother, looks disapprovingly at his younger sibling and stomps over and tries to push Frankie off his mother's knee so he can get the prime spot on her thigh.

'Johnny. Easy.' Maggie pulls one boy on to each knee. They lean their dark, glossy heads back against the cushion of her breasts, entwine their perfect tiny fingers in the gold chains around her neck. Johnny elbows Frankie. 'I saw that, Johnny! Be nice to your baby brother. Stop fighting, you two!'

'It's not their fault,' says Jake sharply, giving each child a nice cake. 'They haven't seen you all day. What do you expect?'

In the drive, Maggie hitches up her trousers, heel flexed at the clutch of the family Audi, and accelerates loudly. 'I don't know what's been eating him. He's getting moodier and moodier. And kind of . . .' She shoots into the main road, fast, like a boy racer. 'Distant. I don't know what I'm doing wrong. All I know is that I'm not doing anything differently to how I normally do.' She shrugs. 'Please promise me you'll enjoy your child-free years, Annie. Honestly, much as I love my boys, big and small, I do look back and think, God, I was happy, I just didn't know it at the time.'

We arrive at the sample sale, following the trail of flushed, feverish-looking women clutching large unbranded plastic bags. We pay our five pounds entry fee. Inside, women swarm around piles of clothes and bags and shoes like clouds of troubled bees. The younger crowd rummage through the bargains, thrilled, determined, snatching arm-fuls of clothes off the rails just so others don't get a chance to grab them. In the changing rooms they throw clothes on and off their lithe bodies with abandon. The older, doughtier women look a bit crosser, as if resentful that they are still in such an undignified scrum, foraging for cut-price handbags and no longer able to fit into the sample sizes. It's greedy, frenetic. And stripped of designer pedantry – the snooty shop assistants, advertising, the flattering Bond Street light-ing – all the products look cheap. It's not the prettiest of scenes.

'Annie, Maggie, you made it!' Vicky, peering over a vast bundle of booty, taps me on the shoulder. 'I'd given up on you two coming. I am buying Christmas presents, en masse.

Thought I'd stick to bags and scarves, you know, given the maverick personal stylist voice in my head that makes me pick out the least fashionable item in the shop. Thanks for the invite, Annie. I owe you a free writ or something.'

Unlike us spoiled masses of glossy magazine hacks, jaded by freebies and cut-price designer items, Vicky appreciates every moment, every cheap belt, every end-of-the-line hand-bag. That she can more than afford the full-price version is irrelevant. Everyone loves a bargain.

'Don't miss their beautiful underwear.' Maggie points to a frothy mountain of lacy garments piled on a low stand, like the emptied contents of an underwear drawer. 'You'll put it to better use than me, Vicky.'

Hmm. Things aren't really happening for me, either. The more available sex time Nick and I have, the less we do it. In an unexpected way I miss the frisson of him being back late from the office, the anticipation of his homecoming, snatching it from between the jaws of our schedules. 'What's sex again?' I say.

'Sex?' A gruff voice stirs the air behind me.

I turn. Don! Christ.

'Sorry to interrupt, ladies. I couldn't help but overhear,' says Don, grinning. 'You're obviously having quite the juici-est conversation in the room.'

'What are you doing here?' The words come out harsher than I intend. Be civil. Act like you're pleased to see him.

'Shopping, Miss Rafferty. Tina gave me an invite. There's stonking menswear here apparently. Don't look so stunned. I'm metrosexual enough to do sample sales, aren't I?'

Hardly. Don looks even more like a comic cartoon today, his stocky body filling out his suit and giving him a square silhouette. No, he is the least metrosexual man I've ever met, sample sale shopper or not. 'Vicky, this is Don,' I say briskly. 'He works at PQ Publishing.' No, I won't kowtow by reeling off his ridiculously pompous title.

Vicky meets his gaze with a flurry of furious eyelash activity. Vicky, please, I want to shout, don't give him the satisfaction.

'Charmed,' says Don, shaking Vicky's hand before kissing Maggie casually on her cheek as if he'd just seen her yesterday. 'You're a mate of Holly's, aren't you? How's tricks?' He turns to me. 'I've just seen a coat that would look perfect on you. Come. I'll show you.'

'No, really. I'm—'

Vicky elbows me sharply in the ribs. 'A man has shopped for you! Annie, don't let him get away. Pickle him in formaldehyde.'

Don laughs. 'Come on. Behave, Miss Rafferty. It's just over here. I promise to return her to the cabal in one minute. No, give us five.' He presses his hand on the small of my back and pushes.

I don't move. Don pushes harder. This is not the way publishing people behave. It is beyond eccentric. He pushes harder again and I relent.

Don reaches into a crammed rack of clothes and pulls out a pink woollen boucle jacket, cut small on the shoulders and swinging out to the hip. 'Ta-dah!'

I laugh. The jacket is pretty. But it is the kind of thing Georgia might wear. And it is pink. I never wear pink. I am a graphic grey-and-black type of woman. 'Sorry, Don. No, not me.'

'Try it on.'

'No, really . . .' Who does he think he is? Shan't.

'Miss Rafferty . . .' Don insists teasingly, as if he's known me for years and this is our affectionate shorthand. 'Do as I say.'

'Only to prove my point,' I concede, realising resistance to be futile. I reluctantly slip my arms into the jacket's skiddy satin-lined sleeves. 'Satisfied, Don? See. Not me.'

He steps back. 'Fucking great.'

Is he gay? Is the maleness camped up? That would explain a lot of things. He doesn't look gay, no, but then so many gay men look straight these days. Or is it that more and more straight guys look gay? 'Really, I don't think . . .'

He puts both hands on my shoulders. 'Just look. Not at me, doughnut. Look at yourself in the mirror.'

Doughnut. Charming. Laughing despite myself, I look at my reflection. I see a tall woman, not fat, not thin, a strong woman with broad shoulders and a hedge of brown wavy hair framing an oval face with an announcement of a nose and navy-blue eyes. Then I look a bit harder, and I see a softer, prettier woman. A woman with roses in her cheeks, eyes a startling blue when contrasted with the pink, her waist nipped in by the tailoring. I see a woman in a pink jacket with a man, a short, dark man with large hands on her shoulders like paws. (A man who suddenly doesn't seem very gay at all.) For the first time in a long time, a very long time, I feel intoxicated by my own femininity, as if I've been whirling too fast around a dance floor in frothing tulle.

Get a grip, woman.

I blink, pull myself together just in time and yank the jacket off so quickly a seam rips.

Eight

My fingers turn the cold key in the lock. The door opens a couple of inches. Warm home smells escape, mingling with the damp cold of the street like two weather fronts. 'Hi.' My boot crashes on to the stripped-pine hall boards, making a disproportionately loud sound, something hard and cold entering a soft, private domestic space. There is no answer. 'Hullo?'

No reply. The kitchen table is still scattered with breakfast bowls and dirty cups. Old food smells. I check the table for post. Just bills. And one opened letter. 'Dear Nick,' it begins. 'Thank you for your application. Unfortunately in this case . . .' I walk into the living room. One mushroom-paint-streaked wall. An empty sofa. 'Nick?'

I push open the door to the main bedroom gently. There is a cloud of grey dope smoke lit by a circle of lamp light. Nick lies diagonally across the bed, his tufty head crushed against the headboard, his long body and legs like a road in a valley of duvet, his large socked feet dangling off the end, as if he's gone to sleep where he fell like a toddler. There is a gleam on his cheekbone. I touch it. It is wet. 'Nick?' I wrap my arms around him and lean my head against his chest. 'Baby, you're crying.'

Nick opens his eyes, rubs them. 'I'm not crying. I'm just feeling low, that's all.'

'Fuck 'em,' I say, thinking about that letter. 'You'll get a job.' I wince a little at the determined optimism in my own voice. It sounds like I am at work trying to enthuse demoralised staff. 'The right job.'

'I don't want a job!' groans Nick. 'Sorry, Annie, but it's hard to explain. Don't you see? I don't want to just be . . . well, another jobber.' 'If I can't get to the top in something, I don't want to do it. I don't want to be a middle-ranker. I don't want to collude in my own mediocrity.'

'That's like saying if you can't have a Ferrari you won't drive. Come on, Nick.'

'Fuck.' Nick shakes his head. 'You don't get it, do you? It's like trying to explain the rules of cricket to a fucking Norwegian.'

I kiss his fingers, try to kiss it all away. 'I don't get what?'

He laughs hollowly. 'It's me. Me!' He slaps himself hard in the chest. 'I . . . I . . . I feel so useless. Just fucking useless, Annie.'

'You're not useless.' I try to make him laugh. 'You make a mean shepherd's pie.'

I realise very quickly that this is the wrong thing to say. Nick doesn't smile. There is a long pause. I continue stroking his hair, the corrugated texture of the crazy shaven bits feels unfamiliar on my fingertips.

He sighs. 'The last bit of my redundancy money has gone.'

Shit. I stop the hair-stroking.

'All gone. Credit cards, records, trainers, usual shit.' He throws himself back on the duvet.

75

Trainers? He has twenty-three pairs of trainers. OK. Be supportive. Understand. It's tough for him at the moment. 'We'll manage.'

He sighs and looks up at me apologetically. 'I don't want you to just manage, Annie.'

'I'll pay the mortgage for the moment. Honestly, it's not a problem.' But as I say this, I realise that actually it is a problem. The mortgage should be our problem, but it is now my problem.

'Thanks. You're too good to me.' Nick's mouth turns down. He looks away and the temperature between us drops.

Could my offer of help be the least helpful thing for Nick's ego? Have I just royally screwed up again? Why isn't there a manual on how to manage men with career crises? Now that's an idea! I make a mental note to scribble it in a notebook later, alongside hundreds of other book and project and article ideas, stored away for later when I've got more time, like when I'm sixty-five.

'Annie.' He cranes his head up on one hand and studies my face thoughtfully. His voice is very quiet. 'I'm not sure I can be who you want me to be. You are so certain of everything, so capable, so . . . so . . . The thing is, Annie, you know exactly who you are. And you know exactly who you want me to be. And I'm not sure I can be that.'

I wince, hurt that he seems to think of me as some unimaginative bulldozer of a woman. Is that who I am in this relationship? Is that who I've been forced to become?

'I'm applying for work because I have to, because we have bills to pay, because of us – this house – but I'm not sure, not entirely sure, my heart is in it, babe. I can't give you the perfect package. I can't give you the house, the babies, the . . . the . . .' His voice trails off. 'I can't do it.'

Please don't say this. Please don't. Rewind. I'm terrified that if Nick carries on speaking now he'll say something irrecoverable, something that will change our relationship for ever. 'By *it* you mean us?' I say slowly.

There is a pause, a rustling of duvet as his foot agitates nervously at the ankle. 'I'm not sure.'

My heart starts to thump. I am filled with panic. The solid floor of our relationship feels like it is sagging in the middle. Nick is my life. Nick is my future. This isn't how things were meant to turn out at all. I've not been unfaithful, nor, to my knowledge, has he. He's not got cancer or a secret love child. Our relationship shouldn't be like this, pitching and keeling, as if about to slip soundlessly beneath the waves.

'Look at your dad, Annie. He worked all his damn life, saving, planning, and look where it's got him. He's got nothing to show for it! Nothing! Or my grandad. Heart attack at the age of fifty-eight. Goodbye and good night. Thank you for paying your National Insurance contributions. We live once.' Unexpectedly, Nick starts to smile, the edges of his mouth curling up slowly. 'Annie . . .'

I am scared of what he will say next. I close my eyes and brace myself. Here it comes, the moment I never thought would come when we were giddy in love. Here it comes, the 'it's not you it's me', the finale, the dismantling . . .

'If I've got only twenty-odd years left, Annie, I should fuck you hard now.'

'Nick!' I sigh, relieved, like we were talking ourselves off a cliff and managed to lurch back and save ourselves at the last minute. And it feels good to hear him say the word 'fuck'. So much sexier and less fraudulent somehow than 'make love'. Not that we've even been doing that recently. Last night I even wore pyjamas, blue check pyjamas: contraception by winceyette. A fuck? Yes, that's exactly what we need.

But first Nick wants a bath, which nips the spontaneity in the bud a bit. While he soaks, bubbles up to his armpits, I undress, dropping the day's work clothes to the floor. Without my work clothes, the uniform of the office, in our humble nakedness I hope we will be more equal again. Shivering, I lift one leg to get into the bath. I've forgotten how hard it is to make an elegant entry into a bath when the other person is already in it and getting a good look at a growing-out Brazilian. (Shouldn't paying the bills cancel out the duty to depilate?) 'Eek. This bath isn't built for two, is it?'

Nick soaps his neck. 'This is the first time we've been in here together, do you realise that?'

'Let's hope we don't end up falling through the kitchen ceiling.'

My legs turn firebrand pink under the water, knees protruding like two white islands. Nick tries to crunch his body into a smaller space to accommodate me but doesn't manage it: no, it really isn't that my clothes are shrinking as I'd hoped, I am definitely getting fatter. The cold tap drops an icy drip between my shoulder blades. Sex suddenly doesn't seem quite so appealing. But I cup my hands around Nick, now also a scalding shade of pink in the hot water. I tug. I stroke. Nothing happens. Nick studies my breasts, as if trying to concentrate on becoming erect. He coughs. His willy springs up and it looks like we have some action – our relationship is fine, everything working normally! – then, as he draws breath, it droops down again, settling back into its slouching torpor.

How about a blow job? The panacea for all puckers in male ego. In desperation, I bend forward and curve my head towards the soap-slippery target that sleeps just above the water's frothy surface. He tastes of kelp and lavender bubble bath and feels animate and slippery in my mouth, like a piece of raw seafood. My jaw begins to ache almost immediately.

'Annie.' Nick touches my hair. 'Annie, it's OK. Don't try so hard. I don't think it's going to happen. Not tonight.'

I release him, feeling humiliated. I can't even get my boyfriend hard. I can't make this relationship perfect. And I'm unable to define the exact something that is driving us apart. All I know is that it isn't just the cold dripping tap, and it hurts.

Nine

Yikes! I find it on the Monday morning when I tuck my feet beneath the desk and they collide with a large white plastic bag. Inside the bag is the pink jacket, its sleeves folded across its torso, clutching itself in embrace. I may as well have opened the bag to find half a million in fifty-pound notes, or a dead cat. I stare at it, taking in its improbable pinkness. It must have come from Don. It is inappropriate. He is inappropriate. I shake it out and become aware of a presence behind me, a long shadow and the smell of hairspray. I swivel round on my chair.

'Oh, new jacket?' asks Pippa, patting her hair like Margaret Thatcher did, a little grooming tic that reveals her age. 'I wouldn't normally put you in pink. You're never going to be a pink person, are you, Annie? But that's cute.'

'Thanks, Pippa. It's a present,' I say, hoping to make the subject drop as quickly as possible.

'Thoughtful boyfriend?'

I nod hard and something in my guts twists, as I remember last night's conversation with Nick.

'We approve,' Pippa says, scanning my computer screen as she talks. 'Now. Cover? Where are we?'

'Sorted,' I say, feeling pleased with myself, having taken over the negotiatyion from Pippa – who was rubbing up the agent the wrong way – and finally got permission to use a photograph of a B-list actress that will just about do as a cover image. Never before has the magazine sailed so perilously close to missing the very last print slot.

'Just as well. I ran with it. It's already at the printers.' Pippa shakes her head. 'Fuck. Don't do that to us again, Annie.'

Thank you. That's OK. Not a problem . . .

'Now, moving on. That celebrity belts feature,' she says. 'No. I'm not feeling it, Annie. Too woolly. Not servicey enough,' Pippa says with a whine. 'Where's the reader value? It needs to work harder, a lot harder. Make every edit your best edit, Annie.'

If the feature worked any harder it would give itself a pulmonary. I've already asked the writer to rewrite twice. This is because Pippa keeps changing the brief, rather than through any failing of the writer. But there is little point articulating this, as Pippa seems to have amnesia about decisions she's made only days, sometimes even hours, before. 'I'll rework it, Pippa.'

'It needed to be done yesterday.'

'It'll be in your in-tray by this afternoon.'

Pippa drops the printed-out feature on to my desk. 'You know what, Annie? I'm thinking spas. I'm thinking we just don't do enough spa stuff. I'm thinking that our readers go gaga about spas. Let's think outside the box here. Right, I've got an idea! How about the world's best spas in eighty days?'

'Great idea.' Is she losing it?

She stands closer to my desk and lowers her voice. 'Also, you should know, Don, Don Wilberforce . . .'

I feel the heat rise on my cheeks. I shove the bag a little further beneath the desk with my foot.

'. . . he's been putting ideas . . .' she rolls her eyes. 'into Tina's head about relaunching. I've got to present her with a bit of a mission statement next week, you know, the way forward with the current format. A relaunch would be a bore. We need to consolidate, not change things willy-nilly.'

'Right.' Actually, a relaunch doesn't sound like a bad idea. The magazine needs to do something. It needs to change. Because sales are slipping, and if they continue to slip much further we will all be out of a job. And I can't afford to be out of a job. I have just agreed to give Nick an allowance every week, until he sorts himself out; I have to pay the mortgage. Also, *Glo* deserves to do well, it really does. I want to see it triumph against its increasing odds.

'So I need some brilliant ideas, Annie. Let's show Tina what the *Glo* girls are made of! I want you to really go for it.'

I nod, looking thoughtful. All senior members of staff have to perfect the art of at least appearing to spark ideas like a hedgie on smart drugs. Good days, I'm pretty sharp. Bad days, like everyone else, I look at what the rivals did a few issues back and re-angle it, working backwards from the cover line. So Ten Tricks for Toned Arms becomes Wave Goodbye to Bingo Wings. ('Genius!' said Pippa, in case you're wondering, which may explain why we lost ten thousand readers last month.)

'I've got stacks of advertiser lunches this week, so . . .' Pippa cradles her chin in her hand. 'Tomorrow morning. That enough time? Of course it is! No, let's say by the end of this afternoon. Let's not sit on this.' She flashes a cool smile, the kind of smile that makes the rest of the staff feel stupidly grateful because it has just enough of a non-smile in it to remind us of the pain of its absence. 'Thanks, Annie. I can depend on you, can't I?'

It is at exactly this point that Alexis shoots up like a rocket launcher from behind the raised desk divider. This is where the back issues of *Glo* are filed and I've long been aware that it is the weak point in my defences. Sometimes the walls do have ears.

'I hope you don't mind me interrupting, Pippa. But I've already scribbled down some ideas,' says Alexis brightly, ignoring me. 'They came to me this morning as I jogged around Hyde Park.'

'Well at least someone's on the money,' says Pippa. She has always had a soft spot for Alexis. She likes skinny, fashionable staff. I think the only reason she didn't give her the deputy job was her comparative lack of experience, and perhaps she saw me as the sturdier, more reliable option. There is a favourability curve where Pippa's affection is concerned. Right now, despite my relative seniority, I have a suspicion I am nearer the bottom, while Alexis is nearer the top. But I know, we all know, that the curve is slippery as lip gloss. Pippa beams at Alexis. 'I very much look forward to reading them.'

Alexis hovers for a few moments. There is the faint whiff of tea tree oil. This is because Alexis has a habit of ringing each nostril with the oil every morning in the winter, 'to catch the germs before they get in', like a civilian-phobic celebrity on a long-haul flight. 'I'll get them to you by lunch,' she says, then strides off towards the features desk, clasping a stack of *Glo* back issues. Golden hair thrown back off her honed shoulders, she cuts a glamorous figure in a grey woollen pinafore dress and knee-high black patent boots. Unlike the rest of the office, who improvise designer looks with

Topshop, Gap and Zara, Alexis kits out in designer every day, bankrolled by a large juicy trust fund. But she's not a silly Sloane. Unlike many trust-fund girls, money seems not to have blunted Alexis' ambition. It just adds to her sense of entitlement.

Pippa strides off to torment the fashion desk. Belle phones. 'Sorry to interrupt. Don Wilberforce on the line.'

I hesitate, collect myself and press the blinking extension button. 'Don, hi.'

'Are you wearing it?'

I laugh, masking indignation. 'I don't really know what to say . . .'

'Say you'll have lunch with me tomorrow.'

Lunch! Gosh. I crunch forward on my desk, suddenly paranoid that somebody can overhear. 'Um, I . . . I . . .'

'It's business, Miss Rafferty.' He starts to laugh. 'Did you think I was asking you on a date?'

'No, I did not!' I say, possibly too forcefully.

I wake up the next morning hot, alert, my forehead shot by a small disc of sunlight that beams through a gap in the curtains with the precision of a laser gun. My tummy is full of the something-is-about-to-happen feeling that I used to get as a little girl for no reason at all. It takes a few seconds to identify it, rather than put it down to hunger or needing the loo or the residue of an excitable dream. Reminding myself that it is a Tuesday, just a plain old cold, sunny Tuesday, I turn on my hip and bridge my body up. The left-hand side of the bed is empty, just a rumpled hollow where Nick has been.

I sit at my mirrored dressing table, my elbows on the cool glass, watching my features rearrange themselves from squashy sleepiness to something more alert. I assess my naked self. Breasts. Not bad. Still conical. Upper arms could do with a bit of work but nothing disastrous. It's odd, because when I looked at my body the other night, after failing to get a rise out of Nick in the bath, it seemed fourteen pounds heavier and ten years older. It's amazing what a bit of office flirtation can do for one's self image.

I find Nick in the second bedroom, standing at the sloped drawing table, painting on a large white sheet of paper, his back to me. A plastic jug full of lilac turps sits on the mantelpiece. Two tubes of thick paint, one white, one pale blue, are lidless, their contents oozing out on to the window frame.

'Hi, sweetheart. You're up early,' I say, screwing the lids back on the paint tubes. He normally surfaces about ten.

'Couldn't sleep. I had dreams about my teeth falling out.' There is a frost in his voice. Things have got palpably chillier between us since the day I found him crying on the bed. He glances over. 'I'd rather you didn't fuss with my paint tubes, if you don't mind.'

I put the tubes down and loop my arms around his waist.

He shrugs me off. 'I'm in flow, Annie. Sorry.'

Oh. OK. A sense of déjà vu confuses me momentarily. It was like this, but so not like this, six months ago. I remember waking up to go to the loo, in the cool, dark early hours of a spring morning, and discovering Nick painting in the living room of our old flat in Dollis Hill. He had his back to me, naked from the waist up, his lean musculature shadowed by the streetlamp light coming through the blinds. Still half-asleep, I put my hands around his waist, on to his smooth, warm skin. He didn't shrug then. He smiled and turned to face me, kissing my nose, snuggling his neck into mine, his hands slipping around my waist. And we made love there, without speaking, and then he carried me back to bed, tucked

85

me up beneath the duvet, kissed me on the forehead and I was asleep. It feels like a lifetime ago. A different relationship. 'I'll leave you in peace, then.'

Back in the bedroom, fired up by Nick's shrug-off, I rifle through the hangers in my wardrobe. Lunch with Don. What should I wear to lunch with Don? Nothing is right. The harder I think about my outfit, the more of my clothes I see, the clearer it becomes that I have absolutely nothing to wear and must go shopping. After a few minutes of trying on (then throwing into a heap on the floor), I settle on one of my favourites, a red wool Hepburn-style shift. Round-toed low heels. A grey cashmere shrug cardigan. I put the kettle on and tackle some honey on toast but find that, most uncharacteristically, I am not in the least bit hungry.

Nick appears in the kitchen and puts on some hip-hop, confrontationally loud. 'Who are you dressing up for?'

'All the gay men in the office, darling.'

Nick doesn't laugh. 'You hardly ever wear dresses any more.'

I guess he might have a point. At home, in recent months, I have developed a rather slovenly habit of slobbing around in ancient Juicy Couture tracksuit or old baggy jeans. And in recent weeks, I've found myself drawn to trousers even when we go out – which is, now I think about it, increasingly rare – as if the trousers are somehow the sartorial expression of my new role in the household. 'I was in the mood for a dress. Any law against it?'

'No.' He shakes his head and smiles.

'Don't you like it?'

Nick smiles. 'You look lovely.' He hovers hesitantly. After a few moments' silence he speaks. 'Can I borrow some cash?' He tries to say this as he always used to say it, as we both used to say it when the cashpoint was out of cash or a cheque hadn't cleared. Except that this time we both know that it is different. His words shoot out too fast. He is staring at his trainers.

'Sure.' I pretend that it isn't different, fixing my voice at a casual pitch. 'How much?'

'Um . . .' Nick looks uncomfortable.

I don't want to put him through it or make it more of an issue than it already is, so without waiting for his reply, I click open my purse and press all the notes I have, about sixty quid, into his hand.

'I'll pay you back.' He scratches his stubble, which is the longest I've ever seen it apart from during a holiday to Pushkar in India when he did his best to go native. He even tried to stand on one leg for a whole day in the manner of a holy man but managed about twenty minutes before getting cramp. 'I was hoping to be sorted by now, Annie.'

'I know. It's fine. Don't worry about it.' Last button done on my coat, I kiss him on the cheek, in a disturbingly motherly way. 'I've got to run. I'll probably be late back tonight.'

'I guessed that,' he says.

Pippa takes off her sunglasses and grins. 'Now, Annie, can you keep a secret?'

'Of course.'

Just as Pippa opens her mouth to speak, an ear-splitting siren blasts down from the speakers on the ceiling.

'Fire alarm.' Pippa rolls her eyes. 'What a bore. Let's speak later.'

Everyone at *Glo* always reacts to every drill as if it were indeed a drill and not a fire: they apply lip salve, refill their handbags, and take the stairs down slowly, coffee in hand, gossiping, pleased at the excuse not to have to work. It takes about half an hour before the entire building is disgorged on to the pavement in the drizzling rain. The inhabitants of the various floors, who rarely see each other at such close quarters apart from in the lifts, check each other out. Is Don around? I can't see him. The single *Glo* staff scan the huddle in the street for attractive male heterosexuals and reports filter back of some talent in IT. The main problem with them, of course, being that they're in IT. The great unwashed from *Quad-Bike Digest* drool after the pretty fashion assistants and nudge each other indiscreetly when Alexis sashays over to me, hips swinging in a mini-skirt. We're discussing the latest feature pages disaster – all the real-life readers on our Miracle Ten Day Diet have gained weight and require serious Photoshop – when Belle touches me lightly on the elbow.

'You look nice in your red dress, Annie,' she says approvingly. 'Colour really suits you.'

'Thanks, Belle!' I'm liking me in a dress right now. I'm feeling hot in the dress. I want to twirl around like a five-year-old shrieking, 'Look at my lovely red dress!'

'Just before the alarm went off I took a message from Don Wilberforce,' Belle continues. 'He passes on his apologies but he has to cancel lunch.'

'Cancel?' I stop still, as if in seizure, the pavement suddenly a vertiginous drop beneath me. It seems preposterous, absurd that he's cancelled. He'd been so insistent. And I've put on this dress . . . I hate this dress. What am I doing in a red dress?

Alexis nudges me. 'Don probably pressed the fire alarm himself to rearrange his schedule,' she says, breaking into an irrepressible smile. 'Aren't men exasperating? Honestly.'

Later, back in the office, not wanting to give Alexis the

satisfaction of witnessing me self-consciously eating a sandwich at my desk wearing an obviously lunch-date dress, I
quickly arrange to meet Maggie, who, luckily, has a meeting
in this part of town. I find her at a small busy café further
along the river at Gabriel's Wharf. She is sitting by the
window. Her olive skin looks paler than normal, her features
tight. Her left hand clutches her mobile, which she keeps
glancing at, as if expecting a call any minute.

'So?' I say.

'So,' says Maggie slowly, taking a sip of a glass of water.
'This woman, this Nicky . . .' She says the name with distaste.
'A neighbour, she lives about ten doors down. I've always
avoided her. She glares at me on the few occasions I get to the
school gate. Gives all the working mothers the evil. Anyway,
today she asked me who my new nanny is. New nanny?
"Oh," she says, "in a really kind of annoying *oh really?* type
of voice. "I keep seeing Jake with this nanny, the pretty
blonde Polish one," she says. "Works in Milverton Road . . ."

'I don't understand.' Try as I might, I don't get nannies. It's
not my world.

'But I don't know what he does all day while I'm at the
office. Who is this bloody nanny?' Maggie ruffles her choppy
black hair with agitated fingers. 'Is she hot? I tell you, I look
around London these days and the girls seem to be getting
prettier and prettier, better and better turned out, or is that
because I'm getting older and frumpier? I mean, look at you
in that fantastic red dress. You look sensational, by the way.'

'Thank you. But Maggie, please. Jake is not going to be
eyeing up nannies. He's got you. He's not insane.'

Maggie stabs her steak with a fork. Blood oozes out of it.
'I piss him off. He says I boss him around. He says he's sick
of being at home with the kids.'

89

'Well, I guess it must be tough . . .' I tread carefully, not wanting to offend Maggie – my loyalty is to her; partners always come second – but hoping to put across the other side. 'Would you really want to be at home with the kids all day, every day? Wouldn't you find it incredibly frustrating?'

'It's not an option, Annie,' says Maggie quickly.

'But if staying at home were an option?'

Maggie interlaces her fingers and rests her chin on her hands. 'Yes, it probably would drive me bonkers.'

'And it would be domestic carnage.'

'Oh, completely. The kids would go feral. We'd all go feral.' She sighs. 'But the problem is, I miss my kids like mad, Annie. I miss cooking them lunch, taking them swimming, to play dates, all the things that full-time mums, and dads, moan about, I guess.' Maggie slices into the steak and cuts out a precise cube of bloody meat, raises it to her mouth.

'I'm sure you and Jake, being you two, will work it out,' I say, picking a fishbone out of my mouth with my fingers. 'As for the nanny, I really wouldn't worry. It sounds to me like shit-stirring by a jealous housewife.'

Maggie bites her bottom lip. 'I know Jake. Something's up.'

Would Jake? Could Jake? No. Not with a nanny. Not when he has the splendid, clever Maggie. Why would he risk it all?

'Instinct,' continues Maggie, looking mournfully out of the window at the Thames, which is vast as a sea and goblin green today. 'Annie, I know this sounds terribly un-PC, the kind of thing Vicky might say, but do you think men ultimately want women they can feel they can protect? Who are on some bullshit level inferior?'

'Maggie!' I'd never have given Maggie those lines. Not

Maggie with her stallion legs and fast, funny brain. 'You're depressing me now. No. No, I don't. No more than all women want to be protected. Do you want to be protected?'

'From hot nannies, yes, I do actually,' she laughs.

For no particular reason I wonder what Don is doing. Why he's blown me out. Who he is with. Am I hot to him? Stop. Stop. Ridiculous.

Maggie leans back in her chair, more relaxed now that she's vented her anxieties. 'The sad thing is, I'm jealous of this nanny, whoever she is, whether she's got her eyes on my husband or not. I'm jealous of her freedom. Of the time she spends with kids. Is that an awful admission? Does that make me a risible feminist?'

'Probably.'

Maggie flicks her napkin at me. We laugh and then sit in a happy silent bubble of mutual understanding for a few moments and I feel full of love for her.

She raises one eyebrow. 'You could probably do with the odd day at home too. You work too hard, Annie. I worry about you.'

Her comment takes me by surprise. 'I am a full-time busy bee. It's in my veins. I don't know what I'd do with myself at home, Maggie. I'd end up reorganising the bathroom cabinet, or stacking my shoes in Perspex boxes and labelling them, or wallpapering lampshades, like Georgia does. In other words, I'd go doolally.'

Maggie studies my face for a moment. 'You've mentioned before that one day you'd like to write a book, do something different. I'd like to see you do that.'

'Oh, that's a retirement project,' I say, dismissing the idea with a wave of my hand. 'I'll be banging out bad novels in my seventies, I promise, in between tours of India and pottery classes, of course. I can't wait! Bring on old age! Sadly, right now, I'm entrenched.'

'Me too.' Maggie grins. 'Who cares! Let's self-medicate. I think we need a cheeky lunch-hour glass of wine to lift ourselves from our entrenchment.'

As the waitress pours the wine, twists the bottle and pulls it away, something catches my attention from outside the café window. I look up. A roller-skater whizzes past. Then a huddle of Japanese tourists excitedly disperse, revealing the figure I sensed before I saw, the square, stocky figure of Don Wilberforce, walking fast, chatting animatedly to – Christ almighty, it can't be, yes, it is – Alexis.

Ten

Mum and I sit, waiting for the show to start, on red-velvet-cushioned gilt chairs outside the changing room, me slumped with my denim-clad legs apart, Mum cross-legged, neatly and a little awkwardly, her hands clasped tight in her lap, like a theatre goer who doesn't go to the theatre very often. Chandeliers drip from the ceiling, shattering sunlight on to the French mirrors that lean against the walls like giant playing cards. Georgia disappeared behind the muslin drapes with the dress designer almost ten minutes ago. We're getting restless.

'If I'd known quite how grand this place was I'd have done something with my hair,' Mum mutters, clicking open her handbag and reaching for a compact of pink pressed powder. She checks her lipstick in its mirror, purses her mouth, twists it from side to side anxiously, then snaps the compact shut and slides it back into her black leather John Lewis handbag. I have given her a couple of nice designer bags over the years, bought at sample sales, but Mum always views them warily, fills them with tissue paper (saved from shoe boxes) and keeps them For Best, which means they rarely, if ever, get an outing. I fear she suspects that having a nice handbag is too great a vanity or a horrible symbol of conspicuous consumption, solely responsible for the melting of the Antarctic ice floes and child labour in the Third World. For this reason, if she asks me how much my new clothes cost, I usually have to shave at least one nought off the end. She leans forward, resting her chin on cracked gardener's hands that have a rim of mud under the thumbnails. 'I wish me and your father were paying for all of this.'

'Many couples pay for their own weddings these days, Mum. It's not unusual,' I say softly, trying to reassure her. 'Besides, Olly earns as much as the GDP of a small developing nation. You are paying for the champagne, Mum. Very generous, considering.'

'Yes, we are.' Mum sighs and fiddles with her wedding ring, a cluster of tiny diamonds set on a gold band, worn down by decades of submergence in Fairy Liquid. 'Rather a lot of champagne, if I may say so. Georgia says she wants it all night. I thought . . .'

'That it would be just for a toast?' Lord knows how much champagne Georgia has requested. Five bottles per guest, probably.

'Just a glass or two, yes. But people seem to drink so much these days.'

'I can chip in if necessary.' I smile at Mum, but as I do so a shameful part of me hopes she doesn't take me up on the offer. I'm suddenly not sure I can afford it at all.

We stare at the drapes as they bulge with a Georgia shape then flatten again.

Mum looks thoughtful. 'How is Nick's job hunt going?'

'Still hunting, I'm afraid, Mum.'

Mum shakes her head. 'Poor Nick. It's been a while, hasn't it?'

94

'Don't get me started.'

'Ah.' Mum smiles. She understands. 'Could he not just get a job at the greengrocer? A little something to tide him over?'

I try to imagine Nick in a smeared apron and laugh. 'I don't think he'd do that.'

'You'd get discounted fruit and veg. Could be very useful.'

'Mum!' I laugh. 'Now what is Georgia doing in there? George!' I shout. 'We're fossilising out here! Give us a butcher's.'

The designer tugs back the drapes. A bare pink foot. A neatly turned ankle. Georgia steps out of the fitting room. The dress – pure white, fluted like a lily, embroidered with a subtle laminate of clear crystals – throws flattering soft light at her happy freckled face. It is as if she has always been destined to inhabit this precise moment, walking out of a changing room, her feet bare, her eyes wide, hair flaming, ready to embrace the awaiting future. It strikes me that Georgia was born to wear a white dress. Was I born to wear black jersey?

'Oh, Georgia,' coos Mum, her eyes immediately watering. 'Goodness me.'

'Doesn't she look stunning?' asks the designer. 'We got there in the end, didn't we, Georgia?'

Georgia has had the dress redesigned at least three times.

'What do you think, Annie?' Georgia turns, showing off her slender, naturally corset-shaped back, neatly contained in the dress by a row of pearl buttons.

'You look completely, heartbreakingly beautiful, sis.' My eyes fill. 'Look, you're making me go all soppy.'

Georgia beams. She knows it takes a lot for me to go all soppy.

'May I?' Mum stretches out her hand to gingerly touch the fabric.

The designer looks uneasy. She's spotted Mum's gardening thumbnail.

'Goodness,' sighs Mum. 'To think I got married in a two-piece from Marks and Spencer.'

She still has that outfit, a rather stiff cream taffeta bodice and tailored skirt that look much better in the wedding photos than in scratchy real life. She also has a hat, a wonderful large white hat made out of some kind of woven 1960s plastic, which once seemed the epitome of movie-star glamour. We fought over it when we were younger, wearing it around the house, its rim falling over our eyes, peeping out through the white grids of plastic. In Georgia's dress I recognise a new heirloom in the making.

After the fitting, Georgia insists we all go to tea at the Connaught, despite Mum's protests that we don't need to go anywhere so fancy, and what is wrong with that nice little cheap café off Green Park? She's worried about money, of course. 'My treat,' I say.

We sit at a small, round linen-covered table in the Connaught's Red Room, next to a roaring fire and an aged silver mirror hanging on the lacquered red wall. I order two set teas rather than three, knowing that Georgia will not inhale more than a mouthful of scone.

Georgia leans back in her chair, shaking her hair between her fingers so it fans out like a comb of coral. Then she twists it round and fastens it at the top of her head in a louche bun. 'I can't believe this is my life. I feel like pinching myself.' If anyone else said this it would sound disingenuous, but she really means it.

'To think . . . Well, my little Georgia.' Mum pats her wrist. 'Goodness.'

'Mum!' says Georgia, enjoying Mum's sentimentality. She

never gets bored of it. She can always handle being loved more.

'You'll always be my little Georgia to me. You're a lucky girl,' adds Mum.

I wonder, for a fleeting second, if this means Mum sees me as unlucky.

'Olly is just . . .' Georgia laughs. 'Oh, I just really love him,' she says. 'It's like coming home.'

I stare at her, in awe of her uncomplicated sentimentality. With her eyes shining and her hair whipped up off her face, she looks like every woman wants to look when they're in love. She's so free of cynicism. And, I guess, because of that, so vulnerable. I hope, I really hope Olly'll look after her. 'He's the lucky one,' I say.

Georgia looks searchingly from my face to Mum's. 'You both love him too, don't you?'

I am a little thrown. It's not really a Georgia-style question. She rarely questions anything. She's non-neurotic in that sense, the opposite of me.

'Gosh, yes. He's such a decent man,' says Mum enthusiastically. 'A sensitive man.'

'Decent' means solvent. 'Sensitive' is Mum's optimistic euphemism for depressive tendencies.

'He is!' Georgia clinks her tea cup against mine. 'You next, sis! It'll be wedding bells for you soon, I bet. I'll bet you a squillion—'

'I wouldn't hold your breath,' I interrupt. The idea that Nick and I are about to splash out on a wedding when we can barely afford our mortgage and haven't had sex in weeks is laughable. Besides, I'm not sure he'd want to marry me right now. I'm not sure I'd want to marry him either. We're in a relationship trough. When will the wave peak again?

'You'll want kids soonish, won't you?' asks Georgia.

'I'm thirty-four, not forty-four. Hit thirty and your ovaries become everybody's business.'

'Don't you want kids?' perseveres Georgia, struggling to fathom the idea. If she could put her unborn kids down on the waiting list for Wetherby Prep, she would do.

'Not right now,' I say quickly. 'No.'

I can sense both Georgia and Mum swallowing 'don't leave it too late' comments.

'I've only just got the promotion. We've just bought a house. Nick's looking for work. It's so not the right time.' I am sensing that most of our issues lurk in between the full stops somewhere.

'It's never the right time, darling,' Mum is unable to resist.

'Mum!'

'Sorry, dear,' she says, dabbing at her mouth with a linen napkin.

'Honestly, while I understand your eagerness for grand-children, this really isn't the right time. I don't believe all those don't-forget-to-have-children headlines. I'm sure it's a conspiracy.'

'Hmmm,' says Mum, carefully crushing a crumbly wedge of yellow cream on to her scone. 'You always did have strong opinions about things.'

'Sorry, we don't mean to upset you,' says Georgia.

'You haven't upset me.' Why does expressing an opinion in this family equate with discord? Other families – clever ones that live in north London – have heated family debates. When I was younger, I always wanted to be part of a family who had heated family debates. I enjoy a debate.

The sound of a mobile ringing. Mum jumps in her seat, immediately flustered. After five years of reluctant mobile-phone ownership, she remains stunned by the shrill of the ring tone. Her hands lurch towards the alarming green flashing thing in the powdery depths of her handbag and grab it firmly, lest it escape. She studies the buttons before pressing them, as if she might launch *Apollo 13* by mistake. 'Hullo?' she shouts. 'This is Marjorie Rafferty speaking.' Her neck flushes. 'Yes! Oh, hullo. Yes, she's here! She's forgotten her phone, you say? Well, it's been such an exciting day for her. We've just been discussing my future grandchildren!'

Mum! I elbow her. 'Shhh!'

'Yes, yes, quite. Gosh, you do sound serious, Olly.' Mum passes the phone to Georgia with a wink. 'Lover man,' she laughs.

Eleven

David emails me: *Hi Annie, how's tricks? Thanks for coming to the Hatch party. I got horribly pissed and had a fantastic time. Hope you did too. Now doing research for a comedy series set in the magazine world, kind of Ugly Betty meets Cold Feet. I know lots of women in magazines, all of them totally mad. Apart from you. Can I bribe you to talk – research! – over a drink? Dave x*

Of course, happy to discuss in confidence. Pop round. Any excuse. I press send and immediately wonder why I haven't had an email from Don. Don. Don. Don. A liar. An Alexis hound. Why on earth did I *ever* feel flattered by his attentions?

I shut my computer down, leave the office and walk along the South Bank. It's a warm autumn evening. As I stroll along, I use the spare brain time to calculate my new mortgage repayments. Interest rates have shot up and the newspapers groan with doom-predicting stories of future repossessions. The digits flick up and down in my head like the numbers on an old-fashioned clickety shop till. So, by my calculations . . . we're skint!

I hear footsteps gaining ground behind me. A loon? A mugger? I instinctively start walking faster.

'Whoa!' Don looks a bit sweaty, as if he's been running, or beating someone up. His physicality is always a bit of a surprise.

'Hi.' Yes, right tone. Very good, Annie. Professional politeness.

'Walking along the South Bank?'

I can't really claim to be walking any other way, hedged in as I am by the river and the National Theatre. 'Quite.'

'I will escort you.'

You will?

'Sorry about lunch the other day,' he says, without sounding sorry at all. 'Had to fire someone.'

Fire someone? Lunch with someone more like it. Should I say that I saw him with Alexis? No. I will let him dig himself in further. 'Oh, don't worry. I was manic anyhow.' I speed up, keeping my eyes firmly fixed on the wide green Thames and the noisy boats that chug up and down its length. I refuse to give Don the satisfaction of looking at him, if only to discomfort his swagger.

'Where are you rushing to?' he asks teasingly, feet thumping on the pavement.

'Home.' I roll my eyes, glimpsing wispy white clouds.

'Where's home?'

'Kensal Rise.'

'Oh. So why are you in such a rush to get back, then?' There are streams of untapped laughter in his voice.

Cheeky bugger. 'Very funny.'

'Fancy a quick drink?'

'Sorry. I've got to get back.' I continue to march, past buskers, groups of tourists, and lovers on benches snogging stagily.

'I do believe you are angry about lunch.'

'Don't be ridiculous.'

'I don't believe you have to rush home, Miss Rafferty.'

'Nick has cooked a meal.' This is a lie. Nick's enthusiasm for cooking has begun to wane. Last night we had fish and chips. When I woke up, the greasy wrappers were still crumpled on the kitchen table, putting me off my Dorset muesli. Knowing me as he does, leaving the wrappers on the table was an act of aggression.

'Then why are you carrying a Marks and Spencer bucket of ready-made Chinese stir-fry?'

'And why are you looking in my shopping bags?' Indignant, head held proudly aloft, heels pounding the pavement, heart inexplicably racing, I do not anticipate the dislodged ledge of Southwark Council paving that rears up at an angle in front of me. My toe catches it and I tip forward, arms outstretched, hitting the cup of my left knee hard on the concrete. 'Fuck.'

Don picks me up, holding me tight beneath each elbow. 'You OK?'

'Fine, fine.' I brush myself down. I am not fine. There is a whoop of pain in my left knee. Of course, I don't want to admit this. I carry on walking. One step. Two steps. If I can just make it to Waterloo Bridge, then I can get a cab and lose him.

'You're hobbling,' says Don.

'I am walking.'

Don quickens his pace so he is standing in front of me, his pupils shrinking in response to the last flare of evening sun. His short stature means that he is almost on my eye level. And his gaze is so intense it reminds me of those weird gazes utilised by ITV hypnotists. I have to look away.

'Miss Rafferty, I insist you sit down. Don't martyr yourself.' He grabs my arm. 'Here, let me.'

Something in me gives up. I rest my weight against his bulk. His supporting arm is as sturdy as a shelf. I let myself fall ever so slightly into his body, just to take the weight off my left knee. He guides me to a free bench. Then he stops, shrugs off his coat and lays it down on the wooden slats. 'A cushion.'

Smooth cheesiness or gallantry? Does it matter?

I sit down and rub my knee. Don reaches inside his jacket pocket and brings out a packet of cigarettes. He smokes! I hadn't had him down as a smoker.

'Cigarette?' he offers.

'No. Don't smoke.'

'Very sensible.' He sparks up the cigarette and inhales deeply. He smokes in short snorts, blowing the smoke out with some force so that it tunnels from his mouth like exhaust from a car. 'How's the leg? Would you like me to have a look?'

'No thanks. I've changed my mind about that cigarette, though.'

'Very sensible.' Don laughs, pulls a cigarette from his packet and lights it for me in his mouth before handing it over.

What would happen if a work colleague – Belle? Alexis? – spots us? What would they think? Yet I can't bring myself to move yet. Just another five minutes. Give my knee a chance to rest. I pull on the unfamiliar cigarette. I haven't smoked for over a year, but after the first three horrible puffs it still tastes good.

Don sighs, uncharacteristically wistful, and stretches out his legs. 'I missed this in New York, you know. The grey skies. The ugly mish-mash of buildings. The hunks of concrete. It's funny the things you miss when you go away. It's not the things you think you might miss. It's not Marmite or the BBC. It's the things that you take for granted when you're here. Simple, ugly things.'

'Right.'

Don takes a final drag on his cigarette before flicking it to the ground and crunching it beneath his shoe. 'I missed English women too.'

'Simple, ugly things?'

'No, the mouthy, defensive, clever ones. The ones who are so seriously unimpressed it's like they've learnt flirting techniques from the Queen.'

I stare ahead, refusing to be drawn into his schoolboy banter. He is my superior. My life is clearly divided in two – home and work – and he is on the wrong side of the line.

It begins to darken suddenly, as if someone has tipped a pot of dark blue ink into the pale sky above east London. A sharp wind blows up from the Houses of Parliament, skidding along the water, surprising me with its cold slap. I pull my coat tight.

'Do you want my scarf?' offers Don.

'No. Thanks. I should be heading back.' Nick will be waiting.

'Hang out with me. Champagne at the Oxo, what do you reckon?'

I shake my head.

'I wanted to talk to you about Pippa. About the magazine,' he says, shamelessly pulling rank.

'Can it wait until next week?'

Don suddenly stands up, brushing down his trousers. 'Christ, you're infuriating.'

'Excuse me?'

He stretches out a hand brusquely. 'Come on, for fuck's sake.'

I take his hand's dry, tight grip and allow him to pull me up. He lets go of my hand once I am up, and part of me is disappointed that he didn't try to hold it for longer. We walk – me hobbling slightly, Don, brooding and silent, kicking up stray bits of litter – alongside the river until we get to Waterloo Bridge. The traffic rushes past with a loud whoosh and the cold air skids off the Thames. It is noisy, bracing. He sticks out an arm at the stream of cars. A black cab signals and stops. He opens the door. I step inside. Where are we going?

'Kensal Rise,' barks Don at the taxi driver. The evening is about to unfold against my will. I am certain Don will jump into the taxi. But he doesn't get in. He slams the door, raps it twice with his knuckles and storms off over the bridge into the dark autumn evening without even a backward glance.

Twelve

'Come in,' Nick hisses as I open the front door. 'Quickly.' He looks drained. His tufts of crazy hair point out from his scalp at confused, contrary angles, as if he's just spent the last hour ruffling it furiously.

'Ow, my knee. I banged my knee. It hurts. I'm getting old.'

'Annie . . .' he says urgently.

A sense of foreboding hits me. I stop rubbing my knee melodramatically. 'What's the matter?'

'Olly's called off the wedding!'

'He's what?' I dump my bag in the hall.

He points inside the house. 'She's in there.'

I gasp when I find Georgia in the living room, crumpled in a sobbing heap in the far corner of the sofa, her feet curled beneath her, head bent into her hands, like a small, terrified animal. I'm struck by a horrible, overpowering déjà vu. Suddenly, it is as if we are children again.

It was a hot July day, a week before the end of the school summer term. I was fifteen, Georgia was thirteen. Normally I'd meet her at the school gates and we'd cycle home from school together. But that day, that baking, cloudless afternoon,

I was late because my library books were overdue and I went to return them at the school library first. By the time I got to the gates, Georgia had gone on alone. When I got back to the house there was no sign of her. I walked inside and, after a few moments, heard gasping sounds from behind the sitting room sofa, and that was where I found her, sitting on the floor, knees bent up to her chest, arms wrapped around them, teeth chattering, trembling. She wouldn't speak to me at first, just looked at me with huge, pleading brown eyes. I knew something terrible had happened. Eventually, I coaxed it out of her. She'd been cycling back from school down the lane that weaves for a few hundred yards behind cornfields. A man, shaven-headed, fat, old to a thirteen-year-old, had leapt out at her from behind a hedge. He had grabbed her by the shoulder. She had only just managed not to fall off the wobbling bike and snaked her body out of his grip, pedalled away as fast as she could, screaming, the man chasing after her, crashing through the corn, his trousers down and his dick hanging out. She had managed to cycle to the main road, leaving the man in the fields behind her. A chill passed over my body in a wave. Was he still there when I cycled past on the same route twenty minutes later? I hugged Georgia and she clasped me so tight I had marks on my neck for hours afterwards. We told Mum, who phoned the police. They never caught the man. And Georgia used to wake up at night for years after, sitting straight up in bed, asleep but with her eyes wide open, screaming. I've always felt that it was my fault. I should have been there for her. I wasn't.

'George, darling,' I say softly, sitting next to her and wrapping my arms around her heaving body. 'I'm so sorry.'

Georgia tries to speak, but the words come out as guttural sobs. I stroke her soft red hair, wishing I could take the hurt away. We sit like this, only sobs breaking the silence, for five minutes. Eventually the sobs become less heavy, less frequent, and she regains control of her breathing. I hold her tighter, test the water. 'What happened, George?'

Georgia sits up, pulling strands of wet hair off her face. 'He . . . he . . .'

'Take your time.'

'He says that he doesn't think . . .' she starts to cry and gulp again, 'we will work. That I've changed or something. And that we are too d . . . d . . . different.'

'No. I don't believe it. Are you sure he means it and it's not just a row? It's easy to say things in the heat of the moment.'

Georgia's shoulders judder. 'He means it, Annie. I swear he means it. I can see it in his eyes. His eyes have gone cold.'

'Men do get nervous before weddings.' But if his eyes have gone cold. Oh no. That's not good. Not good at all, poor love.

Georgia shakes her head, disbelieving. 'He's ruined my life, Annie.'

'No. He hasn't. You'll be OK. I promise you, you'll be OK. Is he depressed again?'

'No. He's not depressed. He's recovering. I blame his fucking therapy!' shouts Georgia suddenly. Georgia rarely shouts. Life has always washed over her like warm sea water across a beach. 'He told me he realised in therapy! But the fucking therapist doesn't make his meals. She doesn't decorate his homes, talk to his boring banking friends . . . She doesn't love him. God, I love Olly so much.' Georgia lets out a horrible wail, half woman, half hyena. Nick, who's been hiding in the kitchen trying to keep out of the way, appears at the door looking alarmed. I shoo him away, and, obviously relieved, he disappears back into the kitchen.

108

'What am I going to do? What the hell shall I do?' The sobs quicken again. 'What will become of me, Annie?'

I try to think fast. But there are no answers. In my experience, there is no salve for heartbreak. You have to live it out, wait for the pain to recede, like floodwaters, until the old self is revealed again, a little damaged but intact. 'Do nothing. Stay here. We will make up the spare room. Stay here and rest. Let me look after you. Please, George.'

'Supper!' Nick has heated up the Chinese stir-fry. We sit around our rectangular oak table, a horrible inversion of a normal happy mealtime. Georgia doesn't speak. Or eat. Her fork trembles when she lifts it. After a while she says very quietly, 'I'm off to bed. I need the obliteration of sleep.'

I cradle her with one arm and walk her to the spare bedroom. She feels shockingly light and fragile, as if sadness has filled her bones with feathers. 'Do you want to borrow a T-shirt? A toothbrush?'

Georgia shakes her head, pulls off her jeans and sweater and slides into bed in pink polka-dot knickers and silk cami vest. I tuck her up like a child, watch as her eyes close and her eyeballs pinball back behind their lids.

I walk back into the living room. 'The bastard,' I say to Nick. 'The absolute bastard. I could murder him.'

Nick shakes his head, bewildered. 'Fuck. I don't know what to say.'

'I do!' I grab my coat.

'Where are you going?'

'To get to the bottom of this.'

'It won't do any good, Annie. You can't fight her battles for her. Shit—'

'Don't say shit happens, Nick. It doesn't happen to

my sister. It shouldn't happen to my sister. Any better ideas?'

Nick shakes his head and walks off, as if I exasperate him. He exasperates me. Why doesn't he ever do something?

I shake the rain from my umbrella and ring hard on the bell. No answer. But the lights are on. I know Olly is in. Eventually the locks crunch and a wedge of light pours across the wet cobbled street. Olly is wearing a grey cashmere dressing gown, black pyjamas and sheepskin slippers. He looks like a man convalescing. I almost feel sorry for him. The insults I thought I'd hurl don't materialise. We walk silently into the cavern of the living room. We both know why I am here. I step towards the fire burning in the suspended designer grate, thankful for its heat, the distracting flicker of its flames. A silence drops over us like a bell jar.

'Is she OK?' asks Olly eventually as he drops heavily on to the sofa, hitching his pyjama bottoms up. His legs are skinny and covered in gingery hairs.

'No, actually. She's not.' I sit down in a modern green armchair, facing him, as if in a formal interview situation, or as if I'm his shrink. 'What are you playing at?'

He slumps forward, head in his hands. 'It's not been an easy decision. I know . . . Christ, I know how this looks.'

'Is there someone else, Olly?'

Olly shakes his head vigorously. 'No, there's no one else. I promise, Annie. It's . . .' He looks up. He really does look as if he's aged ten years since the last time I saw him, his skin grey, purple bags under his eyes. Good. He deserves to suffer. 'We've been arguing quite a bit recently.'

'You and the rest of the world's couples.'

'And I think it's all caused by my frustration with her.' He

110

flicks his hair out of his eyes. 'I haven't offered you a drink. Would you like a drink, Annie?'

From you, no. I shake my head. I realise immediately after the defiant head shake that I am desperately thirsty and wonder if it would undermine my case if I conceded to a glass of water.

'When I met Georgia she had so much going on. Her job, all her publishing friends . . .' he says, the words gushing out as if they've been going round and round his head for hours and have finally found an outlet.

I have a horrible feeling that I know where this is going. 'She's been busy with the wedding, Olly.'

'She has become v' Olly hesitates now, uncertain of my response. 'like a City wife.'

'You wanted a City wife, Olly!' I shout. I cannot believe this man. I cannot believe I ever thought he was good enough for Georgia. He is turning against her when she needs him most, when her expectations are at their highest. She thought he was her safe place, and he's proving the most dangerous place of all.

'No. No, I didn't. I wanted Georgia. But she's changed.'

'You've changed.' Or was there a seed of this betrayal in Olly all along? Maybe, in his heart, even when he was pro-posing, even when he was planning the honeymoon, perhaps all along he knew, he knew he couldn't go through with it. Maybe we all know such things and time and events just chip away at our false intentions until the truth emerges naked, like a statue from a block of stone. 'Or did you always have doubts?'

Olly looks puzzled. 'I don't think so. I mean, I've been over and over it all in my head. And I don't know if I had doubts really, no more than the average guy. But then . . .'

111

'Go on.'

'Perhaps it's the seeds of destruction in me. I don't know. Why are you laughing?'

'Come on, Olly. You're trying to dress up your behaviour. Maybe you should call it what it is, a caddish betrayal.'

Olly shakes his head.

'You encouraged her to leave her job, Olly. You made her become someone you could justify betraying.'

Olly looks sheepish. 'I encouraged her to leave her job, yes. And in hindsight that was a mistake. But we didn't need the money. I thought it would be nice for her to have time to do the house, organise the wedding, just pad around for a bit.'

A glowing ember leaps out of the fireplace, hissing before it hits the floor. We both stare at it. Georgia would sweep that up, I think. Then she'd plump the cushions. There would be nibbles. There would be incense. The house would have soul.

My visit suddenly seems goalless. Why did I come? 'She loves you, Olly.'

'And I love her. Don't look at me like that. I do! But it's . . . it's a lifetime we're talking about here. I don't want to be divorced. I've got so many friends who are divorced. I couldn't bear it. I have to be totally sure.'

'If you loved her, you wouldn't do this to her.'

Olly stands up and starts to pace the room, fiddling with the belt on his jeans. 'It's fairer in the long run, Annie. You know it is.'

'You were due to get married in just over a month.' I think of Georgia in her fluted white wedding gown. The memory is already ghostlike. It makes me want to weep.

Olly stops, places his forehead against the wall and rolls it from side to side. 'Don't.'

'Until yesterday she thought that she'd be a wife, a mother, a—'

Olly looks up. 'I'm not a meal ticket.'

'A meal ticket!' Rage engulfs me, a fireball in the belly. 'Georgia was never with you for your fucking money. You made the money important. You allowed it to spoil her. You let her rely on you! And now you reject her.' I pull on my coat. 'It's despicable. The way you've behaved is totally despicable.'

'Annie, please,' Olly implores, reaching out to get me to sit down again. 'I'm sorry. I can't go through with it feeling like this. How can I? I need more of an equal. A woman with more going on in her own life. I'm not like those other City guys. I want . . . a woman more like . . .' He stops and stares at me intensely. It is time to leave.

Thirteen

It torrents down all weekend, the endless rain throwing itself against the windows, drumming on the skylight, making the days dark as dusk. Nick regularly pops out of the house on 'monsoon missions', and returns with his blond hair flattened wet against his skull, eyes glittery bright, hugging wet bags of croissants and newspapers and slabs of chocolate to his chest, all things intended to coax Georgia out of her tunnel under the duvet. None of it works, of course. Inevitably, I find myself eating the chocolate while Georgia suffers silently, getting ever thinner, listening to the rain, lost in thoughts and broken dreams. I try to rouse her, talk it through, but Georgia doesn't listen. What if she lies like this for weeks? Not eating. Not talking. What if she just fades into skinny nothingness beneath the duvet? 'Fuck, Nick. What do we do?'

Nick is doing press-ups on the floor of the bedroom, a new routine now that he can no longer afford his gym membership. 'Give her time,' he pants, crumpling down on the floor and rolling over on to his side. 'It's only been two days, Annie. Sadness doesn't schedule.'

Is that a dig? I choose to ignore it, not wanting to spoil the unlikely unity that we've forged against the backdrop of Georgia's trauma this long weekend. After his solemn gloom of the last two weeks, Nick has been in a surprisingly good mood. Perhaps he is reinvigorated by being needed. Or maybe he's just happier now that it's not just him and me in the house. But Georgia has not improved. By Sunday lunchtime, she really does seem to be in danger of disappearing. She is bonier and more withdrawn and, setting an alarming new precedent, has stopped attending to her nails. I sit on the side of her bed. 'Please eat something, George. A little soup? Food will make you feel better.'

Georgia shakes her head stubbornly. 'It won't make me feel better.'

'Please.'

'OK. A little soup,' she concedes.

I feel like punching the air but don't want to reveal a sense of victory in case this changes Georgia's mind. I go into the kitchen to heat up the soup. Nick is there, drinking Budweiser from the can and staring into space. 'The lady will inhale some soup!' I whisper.

Georgia sits up in bed, eyeing the tray of food warily, unsure if she really can face it. 'Just a little,' she says. 'But please, Annie, stop fussing.'

I arrange the tray on the bedside table like a nurse.

Georgia manages half the bowl of soup, then closes her eyes and falls back to sleep, the tray still on her lap. I carefully pick it up and carry it back to the kitchen.

Georgia calls out, 'Annie, there's something . . .'

I walk back into the bedroom. 'Yes?'

'Nothing.' She hesitates, looking tearful again. 'It's nothing, Annie.'

115

And so things continue. Gently, gently. A few dry crackers. A lot of daytime on the portable telly I set up in her bedroom. I brush her soft flames of hair. I press her against my shoulder and feel her warm tears against my neck. Shamefully, while I do this, my mind is elsewhere, away from the household's pea-soup sadness. Thoughts of Don. I pull away, but my brain snaps back to him like tugged elastic. I wonder about our meeting. I wonder what tricks he will pull next time. The confrontational nature of our encounters excites me in a way that I don't understand.

Finally it is Monday morning. After taking particular care over my appearance – damn my frizzy hair in this damp weather – I close the front door, and it feels like I am a parent closing the door on a houseful of sleeping children, a parent poised to run free. The weekend's rain has evaporated and the air has a clean, sharp coldness which pleases. I stride towards the Tube, feet click-clacking on the pavement, the wind flapping the hair from my face. I feel guilty for feeling so alive when my fragile little sister wants to die.

'I'm not happy,' Pippa whines, sitting back in her large black leather chair, tapping her red fingernails on her white desk. 'Not happy at all. Apart from the fact that we have a nobody with a nasty coke habit on the front cover this month, putting off the major advertisers, I've lost my best feature writer. Louise is after a three-day week and demanding . . .' Pippa makes quote signs with her fingers, 'flexible working.' She sighs melodramatically. 'Is she under the impression that she's the first woman in the world to have a baby? Talking of babies, it appears that the entire subs desk has conspired to get pregnant at exactly the same time. What is wrong with you girls? Anyone would think you'd rather be lactating at home than working.' She smiles at me, to signal she's half-joking. 'Our sisters fought for this, Annie!'

For *Glo*? Somehow I doubt it. But I keep my thoughts to myself and smile nonetheless. I stand up from the uncomfortable orange chair.

'Wait! Don't get up. I haven't finished. Alexis, yes, Alexis, who is becoming so indispensable to this magazine, Alexis says she feels shut out from the decision-making process, Annie.'

This grates. Since becoming deputy, I've gone out of my way to make Alexis feel important, to salve her sense of injustice at not getting the job. But this isn't enough. The girl wants blood.

Pippa is working herself up now, her Brummie accent burring the edges of her voice. 'And Wilberforce, fucking Don Wilberforce, is shaking up things which he knows f-all about. He's making my life very difficult. It's all such a bloody bore!' Pippa's voice tightens like a belt. 'I expect you, Annie, to hold the fort. I don't expect this level of turbulence among the staff.' She glares at me. 'Don't make me regret my decision, Annie.'

Ouch. I feel the threat. My trial period ends soon. I must be coming up for review. 'I'm sorry, Pippa, but—'

She puts a hand up. 'No buts! I hired you because I thought you were level-headed, serious and capable of implementing order. Do not disappoint me.'

Translation: I hired you because you will do my bidding and do not present a threat to my fabulousness.

'Pippa—'

'Let's not hear excuses.' Pippa glances at her watch. 'Call the editors in for the supplement meeting, will you?'

After lunch I manage to escape for a quick coffee and gossip with Sam from the art desk in the staff canteen – the hottest gossip being that Don Wilberforce is paid almost twice as much as Pippa, information released in a drunken moment by Susan in Accounts and to be repeated on pain of death. So much for equal pay. Don doesn't call me for a meeting. (Was his need for one a fabrication? Why? Why would he do this?) And now it is five. I've still got a stack of page proofs to get through. Lydia, the fashion editor, hobbles over to my desk, a group of young assistants trailing in her wake, like blonde fluffy ducklings. She shoos them away – they return to the dark, boxy fashion cupboard – and turns to grin at me. 'Hi, Annie.'

'You've developed a new walk,' I say, glancing down at her vertiginous patent platforms. Lydia is the most fashion-forward in the office, which means that she wears things a good season before anyone else and before the eye has adjusted to a new look. So she generally looks a bit odd. Today she is wearing jodhpurs. She looks odd. I love her for it.

'I can stand in these shoes just fine. It's moving that's the problem. Any gossip?' she says in her smoker's growl. Lydia is the only person on the fashion desk who still smokes. The others are all too worried about wrinkles. But Lydia would rather be thin and wrinkly than fat and smooth-skinned. The fact that her face, framed immaculately by her dark bob, actually moves when she smiles does give her a real characterful beauty when compared to some Botoxed members of staff whose faces are beginning to resemble hard-boiled eggs.

My inbox pings. I glance at it.

Don: *Are you still there?*

Lydia looks at me with curiosity. 'Sweetie, you're blushing! Who is it? Let me see.' She playfully tries to peek over my shoulder. I minimise my inbox so she can't see it.

'Boring!' she says.

'What can I do for you, my dear Lydia?'

'Nothing, just trying to dilute the tedium of my day.' She sighs. 'Do you think the road to hell is paved with day-to-night wardrobe solutions?'

'Probably.' Go away, go away and let me read my email a hundred times over.

'And if I have to write another sentence about how to care for cashmere, I will implode. Don't put it on a hot wash! Mothballs! Buy cheap, buy twice!'

'Sorry, but can we catch up later?' I laugh. 'I've got to deal with this.'

Lydia raises an eyebrow. 'Bet you have,' she laughs, hobbling off.

My email pings again. Don: *I know you are there.*

In body, I type back, regretful of my playfulness the moment I click send. I make a vow to sit on my emails for at least ten minutes before sending them in the future. Wait for reply. Nothing pings back. So I carry on working, wetting finger and thumb, flicking through sheets of printed-out paper, taking sips of lukewarm coffee and marking my time with glances at my inbox. I make a deal with myself to only check every ten minutes, and invariably check every eight. Then seven. Then six.

Alexis strides up to my desk, hair, eyes, everything gleaming with grooming, like a polished bullet. 'Fill me in, Annie,' she hisses.

'Er, what about?'

'Doh! The redundancy rumours?' Alexis perches her tiny pencil-skirted bottom on the side of my desk, crunching into a mound of paper clips. 'Oh, come on,' she smiles collusively. Her small white teeth are the shape and colour of Extra chewing gum. 'I won't tell.'

'You're plucking the wrong grapevine, honestly. What's going down?'

Alexis leans closer. 'Well, the rumour is, on good authority, that the company is losing money hand over fist and needs to prune its staff, targeting the more senior members on bigger salaries . . .' Alexis pauses, just to make sure I get the full gist of what she is saying. 'And replacing them with cheaper people.'

Keep 'Yikes!' to myself. 'I wouldn't worry, Alexis.'

'I rather doubt I'm paid enough to worry.' Alexis's eyes focus on something to the left of us and her expression softens. She sucks in her tummy so it forms a concave scoop beneath the fabric of her skirt. 'Hi there, Don.'

I freeze.

'Alexis,' nods Don, swaggering into view. 'I need a quick word with Annie.'

'Oh.' Alexis, clearly disappointed, hip-swings her way across the office, sporting, I am rather pleased to see, a paper clip caught on the fraying fabric of a deconstructed hem on her skirt's back pocket.

Don, in a dark blue suit, has an amused smile twitching at the corner of his mouth as if he suspects that I am pleased to see him. 'I've come to whisk you away and show you some fireworks.'

I splutter into my coffee, trying not to laugh. That's a terrible line. 'We have quite enough displays in the office, thanks.'

'Crunch Media, some old contacts of mine, interesting bunch, are having a fireworks party. I want you to meet them. Tonight.'

A bit of notice would be nice. Most likely his plus one has pulled out and I am the afterthought. Anyhow, I want to check in on Georgia. 'Tonight is tricky.'

Don looks bored and stares out of the window. 'Meet you by the lift in ten minutes.' He walks away, not looking back.

Out of the corner of my eye I can see Alexis watching me from her imperious perch on the features desk. Then I see her scramble commando-like towards the door, rushing up to grab Don before he turns out of the office. 'Don,' I hear her hiss under her breath. 'Don, can I have a word?'

Fourteen

The fireworks aren't due to start for another half an hour. To kill time, Don insists on taking me to a pub off Holland Park Road, one of those old London pubs that still retains its Victorian brass and black-painted interior, decades of smoke gilding its flock wallpaper, the ceiling low, the walls bulging, the thick glass windows small, tinted and swirled. I haven't been to a pub in months, apart from the unsavoury local near my parents' house which is generally full of men who look like paedophile criminal photofits.

'My mum used to work in a pub just like this,' Don says, stretching so his chest expands outwards like a shield. 'In Croydon.'

'That's where you're from?' I'm surprised at this volunteering of personal information.

'Me and Kate Moss, love.' And he shuts down again.

'You're enjoying the new job?' I want to steer the subject straight to business so that he doesn't think I think that we are on a date.

'I'm making some inroads.' Don takes a sip of Guinness.

Is Alexis an inroad?

'But there's quite a lazy culture. It needs to be whipped into shape.'

I imagine Don like a pitbull with the company between his teeth, growling and shaking it from side to side like a chewed football. 'Sounds nasty.'

'It will be.'

So the rumours are true.

Don looks at me with unnerving directness. 'I'm looking forward to giving the company a good prune.'

Prune. The exact word that Alexis used.

'What's more fun, hiring or firing?'

'Annie, if someone isn't doing their job properly, they don't deserve to be there, do they? Let's not be sentimental.' Don doesn't apologise. He doesn't wrap things up in politically correct niceness. I like this. 'Your features director, Alexis.' He pauses, looks at me with smiley dancing eyes. 'Seems talented.'

I nod. Inside I am saying, 'Oh no she's not,' like a Punch and Judy act.

'She came to see me the other day.'

I feel my competitive juices stir. I sip my drink and study a group of young women who are talking animatedly in the corner of the bar. Funny, I think, that that's normally me in that group of girls, watching someone like me drinking with a man like Don, sizing up the woman's attractiveness, as we all do, wondering who she is, whether she and her drinking partner are together, what he's like in bed.

'Aren't you going to ask me why?'

'I'll humour you. Why?'

'She has some ideas about the direction of the magazine.'

Crafty. Typical Alexis.

Don laughs, as if reading my thoughts. 'It's a shark pit, Annie. Work in magazines and you enter the food chain.'

I shrug as nonchalantly as I can manage. 'Alexis is in it to win it. She'll do well.'

Don doesn't take his eyes off my face. He looks like a moody TV detective, a kind of younger Ken Stott-like character. I suddenly wish I'd touched up my make-up in the loos, not because I want to look good, not necessarily. Just so I look like a worthy adversary.

'You're the breadwinner, aren't you?' he says, grinning infuriatingly.

What? How does he know that? Oh, the party. Dave and Ig's party. 'At the moment.' I smile brightly. 'Nick's looking for the right job.'

'Don't women want to be looked after?'

Is he serious, or is this some kind of sad frat-boy humour? Whatever, he's digging for a reaction. I stay shtum, knowing this will piss him off more than an exclamation of feminist protest.

'It's a primal urge,' Don perseveres. 'And I think men want to look after their women.'

I think about Dad, who wanted to look after Mum. How humiliated he must feel to have the rug pulled from under him. Poor Dad.

Don's foot brushes against mine beneath the table. The physical contact jolts me. I remove my feet, curling them behind the back legs of the chair. 'You look after yours, do you?'

Don smiles. It is a gentle smile, a new smile I haven't seen before, kinder, with a surprising hint of benevolence. 'Absolutely.'

'I've never wanted to be looked after. Sorry not to fit your stereotype, but I'm not like that.'

Don starts to laugh, a deep, vibrato smoker's laugh. 'Are

you not, Annie Rafferty?' he says, slamming down his pint glass. There is something cowboyish about the way he does this. And it is almost sexy. Weird. He isn't my type at all.

A spray of pink flicks across the sky like paint from a brush. I crane my head back. A shower of green sparks. Gold. Red. Ah! I lift a glass of cold, fizzing champagne to my lips. We are in a communal garden square somewhere near the Lancaster Gate. Glamorous figures, their faces lit by the flare of fireworks, then lost again in the darkness, roam the garden, chatting animatedly. I am on my own. Don disappeared to the bathroom a few minutes ago and people spill around me like a stream of water around a rock. Despite being marooned among strangers, I am suddenly, surprisingly, quite happy here among the spray of light and people. I love fireworks, the colour, the bang, the release. As a child I spent hours crouching on the scullery windowledge on Bonfire Night, chin resting on the window frame, nose to the cold glass, watching the sky explode with the dynamite of village firework funds, willing the bangs louder, the rockets higher and brighter. Georgia always hated fireworks, turning the telly up full blast to drown them out. At firework parties she'd hold my hand, uneasy until the last one had popped.

'Do you want to rest those feet?' Don asks, his breath curling out of his mouth like dragon's smoke in the cool evening air.

'The feet say yes.'

'Follow me.' Don leads me into a quiet corner of the garden to a wrought-iron bench, accessible only through a gap in the dense black-silhouetted hedges. It is cold but cosy. I sit down. Don sits beside me, thigh banging against mine. It is a romantic spot, the sky fizzing, the noise of the party bubbling behind the hedges, the large white moon suspended like a pearl button above our heads. I stamp my ice-blocky feet and wonder what to say.

Don breaks the silence. 'Have you ever felt fireworks inside?'

I laugh. I won't answer that.

'I used to imagine them going off inside, you know, like my stomach was this big black sky with Catherine wheels spinning round and round inside it. I used to think other people must be able to tell. That sparks would fly from my mouth or something.'

'When was this? Last week?'

'Yes, when I was firing the HR assistant.' He grins. 'No. When I was a child, obviously, Miss Rafferty.'

'Obviously.' I blow on my cold fingers, strangely moved by the unlikely idea of Don Wilberforce being a sensitive child. I imagined him to be the kind of boy who enjoyed pulling the legs off spiders.

'You're cold.' He takes off his jacket and slips it around my shoulders. I protest. Don insists.

The jacket's heavy wool is still warm from his body. 'I should get back.'

'I hate that word, "should".'

Sometimes my whole life feels like a pile-up of shoulds. 'No, really.'

'Annie . . .' Don turns to me. His face is so close I can smell cigarettes on his breath. I don't find it unpleasant. In fact, I am aware that I am not finding his company unpleasant at all. I feel quite safe here, locked in his coat, sheltered from the sky. The fireworks and my mood have somehow fused so that they almost seem to be extensions of each other. Goodness, as Mum might say. I should go now. This is my cue. We've both had too much to drink. But my body doesn't move. I will it to but it remains obstinately sitting. Don's face is inches away. The moment seems to stretch and stretch, like a firework shooting starwards without ever fizzing out. Then, suddenly, the moment is blown apart by an ear-shattering bang and the sky explodes into a spectacular firestorm of metallic blue chips of light, like atomic clouds of crushed blue eye-shadow. There is a sound of clapping and whooping from the crowd on the other side of the hedge. 'I think that's the last firework,' I say, standing up from the bench abruptly and shrugging off his jacket. I am no longer the least bit cold.

Fifteen

We're all trying to fake cheerfulness with varying degrees of success. Georgia has lost the millionaire fiancé she loves deeply; identifying the silver lining is proving tricky. Nick heaves the last of Georgia's suitcases, collected from Olly's, over the doorstep. He drops it and wipes his brow. 'Blimey, George. What have you got in there? Olly's dead body?'

'Clothes,' says Georgia quickly, as she walks out of the room.

'Georgia has always been a hoarder,' says Mum, as cheerfully as she can manage. Her true feelings are revealed by pinked eyes, the busy fingers working her handkerchief. But she remains convinced that Olly will change his mind and has come up to London this Saturday – finding the transport system far less confusing without Dad's directions – to try to bring some calm to our fracturing household. 'What is all this?'

'Gosh.' I stare in awe at the mound of luggage and boxes that has piled up in the living room. I pick up a bag, unzip it. Oh. Not a jumble of clothes but a squished stack of plastic bags. A cashmere cable-knit cardigan. As I shake it out, I notice that the label is still attached. Joseph, £257. I open a Selfridges bag. A navy Miu Miu pinafore dress. Again with the label attached. Is Georgia going to take it back? Confused, I rummage through the other bags, finding more clothes that look like they've just been bought. I prise open a suitcase. More clothes. Brand-new clothes, some still in their shop tissue paper.

I examine one of the receipts. August! It is from August. Over three months ago. I unfold another one. Last March! Christ. Something is wrong here.

'How peculiar.' Mum stands up from the sofa, brushing down her grey flannel skirt. (She's been wearing funereal shades ever since the news broke.) 'I'll put the kettle on.'

Nick stares at the bags. 'Weird.' He shakes his head in a kind of exasperated, 'Women!' way and retreats to rifle through his vinyl collection.

I find Georgia sitting up in bed and rubbing her eyes. She looks frailer than I have ever seen her. I open a window. 'Air. Air is good.'

Georgia nods and sips her tea. 'How was your week at work?'

'Usual. Bonkers busy. And . . .' The image of Don, his thick jaw lit by the fireworks, his big hands, hits me unexpectedly. I feel myself flush and change the subject. 'Georgia, Nick's collected all your booty. It's kind of taking over the living room. Do you mind if I move it through to your bedroom?'

'Thanks. Sorry for the mess. I know you hate mess.' Georgia's eyes fill with tears.

'Georgia, there are a lot of bags there,' I say carefully, aware that she is in such a fragile state that one ambiguous comment could be taken the wrong way and drag her further down. 'Shopping bags. With clothes in them. Still labelled.'

'Oh, that stuff? Yeah,' she says vaguely, scratching her nose.

I know that nose scratch. That is the nose scratch from our childhood: I'd confront her after she'd nicked a pair of my favourite shoes or my *Jackie* annual from my bedroom. She would look at me affronted – how could I suggest such a thing? – scratch her nose, then smile as winningly as possible and confess. The process – from scratch to confession – would take about a minute. 'Why haven't you returned the stuff if you don't want it?'

Georgia's eyes seem to get huger and rounder by the second. 'Um. Well, it kind of mounted up and I never got round to—'

'But there's hundreds of pounds' worth, George. I don't understand.'

'I should have taken it back, I realise now, Annie. I should have got my act together.' She begins to sniff, short hydraulic sniffs.

I put my hands around her slight, quivery body and press her to my shoulder. 'It's such a waste of money,' I say, getting a mouthful of her red hair. 'How many Caribbean holidays are in that pile, do you reckon? I am thinking two weeks at Sandy Lane . . .'

'It's not just that, Annie.' Georgia sheepishly twiddles the corner of the duvet, her voice so quiet it's barely audible. 'A lot of the stuff, um, well, I didn't pay for it exactly.'

Oh God. 'Fucking hell, Georgia! You stole it?'

'No!' Georgia shakes her head furiously. 'Store cards.'

I heave with relief. For a moment there I thought my sister had become someone I didn't recognise. But it's all so puzzling. 'Why would you of all people need a store card?'

'I just thought I'd pay them off in one lump, but you

know me, I forget, I'm terrible with numbers and things and . . .'

I wince, sensing that this conversation isn't going to end prettily. 'Oh George. You idiot. The interest rate on those things.'

'We had so much money, Annie, that to be totally honest, it never seemed to matter. It became kind of abstract.' She is blinking at me with those large round eyes. She is becoming eleven again. Sometimes I do wonder if Olly's money has stopped her growing up.

'How much do you owe?' I say softly, bracing myself.

Georgia gulps hard.

'Georgia? Just tell me. I'm unshockable.'

She clears her throat. 'Ten thousand pounds.'

'OK. I am shocked.' I sit down on the arm of an armchair. 'Shit.' Are us Raffertys jinxed or something? What's with the financial crises? We are just not a family who make a habit of financial crises. For years, when I was growing up, we just pottered along, holidays in Brittany, meals out twice a month, never living beyond our means, modest but regular pocket money, university fees paid out of rainy-day savings. And now . . . In normal circumstances Dad would bail Georgia out. Of course, he would be furious. He would make her feel about three inches tall. But he would pay off her debt. Now he can't. He can't even know about it. There will be no handouts. There will be no family house. No parental sticking plasters. That's all gone. Georgia has got to grow up. And so do I.

Sixteen

At the motorway service station's restaurant till, a woman in her sixties wearing a blue nylon overall addresses Nick. 'That's thirty-four pounds exactly, please, sir.'

Nick hesitates helplessly.

I open my wallet and hand over my embattled credit card. The woman looks up, fleetingly surprised, and takes the card. 'Thank you.'

Nick scratches his stubble and looks down at the floor. He's tried to pay a couple of times in recent weeks, but I've said it is pointless due to the fact that I am subsidising him anyway. Now bill etiquette is almost instinctive. We don't even have to have the conversation. I just pay.

I beckon to Mum, who is sitting at the table draining her cup of coffee, which is foul but which she won't waste on point of principle because it costs £2.95. 'Let's get you home, Mum.'

In the car, Mum grapples with her seatbelt. 'What a lot of fuss. We always used to have you girls laid out in sleeping bags in the boot. You survived,' she mumbles. Seatbelt conquered, she stares out of the window morosely. 'I hope your father's been OK on his own.'

I put the radio on quietly.

'The music's a bit loud,' Mum says.

I turn it down, knowing that Nick will be thinking, Can't hear it! because he's damaged his ears by sticking them in speakers. And we drive on. Five minutes later a rumbling sound comes from the back seat. I check in the rearview mirror. Mum has fallen asleep, head bent back, a stream of air from her open mouth fidgeting her hair.

'Nick.' I pause, suspecting that however I say what I am about to say, it will come out wrong. But it needs to be said. 'Maggie says she's got a friend who's looking to recruit people to this new PR company.'

Nick's expression hardens. 'For God's sake, Annie.' He slams the steering wheel. 'I don't want to work in fucking PR.'

'Sorry, but you're broke. We're broke.'

'I know,' says Nick, in a softer voice. 'But I'm busy, what with the DJ-ing and doing the house—'

'The house is almost exactly the same as it was when we moved in, bar one painted wall,' I say tartly. I've had enough.

Nick glares out of the window. We sit in silence. The car interior feels like a very small airless space. 'At least I no longer wake up every morning having an existential crisis,' he says eventually.

'What if *I* want to have an existential crisis? What if I decided to write a book or join the Hari Krishnas? You know what? Maybe I'd like to do that!'

Nick glances at me, fleetingly contrite. 'My mate, Alf – you know, Ladbroke Grove Alf, who's got that building company?' he says more gently. 'He's got a few jobs going on – everyone's extending or renovating – and he needs a spare pair of hands.'

'Your parents will be so very pleased that they spent that fortune on your education.' Shit. I hate myself for sounding like my father. It is as if Dad is a kind of wi-fi box, radiating infectious radio waves that get stronger and stronger the closer we get to Hedgerows.

'Fuck 'em,' says Nick. 'I'm not living my life for my parents.' He quickly looks over his shoulder to check if Mum is asleep. 'And nor should you.'

'What do you mean?'

'Forget it.' Nick fires up the accelerator. 'You're trying to control me, Annie.'

'I'm not.'

'You're a control freak. You have all these ideas about the perfect house, the perfect man, the perfect job. You're a box ticker. And I'm not a box to be ticked. I love you, Annie. But you're driving me fucking insane!'

Dad is leaning against the sideboard in the living room, wearing fawn corduroy trousers and a navy sweater. He looks like the slugs have gorged on all his cabbages. He pushes his glasses up his nose, nudging aside a bushel of nostril hair with his thumb. I make a note to tell Mum to get him to do something about the nostril hair. He pours himself a large glass of whisky.

'It's a bit early in the day for a whisky,' notes Mum, as she walks into the room brandishing a plate of Marks and Spencer's Luxury Selection biscuits.

'Not today, it's not,' growled Dad. 'Don't hover like your mother, Annie. Sit down.'

I sit down on the sofa, pulling Nick with me by tugging on the back pocket of his jeans.

'So.' Dad takes another large swig of whisky. His hands

134

shake slightly. 'Olly, the bastard.' Salivary strands of fury shoot across the room. The large purple vein in Dad's forehead starts pulsing. A bad sign. 'The absolute bastard! Excuse my French, Nick.' When I was growing up, it seemed like the fee-fi-fo-fum giant himself was shaking the earth with his fury. But as Dad gets older, he gets less terrifying, more toddler-like.

'Calm down, Arnold,' pleads Mum. 'Think of your blood pressure.'

'Hell, it's all turned out exactly as I feared. I tell you, once I heard about him paying good money to ponce around that loony bin, I got my suspicions. I thought, hmmm, man or a mouse?'

Nick and I exchange glances and try not to laugh.

'Anyhow,' Dad says, draining his whisky. 'Let's not waste any more time on him. We've got to move on. We're about to put the house on the market, Annie.'

Oh. Oh dear. I swallow hard. My childhood and adolescence are contained within this house's thick stone walls. I wrote my first diary under its eaves. I cried over my first boyfriend in the bathroom and burned his declaration of lust – written on a sheet of maths exercise book, paraphrasing Spandau Ballet – in the living room grate. Later, of course, I gazed out of the leaded windows, dreaming of cities and escape. On the other hand, clicking my rational head back on, my parents are getting less and less capable of maintaining Hedgerows. It is damp and dusty. It is a house that comes alive with children. Not with sixty-somethings. And the grandchildren don't appear to be scheduled any time soon. 'You should get a good price,' I say as brightly as I can manage. 'There's a huge demand for second homes around here.'

Nick looks around him, clocking the damp patches, the wallpaper that is peeling off in scrappy strips. 'Just give it a lick of paint,' he says optimistically.

Dad glares at him. 'We don't have money for fancy decorators, Nick.'

I have a vision of the folks underselling the house – 'in need of modernisation' – to some west London family looking for a weekend retreat that they'll stuff full of Cath Kidston and spanking new Hunter wellies. The idea makes me feel a little sick. Those people would be oblivious to the house's history, Georgia's gerbil's final resting place in the back garden, the pencil marks on the wall in the spare bedroom that recorded our growing heights . . .'Spruce it up a little, Dad. It's looking a bit tired. You'd get the money back.'

Mum's eyes are watering. 'It may not have the wow factor, but it's got – what do they call it? – character.' She takes a neat bite of a chocolate biscuit. 'And we really can't afford to get anyone in. Your father's quite right.'

Dad strokes his beard thoughtfully. 'You really think it would make a difference to the price, Annie?'

'Big difference, Dad.'

He looks thoughtful. 'I always was good with a paintbrush. Wasn't I, Marj?'

Mum and I exchange alarmed glances and start to laugh. The spare bedroom is testament to Dad's DIY skills. The walls resemble a badly iced cake. Each brush stroke is visible, embedded with brush hair, and each goes in a different direction to the last.

Nick looks thoughtful. 'I could do it for you,' he volunteers.

I look at him. You could?

Mum pounces. 'Oh, Nick, thank—'

'Aren't you trying to solve your unemployment crisis?' Dad interrupts. 'I'm not going to make Annie's life any more difficult.'

Mum transmits her disapproval to Dad through their evolved marital language of lip twitches. I think she is scared that Dad is going to have them begging on the streets of Stow-on-the-Wold.

'Well . . . Oh. OK.' Dad pauses a little pompously, so as not to give the impression he is giving in to Mum too easily. 'If you insist, Nick.'

Sorry, who insisted?

Lovely,' says Mum, looking relieved. 'That's settled. Now, anyone for a cup of tea before supper?'

Before we can answer, Dad lets out a groan, a groan so hammy that if a stage actor had done it I'd have got the giggles. I wonder if this is prelude to an expletive eruption. It is not. He leans into the sideboard, steadying himself with his hand. His face chalks. He puts one hand to his heart. Nick leaps up and catches him just as he folds like an old umbrella and crumples towards the floor.

Seventeen

Darker clouds billow in from the west like giant black duvets. By Midday, the skies are so thunderous, it looks like Canary Wharf is a pale paper cutout against a background of matt-grey felt. I cross the office to fill my water jug at the cooler. I realise I am now senior enough to silence conversations as I walk past. Facebook and Ocado sites are swiftly shut down and personal phone calls made to sound official. Is this the kind of power that some people get off on? It just makes me feel a little alienated, slightly cut out of the loop. I check the clock for the third time in five minutes. Mum should have phoned by now. Lydia stops by my desk and I tell her about Dad. She puts her arms around me and gives me a hug.

Belle appears, twisting a curl around her finger. 'Meeting in five minutes, Annie.'

Meeting? I look at her blankly. How can I sit through a meeting when Dad is in hospital and I don't know how he is? I check my mobile again. She still hasn't returned my call. Come on, Mum. Phone me.

'Critique of the last issue,' Belle says. 'It's changed. Didn't Alexis tell you?'

'No.' Damn Alexis. 'No, she didn't.'

Lydia raises one eyebrow at me.

'Typical.' I roll my eyes. 'I'll just have to blag it. Wish me luck, Lydia.'

The doors to Pippa's office open and shut silently, as if on cashmere hinges. Holding my notebook to my chest with one hand, a coffee in the other, I push open the door, cross its threshold into the sharp glare of strip lighting and stop dead. Pippa. Alexis. Kat, the deputy features editor. Claire and Jo, two features desk assistants. And Don! Shit. There he is, glowering at the top of the table, shoulders bulky in his dark suit, like the top half of an action toy. I stand there like a mute loon, hesitating, fighting the urge to run out of the meeting room, giggling.

I notice that my normal seat, which is adjacent to Pippa, is held hostage by Alexis's pert bottom. Everyone knows that there is a secret etiquette to the meeting seating arrangements: the closer you sit to Pippa, the higher up the masthead you are. To brazenly seat-hop is to throw down the gauntlet.

Pippa looks at a features desk minion. 'Open a window, please. It's unbearably hot in here.'

We all goosebump as a stream of freezing air whooshes through the open window.

'Right, let's get this show on the road, guys,' beams Pippa, her voice infused with phoney enthusiasm because of Don's presence. She has extra polish today. Her hair looks as if it's been dipped in sugar glaze. And when she speaks, her red-lip-sticked mouth enunciates each word exaggeratedly, as if reading an autocue. 'Now,' she purrs. 'Who's going to kick things off?'

Fuck. Not me. I look down at my notebook, willing myself to become invisible for a few minutes. Not only have I not prepared properly – Dad's heart attack will not be a justifiable excuse for Pippa so is not worth mentioning – but I feel under horrible scrutiny from Don. I strongly suspect that I am about to screw up.

Alexis rises slightly in her seat. 'I'm happy to start.'

With a slight turn of the head, Don transports his knowing, wide smile from Pippa to Alexis. 'Thank you, Alexis.'

Alexis unclips a pad of notes, annoyingly colour-coded with fluorescent sticker flaps. She makes an efficient click with her tongue, licks her finger and flips towards a lime-green sticker. 'After studying the magazine's last ten issues . . .' she begins, directing a nuclear smile at Don, then at Pippa, and ignoring the rest of the staff, who are less senior and therefore don't matter, 'I've come to the conclusion that the weakest part of the magazine is . . .' She pauses, showmanlike. 'If everyone could just turn to the Scorching section. Page forty-five of the current issue . . .'

Scorching? My pages. I reach towards the pile of magazines fanned out in the centre of the table.

'I think the headline is a bit flabby here,' says Alexis, stabbing at the page with her forefinger. 'The first paragraph doesn't get to the point quick enough . . .' And so she goes on. My brain red-mists over. First with possessive fury – that is a damn fine opening paragraph even if I do say so myself – then with a kind of weary ennui. Alexis's suggestions are not inspired. But I have to concede that they are delivered with confident aplomb. And I know as well as anyone that it is the delivery of a message rather than the message itself that gets you noticed at this magazine: like the staff, ideas need to be well dressed.

'Excellent, Alexis,' says Pippa, leaning back in her chair, biro between her teeth. 'I think we all got a lot out of that.'

I steal a glance at the rest of the table. Kat has a grimace-like smile on her face. She can't stand Alexis but is working out her notice so no longer cares. The features assistants dutifully take notes.

Alexis shuffles her papers, immensely pleased with herself. 'Any questions?'

Don clears his throat. 'Do you mind me asking who edits this section?'

Alexis looks at me and gives a hammed-up apologetic wince. 'Annie?'

Pippa twitches her painted mouth quickly from side to side and looks at me sharply. 'We'll have to take a long, hard look at those pages, I think, Annie. Now, fire away.'

I gulp. Critiquing the magazine is a high-wire act. Because, ultimately, it requires you to critique the work of Pippa, she being responsible for the final product. Make too strong a criticism and you'll insult her. Be too forgiving and she'll assume you are a useless yes-person. 'I think the magazine's looking fantastic,' I say carefully. 'But there are parts that could be better. It's just a matter of a little fine-tuning.' I cough to create a space in which to think of something intelligent to say and stare at the magazine laid out on the desk, mentally freezing over, willing it to shout some ideas back at me. There is silence.

'Yes?' presses Pippa impatiently.

I take a deep breath. Shit. The room feels very small all of a sudden. Small and getting smaller. Full of people staring at me.

'Annie?' repeats Pippa.

Oh, to hell with it. I sit up straighter in my chair. 'Sometimes I feel that we assume too much about the reader. We need to reconnect with who she is. What she watches on

141

telly. I mean, does she really care about a theatre actress on an Islington stage? Are we projecting here?'

Don laughs. Pippa glares at me. She likes to feature acclaimed artistes who she can then invite to the soirées she throws at her home in Primrose Hill to add a dash of bohemian colour.

'The art direction needs an overhaul. It needs to be bigger, bolder, less cluttered. That would change the feel of the magazine entirely. I'd also put a clearer signage through the magazine, so readers know exactly where to find each section. It's messy.' I glance at Pippa. Yes, I've overstepped the invisible line. Pippa is frowning. The art director is her closest ally. 'I think everyone's doing a great job, but perhaps we could all push ourselves just that extra mile – sorry for the Brentisms – to make things sparkier.' I look at Alexis and smile. 'As Alexis rightly points out.' I flick through the magazine, open a random page and describe changes that could improve it, trying not to humiliate the editor of that section as I do so. A process I repeat with two, three, four random pages. Soon I am getting into my stride, rather enjoying myself, the fast click and pop of ideas and the possibility of change is exciting. This magazine could really sell . . . As I continue flicking through, my critique expands, making more sense, until I feel that I could re-edit the magazine there and then and make it a hundred times better. 'So—'

'We'll have to stop you there.' Pippa puts up a hand. 'Or we'll run out of time. Everybody deserves a chance to speak, Annie.'

The silence in the room is stifling. I can't read the faces that stare back from the corners of the table. Have I gone too far? Bored everyone to tears? Even Alexis looks blank. Pippa looks irritated. I dare not look at Don. 'Of course. Sorry, Pippa.'

142

After the meeting, I flop my notebook shut, humiliated. Alexis's method, sure, competent and well prepared, is obviously the way forward. Whereas I've revealed myself – in front of Pippa and worse, far worse, in front of Don – to be impetuous and opinionated. Not qualities prized in deputy editors.

When I get back to my desk, I find a little tissue-wrapped package with a Post-it note attached, scrawled with spidery handwriting. 'A pick-me-up, love Lydia.' It is a silk leopard-print scarf. Bless Lydia. I wrap it around my neck. The office clears for lunch. Only a few subeditors remain, glued to their screens, picking at sandwiches, and occasionally their noses when they think no one's looking. I stare out of the window, tired, drained by the meeting, by the look on Pippa's face. By Georgia. By Nick. By my parents. Life feels like it is crashing in on me, wave upon wave, so that I emerge from one dunking only to have another blasted great wave flop on to my head. I see Dad's face again, waxy pale, a look of disbelief on his contorted features as he crumpled to the floor. He could speak afterwards, though. He could say, 'Gordon Bennett, I'm dying,' which means, I hope, that he isn't. And he had to be practically manhandled into the ambulance, obstinate as ever. Still, where is that call?

'Lunch?'

I look up. Don. The last person I want to see right now.

'Busy, I'm afraid,' I say briskly, rearranging my new leopard-print scarf around my neck.

'You're lying.'

I smile in defeat and shrug.

'Pippa didn't seem to like your critique much,' he says drily.

'So it's not paranoia then.'

'I did.'

'Thanks.' Is this charity? 'I'm big enough to take it, Don.'

'I've no doubt.' He sits down on an empty chair and wheels himself closer to my desk. 'The question is whether you want to.'

'Good point.' I dip my finger in my chapstick pot and smear some on my lips. 'Funnily enough, I was just thinking about running away and spending the rest of my life on a sun-soaked island in the Caribbean.'

Don leans forward on his chair. 'Let's elope.'

'Bills to pay.'

'Come away with me and you won't have to work.'

I refuse to look at him, refuse to let him think I am even close to taking him seriously. 'I'd make a terrible unemployed person, but probably an absolutely brilliant housewife. It's just that I would go out of my mind with boredom by day three and toss the Hoover out of the window like a rock star.'

'I can see you in an apron very easily.' Don leans back in the chair and laughs heartily, as if this really tickles him. 'Maybe there is an unfulfilled part of you hungering, yearning, to be a housewife.' He looks rather pleased with himself when he says this, as if he's really goaded me to react now. I won't rise to it. Oh, how I want to hate him. 'I can't offer you the Caribbean just yet. But I can offer you a trip to New York.'

New York? I sit up in my chair. I love New York.

'Our sister publishers are thinking of opening *Glo* stateside. Just thinking. And they want me and a senior member of staff to go over next week.'

Something dances in my chest. Yes! I want to scream. Take me! Then reality hits. I can't. Can't possibly. Not with

Dad ill. Not until I've heard from Mum. 'Why isn't Pippa going?'

'Too much stuff going down here.'

'The thing is . . .' I consider telling him about Dad. I've got a hunch he'd understand. But I don't. It's generally a bad idea to bring personal problems to work.

Don stands up and starts walking to the door. 'Don't worry if you can't come,' he says breezily. 'I'll take Alexis.'

I watch him walk away. Just as he is about to reach the office door I call, 'Don!'

He turns to face me, smiling, as if anticipating what is coming next.

'Count me in.'

Dad, forgive me.

Eighteen

I always know when it's Mum on the phone. Call it daugh-
terly sixth sense or a matter of probability (Mum typically
calls at the start of the Channel Four news, just as I've sat
down to dinner or, in happier days, just as me and Nick got
down to it), either way, I don't need to see caller ID. So when
the phone finally does ring – just as the pizza comes out of the
oven – I jump it. 'Mum! Why haven't you called? Is everything OK?'

'Oh, I left you a couple of messages, dear,' says Mum.
'Well, I think I did. The phone line made some peculiar beeping noises. As I always say, you can't trust mobile phones. My
one's been playing up. The volume button has gone skew-
whiff.'

I marvel at Mum's ability to focus on life's minutiae at
times of crisis. She'd be in an earthquake and worry about
breaking china rather than the gaping hole that was cracking
open beneath her feet. 'So how is Dad?'

'He's out of the operating theatre. They cleared the block-
age. He's fine. Well, he's OK. One doctor, a very nice chap,
can't pronounce his name, Indian chap I think, says it is a

wake-up call and he should be grateful he has had a small heart attack, to warn him of the big one. Now he has to take these pills, gosh, so many pills, cut back on the booze and avoid stress.' Mum snorts. 'I said to the doctor, how can the poor man avoid stress given what's happened?'

'Georgia blames herself, you know.'

'Yes, I can imagine she might, silly thing. Can you drum some sense into her, Annie? Although between you and me, I dare say news of Olly's atrocious behaviour was like washing a tub of lard down his arteries. It's no laughing matter, Annie,' says Mum sharply. 'How is he going to cope, what with selling the house and all? I mean, really.' Her voice begins to yodel.

'Mum. Sorry. I'll help as much as I can.'

'Would you? Would you really? That would make such a difference, Annie.' She sighs heavily. 'Georgia's bills are worrying me sick.'

I immediately regret confiding in Mum about Georgia's store card debt. But she was so puzzled by all the shopping bags. And I really needed to share the horror of the whole thing with someone other than Nick.

'I'm terrified your father will find out,' she continues. 'It would drag him to his grave, I'm sure of it.'

'I'll sort them out.' I gulp. Ten thousand pounds. That will wipe out my savings. Still, family comes first. Bloody Georgia, though. Honestly.

'Oh! There's that nice doctor going into the ward. I better catch him. Bye, darling.'

I put down the phone and drop my head to my hands. Making everything so much worse somehow is the sight of one of Georgia's old cups of tea (a vastly expensive brand from Fortnum and Mason, identifiable by the rose petals in the tea leaves, that Georgia insists is essential to her recovery), which has left a pale yellow stain on my new copy of American *Vogue*. Georgia's mess sits somewhat uneasily with the demands of the romantically wounded. Yes, I am sympathetic but not so sympathetic that I can ignore the way she uses my bath towel and then leaves it in a smelly heap in the corner of the sofa.

In truth, I am beginning to feel invaded. Georgia's washing has been festering damply in the barrel of the washing machine for almost twenty-four hours now. Georgia's eye cream is in the fridge. A hairy hairbrush, three different exfoliating scrubs, an exploding make-up bag and a huge pot of Crème de la Mer have taken up residence in the bathroom. ('God, you really are like an older brother in comparison,' Nick joked yesterday. Not funny.) Years of being looked after – cleaners five times a week, space enough to absorb her mess and, crucially, her own bathroom – has not moulded my sister into the ideal house guest. Not that Nick seems to notice. Domestically, he's worse of course. So much for Nick the wife.

'Hi, Annie,' yawns Georgia, stepping into the kitchen, all long tawny legs and tousled hair and . . . She isn't! She bloody well is.

Georgia is wearing a pair of pink stripy knickers, a white vest that barely covers their gusset and the pink jacket Don bought me from the sample sale. 'You're wearing my jacket!'

'You don't mind, do you? I found it at the bottom of the wardrobe in my room. Looks like it's hardly been worn.'

The sight of the jacket makes the blood rush from my head. I'd hidden it away in the spare room and had begun to imagine that the jacket – its pinkness, its impertinence – was a figment of my imagination, but no, here it is. It exists.

'Except one of the seams has ripped.'

'Yes. I know that.'

'Just thought I'd point it out so you don't blame me for it,' says Georgia. 'It's not your normal style, is it? I like it, though. Cute.'

What if Nick should walk in now? I've never shown him the jacket. He might ask where it is from. He would notice, as Georgia has, that it isn't part of my normal black-to-basics look. I glance nervously at the bathroom door. Steam is puffing out of the gap around its hinges. He is still in the shower. 'It suits you. Have it.'

'Don't be silly.' Georgia laughs. 'Hey, I'd kill for a cup of tea.' She collapses her teeny frame into a kitchen chair as if the very act of getting up has already exhausted her for the day.

I flick on the kettle. 'Would you mind taking off the jacket? The kitchen is a mess. I don't want the jacket to get sticky.'

Georgia shrugs it off. I quickly hang it on the back of the door, hiding it beneath my coat. I relax a bit.

'How are you feeling, George? Any better?'

'Olly phoned.' Georgia sniffs. Is she going to cry? She always cries in the mornings; her mood gets better as the day progresses and the television programme schedules improve. 'Just to check that I was all right, nothing more. He says he misses me horribly but that he's done the right thing. And . . .' She stops and bites her nails, looking up at me coyly. 'He's offered me . . . er . . .'

'The entire contents of the house. He should do, you know! All that stuff! What's a man going to do with—'

'. . . thirty-five thousand pounds,' George interjects. 'He's offered me thirty-five thousand pounds, Annie.'

'Oh my God!' I crush my hands to my mouth. 'Thirty-five thousand pounds! That's . . . Gosh. For what?'

'To say sorry.' I can tell as Georgia speaks these words she's not convinced by them. 'To help set myself up again.'

'Blood money?' I say slowly, as it dawns what Olly is up to, paying off his conscience.

Georgia looks at me uncertainly. 'Do you reckon?'

I sit down on a kitchen chair, shaking my head. Olly's got some cheek, he really has. 'Why the precise thirty-five thousand? Why not fifty pounds and forty-seven pence? Why not two hundred thousand, dammit. Does he think he can buy his way out of everything?'

'Probably.'

'You're not going to accept it? It'll make you feel horrible.' A real part of me fears that if she takes it, her self-esteem will hit rock bottom, that by accepting the money she's accepting herself as a commodity in some way. Or am I being naive?

'Well . . .' Georgia flushes. She obviously is thinking about it.

I reach over and squeeze her hand. 'Don't give him the satisfaction. Listen, I'll sort you out. You're not alone. You've got family. You've got me. I know it must feel like a bit of a consolation prize, but . . . Well, I'll always make sure you're OK, you know I will.'

Poor Georgia probably (rightly) imagines I will not be able to sort her out in the manner to which she has become accustomed. 'Thanks, Annie. But . . .'

Am I being too pushy? Probably. 'How does the offer make you feel?' I ask, softer this time.

'Like a tart. A well-paid one, though.' Georgia pulls her knees to her chest and wraps her arms around them. 'Listen, I said to him I would think about it, that's all.'

I put a piece of toast on her plate.

150

Georgia is silent for a few moments. She drops her head on to her knees, a curtain of red hair swinging forward. 'I'm not like you, Annie. You wouldn't be here. You wouldn't be in this mess.'

I put a hand on her shoulder. 'Anyone could be where you are. It's just bad luck, really bloody bad luck.'

Georgia sits up and looks at me. 'But you have a functional life, Annie. You always have done. You're so self-contained. You've got stuff under control. You always have everything under control. Things happen to me, and when they happen I just cling on for dear life until they drop me somewhere and I land with a bump!'

I laugh. 'George. That's rubbish.'

Georgia sighs and looks up at me with doleful brimming eyes. 'How come you and Nick have got things so sorted? What's your secret, Annie?'

An image of Don, his dark face framed by fireworks, floods through me. Is Don my secret? 'I don't know.'

Georgia looks thoughtful. 'You know what I think? I relied on Olly too much, played the wee wifey. Whereas you and Nick have a totally modern relationship. He's not threatened by your success. And you don't mind the fact that he's not successful . . .'

I raise an eyebrow. 'You're on shaky ground.'

Georgia whacks me on the arm playfully. 'I mean successful in a career way. I mean, you haven't confused masculinity with . . . oh, what's the word? . . . Um. I just mean you haven't confused it with power, I suppose. And your relationship is all the stronger for it.'

Some hours later, while Georgia stews in her Space NK organic sage and seaweed salts in the bath, I crumple into an armchair next to Nick. 'It's only for a couple of days. I'm hardly going on a round-the-world trip.'

'Suppose,' he says, drowsily. He has been smoking skunk all afternoon. 'You're not worried about your sister? Or your dad?'

'Oh come on, Nick. It's work. I don't want to go.' This is a shameless lie. 'It's so tough at the moment. I've got to look committed.' This is true.

Nick cracks open a beer. 'And your job is more important than your family?'

'That's not fair.' This plays right into my guilt. Am I being a thoughtless daughter? What if there was some unexpected medical development and Dad deteriorated? Shit. Maybe Nick's right. I shouldn't go. Hell. I am a good person. But if I am a good person, why does Nick make me feel like a lump of shite?

Nick sticks his hand in his pocket, then thumps a wedge of crumpled twenty-pound notes on the coffee table. 'Here!'

'Wow! Where did you get those from?'

'Selling my body. What do you think, Annie? I've done two days'. With Alf.'

'When? You never told me.'

'You never asked.' Nick sighs. 'Or is money that comes from building work not good enough for you?'

I roll my eyes. But as Nick storms out of the room, I realise that I am probably making him feel like a lump of shite too.

Nineteen

Don's thick thigh judders as the taxi revs up and speeds away from JFK. There is something so intriguingly other about his thigh, something so bullish and male. It makes mine look skinny, which is a first. Nick's makes mine look like a rugby prop forward's. I wind down the window. The air pours in like icy water. I pull the lovely leopard-print scarf that Lydia gave me tighter around my neck.

'All right?' asks Don gently.

I nod and smile. The New York skyline stirs in me, as it always has done, an excitable feeling, a little like falling in love. Being in the car with Don in the middle of such a moment is confusing. We pull up outside a hotel amongst the barking traffic, blinking neon and crowds of midtown, just off Forty-Third Street.

'Booked by the travel department,' Don says, holding the door open for me. 'Not the Mercer, I'm afraid.'

We check in. Our rooms are on different floors. Don says he'll see me in the lounge at eight. My room is white and taupe, not too small, with a large window that looks out on a parking lot and advertising hoardings. I hang up my clothes, pull a Diet Coke from the minibar and prise my swollen feet from my shoes. There is a taste of plane in my mouth. I put on the telly and fling myself back on the bed with a sigh. I shut my eyes. Alone at last. I almost feel as if I can pan back like a Google Earth map, so that midtown, then New York state shrinks to a dot, then America, then it is just me on a revolving planet, an anonymous person in a little room thousands of miles from home. Bliss . . .

Ring ring! The telephone makes me jump. A shrill American voice: 'Mr Don Wilberforce is waiting for you in the bar.'

Shit! I look at my watch. Disaster. How on earth could I have slept so long? 'Thanks. I'll be down in five minutes.'

I leap into the shower, despairing at the ravaged reflection in the mirror – the pores on my nose look like craters in Swiss cheese – before rushing into the lift outside my bedroom, body still confused by the disturbed sleep and differing time zones. How unprofessional. How completely crap.

Don is sitting stoutly on a bar stool when I get downstairs, sipping a pint of lager, cigarette-less fingers fidgeting a beer mat.

'I'm so sorry to keep you waiting.' I slide on to a stool next to him. 'I got stuck on the phone.'

Don turns to look at me. He looks unamused. But as he stares at my face, his expression softens. He starts to laugh.

'What?'

'You've got a great fuck-off pillow mark on your cheek.'

Foiled! I start to laugh. 'I just lay down, shut my eyes for one second . . .'

'Yeah, yeah.'

'Jet lag. Sorry.'

'I always suspected magazine women couldn't cope with

154

business trips. And before you say it, fashion shows don't count.'

'Well I regret that I have reinforced your prejudices.' I look around the bar. It is wood-panelled. Leather seats. Black-and-white photographs of 1930s New York on the wall. Kensal Rise is another galaxy.

'You know you won't sleep tonight now,' says Don, sipping his beer.

'Thanks for planting that seed of insomnia in my head.'

We sit quietly in the bar, Don laconically briefing me about the early-morning meeting tomorrow. He stretches, his chest tightening the suiting of his jacket. 'I've booked a table for tonight. Little Italian a few blocks down. Move it, Miss Rafferty.'

We are seated at a candlelit table in a busy dining room with red banquettes and a mushroom cloud of chatter hovering over the restaurant. It's buzzy and comfortable. 'Is this an old favourite?'

Something flickers behind Don's eyes then disappears. 'Kind of.' He coughs and scans the room quickly. 'I haven't been here for a while, though.'

'Where did you live in New York?' I lean forward eagerly, elbows on the table, chin in my hands.

'Oh. Kind of Tribeca way,' says Don, rubbing his jaw. His eyes are dark, impenetrable pools in this restaurant half-light. When he smiles, they dance. When he doesn't, they are intimidating, like an animal who hasn't quite been tamed and could turn at any minute. 'I worked near here, though.'

'Tribeca? Is that . . .' I try to work out the geography and unfold a New York City map in my head.

'West of SoHo, darling.' Don wraps this thick dark fingers

around the stem of his glass and takes a hearty gulp of his wine.

'Did you have a loft?'

'A nice apartment.'

'What street?'

A frown creases his shallow forehead. 'What is this? A hundred personal questions?'

Oh. I lean back, embarrassed. Sensing my discomfort, Don smiles at me softly and I immediately realise that I haven't offended him at all. We exchange a look that acknowledges: he's a grumpy git, I'm banging on. Understood.

'Hey, Don!' shouts an American voice behind us. A blond man in a stripy shirt is waving two tables back. 'Hell. Isn't it you, Wilberforce?'

Don immediately tenses. He doesn't turn round. He looks like a little boy convinced that if he stays really still no one will notice that he's there.

'There's a guy . . .' I gesture behind him.

Don turns reluctantly, slowly. 'Hi, James.' He speaks slowly, without enthusiasm, as if trying to deter the man from walking over to our table. It doesn't work.

The man is tall, well dressed in a preppy kind of way. He seems perfectly nice and very pleased to see Don, clapping him on the shoulder. 'Jeez, man,' he says. 'Haven't seen you for months. Where did you disappear to?'

'London. I'm back in London.' Don is smiley, civil and controlled. He pauses, and in this pause he lets James know that he won't be furthering the conversation.

'Right,' says James hesitantly. He looks at me and smiles. 'And—'

'This is Annie,' interrupts Don. 'Annie. James.'

James looks momentarily confused before sticking out a

hand. 'Good to meet you, Annie.' He smiles at Don, hesitant. 'Well, nice to see you again,' he says, more awkward now, staring at me, as if something about me intrigues him. Have I got spinach on my tooth? I wipe my mouth surreptitiously with my napkin. James walks back through the jostling restaurant to his table and his dining partner, a blonde woman, who looks none too pleased at being left alone with the water jug for company.

'Right, let's eat,' says Don, relaxing once more.

We eat, alternating gossipy magazine talk with comfortable silence. I realise that Nick and I never talk about work any more. I feel, rightly or wrongly, that it alienates him. It's a relief not to have to underplay my day. It's a relief not to have to be the one in charge. I gaze at Don, the jet lag lapping at me now, and tune in and out of the conversation, watching his mouth move without listening to the words, noticing for the first time the way his nose crooks slightly to the left as if broken once long ago . . .

'Are you listening?' asks Don, pointing his knife at me. 'Earth calling Miss Rafferty.'

'Oops. Yes, in another space-time continuum. The wine, I'm afraid.' As I pick at my plate of pasta – the size Mum would serve up for the whole family – I am struck by a sense of dislocation, as if my brain hasn't yet caught up with the new time zone, nor circumstance. Nick and Georgia and London life suddenly seem so far away, it's as if there is a possibility that they don't exist at all.

'I'll get you back to the hotel,' he says.

No pudding then? I rather fancied one. The chocolate pot incident seems like a lifetime ago. He seemed like a stranger then. He doesn't now.

Don pays the bill, slamming a wad of dirty dollars on to

the table with casual machismo. He holds up my coat: I tunnel my arms into its sleeves. He holds the door open, waving to the James guy with one hand, his other hand on the small of my back, pushing me forward. Bone tired now, I am grateful for the offer of his arm. We walk quickly, our breath clouding in front of us like fine lace. Don lights a cigarette and pulls heavily as we walk. Something about the evening nags me. 'Don?'

'Huh.'

'Who was that?'

He quickens his step. 'Oh, just some guy. Old acquaintance.' He blows out a scarf of smoke dismissively and speaks so quietly I have to strain to hear him. 'A different life, Annie. That's all.'

Twenty

'Yes, you were good, Miss Rafferty,' says Don, as we whirl through the revolving door of the publisher's gleaming large offices and break out of our temperature-controlled environment into the icy sunshine. New York is beginning to feel like the backdrop to our own very personal cinematic drama.

'Really? I thought . . .' I am grinning stupidly.

Don stops on the pavement and touches my hand lightly. 'First lesson Brits must learn over here. False modesty doesn't work.' He laughs. 'Anyway, I said you were good, not brilliant. A bit too candid at times.'

'Oh.' I deflate again. I hate this power Don has over me, that he can raise me up with a little comment, then smash me down just as easily. And I hate the way I am becoming almost puppyish in his company. He makes me feel like a twenty-year-old work experience. And yet, if I am being brutally honest with myself, this is part of his growing attraction. I quite enjoy his domination. It is an unfamiliar dynamic; the opposite to how things are between me and Nick: I am a road map Nick memorised long ago.

We turn on to Fifth. 'Let's hit the shops, girl,' says Don, slinking his arm through mine.

'Shouldn't I go back and write up a report for Pippa?'

He tugs me, laughing. 'Oh, Annie. Later.'

My feet are tired, but I have uncovered a new, restless energy from somewhere, an excitability that makes me feel that I can walk the New York City streets for ever. The stores blink with Christmas lights, and gigantic white snowflakes dangle high above the street. It is a magical cocktail of festivity and consumption that only New York ever pulls off. Whereas in London, Christmas shopping feels a little obscene and wasteful, here it feels good, a moral imperative. I spend far more on Nick than I would at home. But I don't spend as much on presents as Don, whose Amex flashes at tills up and down Fifth, in Barneys, in Bergdorf's. We start to dawdle more as the day goes on. In Bloomingdales I'm entranced by a display of jewellery, a luxurious row of hanging blue stone and silver necklaces. I run my fingers over them, cooing, while Don waits patiently.

My phone starts to ring in my bag. I rummage to get it.

'Hi Babe,' says Nick.

Other life calling. 'Hey!'

'Have I disturbed a meeting or something?'

It's hard to hear him. A shop assistant is talking in a very loud voice right behind me. 'Sorry. One minute . . .' I step away from the jewellery display stand.

'Obviously not a meeting,' Nick says.

'No. I was just doing a spot of Christmas shopping.'

'Oh.' Long pause. 'Right.'

Can I feel the static of resentment down the phone, or am I imagining it? 'Is everything OK? How's George?'

'The same.' Nick coughs. 'We miss you.'

'Ah,' I say, realising the unsettling truth that I don't miss them at all. Not Georgia. Not Nick. Not even poor old Dad convalescing at home. I say, 'I miss you,' back, sensing that Nick knows that I am lying.

Don nudges me. I turn around, awkward at dealing with both worlds at the same time, the thudding collision. He holds up a necklace to my neck, its beautiful glossy chunks of dark blue stone cool against my skin, his fingers brushing my décolletage. 'Not now,' I say. Don snorts like a boar and steps away.

'Who's that?' asks Nick, quietly.

'Don. Don Wilberforce. The exec I'm here with. You know, I mentioned . . .'

'You didn't, actually.' There is a catch in his voice. 'I presumed you were going with Pippa.'

Come to think of it, I didn't say anything. I studiously avoided the subject because I thought about it so much it felt as though I had in fact mentioned something. 'I'm back tomorrow. Crack-of-dawn flight.'

A long, awkward pause straddles the Atlantic. Normally I would chatter on about what I've been doing, but Don is still in earshot and I am also sensitive to the possibility that Nick might think that I am boasting. Don looks at me unnervingly intensely.

'I guess you're busy,' says Nick, sounding put out. 'Don't want to hold you up.'

'Yeah, I better go. I'll call you as soon as I touch down tomorrow.'

The phone goes dead. Our close shorthand has gone. Poof! What has happened between me and Nick? I look up. Don is watching me. He is smiling, one of his enraging, lazy smiles.

'I'm beat. I'm going back to the hotel,' I say. The phone

161

call has siphoned away the energy I felt a few moments ago. I feel disloyal. I can feel Nick's hurt, hurt that I am here, having a fabulous time, while he is left looking after my sister at home in London.

'Boring.' Don ruffles his black hair. 'I won't see you later. I've got a supper.' He looks down at the polished shop floor. 'Old friend.'

'Of course.' I try to mask the disappointment in my voice. I have no right to be disappointed that he isn't available for supper. We're not on a mini-break.

'I'd invite you along, but . . .' he says awkwardly.

'Don't worry,' I say brightly, not wanting him to think I expected him to be available for supper. 'I could do with a night in on my own with the minibar. It will be a rare treat.'

I do work hard at making my solitary evening enjoyable. I pack my shopping, scissoring off the labels so that I can claim they are mine and won't have to pay tax if I get stopped at Customs. I order room service, spinach risotto. I crack open a small bottle of cool white wine from the minibar. I have a bath. But after the slightly forced me-time rituals are over, something akin to homesickness balloons in my chest, though it's a yearning for something indefinable rather than a yearning for home. I wonder where Don is right now, and imagine his stocky legs pounding towards some glamorous restaurant downtown. Who is he dining with? A man? A woman? A woman, of course. That would explain why he didn't want me gooseberrying along. Yes, it will be a polished New York woman, all airbrushed skin and paper-white teeth. She will laugh at his jokes in the right places, find his accent endearing. Don will order champagne. He'll be showing off, of course, the one-time New Yorker proving that he has gone on to better things, hasn't downsized by moving back to

162

London. Then they will get in a yellow cab together, fire down Broadway, piercing through the romantic New York night, and then . . . and then . . . Stop it.

If only I could tweezer the man out of my head. I pour myself another glass of wine, slip into my new white silk nightie from Banana Republic, and flump down in the bed, telling myself how nice it is to rest my head on crisp linen pillowcases, sapped by the increasing sense of dislocation from normal life. All the Christmassy feelings that bubbled up inside as Don and I shopped have flattened. I pull the light switch, plunging the room into blackout-blind blackness.

There is a knocking in my dreams. It gets louder and louder until I realise it isn't in my dreams after all. It is external. Although what is external and what is internal is confused as the room is still so black it feels like I've woken up with a thick woollen sock over my head.

'Annie,' Don's voice hisses from the other side of the door. 'Are you awake?'

I pull the light switch, blinking as the light splashes against me like cold, bright paint. Rubbing my eyes, too tired to feel surprised, I open the door. I don't need to say come in. Don strides through into the room, launches himself at the edge of my bed, making the whole thing tilt. He brings outside smells into the room. Cigarettes. Wine. Beer. Traffic. Food. I wish I'd thought to smooth the quilt before answering the door. It looks like a large animal has rolled about in it, and my unsexy Marks and Spencer nude T-shirt bra hangs off one end. I fold myself into a taupe velvet armchair by the side of the bed, aware of the skin exposed by my insubstantial nightie, pulling my legs beneath me. Should I cover up? What with? The dressing gown is hanging on the back of the bathroom door, and retrieving it will entail a self-conscious sashay across the room. No, I am better off staying put.

'Sit here. Next to me,' says Don, patting the bed.

'Fine here, thanks.'

'I missed you tonight, Annie.' He pulls his pack of cigarettes from his inside jacket pocket.

'This is a smoke-free zone,' I say rather pompously, pointing to the sign on the back of the door.

He holds up a hand in mock-surrender and puts the cigarettes back into his jacket. 'Take me through your evening.'

'Bath. Bed.'

Don smiles, a lopsided, inebriated smile. 'Exactly how I imagined.'

I blush, a little uncomfortable. I am properly, rudely awake now.

'That nightie suits you.'

'I'll make a point of wearing nightwear to work in the future.'

'Ah.' Don falls back on the bed, supporting himself on one elbow, resting his chin in his hand, staring at me. 'All that glossy magazine black.' He wags a stout index finger. 'Let me tell you, Annie Rafferty. Black polonecks are not sexy. Nor are those weird tunic things all you girls wear. And flat ballet shoes don't get the heart racing either.'

'Weirdly enough, we don't dress for you.'

Don starts to laugh. 'No. I don't suppose you do. Can I get a drink?'

Before I answer, Don is tugging at the minibar, the door sucking as it opens. He takes out a beer, breaks open the can and slurps noisily. He has no manners. Why don't I find him more repulsive? 'Who *do* you dress for? Nick?'

'Pippa, probably.' I laugh.

'Travesty.' Don is now standing in the no-man's-land between bed and minibar. 'If I had you all to myself I would wrap you up in ribbons and lace and glue you into a towering pair of heels.'

He will regret this talk in the morning. If he remembers. He's drunk.

'Do you ever wear that jacket?'

'Afraid not. My sister does, though. She likes it very much. It suits her.'

Don puts his hands to his chest, like a wounded Shakespearean actor in his death throes.

'It's not me, Don.'

'You know what I think? I think . . .' He is really slurring now. 'I think that it is you. It is you really, Miss Rafferty.'

I sit up straighter, realising that at this very moment I feel exactly the opposite of how I feel at home: vulnerable, erotic. 'I wish I had another fascinating self buried somewhere, Don. But I fear I don't.'

Don staggers towards me, as if in slow motion. Suddenly he is squatting beside me. Then he's on his knees. I am riveted to the chair, scared of misinterpreting him, wondering what the hell is about to happen, not willing to stop what might happen before it does. He drops his head into the cradle of my nightie that is stretched across my crossed bare legs and lays it there like a child. 'Oh, Annie,' he says softly, the wet warmth of his breath penetrating the silk to my thigh.

I try to nudge his head off my lap. It doesn't work. I have to grip his head between both hands as if it were a large coconut and lift it up. It drops back down again. 'Don. You're drunk, very drunk.'

'Not that drunk.' Don reaches up and yanks the sidelight's

165

string pull. The room is swallowed by bat-cave darkness. The weight of his head lifts off my knee. Then his hand is on my cheek. I can feel the pulse in his palm. He pulls me towards him roughly. I can smell him, intriguing, musty, male. Then his hand is in my hair. He is breathing heavily. This all happens in microseconds: I'm flipping upside down on a fairground ride. I must do something. I must stop this. But I am rendered passive by an overriding desire to yield to him, to let him do to me what he will, to absolve myself of all responsibility. 'Don . . . I can't . . .'

Don ignores me, stroking his hand down my collar bone, across my breasts. I gasp as it skims over my nipple, circles it with his fingers. Then – ohmygod! – he pinches it. It is just, and only just, the right side of forceful. He is so hungry.

Is this how date rapes happen? I push him away. I am scared that he won't stop. That he will. 'Don. Please. No. We can't do this.'

'We can.' He does not move his hand.

I push him again. He still doesn't move. His lust is beginning to slightly scare me. 'Don, please.'

Finally he loosens his grip, slowly, reluctantly, and pulls his body away, breaking our electrical circuit. He gets up.

'I think you'd better leave.'

'I know you don't want me to.'

I stare back hard at him, as if we're daring the other to look away first. Don breaks the spell by opening the door, a slice of light from the hall spills into the room. The door clicks shut and he is gone. I lean against it, pressing my forehead on to the cool wood in the darkness, relieved – close shave! – but actually, overwhelmingly, shamefully, disappointed that he has gone.

*

I emerge from the Nothing to Declare tunnel at Heathrow feeling so guilty I am amazed that I'm not pulled aside and the contents of my bags and stomach investigated. My eyes stick to the rubber wheels of my trolley, unable to meet Don's full gaze. The events of last night have yet to be mentioned. Instead I've had to endure hours of Don's amused, teasing looks, as if he is daring me to bring up the subject. But I won't. I can't. Because I have no idea what I'll say. And in the cold, sober light of day I am rather unsure as to what happened exactly. It's like falling asleep halfway through a film and waking up at the end with no understanding of how you got to the denouement. All I can clearly remember is the exact weight of his head in my lap, its skull-dense heaviness.

'Meet me next week,' instructs Don, pulling his bag off the trolley, bending down and tightening its strap. 'We'd be good together. You know we would.'

'Don . . .' The other travellers are bustling past us now, excitedly looking out for relatives in the crowd, squinting for the taxi sign. They become dashes of colour and movement, incidental to the main action.

'Not another word. Just come round for a drink at my place. Wednesday.' Don leans forward and kisses me, lightly, on one cheek, then the other. He lingers not on the kisses but beside my neck as if sucking in my scent. 'Or you're fired.'

Twenty-one

OK. It is Wednesday. It is the Wednesday on which I will not go to visit Don in Bermondsey in the evening. I need to get my house in order first. I need to try to make things better with Nick. I've got to fix the relationship. And I cannot avoid having sex with Nick for ever. I've exhausted my excuses – period pains, bad back, feigning sleep – and need to find a way of getting things back on track. It all goes round and round my head. Am I willing to throw away three years with someone because of a silly schoolgirl crush? Am I willing to throw away the potential father of my children and end up having to filter through an ever-decreasing man pool in my mid-thirties? For what exactly? The problem is that however much I remind myself that Don is just a roguish charmer whose interest in me won't outlast a light bulb, there's another voice inside my head whispering, 'Maybe he's more than that . . .' And I just can't escape him. I am editing an article on holistic cures for adult acne, but Don – the memory of our encounter in the hotel room – hovers around my head like the smell of a night out on an unwashed party outfit. I cannot escape him at all.

'Annie!' Alexis shouts from the other side of the office and strides over to my desk in short steps, her speed clipped by her tight pencil skirt, like she's got a million things to do and no time in which to waste her many prodigious talents. She has become bloated with renewed confidence since her triumph in the last issue-critique meeting and, the features staff inform me, is being insufferable.

'So much has happened while you were away,' she sighs theatrically, sitting down at my desk, tiny bottom imposing itself into the circumference of my personal space. She's wearing a short sixties-style tunic dress, black opaque tights and high, very high snakeskin heels. The girl looks good, no denying it.

I am suddenly aware of my own rather unimaginative black trousers and grey boy sweater combo. Must try harder. 'What's been going down?'

'Pippa gave us a big pep talk on Friday. She says that we should, like, trust our instincts and continue doing what we are doing, rather than try to change things unnecessarily, just because . . .' Alexis makes annoying quote signs with her fingers, 'the powers that be say so.'

It is undeniably annoying that it is Alexis, not Pippa, who is imparting this information. It makes me want to shoot the messenger.

'And the new sales figures are about to be released.' She glances around the room, looking out for potential eavesdroppers, as if confiding secret military intelligence. Surely she hasn't got hold of them before me? 'Wave goodbye to another fifteen thousand readers,' she says.

'Shit. Really?' This is bad. Very bad. I wonder how much longer Pippa will be able to maintain her fantasy of being a media genius, contradicted as it is by the full force of the

169

diabolical sales figures. And I wonder how much longer I can maintain my fantasy of being a home-owner. What was I thinking, taking out such a monster mortgage?

'I'm staying positive for my team, of course,' crows Alexis. 'Boost them, you know. I told them that there is no place, absolutely no place, for negative thinking.'

'That's the spirit.' Lordy. How long will Alexis's features desk be able to endure her?

'You know what, Annie?' Alexis rubs her chin. 'The magazine is having such a tough time, but the funny thing is, I'm enjoying my job more than ever. It's like . . .' She gazes wistfully across the carpet tiles. 'I feel like I've finally got some recognition. The people who matter have finally noticed me! Hoorah. What took them so long, eh?' She says this like she's joking. But we both know that she is only pretending to be joking and beneath the unfunny joke lies a trickle of sticky dark ambition. 'Anyway, I better skedaddle, I've got a meeting with old Wilby.'

'Wilby?'

'Wilberforce. Don Wilberforce.'

My hands freeze mid-air above my keyboard. 'How . . . how come?'

Alexis's smile is irrepressible. 'Oh, he wants to discuss something or other. You know, he wants a trusted opinion from the shop floor, I guess.' She takes small steps back to the helm of the beleaguered features desk, head aloft, stopping on the way to mortify a painfully shy new subeditor about an 'unforgivably lame' headline.

My email pings. Finally.

Meet you at 7. Address below. The blue letters streak across my screen like a fox marking territory with his scent.

A part of me – waist upwards – was dreading a tussle with

the appalling immorality of this dilemma. I had a plan, of course: if he did call, which he probably wouldn't, then I'd laugh it off lightly, pretend it (the incident of the nightie at nighttime) was one big joke, a drunken escapade that was better off dismissed and forgotten. I bite into a paper clip, pull it apart with my teeth until it is a sharp wiggly wire stick and stab it against the desk. But the idea of Don and Alexis having cosy meetings *à deux* has awoken a dark, competitive creature within me.

My brain whirs. OK. Plan. How about if I turn up and use the opportunity to finish the thing before it starts? Deprive it of light and food and air before it can scamper to its legs and run off, creating its inevitable chaos. I cannot work like this. I've spent the week haemorrhaging anxieties, on email-watch, listening for the heavy tread of his brogues. No. I absolutely cannot let this drift on any longer. I must confront him. Tell him that I am not, so not, available. And can we just return to normal, please? I am Annie Rafferty of Lower Dalton. I will always be Annie Rafferty of Lower Dalton. Sensible Annie. Like a shire horse. I need to get my house in order and stop behaving like a teenager.

See you there, I type. My fingers hesitate over the send key. Then I look up: Alexis is pouting into a hand mirror, one heel perched on the black mesh waste bin as if it were a stage accessory from a production of *Cabaret*. This clinches it. My finger whacks the key and the message shoots off, irretrievably, into the wireless motorways of the building. I imagine it whizzing through the office equivalent of the M25 before turning off a trunk road and parking on Don's expensive flat-screen computer on the fifteenth floor. I sit back in my chair, waiting to feel some kind of release or relief. But I don't feel better. I feel worse. Three hours to go. Three hours before

171

some kind of resolution, three hours before I make everything go back to normal and my life can continue as planned.

When I get out at Borough Tube station it is dark, the street patched with yellow circles of lamplight. I walk fast towards Bermondsey Street, powered by something that I can't control. I turn left, turn right, my heart punching, until I get to the apartment block. It looks like an old warehouse conversion. With its CCTV cameras, locks and wide door it appears hermetically sealed off from the rest of the street. Flat five. I depress the polished brass button, wondering where in the building the sound will trill out my arrival, and lean towards the intercom grill, clearing my throat so my voice will sound casual. I wait. Don's voice doesn't boom out as I expected. Instead, the big black door that I press against releases with a buzz and I fall forward into the warm, laundered scents of the hallway. Partly to calm myself down and partly out of curiosity, I decide to take the stairs rather than the lift. This, it quickly transpires, is a mistake. By the time I reach the fifth floor, my armpits are slippery and I am panting. Not quite the entrance I was hoping for. I stand, collecting myself, outside the dark walnut door of flat number five for a few moments, and wipe the beads of sweat off my nose with the sleeve of my coat. Without me knocking, the door opens.

'Come in, Miss Rafferty.' Don is wearing jeans and a patterned navy shirt with the cuffs rolled up over his wrists, exposing a bright pink interior fabric. He looks so different without his work-suited skin. I'm suddenly not sure I can relate to him in a private space. What will we talk about? What am I doing here?

'Hi.' I step on to a dark floor, glassy and smooth as an iced lake. Goodness, this is grand, as Mum might say. It is a slick warehouse apartment: polished wood, vast frameless windows, textured taupe and exotic plantings in oriental-style matt-black pots.

'My gay pad,' says Don drily.

'It's definitely got a man's touch.'

'Here, let me take your coat.'

I wish I had had the foresight this morning to guess that I might indeed be weak and relent on my earlier fiery conviction that I wouldn't visit him, and therefore paid a little more attention to my dress. In this shiny new context, last year's Reiss coat looks tired, scraggy and shapeless. It looks like the coat belonging to a woman who doesn't get invited to swanky apartments in Bermondsey very often.

'Champagne?' He presses a cold, fizzing glass into my hand.

The dry blond bubbles hit my tongue, then my blood stream, almost instantaneously. I feel myself start to fizz. I am old and wise enough not to have my head turned by a glass of Krug and a designer interior. Or am I? It is quite an apartment. The sofa is stupendous, a vast L-shape the colour of thick cognac cream. It is exactly the kind of sofa I am likely to spill red wine over.

'Sit down.' As always with Don, this sounds more instruction than polite invitation.

I sink into the pristine sofa. We chat politely for a few minutes, slightly inanely, considering the subtext of my visit, about the glories of living in Bermondsey – Borough market, great restaurants, interesting creative people – and the cold snap. The small talk only seems to draw more attention to the bigger issues swirling overhead like the vast, spacey contemporary chandeliers that hang from the ceiling like models of the solar system. It makes me nervous. Within five minutes, I have uncouthly drained my first glass of champagne. Don notices and glides back across his slippery square footage to pull the bottle from the fridge. His fridge is stacked with champagne, the bottles' cold noses pointing outwards like a cluster of warheads. When are we going to have The Conversation?

'You are distracted, Annie.' He leans against the wall and studies me casually.

My self-consciousness and the directness of this observation ignite a pointless but instinctive defence. 'Only by the sofa.'

'Stuff going down at home?' Those eyes are dancing again.

'Well . . .' For some reason I'll never understand, this is the question that pops the cork on my problems. My tongue, loosened by champagne and agitated by the oddness of the situation, begins to overdevelop any line of conversation that avoids the main issue of our New York Moment. So I talk about Olly. My parents' pension crisis. Nick working as a builder. Dad's dodgy ticker. When I explain about my parents having to sell Hedgerows, to my horror my eyes begin to brim with tears. I am appalled by this uncharacteristic loose verbosity, but cannot stop. Like a river bursting its banks, the talk keeps coming, gaining momentum, whooshing into his living room, flooding our professional relationship with unnecessary intimacy. What on earth has come over me?

It's enough to send any man not paid by the hour fast asleep. But Don's eyes never once leave my face, as if I am the most interesting raconteur on the planet, as opposed to a nervous woman with sweaty palms haemorrhaging anecdotes which are of no interest to anyone other than the Raffertys. 'It means a lot to you, Hedgerows, doesn't it?' he says eventually, when he can get a word in edgeways.

I nod, swallowing the lump in my throat, and start to describe the way the ivy curls up the outside walls. The covered well beneath the pink hollyhocks. The view of cornfields from my bedroom window. And on and on.

'Heavenly.' He sighs. 'I almost bought a run-down cottage outside Bath last year, in a rather laughable attempt to create the rural dream, at weekends at least, but I got gazumped. God's way of telling me to stay in the city. Where it's safe.'

I laugh. 'I can't really see you in the country, Don.'

'Why not? I am most offended, Miss Rafferty. I know that I appear to be a horribly successful slick urbanite, and I am, of course, but there is a wilder, muddier side to me.'

This comment makes me blush for some reason.

'My grandad came from your parts, you know.'

'Really? I thought you were from Croydon?'

He laughs. 'Yes, born and bred. But my grandparents lived in the Cotswolds. Grandad used to work at Shipton rail station, near Burford. Nan was a housekeeper for a big posh family down there. We used to trog down there regularly, all six of us, any chance we could.'

'Six? You're one of six?'

'I've got five older sisters, Annie.' He grins. 'That, my dear, is why I understand women so damn well.'

I laugh. 'All is explained. You are a pampered youngest son!'

Don raises an eyebrow. 'But of course. Some of my happiest times were spent in the Cotswolds with my sisters. Although . . . you know what? I do have a confession to make.' He pauses. 'I have a thing about cows.'

'Oh do you indeed?' I laugh.

'It's more embarrassing than that. Annie, I am shit scared of cows, always have been.'

175

'Bulls? No one likes bulls. To be a little wary is acceptable.'

'No, not bulls, Miss Rafferty, the black-and-white things with those huge pink udders like whoopee cushions.' He shivers. 'They're demonic. I look at them. They look at me. And there's an understanding. I stay out of their way and they agree not to trample me to death. It happens, you know! In the green pastures of merry England, three or four people get trampled by psychotic herds of bloodthirsty cows every year. '

I am giggling now. 'You definitely need to stay in the city to be safe from cows.'

'Did you have any of the foul beasts?'

'Hedgerows has a lovely big walled garden. So, no, we didn't have cows. My dad is a keen gardener. We had enormous prize turnips.'

'Aha, a Cotswold man with good sense. Give me a turnip over a cow any day.' Don stares at me and lets the pause empty out to a proper baggy silence. He rearranges himself on the sofa, shuffling closer to me until his wide square knee lightly touches mine and my skin sparks like a match. 'Do you ever wonder how all these things could have turned out differently?'

'How do you mean?' I ask suspiciously, sensing a provocation brewing. The mood in the room has flipped from playful to something a little more serious. He often does this, switching lanes in the conversation, keeping me on my toes.

'Well, you could have married a rich guy like your sister. Always was the simplest solution for an attractive young woman.'

I laugh. 'I don't think so.'

'Oh, come on. Imagine. No need to work. Endless holidays, shopping, lunches . . .'

176

'Lipo in my lunch hour. Divorcee at forty-five. No thanks, Don.'

'Divorce settlements are far more generous than any company pay-off.' Don lights a cigarette and exhales the smoke with a laugh.

'You really are a cynical unreconstructed male, aren't you?'

'Just realistic.'

My hackles rise. 'All this "it's a man's world" stuff. It's so . . . God, it's so eighties!'

'Come on, women's magazine journalist, how come women still earn about twelve per cent less than men for doing the same job then? How come I can count the number of truly influential female execs on one hand? Keep up.'

Is he playing with me? I will not rise to the provocation. 'OK. But that's partly because women are sensible enough not to want to sacrifice their lives to make other people rich,' I say in a measured voice. 'Besides, publishing is different.'

'Yeah, right.' He smiles gently. 'Most female journalists, especially those in magazines, don't get to fifty and receive a pat on the back or a golden pair of Jimmy Choos, you know. The industry is still a fucking finishing school for middle-class twentysomethings and you know it. Only the very best get to the top, let alone make decent money. The majority of you soon realise – when a cheaper, prettier, younger colleague happy to do a naked byline picture has been promoted above you – that the best thing you can do is use your contacts as a springboard to a half-decent husband, preferably not a fellow journalist because he'll be unable to pay the prep school fees and you'll end up living in Hackney.'

'Very funny, Don.' I bristle at him. 'You know, you really are intensely annoying.'

'Oh don't be so uptight. Where's your sense of humour?'

I am beginning to feel that I have a moral duty to leave. It's just that I'm rather enjoying the heady cocktail of confrontation and Krug, cut through as it is with the unspoken erotic chaser of our New York encounter. 'And what happens to men as they get older? Hair transplants, mistresses, mid-life crises. Bad columns about hair transplants, mistresses, mid-life crises.'

'True. But at least in general our salaries rise as our hair falls out. For women in this business, it's unfashionable to get too old.' He stretches out his legs and yawns as if this is all so obvious it is tiring him. 'Wrinkles work against women. They work for men.'

'Right, well, thanks for the corporate pep talk, Don!' I say, standing up and smoothing down my skirt. 'I'll book myself in for a face lift. You do know, don't you, that if I were recording this conversation you would be fired?'

Don grins, unruffled. 'Miss Rafferty, I'm not saying this is the way things should be – I'd much rather they weren't, I love working with women – I'm saying this is the way things are. I'm looking out for you. I'm arguing the case against complacency.' He smiles. 'Oh, don't look at me like that. Everyone knows I shoot my mouth off. It's the silent ones you need to worry about. Now sit down, for God's sake. Stop being so melodramatic.'

I sit down again and take a large slug of champagne. Where is this conversation going, and much more interestingly, where has it come from? What eats Don up inside? I glare at him for a few moments. I realise I haven't enjoyed myself so much in ages.

Suddenly Don reaches out and grabs my knee. 'Fuck, Annie. Put me out of my misery here.'

'I beg your pardon?' But I know. I'm playing now.

'Kiss me.'

'No! Don't be ridiculous.'

His face is inches from mine, his pupils have spread so his eyes look totally black. His non-knee-gripping hand dangles a burning cigarette a millimetre from the sofa arm. I suddenly visualise a disaster-scenario vision of everything going up in flames, of the fire brigade coming, of ending up in hospital and having to explain to Nick and Georgia how I got there. Don's hand grips my knee harder. The grip reminds me of the ferocity of his embrace in New York. It sends a shiver up my spine.

'It doesn't take fucking Irma Kurtz to see that you and whatshisname are on the rocks. It's over, Annie. Accept it. You know what?' He drags a finger roughly across my bottom lip.

Oh, the arrogance. But my imagination has already roguishly transported me: what would he be like in bed? Then it suddenly occurs to me, what if me and Nick *are* on the rocks? I shut my eyes and squeeze my nose bone with my fingers. 'Don, please.'

Don stands up and walks away. The sudden physical distance feels like a loss. He smiles, a slow, lazy smile. 'I could seduce you now, you know that, don't you?'

Damn him. He's right. 'In your dreams, honey.'

'But you know what? Because we work together, and because I rate you, I'm going to let you go.'

'Very big of you.'

Don walks over to the coat stand and pulls my coat off a hook.

That's it? I was thinking he was going to try a bit harder. I'm the one who should be rejecting him after all. Feeling slightly short-changed, I walk out into the corridor and press the lift button. Don leans on the door frame, watching me, a smile playing around his lips. The lift doors shudder open. I make myself step inside. They begin to slowly close. I consider putting a foot out to stop them, freezing the moment until I feel certain that I am doing the right thing. I imagine Don bursting through the gap like a superhero and pushing me against the lift wall like a scene from a movie. Then the doors shut. The lift glides soundlessly to the bottom of the building. I fall out of the front door to the apartment block into an icy cushion of winter air and burst into tears.

Twenty-two

Maggie and I watch Jake and the boys amble through the park gate, along the road – dropping, picking up a hat – and into their Audi. The wind whips up and the trees swing against an orangey city sky. Maggie pulls her sheepskin coat tight, blows on her fingers in their black cashmere fingerless gloves and huddles forward over the wooden café table. 'Time to swap coffee for something a little stronger?'

'I should think so,' I say.

We stand up, shake ourselves down. Handsome dads glance over, keeping Maggie in the periphery of their vision as those long, lean legs of hers move in and out of her sheepskin coat. She links her arm in mine as we walk through the park, up the road to the pub. 'You are a good sister, Annie.'

'Someone had to pay it off.'

'Ten thousand pounds from your own savings? Blimey. I don't think so.'

'She is my sister. She's beyond making plans, Maggie. She's in decline. It's scary.'

Inside the pub – rowdy, noisy, full of thirtysomethings – we are immediately hot and overdressed. We sit at a small round

181

wooden table, peel off our layers and order a bottle of wine.

As Maggie loses her coat and hat and gloves she sheds her park-mum skin and looks five years younger. 'So she hasn't accepted Olly's offer?' she asks, dark eyes glittering with outdoorsy brightness.

'Not yet. Thinking about it. Nick thinks she should definitely take the money and enjoy spending it. I think no. It's yucky. The right thing would be to say no.'

'The right thing for Olly's bank balance! Annie, if she'd married him, she'd be in line for a seriously large whack of money. He's used up some of her valuable fertility years. He's messed her around. Personally, I'd take the money and demand interest. Come on, Annie. Don't look like that. We all have our price.' Maggie puts an arm around my shoulder and squeezes as if hit by a sudden rush of girlie warmth. 'You,' she says and lets out a low whistle. 'You and your bloody morals.'

Morals? Hmm. Yes, quite. I take a long sip of wine and try not to think about Don. 'You saying I'm uptight, Maggie?'

'Oh, totally, completely uptight,' laughs Maggie. 'Funny, isn't it? I always thought that Georgia had it sewn up. That she'd escaped the slog. But it must be far worse having all that, then losing it, than never having it.'

I run my fingers around the rim of the wine glass and laugh. 'If I hadn't had such riches I could live with being poor ... Yes, let's pretend being married to a millionaire would be rubbish.'

'Imagine the agonies of deciding whether to shop in Prada or Pucci. It would be torment! Daily torment.'

We laugh. 'Still, in all seriousness, Maggie, I can't see you married to a banker, wondering why his secretary keeps phoning at the weekend.'

'Indeedy. I am not the City boy type, so we've both been spared the pain. The problem with being a City wife – and I know this, Annie, we've got two on the street – is that you are a depreciating asset.' She slugs back her wine. 'It's horrible. It can only end messily.' Maggie stares a little wistfully into the animated crush in the interior of the pub. 'Still, maybe City bankers aren't the only men who trade their wives in.'

'Maggie! You are obsessing about that hot nanny again, aren't you? This must stop!'

'Yes, of course I'm obsessing. Wouldn't you?' She looks at me and grins. 'But I have taken action.'

'Aha. Action. I like the sound of this. Go on.'

'Jake's been saying for a long time that he feels trapped, starved of adult conversation, and he's got a bee in his bonnet about what's being going down at the Browns'. Remember Danielle Brown? The one with the Pekinese nose job? Lives down the road from us, number twenty-three.'

'Think so.' I vaguely remember a very well-groomed tall woman at Maggie's lunch party last Christmas. She was wearing a bold-print red dress. I can't picture the husband. She totally overshadowed him.

'Three kids. She works for Samsung or something, grand fromage. Tom's the house husband. Or was.' Maggie takes a sip of wine, mischievous smile playing at the corners of her mouth. 'Forget hot nannies. Danielle is the one who has just run off with their twenty-three-year-old Swedish male au pair!'

'Hoorah!' I lift my glass. 'Or is that horribly sexist of me?'

'Probably. Anyway, things have come to a head.' She stops and pauses. 'Jake has got a job, Annie. A proper, paid job. Back at the newspaper. I pulled a few strings.'

'Well, that's great, isn't it? But who is looking after the kids?'

'I've employed a nanny, live-in, Magda. She is built like a hay bale, has ginger facial hair and stained teeth.'

'Genius.'

Maggie stares at her wine glass, straddling the stem with her fingers. 'But it's all a little sad. I mean, Jake is really chuffed about the job, but neither of us wanted to bring up latchkey kids. The only reason I felt OK working the hours I do was because I knew Jake was at home looking after the kids, that they've got the love and attention of one parent at least. Now,' she sighs, 'they've got the attentions of Magda with ginger facial hair.'

'I wouldn't beat yourself up. You know, when I was a girl I thought that Morag, who was my childhood friend's nanny, a fearsome old Scot with one black thumbnail, well I just thought that she was the most glamorous thing ever. A nanny always sounded like an enviably big adventure that happened to posh girls. I yearned for a nanny. I yearned to be packed off to boarding school too.'

'Now why doesn't that surprise me? God, you must have been an eccentric child.' Maggie laughs and hunches forward over the table. 'But you know the worst thing? Magda is almost earning more than Jake. No. I'm so not joking. It is the only way to secure anyone half decent. Gosh, this is all so depressing. I'm going to have to order some potato wedges to make myself feel better.'

Suddenly I feel a lot younger than Maggie, the friend who hasn't quite grown up. The days of childcare conundrums seem so far off as to be totally abstract, and as I get older, they seem to be getting further away, not nearer. I am hit by a nostalgic pang for a life I've never led. It's weird. An image of me and Nick curled up in front of a roaring fire hits me hard, almost physically, in the stomach. Last winter we hired a cottage near the Black Mountains. We were lying on a lovely old rug, having drunk a bottle of red wine. And we were talking about our children. He told me that he wanted four children. Four! I exclaimed. No way! But I remember inside feeling ridiculously blissed-out that he wanted me to have four of his children. He rolled a spliff and we started smoking and playing silly baby names. Ickerbod, he said. Gertrude, I said. Caesar, he said, and on and on we went, giggling, getting stoned and silly, as the wind whipped up outside and we snuggled into each others fire-warmed bodies. We haven't had a baby names conversation since that weekend.

As if reading my thoughts, Maggie looks at me, her black eyes wide and gentle. 'Annie, don't do as I've done.'

'What do you mean?'

'Don't force yourself into a corner, away from your kids, unless you're absolutely sure that's what you want. I love what I do, don't get me wrong. I really love it. But I do sometimes wish that all the financial responsibility wasn't on my shoulders. I do sometimes wish I could be Mum. That's all.'

I nod, appreciative of Maggie's advice, unsure how to respond. Right now, this is very much a hypothetical problem, considering the fact that pandas see more action. I point to the door. 'Look! It's Vicky Vick Vicks!'

'Hi, my old muckers!' Vicky strides into the bar, carrying a mixture of perfume and cold winter air in her voluminous coat and curls. 'I've only got time for a quick glass, I'm afraid.' Grinning her gap-toothed grin, she kisses us both on the cheek, pulls out a chair and shrugs off her black velvet coat to reveal a tight-fitting dark grey satin dress.

'You disappoint me with your chicness, Vicky Vick Vicks,' says Maggie. 'Where are your fuck-me red shoes?'

Vicky laughs, mouthing 'another glass' to the bartender. 'I'm off to a dinner party thrown by a couple from work. Thought I'd better tone it down. Us single girls rarely make it on to the coupley invite list anyhow. Especially in red fuck-me shoes.'

'Bah humbug,' I say. 'I think you have a moral obligation to wear your red fuck-me shoes to smug couples dinner parties.'

'Actually, so do I. So – ta da! – I've brought these to change into . . .' Vicky rummages in her vast black buckled handbag and pulls out a pair of leopard-print platforms. 'Christ, I'm not about to turn up anywhere in flats. One must maintain some standards.'

'Thank God for that. Now, drink vino and tell us all about your shenanigans,' says Maggie. 'Some vicarious entertainment, please.'

Vicky puts her head in her hands in mock despair. 'Girls, I've struck a drought.'

'No!' exclaim me and Maggie simultaneously. The table adjacent to ours looks up.

Vicky swivels on her seat, flinging one leg exuberantly over the other. 'My latest date was really rather nice actually, filthy rich, City boy.'

'Promising?'

'I thought so. I really did. But then when it came down to the basics . . . well, he just couldn't get it on. Too stressed out, he said. We tried again last week. We got back to his place in Notting Hill. Champagne. Lights low. It still would not wake up!' Vicky sips her large glass of white wine, smudging its rim with pink lipstick. 'I've decided not to take it personally. And I've moved on. I'm online dating now. Far less labour intensive. More room for creativity.'

186

'Aha. What's your USP?' asks Maggie.

'Adventurous—'

'Will sleep around,' says Maggie drily, arching one black eyebrow.

'Maggie!' I say, giving her a sharp nudge with my elbow.

'I'm just translating it into man lingo,' she says. 'You don't mind, do you, Vicks? Go on.'

'Compassionate,' says Vicky, more reluctantly now.

'Neurotic,' translates Maggie. 'Likes cats.'

Vicky rolls her eyes. 'I can see where this might be heading.' She takes a sip of wine. 'Fun-loving.'

'Loud and irritating with huge credit card debts.'

'Curvy. God, that's a corker, isn't it?'

'Yup. Curvy means size sixteen plus,' says Maggie.

'Solvent.'

'Wa-hey! Tight career bitch from hell!'

Vicky groans. 'Enough already.'

My phone beeps. A text. *Am at your house, drinking wine with Georgia. You are not. Dave x*

'Oh shit. Shit.' I slam my drink down on the table and sit bolt upright. How could I have forgotten?

'What's all the drink-slamming for?' asks Vicky.

'Dave. You know, Mr *Hatch* TV, my old mate Dave? He was popping round. Anyway, I'm not at my house. I'm here.'

'Oh, sit down, admit defeat and have another glass of wine,' says Maggie. 'Vicky's travails are much more interesting.'

'No, I've got to go. I promised.' I throw on my coat and put my left arm in the right armhole in my rush to leave. 'Sorry, gals.'

'Not so quick!' says Vicky. 'I've been hearing things about you, young lady.'

'Eh?'

'I actually bumped into Ig last week at this do in Belsize Park. He was full of gossip. Are you sure he's not gay? Anyway, he said that Don Wilberforce has been getting on well, particularly well, with a *Glo* gal . . .'

Maggie turns to stare at me. The pub clatter seems to cease. I feel the incriminating heat rise on my cheeks.

'Whoa.' Vicky looks at me quizzically. 'Have I said the wrong thing, darl?'

When I finally get home, panting, having run all the way because I didn't manage to flag down a taxi, David is walking away from the house. I apologise profusely for forgetting our meeting but he doesn't seem at all bothered. No, he says. Don't worry. Georgia looked after him and told him everything he needs to know about magazines.

Twenty-three

I've already told Nick that I am not feeling very well. This is a lie. But it is a lie on which to build the foundations of another lie so that I can say I feel really unwell later and need to leave the *Glo* Christmas party early. Nick is happy to collude with the lie because he doesn't want to go to the party either. In fact, until a few minutes ago, I didn't think he'd make it at all. I phoned him at about seven, just after me and the girls from the features desk had changed into our sparkly party outfits and powdered our noses in the office loos, muttering about how the harsh strip lighting gave us the complexions of the undead and taking bets on who would get drunk and humiliate themselves later. (Even the wilder members of the fashion desk tend not to drink that much because booze is fattening, so my bet's on Melanie, the glamorous new girl on the subs desk who always looks absolutely shattered on a Monday morning after her Sunday night Hoxton socials.) So it was seven o clock and Nick was still poncing around the house. I told him to shave and get himself down here.

When I meet him, he hasn't shaved. We stand outside the

private members' club, borrowed for the night: fees traded for a shameless syrupy plug in the magazine. 'You look nice,' he says, running his hands down my satin midnight-blue shift dress.

I smile gratefully and for a moment I miss him – the old him, the old us – even though he is there right in front of me.

'Ready?' I breathe in, readjust my Magic Knickers and ring the bell.

Inside, to my great relief, there is no sign of Don or Pippa. My toes uncurl in my shoes. Everyone is an upbeat, silly mood, drinking far too much, gossiping, clustered in cliquey knots around low round tables. The soft lighting and the sparkling dresses give everyone a 'Why Miss Jones you're beautiful . . .' moment. Even the girls who in the office normally look quite plain assume a new luminescence and glamour. (I suspect I fall into this category.) The barriers between different desks and hierarchies dissolve like the sugar in the cocktails. Not everyone has brought their partner. This is because most of the girls in the office are single. They're in their twenties and aren't about to drag along the last guy, or woman, they slept with. But there are partners who should be here and aren't – yet anyway – because they're at work. Nick is the only guy whose schedule, or lack of one, allows him to be unfashionably punctual.

We stand at the bar and order champagne. Having helped organise this party, I know that there will only be one or two glasses of champagne each, then it's on to the cheap wine and beer. I would like to sit and gossip with the features crew – Lydia is always late, late – but stand next to Nick, chaperone him. Sadly, right now, it doesn't feel like we've got a lot to talk about. We're stilted. The silly shorthand that we might once have whispered to each other in this situation has gone.

Nick looks alienated, which translates into looking blank, a little bored. This puts me on edge. And me being on edge makes him more alienated, which makes him look more bored. I persevere with my forced smiles and light chat because I don't want everyone else looking at us and noticing anything is wrong. I want us to look like 'a good couple'.

Suddenly, Alexis spins across the room in a silver sequin-scaled dress, like a fish across a deck. 'Annie!' she squeals, as if I'm her favourite person here.

'Alexis!' I squeal back, because it's Christmas and that's what you do at Christmas office parties and I don't want it to be obvious that she's my least favourite person here.

'Oh.' She stops. 'Nick, what happened to your face?'

'It's called a beard?' Nick says.

Alexis looks baffled and turns to me. 'Pippa's just arrived.'

I squint. There, emerging from the clubby gloom, is the unmistakable blond crystalline do of Pippa Woodside. Blow-dried and Elnetted to rigidity, it judders under the mood lighting as she stamps forth on her heels, fanning herself with her invitation. Following behind her is husband Martin, stiff and patrician in a dark suit, smoothing his silver-fox hair away from his lightly tanned face, looking like a kind of non-worked-out (and non-worked-on) version of Michael Douglas. As he and Pippa stride through the bar area, like royals on an official engagement, conversations grind to a halt, smiles stretch wider and tighter across faces, people study their drinks, willing her not to stop and sit at their table. If there's one thing that sobers up a *Glo* social, it's the prospect of Pippa Woodside and her fearsomely successful husband threatening to join in the fun.

'Oh my God, Pippa! You look totally amazing,' exudes Alexis.

191

Pippa doesn't look amazing. She looks expensive. She is wearing a tailored black shift dress encrusted with large chunks of coloured stone and crystal around the cuffs and neck. She smiles first at Alexis, then me. This is not a good sign. Pippa always addresses the person she deems most important first: you just have to follow her sightline to understand the current office hierarchy.

Alexis picks up on the status signal and steps towards the centre of the invisible social circle. If she were a drink she'd be fizzing over the sides of the glass. She turns her attention to Pippa's husband. 'Martin, lovely to see you,' she coos, flicking her hair back off her face.

For one delicious second I wonder whether Alexis is going to ruin all her good work by flirting with Pippa's husband. Will she cross the line between sycophancy and flirtation? Her bosom heaves beneath the silver sheaf of her dress. She's twiddling her hair. Go on, Alexis. Put your Choo in it. But, argh, no. She's pulling back. She's realised just in time. She steps back out of the invisible circle and straightens her dress demurely.

Martin turns to me. His mouth opens then shuts again. He has forgotten my name.

'Hi, Martin, it's Annie,' I volunteer. 'Annie Rafferty. Deputy editor. This is my boyfriend Nick. Martin, Nick.'

Pippa edits Nick with her eyes, sweeping a glance from his beard to his . . . to his . . .

Oh. Nick is wearing his old, paint-spattered Adidas trainers beneath his suit. Pippa's eyes linger on the scuffed shoes for a few painful moments. 'So how are you, Nick?' she asks. 'It's been a long time. You didn't come to the Christmas party last year, did you?'

Nick coughs. 'Nope. Sadly not. Working late, if I remember rightly.'

Martin laughs, a deep macho rumble from somewhere inside his suit. 'Oh, I'm not allowed to work late on the night of the Christmas party, am I, darling? Alan Yentob can wait. Clive James can wait. The girls from *Glo* are waiting. Lipstick ephemera calls.'

Is this meant to be funny?

Alexis splutters laughter over her cocktail. 'Oh, Martin.'

'He's learning his priorities,' says Pippa archly, almost coquettishly. She bats spidery eyelashes and giggles.

Pippa Woodside giggling! Flirting! I'm hit by a runaway train of inappropriate thoughts. Do they have good sex? Who is the dominant partner? Before or after discussing their share options?

'I loved that pink jacket you bought Annie,' says Pippa to Nick.

Oh God. Rewind. Rewind and exit.

'Er . . .' Nick looks confused.

'I usually loathe pink, the chav's navy blue,' Pippa goes on. (Because Pippa is no fashionista and this makes her insecure, she likes to talk about fashion to people who clearly don't know much about it, trying on opinions for size.) 'But it was cute. You've got a good eye, Nick.'

Nick nods in a befuddled fashion. 'Thanks.'

Make the conversation stop. Make it stop. I stare at the floor.

'You're in hotel PR, aren't you?' continues Pippa. 'I can never remember.'

Nick shuffles uneasily for a moment. He clears his throat. 'Not any more.'

I am beginning to knot up. It occurs to me that there are a hundred ways that this conversation could end really badly.

'What are you up to, Nick?' asks Alexis, who has picked

up on my unease, smelling it like a piranha might smell blood and moving in for the kill, bleached teeth gnashing.

'He's—' I am about to say in between jobs or a variation on this theme, anything to fill the anticipated silence.

'I'm working as a builder,' he says.

My stock falls.

'You never told me you had a builder husband, Annie,' says Alexis, as if being a builder was the same as having a contagious skin infection.

'Boyfriend,' I say.

'Oh,' says Pippa. A chill begins to radiate from her like cold air from an open fridge door. She stares over Nick's shoulder, glancing around the room, checking that none of her staff are enjoying themselves too much.

Martin glances at Nick, bemused, then starts to laugh heartily, as if a great joke has just occurred to him. 'Gosh, you don't sound like a builder. Are builders the new plumbers or something, Rick?'

'It's Nick.' Nick taps his left foot, agitated.

'We've had terrible problems with our downstairs loo,' Martin snorts. 'Smells like a cesspit, water draining everywhere . . . some Polish guys did it . . .'

Just when things couldn't get any more awkward, I spot Don in the corner of my eye, boxy in a black suit, stampeding through the crowds. He's looking around. He's looking for someone. For me? He spots us. Shit, he's coming over.

'Don!' squeals Alexis. A soft pink flush spills over her cleavage.

'Ladies.' Don nods to me, then Alexis, then Pippa, who applies her widest, fakest smile, then Martin. 'And a gentleman.'

'Only just,' says Martin, and roars with laughter, spraying

a fine mist of saliva over my right arm. 'I feel my testosterone evaporating by the second in this place.'

Alexis giggles, sending a wave of shimmer over her sequinny dress.

'Have you met Rick, Don?' booms Martin. 'I was just trying to get him to agree to fix our downstairs loo.'

Christ. The loo conversation has bobbed up again like a turd that won't flush.

'He's a builder, Don!' exclaims Alexis. 'Isn't that cute?'

Don glances at me. I daren't meet his eyes. Having Nick and Don standing a metre apart in the same space, damn it, the same universe, is beyond disturbing. Don doesn't say anything, which makes it all somehow a lot worse. There is a silence that goes on two seconds too long to be comfortable.

'So, Rick,' perseveres Martin, warming to his theme. 'Could you work some magic with our downstairs loo?'

'I'm sorry, Martin. I tend to draw the line at sorting out other people's shit,' says Nick laconically, before walking away.

Don grins so widely and approvingly he exposes gum. He looks like he wants to take Nick's hand and shake it. Alexis and Pippa stare at me intently, astonished, as if I've just revealed a bizarre personality disorder hitherto kept under wraps.

This is like an anxiety dream. Except I'm not naked.

Our awkward group disperses, everyone but me and Don.

'Nick has balls.' Don looks me up and down. 'And you have the most amazing breasts. That dress is fantastic.'

Despite myself, I grow two inches. I also become aware of other people staring sideways as they talk. Lydia. Belle. Louise. Or is it my imagination? Alexis ends her conversation with the magazine's sales director and breaks into ours, swivelling her hips towards Don so that she is so close he must be able to feel her body heat. Go away, Alexis! But she doesn't. I wonder if the evening is going to get worse and decide that, surely, it can only improve.

I am wrong.

Jerry, a petite blonde assistant on the beauty desk, doesn't realise that Nick is with me – he evidently doesn't tell her – and starts to flirt with him conspicuously by the bar. There is a blue spotlight beaming down on them as if they are the evening's hired entertainment. Then I bump into a freelance writer who I've recently dumped because the last two features she filed were crap. She has drunk too much free wine and wants to know why I haven't returned her last two emails. Then she bursts into tears and tells me that her favourite ex-boyfriend has just died in a motorbike accident and she really wants to do more work for *Glo*, as if these things are some-how connected. I don't know what to say and escape to the loos. In the loos I notice that Isla from features is wearing exactly the same dress as me – Topshop, £56 – but looks much better in it because she's thinner, taller and has legs like a shop mannequin. She says to me, 'Shit. Thanks for the stiff competition . . .' We both laugh. We both know she is trying to be nice and that she looks better in the dress than I do. I'm jogged by Melanie from the subs desk tumbling bath-room-wards (I win the bet, she is legless). She spills a lurid raspberry-pink cocktail down my front. Dabbing at my dress with a bit of loo roll, I come out of the bathroom to see that Jerry is still flirting with Nick. I talk to Pam. Over the black silk corsage on her left shoulder I see Don. Don is flirting with Alexis. Yes, he is. Is Alexis actually the *Glo* girl that Don is getting on with particularly well, that Vicky referred to last night?

When Don turns to talk to someone else, Alexis strides over to me, dress sparkling in the dusky lighting. 'Can I have a word?' She winks. 'In private.'

I get up and follow her to the loos. But there are huddles of staff there applying make-up. Alexis steers me towards the emergency fire exit, shoves down the bar on the door and we fall into a cold, gloomy corridor, its walls rough grey concrete, a flight of escape stairs tunnelling downwards into a dark basement.

'I'm going to let you into a secret, Annie,' she slurs, her breath alcoholic. 'I'm going to do you a favour. It's Don. I can see you're in awe of him.'

'I am not in awe of him!'

'It's just that you don't want people getting the wrong idea. I don't think Pippa would like ...' Alexis laughs, not unkindly. 'Look, I've known him for a while, before he started here. And I know he is not to be trusted. The guy's a player, Annie.' She puts her hand on her hip and looks at me intently. 'Honestly, if I were you, for the sake of your career, I'd keep your distance.'

Twenty-four

It's three days before Christmas. I squint at the cup of posh petal tea that Georgia has made me and feel dicky. Something about the way the sodden rose petals cling to the sides of the cup . . . There is nowhere to look that doesn't hurt my eyes. Nick and Georgia have decorated the house with plastic baubles, sprays of fake snow and multicoloured bits of cheap tinsel. (This is a radical departure for Georgia, who in recent years has only ever handled hand-blown glass baubles and silver garlands from Liberty.) I stretch and my feet scuff against Nick's painting outfit, a soiled heavy heap beside the washing machine. The place is a mess. There is an empty Corona bottle rolled against one of my furry slippers, a fast-food wrapper crowning a mountain of unopened post. Boom. Boom. My head throbs. My life throbs. It's all so wrong. I've got a terrible hangover.

On cue, Nick walks into the kitchen, unaware of his starring role in the crisis in my head. He yawns and smells vaguely of stale sweat. 'Hi, babe.'

Babe? Can I be both babe and breadwinner? I don't know why the 'babe' thing is beginning to rankle but it is. Perhaps it's just because it's the language of our old love and it doesn't translate so well in these new, leaner times.

'My ma phoned.' He sits down with a heavy huff on the chair and rubs his eyes. 'She's miffed that we're not going to France this year.'

'We did France last year.' Ten days we spent hunkered down in their telly-less chateau while an unprecedented rainstorm showered down outside. There are only so many goose sandwiches and fish soups and stiff conversations in the company of Nick's parents that I can endure without getting restless or stark raving bonkers.

'She's very keen. She's says she's got some amazing wine and foie gras and . . .'

'This is a Hedgerows year, Nick. It will, after all, be the last time we have to endure damp bedrooms and carbonised mince pies and quite possibly my father.'

'I know. I know.' Nick leans his lanky frame against the kitchen unit, his long body bending in the middle like a boomerang. 'It's just that you know what Ma's like.' He puts on his mum's posh accent. '"You simply must come, darlings, you know what a bore your father is at Christmas if left to his own devices . . ." Anyway, I said that I thought maybe we could pop over there in early January.' He looks up at me and says, without sympathy, 'Quite frankly, you look like you could do with a holiday.'

'Thanks. Unfortunately, January is not good,' I say hastily. 'We've got to prepare a relaunch dummy in the new year. I'm going to be frantic.' This is true. But it's also true that I don't really want to hang out with Christa and Ian. It feels vaguely hypocritical while I am entertaining doubts about Nick. Despite the fact that Christa is one of those psychotherapists who seems literate in everyone's emotional state bar that of her own family, I fear that even she would smell the discord on us somehow.

Nick stands up and rakes his crazy hair. 'For fuck's sake, Annie. Your job is taking over our lives.'

'It's paying for our lives actually.'

Nick's hazel eyes harden. 'Fuck you.'

At this moment Georgia strides into the kitchen, her lovely face sleep-smudged and her slim limbs only partially covered by a pink t-shirt and white knickers, as if bunking up for a girlie student sleepover. 'Sorry, is it a bad time, guys?'

'No. Good time,' I say, relieved at the interruption.

'I feel like I've hardly seen you recently.' Georgia lays a soft, light arm across my shoulders. 'But at least the *Glo* Gestapo have released you for Christmas.'

Nick huffs and fills the espresso machine with coffee, clattering every implement to make as much noise as possible.

Georgia's lower lip starts to wobble. My heart sinks. Not this morning. Not with this head. 'What is it, George?'

'Cynthia told me that Olly . . .' Georgia starts to gasp. 'That Olly is seeing someone else.'

'Georgia found out two days ago, Annie,' Nick says pointedly, tipping a rush of golden cornflakes into a bowl. 'You haven't been around.'

'I'm so sorry, George.'

Georgia pushes her hair out of her eyes. 'It's so awful. It's so final. But . . . well, in a horribly sick way, you know what, Annie? It's like a wake-up call. There will be no wedding. There will be no Mr and Mrs and babies and all that shit. I will remain a Rafferty.' She collapses into a kitchen chair. 'I've got to sort myself out, haven't I?'

'Yes.' I feel a flush of pride. Acceptance! Progress!

'And maybe I have changed. Maybe Olly's right. Maybe I'm . . . I'm . . .'

Nick shakes his head. 'Don't flagellate yourself, Georgia. We've talked about this . . .'

We? They've struck up collective shorthand in my absence. I know I have no right to mind, but it bites a little. It feels exclusive. I should have been here more for Georgia. I should be looking after her more. I'm letting her down.

Georgia smiles warmly at Nick. 'I'm going to get the old Georgia back. I promised you that, Nick. And I will.'

I smile too. The old Georgia never went away, not in richness or heartbreak. My sister has not been changed by affluence, it was merely the peat in which innate parts of her personality bloomed. She's always been a bit of a princess.

Georgia digs into her quilted black handbag and hands over a crinkled slip of paper. 'Here, Annie. Thank you.'

It is a cheque for £10,000. I stare at it.

'Yes, I took his money! Every last penny!' says Georgia defiantly. 'All thirty-five thousand of it.'

Nick looks at me sharply. 'I made her see sense, Annie. I don't see why she shouldn't take it. I can't believe you advised otherwise.'

I think back to what Maggie said about me and my misplaced morals. Maybe Maggie's right. Maybe Georgia should get something out of the relationship. Who am I to advise anyway? 'Your life, George.'

'My bank balance,' she says.

'Indeed.'

I kiss her on the cheek.

Georgia looks relieved. 'I was scared you'd be so cross.'

Does everyone see me as so horribly self-righteous? My

hangover seems to escalate by the second. I put an arm around my sister. 'Don't be nuts.'

Christmas morning is damp and mild. One immense sponge-shaped cloud spewing drizzle follows our car down the busy motorway emptying London. It makes me yearn for the ice-bright clear skies and vertical vistas of New York. That particular moment when I walked down Fifth, my arms loaded with presents, the steam billowing from the pavements, Don stomping beside me. That anticipation in my throat.

When we arrive at Hedgerows, my mother is already tipsy on Baileys and humming along to the carols on the radio. Dad is slumped in a kitchen chair working his way through a row of After Eights, wearing a beige tracksuit with elasti-cated cuffs around the ankles, in the manner of Jimmy Savile. It's a strangely upsetting sight, almost more upsetting then his heart attack in a weird kind of way, as if the slow slide towards old person's casualwear is representative of the slow slide towards infirmity and dependence.

Christmas lunch, in the best Rafferty tradition, is plentiful and a little burned. Nick finds a small snail in his garden-grown kale. He removes it from his mouth and puts it on the side of his plate like an olive stone. Georgia giggles. Dad glares at him, as if he should have eaten it out of politeness. Dad is the kind of man who is not squeamish about eating the odd snail. We pull crackers, tell jokes, hunt for the twopenny piece in the pudding. Olly's absence is not referred to but is the great white elephant in the room. Dad's health also hangs heavily over the table. It has had an unfortunate effect on Mum's cooking, because with Dad's aorta in mind, she's tried to reduce the fat in things that need fat in them, such as gravy. Nick sulks quite a bit and picks at the overcooked turkey, letting me know that he's cross that we're not eating posh goose in France. Does he wish that he could send me back, like a badly chosen Christmas present?

After the meal, me and Dad retire to the living room, while Nick and Georgia sort out mince pies and drinks in the kitchen. Dad sits down on his favourite blush velour arm-chair and stretches out his legs so that the elasticated cuffs ride up his hairless shiny old-man legs. 'Annie, love.'

'Yup.' I sit on the sofa amongst a pile of foamy scatter cushions, sensing a father-to-daughter chat coming on.

'My time on this blasted planet is limited, Annie.' He slams his palm melodramatically to his chest. 'This old ticker has served me well. But I'll be damned if I'm going to spend the last of my days stone-cold sober without bacon in the morn-ing. I'd rather die happy. I'd rather die drunk. Your mother's fussing will be the death of me.' Dad sips his whisky slowly, taking his time. It smells so strong I wonder that it doesn't singe his nostril hair.

'She's looking out for you.'

'She's driving me to distraction. It's enough to make me hunger for the other side. At least I'd get some peace and quiet.'

It's horrible hearing Dad talking about dying. I suddenly can't imagine life without him. When I think about it, it's as if something is hollowing out in my tummy. 'Dad, please.'

'Oh, don't get all soppy on me, Annie. Out of all the mad-women in this house, I thought I could trust you to be sensible about this. Anyway, I wanted to have A Chat.' He clears his throat. 'Before I expire—'

'Dad! You're not about to pop your clogs. It's a mechani-cal fault. They've fixed it. They can fix it again if it goes wrong.'

'I'm not a lawnmower.'

'Sorry, but you kind of are, Dad. In cardiac terms.'

'Annie, Miss Know-It-All, if you will let me speak, I'm trying to impart sage patrician advice here.'

'Sorry.'

'As I was saying, before I expire, I want to see my girls happy. I want . . .'

'. . . to make sure that I look after Mum?'

He smiles gently. 'I don't doubt that. I know you will. Actually, Annie, I'm more concerned about you.' He angles his tumbler towards me.

'Huh?' I stand up and move closer to the fire, squatting down on a low stool beside the chimney breast, enjoying the sear of heat against my skin.

'Georgia's got her knickers in a twist at the moment. But she will be OK, once she's calmed down a bit. I dare say it won't be long before she's leading another great chump down the aisle.'

I smile, thinking of the strings of besotted men who have trailed behind my sister over the years. 'Nope. It won't be long.'

He points his glass at me. 'But you, Annie, you worry me.' He looks at me and he looks sad. 'I want to see you settled with a good man.'

I glance at the door anxiously. 'Shush! Dad . . .'

Dad shakes his head. 'Don't worry, they can't hear us. Nick's a nice chap,' he whispers. 'I like him. I thought he was really going to be good for you. But he's . . . he's a drifter, love. A father wants to see his daughter looked after.'

I don't know what to say to this.

'I know you're . . . well, you're a modern woman, Annie.' He looks up and smiles gently so that his face crinkles benignly in the glowing orange firelight. 'And I am proud of you. Really bloody proud of you, love, of everything you've achieved. But I don't want a daughter of mine supporting her man. It twists something in my guts. It's not right.'

'It's a temporary state of affairs, really.' I sound like I am pleading.

Dad shakes his head. 'Backbone. You need a man with more backbone. A good honest worker. That's what you need.'

'Miners are thin on the ground in north-west London.'

'I'm not joking, Annie.'

I think how much Dad would like Don, appreciate his straightforward testosterone-ness. 'You're being unfair.'

'Annie . . .' He leans forward. 'It's not about money, it's about finding an equal. Some men, they're passengers not drivers. And I think Nick, through no fault of his own . . . for argument's sake, let's blame all those silly schools he went to . . . well, he's . . .'

I begin to blank out as Dad talks. I want him to admire my boyfriend. This suddenly seems incredibly important, even though it shouldn't be, even though as a teenager I enjoyed Dad's disapproval and ran around with deliberately unsuitable messy-haired boys who rode clapped-out scooters and smoked Benson and Hedges and smelled of cheap lager. But Nick is the man I thought I'd settle down with. Have children with. One day. The man who made my heart flutter. Who painted me a picture for Valentine's Day, a picture of me lying on a beach, all spare brushstrokes and creamy skin under Riviera sunlight. Who has a V of dark blond hair that sweeps up to his belly button like magnetised iron filings. Who can make me laugh like no one makes me laugh. Except he just hasn't done it for a while, that's all.

'I don't mean to upset you. I'm just looking out for you.' Dad crosses one leg creakily over the other.

I stare at his elasticated ankle cuffs.

Mum, Georgia and Nick come back into the room. I glance guiltily down at the floor, feeling like a traitor just for listening to my father's comments, considering them even, without offering more vigorous defence.

'What have you two been plotting?' asks Mum, her voice lent a higher pitch by the Baileys, which she's now chasing down with liqueur chocolates. 'You look quite secretive.'

Nick is looking at me sharply, like he just knows.

'Arnold! I hope that's not a fresh glass of whisky in your hand. Dr Uptah—'

Dad puts his hand up. 'Please. If a man can't drink himself under the table at Christmas . . .'

My mother shakes her head. 'Time for presents,' she says. 'I'll put the kettle on and get the Roses.'

My parents (well, really just Mum, as Dad never has had any input in present-giving because we are not sons and therefore out of his orbit of comprehension) give me and Nick six coasters, each displaying a different wildflower print. As Georgia whispers to me drunkenly, it would never occur to her that I've survived thirty-four years without owning floral coasters and that if I ever felt a great lack of coasters in my life then I would buy them myself. Mum gives Georgia Nigella's latest tome, which delights her. Dad seems quite pleased with our gift, a new book on kit cars, a personal passion of his, and a large box of Liquorice Allsorts. He picks the bobbly blue ones out of the packet, wolfs them down with whisky and falls asleep in his armchair, snoring lightly. My mother's eyes light up at the cashmere cardigan I brought from the Burberry sample sale. It is teal with grey buttons and makes her eyes look pretty and young, like the blue Liquorice Allsorts. She puts it on, snuggles into the scatter cushions and is also soon fast asleep. Georgia loves her embroidered Burberry shawl and holds it up delightedly.

'You really like it?' I ask her. It's hard to tell with Georgia. Her enthusiasm can be quite indiscriminate at times.

'I love it!' Georgia wraps it round her neck. It looks beautiful on her, as most things do. 'Come on, you two, exchange,' she laughs. 'Or would you rather do it in private?'

'Don't be silly!' I say, not wanting Georgia to feel excluded.

Nick holds out a small package wrapped in spotty red and white paper.

'No, you first, Nick. Here.' I reach behind the sofa and pull out a large brown paper Bloomingdales bag. Inside are four presents.

'Oooh, that looks exciting!' coos Georgia. 'Open them, Nick. Go on!'

Nick shifts uncomfortably on his chair. 'Annie, I don't deserve this many presents,' he says.

'They could be a selection of loo rolls for all you know. I wouldn't get too excited.' But I do suddenly wonder whether I've bought him too much.

His long, lean fingers pull slowly on the Sellotaped seams.

Present one: a new attachment for his iPod. 'Cool!' he says.

Present two: a grey speckled cashmere scarf from Mulberry. 'I like it,' he says, not sounding like he loves it.

Present three: two Prada shirts, one blue, one soft grey stripes. 'Nice,' he says.

Present four: 'Christ. There's more?' he says, fingering the last package. A Prada tie in two-tone blues. 'Oh.'

'You've done well!' says Georgia, pouring herself another glass of wine.

Nick doesn't say anything.

'What's the matter?' I ask. But suddenly, without him saying anything, I know. Shit. I've bought him stuff for an office job. It looks like a dig to get back him into work.

'I don't really know what to say. I didn't expect so much. What happened to our One Present Rule?'

We established the One Present Rule the first Christmas we were together. We both decided that we wouldn't buy into the commercial Christmas bullshit and give each other things we didn't need. But this year, for some reason, I felt the need to buy more. I wanted him to feel good. And he had no money, I rationalised. He couldn't buy this stuff for himself. I now see that this was a grand error of judgement. 'I kind of ignored it, sorry.'

Stern-faced, he gives me the red-and-white-packaged parcel. 'I haven't been able to afford much. It's not . . .'

I open it. Inside is pale pink lace underwear. It's the first time he's given me underwear. And the first time he's given me anything pink. Something inside sinks. 'Wow! Thank you.'

Georgia stands up. 'I knew I should have removed myself. I'm going to leave you two to it,' she says, giggling as she leaves the room, closing the door behind her.

Nick looks a little irritated. 'You don't have to say wow.'

'I mean wow. It's lovely.'

'It's pink.'

'I know.' I feel uneasy.

'I thought . . . well, after Pippa mentioned that pink jacket, which you haven't shown me, actually . . .'

I freeze.

'Who gave it to you anyway? It wasn't me.' He is studying my face intently. I don't know where to look.

'Oh. I bought it. Sample sale. A misunderstanding.'

'Yeah, thought as much,' said Nick, loosening up and stretching his legs out in front of him. 'It got me thinking. I like the idea of you in pink. I want you to wear pink for me.'

Twenty-five

Georgia is in concentrated decline in her bedroom, eating Matzo crackers and Marmite and watching repeats of *Hollyoaks*. Nick is flicking through his records, pulling on a long, thin spliff. My mother phones. She says that someone has looked around Hedgerows. Twice. He is thinking of making an offer. Given this wonderful new turnaround to events, does Nick think it's still worth painting the bathroom that fancy shade of magnolia?

I mutter that I don't know. I am so pissed off that Nick hasn't yet painted Hedgerows. That he has prioritised practising DJ-ing for a nu-rave disco over my parents' future. The moment I click my phone shut, the doorbell rings.

'Answer it, for God's sake,' says Nick, switching on the telly and searching for the football with the remote. 'It's probably *Glo*'s secret service checking that you aren't enjoying the last scrap of your holiday.'

Maggie stands on the street muffled like a toddler, pink beanie hat pulled down over her ears, fuzzy grey-and-white stripy scarf wrapped almost to her nose, so that I can't see her mouth at all. She stamps her feet.

'Come in! What a lovely surprise.' I open the door and she comes into the hallway, pulling the scarf away from her mouth.

'I can't stay. I'm in a manic rush. Jake's about to take the boys to this panto and . . . well, it's all very boring. But happy new year!' Maggie kisses me. 'All cool?'

'Fine, fine,' I say, trying to look cheery and happy like you're meant to look after the Christmas holiday. 'Gearing up for work tomorrow. Would rather be gearing up for two weeks in St Barth's, obviously. You know how it is. Are you sure you won't come in? Tea?'

'I'd love to but . . . I've got a bit of a crisis on my hands, Annie. The nanny's been kidnapped by her boyfriend. She never returned from Warsaw.'

'Shit. Kidnapped?'

'Well, loosely speaking.'

'Ah, I see. Mutiny! Have you tried bribery?'

'Tried and failed, Annie,' sighs Maggie. 'I offered God knows what – car, pay rise, frankincense and myrrh – but no, no thank you, she misses her boyfriend too much, the little vixen. I can't believe I chose the most unattractive nanny in the entire world and she still gets a bloody boyfriend! Listen, I've got these critical meetings next week and I don't know how I'll get the kids to school or . . . It's a fucking mess, actually. And I was wondering . . .' Maggie looks uncharacteristically hesitant. 'Jake met Nick for a beer last week.'

Did he? I try to think back. A murky memory of Nick popping out for a beer emerges from somewhere.

'And he seems to think that Nick wouldn't mind us asking if he might like to step in for a bit, you know, just until we find someone else.' Maggie's eyes are large and black and studying me for my reaction.

I laugh, disbelieving. 'As a nanny?'

'Well, kind of,' she says apologetically. 'Just for a short while. We'd pay him, obviously. Er . . .' She's clearly desperate. 'I just wanted to run it past you before I mentioned anything to Nick.'

Nick working as a nanny? Too preposterous. 'It's really not up to me. Nick's around. I'll get him. Nick!' I shout. 'Maggie wants a word.'

Nick emerges from the sitting room, bleary-eyed and sluggish after his never-ending holiday.

'I'll leave you to it,' I say. 'I've just got to check the lamb.'

From the kitchen I hear a bit of laughter and Nick muttering, 'Yeah, that's no problem. No, seriously. It's fine.'

Maggie pokes her head into the kitchen, doing a thumbs-up. 'Nick is a life-saver. Thanks so much, Annie. I'll call you soon. Gotta run.'

I join Nick in the sitting room. He is slumped on the sofa, watching me, as if trying to goad me to say something. 'Oh, for fuck's sake, Annie. Don't look at me like that. I'm not about to start lactating.'

Twenty-six

The desire is dizzying and unexpected. Fidgeting with the sticky bit of a Post-it note, I watch him as he walks across the carpet tiles and stands, one hand on the water cooler, the hand paw-like and chunky and olive-skinned against the ridged blue plastic. He gazes out of the window, the underside of his jaw lit by the flickering light from Isla-from-features' beach scene screensaver. He doesn't look over at me. I rustle some papers loudly. It makes no impact. Nor does me walking to the printer to check a nonexistent document has printed. Don is gazing out of the window.

Alexis perches on my desk and obscures my view.

'Good Christmas?' she says.

'Yes, lovely, thanks. How was yours?' I say. Damn it. Don has now disappeared from the water cooler. I can't see where he's gone.

'Verbier. Glorious.'

'Ah, skiing, no wonder you look so buff.' Alexis is the only person I know who looks thinner after Christmas.

'Have you heard?' Alexis bends low and whispers in her special gossip voice, distinctive and hushed so that everyone in the vicinity knows that juice is being imparted and pricks up their ears. 'Word is that the powers that be are planning a media assault, giving us one last push, kicking off with a cocktail party for PRs in a couple of weeks.'

'Pippa mentioned that,' I say, childishly pleased to be pre-armed with at least some insider knowledge. 'I sent her a guest list. You should check over it and see if there's anyone you want to add.'

'Already have done,' says Alexis smugly. 'I'm overseeing the hospitality side, didn't Pippa tell you? Oysters. Pippa wants oysters and champagne. Even though she doesn't eat them, she's decided they are the height of chic.' Alexis laughs. 'Sushi is so over, apparently.'

'As long as the PRs turn up I'm happy.' No-shows have been something of a tradition at *Glo* magazine parties. The worst one was our Fabulous British TV party which Pippa threw last year, an attempt to attract celebrities in order to get them photographed against the *Glo* logo – since then known in the office as No-Glo – in the vague hope that a newspaper might use the pictures. They didn't. Only a handful of recognisable faces turned up, mostly from the wrong end of the alphabet. The one B-list actress who actually made the mistake of stumbling into our party didn't stay long. As we all joked bleakly afterwards, 'She came. She saw. She left.'

There is a clatter of heels. Lydia, in a beautiful pleated taupe dress with a gold sequin cape and heels. But she doesn't look happy. 'The fucking fashion cupboard thief has struck again,' she growls.

'No way!' Alexis stands up from my desk. 'What this time?'

'Chloe smock.' Lydia runs her fingers through her dark

bobbed hair. 'Of all things. It took us weeks of grovelling to get that. Now the return is late. The PR is phoning every five minutes. I haven't told her it's gone missing yet. Christ.' She looks up at the ceiling tiles, as if for divine intervention. 'It's making me suspicious of all the workies, which is horrible. I need to be able to trust them or I'll have to do my own returns.'

'It's not uncommon for assistants to nick stuff,' patronises Alexis. 'There was a real klepto at *Marie Claire*. *Cosmo* . . . they all have problems. It's always the keen, quiet ex-St Martins gals.' She shoots a look at the underpaid industrious assistants humming around the fashion desk. 'They sell them on eBay. Have you checked eBay?' Suddenly Alexis stops and blushes and smiles, displaying her chewing gum tablet teeth. She is looking at something behind me, staring wondrously. I swivel around in my office chair and glance over my shoulder.

It is Don, marching over. Everything suddenly looks giddier, brighter, like when the colour resolution is wrong on telly. 'Fucking unacceptable,' says Don gruffly. 'I hear that more stuff's been nicked. How are you organising your cupboard, Lydia? Is it organised? Have you got unauthorised people coming and going? It's not a Topshop changing room.'

'It's pretty organised,' lies Lydia politely.

Don turns to me. I suddenly notice a smile creasing the corner of his eye. 'Is it, Annie?'

I nod, out of loyalty to Lydia, making a mental note to get the fashion team to get their act together as soon as Don leaves.

'Right,' booms Don. 'Come on, Miss Rafferty. Let's go and cast objective non-fashionable eyes across the scene of the crime. We'll find the weak point in your defences, Lydia.'

I stand up and nervously follow Don across the office, aware of the pairs of eyes following our every move over the carpet tiles, past the water cooler, the printer, the stationery cupboard. As we pass each new mundane marker in the office landscape, something in me quickens. Don pushes open the fahion cupboard door and shuts it behind us gently. Inside, there are three long rows of clothes on hangers. Shelves heave with handbags, belts and accessories. Brightly coloured high heels trip over each other on the floor. It is chaotic. It is also, it strikes me for the first time, weirdly intimate. The over-stuffed room feels padded. The light that thrums through the small window is milky, as if diffused by handmade lace, then bounced around by gleaming satins and sequins. Sounds are muffled. Everything is softer and denser in here. It's like being under the folds of a huge petticoat.

'And why aren't I surprised?' Don smiles. 'It's like a bloody help-yourself pick-and-mix.'

'There's a system behind the chaos, Don. They have to sign things in and out. The assistants do the returns.' I pick up a piece of paper with the details of shoot, designer item and PR. My hand shakes slightly.

Don doesn't seem very interested in the workings of the fashion cupboard. He is staring at me.

'These are return sheets . . .' I continue.

'Annie . . .' He plucks the return note out of my hand and drops it so it flutters down to the floor and nose-dives like a paper aeroplane into a green Gucci pump. He glances at the door.

Then it all happens so quickly. I am pressed against the cold hard rail, a wire hanger digging into my shoulders. I fall further back into something blue and soft and I hear the hangers crashing against each other, skidding back along the rail until the clothes are compressed against the wall and become a firm, soft ledge, like a mattress. Don holds my face, one hand gripping each cheek. It almost hurts. 'Annie . . .' he says quietly.

There is a squeak. I glance over at the fashion cupboard door, just as it begins to open.

Twenty-seven

Nick is ten minutes late. Late for what, I am not entirely sure. This morning, before I left for work, he made me promise that I'd meet him at one o clock – precisely – on the Embankment, near the Tube, directly beside the Thames. A surprise, he said.

A pair of arms grab my waist. I jump. 'Argh! Nick!' I whack him on the arm, playfully. 'I thought I was being assaulted.'

Nick looks bright-eyed and happier than I've seen him for ages. He has shaved and he is wearing aftershave. He never wears aftershave. 'Come on,' he laughs, tugging me forward. 'We've got to run if we're going to make it.'

'Make what?'

He doesn't answer, but pulls me by the hand and we run and run, panting, my heels click-clattering along the pavement until we stop opposite a big pleasure boat. There is a man in uniform closing down the entry point, about to pull up the gangplank. Nick waves two tickets in the man's face.

'Walk the plank,' he says to me.

'You're not serious?'

'I've never been more serious in my life.'

The boat is shaped like a big Victorian bathtub. It is noisy and it smells of oil and exhaust. Rows of tourists sit inside under a glass canopy. The gangplank is pulled up, the gateway closed. There is a loud hoot and we're off. We stagger along the wind-lashed deck to the back of the boat, which is deserted, splattered by spray and vibrating with the roar of the engine. London unfolds on both sides at once and seagulls scream around us.

'This is fantastic, Nick!' I shout above the engine's rumble. 'Love it!'

He grins and slings an arm around my waist. 'I thought we needed to do something different. Get out of Kensal Rise!' He sniffs the air. 'Ah! This is more like it!'

I smile at him and rub my arms vigorously. It's bracing out here. I realise that Nick and I have hardly seen each other this week. He's been looking after Maggie's boys and coming back in the evening full of talk about their cute mannerisms and temper tantrums and cool toys. He'd forgotten how much he loved Lego and remote-controlled cars.

I sit down on a bench beside the lifejackets. Nick sits next to me, our bodies sandwiched together against the cold. He leans towards me, kisses me on the cheek. 'I'm sorry, Annie.'

'For what? Don't apologise. This is great. What a way to spend a lunch hour.'

'I've been a pain, I know that,' he says, his nose pinking in the wind. 'You deserve more than this. You deserve to know where you stand and where we are going.'

I look up at him, a little startled at his turn of phrase. 'Oh, don't worry. I haven't been the easiest to live with either, I'm sure.' I laugh and sniff. My nose is beginning to run in the wind. We gaze backwards, as the boat chugs beneath one of

Blackfriars Bridge's arches. Nick's foot starts tapping, as if to some internal percussion. Beneath the bridge the tap-tapping is followed by its echo. We emerge from the shadow of the bridge into milky winter sunlight.

'Annie, I've got a surprise for you,' he says, shaking off his jacket.

'What are you doing? You'll freeze!'

'Look at this.' He tugs up his sweater. 'Take a look, Annie.' He twists himself round on the wooden bench, showing a goosebumpy back. Peeking out below his T-shirt is something red, like a birthmark. Has he hurt himself?

I bend in closer, run my fingers over his skin. 'It's a tattoo! Oh my God, you have a tattoo!'

Nick's tattoo is the size of my palm, a red heart, still bubbly and bleeding from the needles. Inside the heart is written in pink swirly writing, *Annie* Smiling, Nick slowly lets his jumper fall over his back again. Not saying anything, he digs inside his front jeans pocket and pulls out a small box. It is an oval jewellery box made of blue velvet.

Something twists deep inside. I'm not sure this should be happening. Not like this. Not now.

A spray of water hits the back of my coat. The seagulls scream a frenzy. The engine seems to get louder and louder, more and more deafening. Nick stands up off the bench, kneels on the cold wet decking and flips open the box. 'Annie, my dear clever Annie,' he shouts. 'Will you marry me?'

Twenty-eight

Dad zips his tracksuit jacket right up to his jaw like an ageing football coach. The pale green of the tracksuit makes his face look very pink. 'I most certainly did not give my blessing!' he bellows.

'Arnold!' says Mum, looking distraught. 'Please. Let's all have a nice cup of tea and talk about this.'

I sit down, reeling. 'So Nick phoned you and asked for your permission and everything, Dad?'

Dad sips his sherry. 'He did, Annie. Which was a nice touch. I told him that. I liked the old fashioned decency in his approach. But this does not, most certainly does not, negate the fact the man is unemployed.'

'Daddy. He is not unemployed.' Georgia sits on the edge of Dad's armchair. 'He's working as Maggie's nanny.'

'My God.' Dad splutters out a mouthful of sherry.

Mum reaches for a Garibaldi biscuit, agitates it in her hand. 'Arnold. Please. Your heart.'

'He's also doing a bit of PR for Maggie's company. Working there a couple of days a week. Isn't he, Annie?' says Georgia, sweetly trying to drum up support for Nick.

I nod weakly. Nick says he's doing it for me. He's putting on a tie and jacket a couple of days a week to work in an office and bring some money in. He's also been tidying up and has stopped playing his music so loud and smoking weed before 7pm. I can't fault him.

Mum shakes her head and dips the Garibaldi into her tea. 'Poor, poor old Nick. So, let's get this straight. When he proposed your answer was . . .'

'I'm not sure,' I say quietly.

'What a dreadful answer,' Mum says, shaking her head.

'I know, Mum, please.' I'm squirming now. Poor Nick. He deserves better than that.

'Most sensible thing she's ever said,' mutters Dad. 'To say yes straight away sends out all the wrong messages. Make him prove himself first. Pass the peanuts, George.'

'Arnold!' exclaims Mum. 'No peanuts.'

None of this is helping. I stand and press my head against the cool glass of the window pane. Damp ivy leaves stick to it like little green hearts.

'Listen, Marjorie,' says Dad. 'It's one thing marrying money. It's another thing being married for your—'

'Dad, I hate to break it to you, but I really am not paid that much,' I say. 'Besides, Nick is not materialistic. It's not about money.'

'Lots of women are the main breadwinners now,' says Georgia. 'It's just not an issue.'

From outside comes the hiss of hard rain.

'You are being terribly old-fashioned, Arnold,' says Mum. 'No man is perfect.'

'I am,' snorts Dad, only half joking.

Mum ignores him. 'Listen, Annie, it's easy to take what you have for granted. If someone said to you five years ago that an adorable blond, handsome man – good genes, dear – who was sensitive and lovely and loved you for who you are, with all your faults—'

'My faults?'

'Yes, dear. Stubborn. Bossy. Headstrong. These are not qualities prized in women of a certain age, let me tell you.' At this point, Mum's voice starts to warble slightly. It becomes clear that she is trying not to cry. The tension of trying not to cry makes her crush her Garibaldi biscuit in her hand, shattering crumbs on to her velour settee. 'I'm sorry,' she says, sniffing. 'Goodness me.'

'Oh, Marj,' says Dad, aghast, terrified he has upset her. 'Marj, darling, what's the matter?'

Georgia and I sandwich her between us, our arms over her shoulders. 'Mum,' I say, bewildered. 'What on earth's the matter?'

'I am a soppy so-and-so, really I am. It's nothing, honestly.'

'Mum . . .' I say.

Mum takes a heaving inhalation. 'Grandchildren. I was so hoping for grandchildren. That's all.'

Everyone is intent on dooming me to marital bliss. Nick is lurking around the house, looking both hurt and hopeful in equal measure, like an abused puppy. (Piling further humiliation on his plight, his tattoo appears to have become infected and has started to ooze yellow stuff.) The guilt of it all is almost enough to make me say yes. My mother has been on the phone again. She tells me that they have exchanged contracts on Hedgerows and she's found this lovely little flat in Brighton which she loves and Dad hates but he's coming round because it's near a good pub and that

I must seriously consider Nick's offer. She makes Nick's proposal sound like a promotion. Georgia has offered me her wedding gown, which is a sweet gesture, but of course it wouldn't fit even if I did want it. Maggie has phoned saying how amazing Nick is with children. As if this should be the deciding factor. Vicky phones shrieking, 'AHHH! I've heard your news! Congratulations.' When I tell her I'm not sure and that we are definitely not engaged, there is a long silence down the phone.

'Are you out of your mind?' she squeals.

Quite possibly. All I know is that when Don gripped his hands on my jaw I didn't want him to remove them. And I imagine if Nick did the same thing right now I *would* want him to remove them. It's horribly confusing. 'Don't, Vicky.'

'I can't tell you how many of my friends dumped men who they imagined weren't quite The One when they were in their mid-thirties. Did they go on to meet The One? Did they hell! They look back in anger, Annie. They're angry that no one told them. And when it all dawns, about the age of thirty-eight, and Mr Almost The One is married to someone else five years their junior and the men they meet are not even nearly as nice as Mr Almost The One, they realise they cocked up. Listen, I know men who make the same mistake. Remember that cute City guy I had a dalliance with? He came crawling back to me last week but then got horribly drunk and banged on about his ex-girlfriend all night. Hopeless. I don't know why we all squander what we've got but we do. It's a Darwinian fault in our make-up.'

'I've got to do the right thing, Vicky.'

'Stop being such a perfectionist romantic.' Her voice becomes stern. 'Do you want children?'

Here we go again. 'Listen, Vicky, I've got to go. I've got a

Glo party tonight. For PRs only, I'm afraid. Yeah, yeah. Otherwise, of course, I'd invite you. I've got to . . . OK. Will think about what you said. Bye.' I slide down the wall, head in my hands. Gulping back tears, I make my decision. Then I put on a black Miu Miu party dress, my heels, my lipstick. I wipe my nose, jump in a taxi and take a deep breath, fearing that I won't be able to come up for air for a very long time.

Twenty-nine

I don't stay long at the party. I don't eat or drink. I am on PR autopilot, and my smiling, chatting professional face is just a mask. I can't believe that I once found this kind of event glamorous. As soon as it is not rude to leave, I leave. In the taxi I keep hoping that when I get home Nick will be in bed already. But as the taxi pulls up outside the house I can see that the living room lights are on and I can make out Nick's long, lean, lolloping silhouette as he moves from one side of the sitting room to the other. Once I'm inside, we both sit on the sofa, tired, bleached out by the week, by the lack of my effusive 'Yes!'

Nick puts on Lou Reed's 'Perfect Day', which just sounds horribly ironic given the circumstances, and offers me a lug on a spliff, which I refuse. He looks emptied, as if I've sucked the last bit of hope out of him. There's a temptation to say, 'Yes, I'll marry you,' just to make sure life funnels forward to a safe and tidy future.

'It's a no, isn't it?' he says, staring at the floor.

I don't speak. I don't want to say the words. I don't want to hurt him.

226

'Isn't it, Annie?' he says more forcefully this time. 'Say something.'

'I'm so sorry, Nick.'

He stands up from the sofa. 'Nothing I do will ever make you fucking happy, will it?' It is the first time I've heard real hate in his voice, and it scares me. That night he sleeps on the edge of the bed so that our bodies don't touch at all. I don't sleep a wink.

The next morning Georgia and Nick hug on the doorstep, holding each other for such a long time I look away. Georgia weeps. Nick tries not to cry. He nods at me and, carrying a holdall mostly containing records and trainers, shuffles off to Alf's spare room in Ladbroke Grove without looking back. He cuts a forlorn figure, his bounce gone. Even his hair seems flattened. I am a queen bitch. Why can't I make myself want him more? As I watch his figure retreat down the street, I am struck by a peculiar and powerful sense that my life has taken a detour, that parallel to me is another Annie Rafferty who accepts Nick's proposal and lives a happy, different kind of life. I'll never know, of course.

Later, I cry quietly in the bathroom with the door locked. I think about his tattoo and I cry harder, catching sight of a horrific figure in the mirror with puffy eyes, a red swollen nose, making a gluggy noise like a blocked toilet. I hardly recognise myself. Maggie's Jake phones me to say I've made a terrible mistake. My mother phones to say I've made a terrible mistake. My dad phones to tell me that I've done the right thing: 'Hold your nerve, girl. Hold your nerve. The road less travelled, or whatever they say, well, it's never the path of least resistance.' Later that evening the sofa I chose all those months ago finally arrives. It is beige and squashy and

227

everything I want from a girlie sofa, but it looks too large just for me and Georgia. I can't bear to sit on it. What the hell have I done?

Monday morning, the day breaks like an early spring, sunlight spilling over London like sparkling water. I take comfort from the weather. I tell myself it's symbolic of a new start. I keep this feeling up all the way to the office, but when I get there it dissipates. The office is curiously empty. I put it down to a collective hangover. But Pippa is sitting at her desk, fanning herself with an invite to a fashion party.

'Belle!' Pippa shouts. Belle jumps to attention at her office door. 'Get those useless guys on the eleventh floor to do something about the heating. I can't start the goddamn year like this.' She looks at me. 'Sit down, Annie.'

I study the fresh bunch of peonies on her desk and am about to make a benign comment about their prettiness when Pippa clears her throat.

'I feel like I've hardly seen you since the new year,' she says, smiling broadly like I'm her best mate, which immediately makes me wary. 'Don't those Christmas holidays just drag? I bet you were itching to get back to work?' She pulls back from the desk and stretches out her legs, rotating her feet at the ankle. 'I'm pleased that someone has deigned to make the effort to actually come to work today. Half the office appears to be ill.' Pippa has no time or sympathy for sickness, never taking any days off herself and having the constitution of a prize bullock. She treats the sick as she treats the ugly, warily and dismissively. 'Annie . . .'

I look attentive, but inside I am whirling. I am pushed against something soft and blue. I can smell new shoe leather. I can feel his hands gripping my face. I am back in the fashion cupboard. 'Yes?'

'I wouldn't say this to anyone . . . it needs to be strictly *entre nous*. Understood? It's a delicate matter. I wonder if you could shed light on it for me. It's about Alexis . . .'

'Yes?' Has she seen the light? Exposure at last!

'And Don.'

Don?

'You see, I've heard rumblings along the grapevine that there's something, well, something going on, shall we say, between the two of them. And I was wondering if you knew . . .'

Alexis? Please, no. I shake my head. 'No. I don't.'

Pippa looks disappointed. 'You know me, I don't like to gossip. But in this particular case . . .' She stands up and gazes out of the window. 'It's a shame, if it's true, I mean. Because as you know, I simply adore Alexis. She's such an asset to this magazine. She's got real class. A great contact book. Such style.' She sighs. 'I'd hate her to compromise her position. Or Don's.' She looks at me conspiratorially. 'I would like you to keep me informed of all developments.'

I manage to nod. The carpet is rushing up to meet me. I want to put my head between my knees. I want to be any-where else in the universe.

'Are you OK, Annie?'

'I feel a little unwell . . .'

Pippa flinches. 'Euw. Not another one. There's something going around. Go. Go, Annie, for God's sake. I don't want to catch anything. And let's keep this to ourselves, no?'

Thirty

'Nick has de-friended me on Facebook!' I shout to Georgia, who is in the kitchen, making the kind of homely domestic noises – kettles, tea stirring, radio – that I'd go mad without hearing right now.

Georgia runs in and pushes the lid of my laptop down. 'Enough.'

'It's not as if I want a drip feed of information about his new mates – new women, yuck! – or a picture gallery of him throwing shapes at parties, but this feels brutal, George.' Compounding this strange, messy bereavement will be a Nick-shaped hole on my computer, adding to the yawning gap in my bed, on the sofa, in the air where his thumping bass used to blast. Terrible to admit, but part of me needs the comfort of Nick, ex or not, to get me through the horrible-ness of discovering the truth about Don and Alexis. Nick is where I feel safe. He is the person that wanted me, that vali-dated my own attractiveness with his proposal. Which, I know, is all totally fucked up.

'It's OK,' says Georgia gently. 'I've got something for you. Wait here.'

She disappears back to the kitchen and reappears with a tray of rose petal tea and charred rock buns. 'I've baked you buns.'

'Buns? Are you feeling OK, George?'

Georgia laughs. 'The first buns I ever cooked.' I notice that she has a smear of bun dough on her freckled nose. 'Sorry, they're a bit burned. I couldn't work out that funny timer thingy on the cooker.'

I suddenly realise that something a little remarkable and totally unprecedented has happened to our relationship. Since Nick left, mine and Georgia's roles are beginning to reverse. I'm the wounded one, Georgia is the empathiser. She is becoming a huge, unexpected support.

'I'm afraid there's a bit of a mess. I'm warning you now so you don't go mental. The flour bag just self-destructed as I was holding it. Sorry, Annie.'

'Oh, don't worry. It doesn't matter?' Did I say that? Bizarrely, I'm finding all signs of human habitation kind of comforting right now. I take a bite into carbonised raisins. 'Delicious.'

Georgia eats hers all up with gusto. It strikes me that I haven't seen her eat a bun for decades.

'Dear me,' she says, curling into the corner of the big beige sofa like a beautiful red tabby cat. 'Look at the pair of us.'

'No wonder Mum keeps sobbing.'

'She'd have been better off having gay sons.'

Georgia and I start to laugh, really laugh, bits of bun spluttering out of our mouths as we try and contain our hysteria, which springs less from hilarity than a need for some kind of physical release from our respective romantic débâcles. What's that? We stop and listen. There is someone banging hard at the door.

'Chill. I'll go.' Georgia leaps off the sofa. A few moments later she reappears in the sitting room with, no, my God, Alexis, angular and anxious in her knitted grey dress and enormous red patent handbag. Her pupils are enormous. Her cheeks are blotched with red eczema. 'Hope you don't mind me dropping round, Annie.'

I choke on my bun. Mind? I'd rather it was a church full of Jehovahs at the door.

'I was at a shoot five minutes up the road. I have to speak to you,' she says urgently.

'Right.' Fuck, is she going to confide to me about Don? I can't imagine anything more hideous. 'Have a seat,' I say, trying to be professional. Act like a grown-up, Annie. 'Excuse the mess. What's the matter?'

Alexis collapses on to the sofa, shaking her head from side to side. 'I'm in the dog house. Seriously fucked.' She drops her head into her hands. 'The party, Annie. You know the party for the PRs, the one we threw last week? Remember the oysters?' She is gibbering now. 'Well, you'd remember them if you ate them, I promise you. Everyone was sick, Annie. Everyone who ate oysters was sick, horribly, violently sick, all over the weekend. It is a PR catastrophe.'

'Oh. Shit.' I must not meet Georgia's eye. We must not smile. I must not enjoy Alexis's pain. That would not be nice. Still . . .

'Pippa is going fucking mental, completely beside herself. She says the magazine is going to fold. She says she'll never live this down! That I'll never work in magazines again!'

'It's not your fault,' I say without much conviction. No, I want to shout, the oysters are not your fault, but mucking around with Don is!

'Of course it's not my fault!' she shrieks, as if the very idea

232

is beyond comprehension. 'It's the fucking catering company! The one I wanted to use was deemed too expensive, so in a typically short-sighted cost-cutting exercise—'

'Bun?' offers Georgia.

Alexis ignores Georgia's offer – does she look like the kind of woman who does carbs? – and pleads with me. 'You've got to save my arse, Annie. I know you've taken a day off, but will you come in? A favour. Please, Annie.'

Pippa is pacing around her office, kicking against the skirting board with the toe of her Prada knee-high patent boot. She has a smudge of red lipstick on her tooth which looks like blood, and is pulling at her mouth anxiously, revealing sore red gums. 'Where the fuck have you been?' she shrieks.

'I took a day off.'

'Listen, eat and breathe this job, Annie. Or I'm not interested. *Glo* is in CRISIS!'

'I heard about the oysters.'

'Don't!' she shouts, putting her hand up. 'Do. Not. Mention. Oysters.'

'Damage limitation. There are things we can do. People will understand. We'll sue the pants off the catering company.'

'The director of Moke PR, the *director*, spent the night projectile-vomiting. Julia Waring from A-G PR was so worried she called an ambulance. Do you think these people will ever *ever* forgive me?' Her accent is pure Brummie now. She glares at me, as if I am solely responsible for the entire disaster. 'Why didn't you oversee the party, Annie? Eh? Why did you shirk the responsibility and give it to Alexis?'

I've never seen her this angry before. It's genuinely terrifying. I take a step back. 'You asked Alexis to organise the catering side, Pippa.'

'But you should have pre-empted me.' Sweat beads on her nose. 'You should have just got on and done it. I shouldn't have had to ask. If I have to ask it's too fucking late!' she screams.

Defence is futile at this point. I just nod and say as little as possible because Pippa obviously needs to seriously unload and she might as well unload on me. It strikes me that a few months ago I would have been poleaxed with mortification by her rage, blaming myself, blaming her, tying myself in knots with Lydia as I worked out the rights and wrongs of the situation. But I'm learning to step back from the situation. The sky is not falling in, after all.

'And that's not the only disaster. Oh no.' She lowers her voice to a whisper. 'There's worse.' Pippa steps towards me. Her breath smells bad, meaty. 'One of the PRs mentioned to me that they'd heard that some television production company are doing a spiteful magazine spoof pilot for Channel Four.'

'Oh.' I stop very still. I don't feel quite so relaxed now.

'Same guys that wrote that moronic *Hatch* series apparently. The PR thought it bloody hilarious. Do you know why, Annie? Do you know why? Because, Annie, because the spoof is based on *Glo*! Apparently they have based it on insider anecdotes delivered by one of our senior members of staff! Any idea who, Annie?' She is almost spitting in my face. 'Come on, Annie. Is it Alexis? Is it that damn Alexis? Maybe she schemed it all up with Don Wilberforce? Nothing would surprise me. This is not the time for misplaced loyalty.'

Oh God. Georgia. For a moment, I wish I was the kind of person who could hang Alexis without conscience. 'No, Pippa. It wasn't Alexis.'

'Who? Who then?' she shrieks, sweat dripping off her nose.

'I don't . . .' And I am about to say I don't know. This is what I'd normally say, what any journalist worth their salt would say, if they hadn't already blamed another member of staff, they'd proclaim ignorance, walk out the office, get on the phone to David and pummel him with expletives. But something in me is not playing ball. Something in me does not want to be that person any more.

To hell with it.

'Well, it's kind of complicated . . .' I begin.

Thirty-one

That time David came over to see me? Well, he saw Georgia instead. Apparently he was just so sweet and so funny and wearing the most darling little stripy sweater that reminded her of him as a thirteen-year-old hanging around the rec in Lower Dalton and offering her fizzy cola sweets. And she hadn't seen him for millennia. And he loved all her stories. Just silly stories, things I'd told her over the years. Small, inconsequential details like how Pippa keeps the office windows open all year round because she's going through The Change. And how we can't get celebrities to our parties even if we offer them free spa trips. It's bad. But as Georgia explained in tearful, profuse apology, 'I had no idea!'

Unsurprisingly, the mood in the car is sombre as we drive to the Cotswolds for the last time, funnelled from motorway to A road to the drive of Hedgerows in a mere fifty minutes. It is raining lightly and the trees are wet and brown and leafless. The house looks different. I realise that it's because there are no curtains hanging at the windows. There is a removal lorry in the drive. When I open the car door the smell of damp soil rushes up to meet me. I take a deep breath. It is a lovely smell. My foot crunches on to the gravel. I listen to the micro-sound of pebbles jostling each other before settling down into their new position. It is a sound that I've taken for granted for thirty-four years. Now, hearing it for the last time, it seems almost musical.

Georgia sniffs and breaks my reverie. 'Oh fuck. I'm not sure I can cope with this.'

A burly guy carries a large removal box out of the front door. He raises his eyebrows in greeting and heaves the box into the removal lorry. He slams shut the back door of the lorry and whacks it twice with the palm of his hand, then gets into the cab with his mate. My mother appears at the front door. She waves at the lorry driver. 'See you at the other end,' she says faux-cheerfully in her speak-to-the-workers voice.

Georgia rushes over to Mum and hugs her tight in silence, and they walk into the house.

'It's ridiculous,' Mum says, stopping in the hallway and glancing around. 'It's just bricks and mortar after all. And this little flat in Brighton . . .' She looks at me and smiles. 'It's charming, really. It is.'

'You can't swing a bloody kitten in it!' booms my father from the sitting room.

Me and Mum roll our eyes at each other and walk into the room, which has been stripped of its previous identity as the tired but homely Rafferty sitting room to become something twice the size, cold and empty. Dad is leaning against the fire surround wearing a dark blue suit. 'But you know me, Annie,' he says. 'Anything to make your mother happy. She has always wanted to live by the seaside.'

'Isn't Brighton a bit random, Mum?' says Georgia. 'Why Brighton? Why not Cornwall?' She sighs. 'I love Cornwall.'

'Cornwall?' splutters Dad. 'It would be quicker to get to Spain.'

Mum laughs. 'Brighton's near London. And we do know a few people there. Peggy Horsham lives just down the coast in Hastings. There's Sue and Ted. They've actually retired just outside Brighton, near Paul McCartney. Remember Sue and Ted, Annie? Lovely couple. Very sociable, which is great, because they'll be able to introduce us. Sue's going to throw us a welcome-to-the-seaside party!'

'Daddy, do you mind me asking, why the suit?' asks Georgia.

'I always said I'd only ever leave this place horizontal in a box. And as by some miracle that hasn't happened, I am determined to leave it vertical in a good suit.'

'OK,' I say. Best just let Dad get on with his eccentricities. He knows what he means, even if we don't.

'I can't even offer you girls fresh tea,' Mum says sadly. 'But I've managed to improvise.'

'Don't ask,' says Dad shaking his head in bemusement.

Our steps echo in the hallway. The house looks twice the size without Mum's knick-knacks. But it also looks twice as decrepit. There are no school photos to hide the blooming damp patches or the cracks in the plaster. But it is still the place I grew up. I suddenly feel very sad indeed. In the kitchen we each sit on an upside-down cardboard box stickered with the words, 'We take the hassle out of moving.' Mum has fashioned a table out of another box, which is adorned with paper plates full of cakes and quartered shop-bought sandwiches. There is also, inexplicably, a plate of Wagon Wheels, their cracked milk chocolate skins gleaming under the light of a bare bulb.

'Your favourites, for old times' sake,' says Mum, pouring dark stewed tea from an old thermos into four plastic cups. 'I

238

saw them in the supermarket and got all sentimental.' Bless her.

'How weird to think that this will be some new family's kitchen,' says Georgia.

'That's a point,' I say, suddenly imagining a removal lorry loaded with someone else's stuff arriving any second and the new owners discovering Dad in a suit sitting on a cardboard box munching a Wagon Wheel. 'When are they arriving?'

'Agent was useless,' says Dad, tugging at his beard. 'Not today at any rate. Possibly next weekend. It's a second home, of course.' He huffs and shakes his head. 'Still, can't complain. They paid the money without any haggling. Didn't even try to knock money off when the surveyor started banging on about woodworm and the damp or some such nonsense.'

'You were lucky,' I say.

'Yes, Annie,' Mum says, trying to be positive. 'We're terribly lucky.' She takes a mournful bite of a Tesco prawn sandwich. 'Considering.'

After the last room is double-checked for what Mum calls 'mislaid treasures' (one of Dad's navy socks, an ancient Pritt stick and thirty-three pence in change), it is time to leave.

'Ready, Marj?' asks Dad, squeezing Mum's hand.

Mum nods bravely, applies some peachy lipstick and readjusts the curl at the back of her head, as if preparing to walk out of the house into a scrum of flash-bulbing paparazzi. I prepare myself to comfort Georgia, who, any minute, is surely due to implode with tears. Georgia sniffs.

I open the front door for the last time. Then a weird thing happens. It is not Georgia who implodes into a howling water bomb. Nor my mother.

It is me. Something inside has come unplugged.

Thirty-two

'Stop if you feel faint, dizzy or short of breath,' it reads on the front of the cross-trainer as I push down on the pedals feeling faint, dizzy and horribly short of breath. But I keep going, arms batting back and forth, legs paddling mid-air, getting nowhere. Panting, I reach for my bottle of water, which drips down my T shirt because I can't master the leg thing and the drinking thing at the same time.

The office gym, housed in the basement of the building, is a misery box. It's small, low-tech – there's not even a telly, only Radio One blaring – and smells of stale sweat, and I generally avoid it at all costs, firstly because it's unpleasant and secondly because the idea of bumping into someone I work with while wearing my Sweaty Betty gym pants and trainer bra is pretty horrific. But with Nick and I smashed on the rocks, Hedgerows sold, and a big flashing red question mark hanging over Don and Alexis's professional relationship, I am in need of a distraction, a serious uplift. And nothing is a better tonic than dropping a dress size. So this morning, after drinking a rocket fuel dose of espresso, I thought, today is the day my bum and life will start to lift: take me to the cross trainer!

Seven minutes. Eight minutes. The ninth minute is the longest. Ten! Enough! I try to leap off the machine but only manage a partial leap, so although I stop moving the pedals don't. I trip over and stumble to the rubber-tiled floor. That hurts. Gripping my sweaty palms on the machine's main stem, I pull myself up slowly, coming to an exhausted slump against it, feeling in desperate need of a lie down and a glass of wine.

'Nice moves, Annie!'

I look up, take in the Puma trainers, the soft grey Lycra. Alexis. Oh God. Screensaver in my head. Alexis and Don fucking.

'I haven't seen you down here before,' she says.

'And you won't see me down here again,' I say, trying to catch my breath.

'Are you OK?'

'Fine,' I say, trying to ignore the thrum of pain in my right knee. I notice that Alexis is wearing bright red lipstick. I am just bright red. 'Absolutely fine.'

'Are you sure?' Alexis stands and stares at me for a moment. 'Thanks, Annie. Thanks for coming back into the office to deal with the oysters crisis. I appreciate it.'

This is possibly the first time Alexis has thanked me for anything. Is now the moment to ask her about Don? Should I even go there? I dug around a bit this morning. Lydia thought the idea of Don and Alexis laughable. She said that Don was not handsome enough for Alexis and that Alexis was not smart enough for Don. Louise told me that the last she heard, Alexis was dating some hotshot advertising guy. But, as she rightly pointed out, Alexis gets through so many men, it's impossible to track them all. Still, no smoke without fire. 'Alexis, do you mind if I ask you something?'

'Fire away.' She looks at me quizzically.

'Are you . . .' I suddenly can't think of any way to make the question sound all right. 'Um, have you got a boyfriend?' I balls it.

'Are you propositioning me, Annie?' she laughs. 'I'll try everything once.'

'Very funny.' I stretch out a leg in front of me, bend down, feel the calf muscle ping and wonder if this is a good thing. 'I was just wondering if . . .' I stop. This is hopeless. She's not going to tell me the truth anyway. 'Oh, it doesn't matter.'

'Why? What are the rumours?' says Alexis suddenly, her face hardening.

How does she know there are rumours? 'Um.'

'There are rumours about me and Don, aren't there?' she says. I have a suspicion that part of her is delighted that such rumours are percolating.

Oh. Right. I look her in the eye. 'Yes.'

Alexis laughs. 'Oh, rubbish! Isn't it ridiculous that in this day and age a woman can't have a few meetings with a powerful man without everyone jumping to conclusions!'

Meetings? What meetings?

'Honestly,' she continues, looking more and more pleased with herself. 'I do have some standards! Do people really think I'd put my career on the line for a shag with an overweight publishing executive?' She starts to walk away, then stops and turns to face me. 'Honey, he is small fry!'

Small fry! Something inside me bristles on Don's behalf. Or is she calling my bluff? I'm not sure what to think. As I limp toward the changing room, Alexis springs up on to the running machine and starts hitting buttons, beep, beep, beep, making it go faster and faster, her ponytail swinging rhythmically from shoulder to shoulder, her thighs and bottom firm as her feet rise and fall. This, I realise, is a woman with drive. She is a fierce opponent. Must try harder.

Pippa appears to be in a state of unnatural clinical calm, which is somehow more malevolent than her rage. 'Sit down, Annie,' she says in a quiet, restrained voice. 'As you know, your trial period is up.'

Shit. It is? I guess it must be. My mind has been on other things. 'Yes, Pippa, of course.'

'How have you found the role of deputy?' She sticks her hand into the latticework of hair and hairspray.

'I've loved it.' It suddenly occurs to me that I could be lying to myself here. 'I've loved the challenge.'

'Indeed. There have been a few of those.' She looks at me and narrows her eyes. 'Do you really feel this is working out, Annie?'

'I'd like to think so.' I smile my biggest smile.

Pippa stands up and readjusts the waistband on her trouser suit, tucking in her white shirt with one hand. 'There are things I can forgive, Annie. A bit of staff misrule. A few cock-ups with agents. I can even forgive poisoning London's most important PRs with radioactive oysters.'

'I didn't—'

She holds her hand up to silence me. 'What I cannot forgive, Annie, is indiscretion. And I am afraid that you leaking things about the magazine to the media, well, that crosses the line.'

I gulp. I should never have confessed. What came over me? I have a horrible feeling I am going to cry. Don't cry. Don't cry. I stare at my shoes instead, studying the shape of my toes beneath the leather.

'I will not be made into a laughing stock, Annie.' She sits

down again and pulls one of her photo frames towards her, spits on it and polishes it with a white tissue. 'However . . .' She smiles. 'You have been good in other areas. Editing. Ideas. Et cetera. And the staff like you. So I'm not going to read you the riot act . . .'

Phew. I smile at her gratefully.

'But I am going to declare that this trial has not been successful. Henceforth you will resume your previous role of senior editor.'

'What? No!'

'And I am going to try out Alexis.'

'You're not serious?'

'I am sorry if this upsets you, Annie. I know it's a blow. But Alexis gives off all the right messages. She's stylish, extremely well connected and a great networker. A good name to have on the masthead, if you get my drift.' Pippa stands and stares thoughtfully out of her vast sheet windows. 'Yes, she sends just the right *Glo* message to the world.'

Oh my God. She is serious. I am speechless.

'You will still be doing the editing work that you do now,' she says brightly, as if she's doing me a huge favour. 'Don't worry, I won't take work away from you. And I still want all your great ideas. But we'll return to your old pay structure and you can take Alexis's title of features director.' She spreads her hands on the white desk and looks at me thoughtfully. 'Yes, I think you and Alexis will complement each other very nicely indeed.'

Thirty-three

Lydia and I steam out of the security barriers at reception, Lydia trailing an enormous dark grey cape, her biker boots crashing against the polished marble floor. 'Hon, I think it's time to come clean with Pippa about what a fucking nightmare Alexis is. Rip the scales from her eyes. Stick the knife in. Let's face it, it is well overdue.'

We stop outside the building, a cold wind whipping around us in circles, Lydia's cape flapping like a flag. I begin to shiver. I'm not sure if it's the cold or the idea of losing the job I worked so hard to get.

'Don't give up! You're an ace deputy, Annie. Everyone loves you.' Lydia clasps my hands tight with her black kid-leather gloves. 'I'll talk to Pippa. Let me set the record straight about Alexis, hon.'

I shake my head. 'I appreciate the offer, Lydia. But it feels so underhand. Oh God, I don't know.' How can I go back to being in features? How will I survive on my old salary? But I don't want to be somewhere where I am not wanted or valued.

'Alexis would do it to you!' exclaims Lydia passionately. 'You must fight back.'

But is the job worth fighting for? I'm just not sure any more.

'Annie,' Don booms, dunking us in his baritone, as he strides out of the foyer.

Lydia looks from Don to me and back again. 'I need to shoot, Annie,' she says tactfully, kissing me on my cheek. 'Call me tonight if you want. And please, think about what I said.' And she rushes off down the street.

'Whoa! You have a face like thunder,' Don says, putting his hand firmly on my arm. 'What's eating you?'

'I'm fine. Just fine.' I start to walk. The 'Don and Alexis merrily fucking' screensaver pops up in my head. If it's true about him and Alexis I will never forgive him.

'Miss Rafferty,' he says. 'Please don't feel you have to put on a show on my account. I thought we'd got beyond the theatrics.'

I stop, turn round and glare at him.

'Ah, now I've got your attention.' I notice, for the first time, that he has enormous gnomic ears that call out for pulling. 'Coffee?' he asks gently.

'No thanks.'

'Please?'

'No.'

'I'm begging.'

'OK.' Indignant but also, disappointingly, rather pleased to see him, I follow Don to the local branch of Starbucks. Over a skinny cap I tell him about the Great Oyster Poisoning, Georgia's indiscretion and my conversation with Pippa.

Don sinks his jaw into his large square hands, looking genuinely shocked. 'Fuck me.'

'I'm screwed, you see, Don.' I look up at him and probe him for the answer I've been dreading. 'Did you know?'

'No.' He shakes his head, pauses. 'I'm not allowed to say it's grossly unfair, Annie. I shouldn't say that Pippa's a bitch. Bloody hell, the magazine could do with the free publicity. I could have a word with Ig, but it wouldn't make any bloody difference.'

Ig. Shit. Of course. Don knows Ig. Then it occurs to me: what if it wasn't Georgia and Dave after all? What if all this time Don has been feeding Ig insider stories?

'That's the rules of the game. And it is a game, Annie. Forget that and it's a fast track to the Priory.' Don laughs and nudges me with his elbow. 'Fuck, I can't wait to see it. I hope you told your sister some good incriminating yarns.'

Game? Is this all just a game to Don? I drain the coffee quickly and decide to confront him. 'You're not the mole, are you?'

'The spoof media mole!' Don looks at me in astonishment, then starts to roar with laughter. 'I wish I was.'

'Is that a no?'

'You have a very curious idea about me, Miss Rafferty. Do you really think I would stand by and let you take the rap if I'd done it?'

'Well . . .' I feel a little embarrassed now. It does seem rather absurd all of a sudden.

'You don't know me at all, do you?'

'Um . . .' I skirt the rim of my coffee cup with my fingers.

'Annie, you were brave to come clean with Pippa,' he says, suddenly sincere. 'You did the right thing. Look, it's a bit of an awkward position for me. I don't want it to look like I'm interfering in her staff management. But I want to help.'

I stand up to leave, pulling my coat on with unnecessary vigour. 'I don't need your help.'

'Whoa. Sit down, for Chrissake.'

I don't sit down. I feel the heat rise on my cheeks, ruining the dignity of my dramatic exit.

'I'm very flattered that I can cause such a reaction.'

'Oh shut up, Don.' I hate him.

'I'm your superior.' He laughs. But the joke's not funny any more.

'Whatever.' I sling my bag over my shoulder. 'You're Alexis's superior too, aren't you?'

Don shuffles uncomfortably in his seat. I know I've hit a nerve. I know that Pippa got the gossip right. My heart sinks. 'I know, Don,' I say wearily, as if the subject completely bores me. 'I know about you and Alexis.'

'Sit down.'

I hover.

'Sit down, please.'

I sit down.

'Annie, there's not much to know.'

'Funny, that. The grapevines are humming with gossip,' I exaggerate to get a reaction.

'Annie . . .' He lowers his voice and scans the people in the café for fellow workmates. 'You mustn't think . . . Oh God. You do, don't you? It was a long time ago. Before I started working at this place. I'd just come back from America and I met Alexis at a party—'

'She does good party,' I interject, and wish I could retract it because I sound jealous. I am jealous.

'It was nothing. We just hung out for a couple of weeks.' He blows air out of his mouth and looks exasperated. 'It was meant to remain a secret.'

'Don. It's a magazine. Nothing remains a secret.'

He shoots me a look. Is that fear in his eyes? Is he scared

I'll start trumpeting our frisson around the office too? 'Sorry you had to find out about it like that.'

'You could have fucking told me.'

'I couldn't.' He smiles softly. 'You are one scary lady.'

He leans forward over the table and cocks his head on one side. His eyes gleam behind a thick fan of black lashes. I'm not going to fall for them. 'Annie . . .'

'Nice to know that I'm just another notch on your dossier of sexual harassment.' I say this quickly and spitefully and immediately regret it.

'Let's go.' He pulls on his thick winter coat and turns his back to me like a blockade. 'I'm sorry, Annie. I can't rewrite my past.'

At this point I should walk away, dignity intact. But I don't. Something makes me reach towards his arm, turn him round, lift my face and kiss him long and hard on the lips. Appalled and shocked by my own crass behaviour, I walk away briskly, dignity in shreds.

Thirty-four

Maggie and I are sitting in a café on Hampstead Heath, drinking cappuccinos and trying to protect our shared chocolate muffin from predatory pigeons. Maggie's two boys play nearby on their scooter, falling off in puddles and rolling around in the mud like puppies. A group of girls buzz around them, licking improbably coloured ice-creams, their cheeks slapped pink by fresh air and sugar. For a moment I think, for no particular reason and without bitterness, that this could have all been mine. I can see them clearly, the pretty children with their blond thatches of hair and endearingly goofy Nick smiles. Then, just as quickly, like a photograph lit by a match, the image curls inwards, fades and dies. I sip my coffee. 'How is Nick?'

'He seems OK, Annie,' says Maggie in a soft voice that suggests that she will only offer anodyne information about my ex if I demand it.

'He's still looking after the boys?'

'No. I've got a new nanny.'

I smile. 'He was that good?'

Maggie laughs. 'The boys loved him, adored him. They ran

rings around him, of course. He taught them all about the pleasure of a good kebab and how to DJ and introduced them to the delights of New Young Pony Club turned up really, really loud. Frankie was deafened.'

'Oh, right.' I smile, seeing him so clearly. 'A better PR, then?'

'He's doing a good job,' nods Maggie, staring into the mid-distance in a way that makes me think he's not setting her world alight. 'And the company's doing really well at the moment. Better than I ever could have imagined, actually. Frankie, share with your brother! Remember what we said about sharing?'

Frankie glares at his brother and runs off with the scooter, not taking a blind bit of notice of Maggie.

'That's fantastic, Maggie. You are clever.'

'I have some more news.' She smiles uncertainly. 'We are going to move out of London.'

'No!' I put down my coffee. 'Not the flight to the provinces, Maggie. Not you!'

'I've spent the weekend checking out property porn. Honestly, it's amazing what you can get. We could be mortgage-free, Annie. It would allow me to take more time off from the business, spend more time with the kids. Jake and I would get to hang out more. He'd stop hating me for working so hard. I'd stop hating myself for working so hard . . .'

'But you love working!'

'To a point.'

'You've built up this amazing business. You should be proud, Maggie. Not apologetic.'

Maggie slaps the table. 'I am fucking proud! I am proud that I've worked so hard that we can live mortgage-free in a nice big house in the country, that I will be able to dictate my

251

own hours, be my own boss. God, I don't ever underestimate the joys of being self-employed, however bloody hard it is, give me self-employment over some despot boss any day.' She sighs. 'But even so, Annie, it was all only ever a means to an end. One day I'll sell the business and be able to build a swimming pool and spend every summer in Tuscany. That's the plan, anyway.' Maggie leans her lovely aquiline head back in the sunshine and shuts her eyes. Her hair is glossy black, sleek as a seal. It's such a familiar head. London will not be the same without her. I hate the thought of her leaving. 'I know it's dreadfully boring. I never thought it would happen to me either.' She suddenly looks worried. 'Tell me, is the countryside dull? Be honest with me, Annie.'

'Well, having grown up in the metropolitan environ of Lower Dalton, I can vouch for the fact that yes, unless walking dogs across muddy meadows is your idea of a wild time, it is pretty damn dull.'

Maggie winces. 'There I was imagining I'd have a life like the Toast catalogue, you know, all Agas and poplin blouses and roaring wood fires.'

'Sorry. Don't let me rain on your parade. The countryside, Maggie, as well as being slightly dull, is also beautiful, life-affirming, and you'll wake up feeling five years younger even if you do start to dress in Boden.'

'I'll never wear Boden.'

'Hmm, that's what they all say,' I laugh. 'Listen, if I didn't have to be in London for work – yuck, work, what a horrible thought – I wouldn't mind a lovely little sabbatical in the country,' I say, waving a bit of chocolate muffin. 'Forget the Toast catalogue, I'd just like to live somewhere without yellow crime-scene placards every two hundred yards.'

We both sigh at the same time, the way friends do, and

gaze out at the heath in comfortable silence. It is time to tell her everything about Don in full gory detail so that she can shed some light on the whole escapade. 'Maggie, I've got a confession to make. Talking of crime scenes—'

Maggie interrupts me. 'Annie, there is something I haven't told you.' She suddenly seems unnerved. Frankie jumps up on her knee and nestles into her neck. 'It's Nick,' she says, cuddling her son.

My stomach knots. Something about the tone of her voice. 'Is he all right?'

She takes a deep breath. 'He's dating Sadie Zuckerman from the office.'

'Mum, Mum,' Frankie pulls at Maggie's face with his little hands, trying to get her attention. 'Who's Sadie? Is she a princess?'

It takes a few moments before it sinks in. 'Sadie? Your production manager, Sadie? The tall, slim one with the loud, annoying laugh?'

'That Sadie, yes. I'm sorry to be the one . . .' Maggie says, wincing. 'It's just that I thought you would want to know.'

'Oh. OK. Thanks for telling me.' My eyes brim with tears. I blink them back. How did he get over me so quickly? With Sadie Zuckerman. If he likes Sadie Zuckerman, how come he ever liked me?

Thirty-five

Don presses the buzzer and the heavy front door swings open, like an escape hatch. I walk off the street and into the building. I stare at the lift's polished walnut panelling and think about Nick. The Sadie Zuckerman revelation hurts. It makes me feel jealous, dispensable, too quickly replaced. But the realisation that Nick has moved on so fast is also, I'm discovering, unexpectedly liberating. I no longer feel guilty. It is just me now. I can do what I want to do. I can see whoever I want to see. I owe nobody anything.

When I get to the fifth floor, Don is there, leaning against the apartment's open door. There is a little curl at the corners of his mouth. Neither of us speak. He grabs me. I grab him. It feels like we are holding on to each other for dear life. We stagger from the front door across the glossy wood floor and fall on to the enormous white sofa. He smells like how he tastes, salty, musky, like a dark bitter olive. We are tangled completely. We come up from the snog for air. He kisses the top of my head.

'It's been a very long time since I've wanted to kiss anyone's head,' Don says. He kisses my head again. 'You smell of buttered crumpets.'

'How glamorous.'

'Glamorous is boring.'

I trace my finger along his arm, enjoying its gym-honed topography, the rise and fall of muscle.

'I am very pleased you decided to forgive me, Miss Rafferty.'

'I didn't decide anything.'

'Ah, you were thrown to my door by the category five gale force of your passion.'

'Don't flatter yourself.' But this is actually kind of what happened.

He kisses the top of my ear. 'What took you so long?'

'Oh, shut up, Don.' I smile and turn over lazily, enjoying the smell of our bodies, the squashed warm patch we've made in the sofa. I thought I'd feel weird about him and Alexis. But I don't. It's as if no one exists but the two of us.

'You know what? I haven't even offered you a drink. Not that I need to now, of course. Not now that you're in my clutches.'

'I'm a cheap date.'

He walks to the bedroom and comes back with a pale grey throw that he tucks over me gently. 'Don't want you catching a chill.'

'Have you had a personality transplant or something?' I laugh.

He laughs. 'I've always been like this. You were always just too chippy to see it, Miss Rafferty. Now, is madam hungry?'

'Ravenous.'

He looks at his watch. 'Well, it's pretty late. Um . . . there's a mean Indian down the road, great takeout. Or this funny little Greek that has strange-looking menfolk playing stringed instruments after a certain hour. It's a blast.'

'It sounds dreadful,' I laugh. 'Anyway, it's a school night. Let's eat here.'

He jumps on top of me and ruffles my hair with his hand. 'Do you have to be so bloody cool, Miss Rafferty? Where's your sense of adventure? Let's go out.'

'I'm not cool!' I protest, thinking how uncool Nick has always told me I am. A whole party can be pumping with narcotics and I'll be the one dreaming of a nice cup of cocoa in front of an *EastEnders* special. 'You don't know me at all.'

He kisses me on the eyebrow. 'Ah, but I do. I know that you think too hard. That you like everything just orderly. But inside . . .' He traces his hand around my jaw. 'Inside, Miss Rafferty, there's a wild beast of a woman trying to get out! Let the Greeks release her!'

The Greek restaurant is tiny, tucked away in a narrow Dickensian street near Borough market. Through its small steamed-up windows I can see that it is crammed full, very dark and lit almost entirely by candles. The other diners are a hip, young, scruffy crowd, huddled in noisy groups, drinking lots. We'll never get a table. We walk inside into a wall of heat and loud laughter. Don taps one of the waiters on the shoulder. The waiter spins around and grins at him. 'We're busy, Don,' he says, gesturing around at the heaving tiny restaurant.

'Come on . . .' badgers Don.

The waiter gives him a macho Mediterranean whack around the shoulders and leads us to the one empty round table at the side of the room, its white tablecloth lit by a solitary flickering candle and decorated with a wilting carnation in a tiny blue vase. We order dozens of little dishes and get stuck into some rough red wine that comes by the jugful.

Don nudges me. 'Check this out. You won't be disappointed.'

I look over. At the very back of the restaurant a bearded man with a guitar is standing on a podium the size of a small desk. One of the waiters is moving some of the diners' tables near the stage backwards, crushing us all up further, but no one seems to mind. As soon as the man starts plucking his guitar, there are whoops from the other diners. And then the bearded man is joined by another bearded man on an accordion, and they sing in Greek, they strum, drink and improvise. The music is so loud that it's impossible to have a conversation. So Don and I drink too. A lot. Don whoops and claps and whistles and drums his hairy fists on the table. I glance over at him, catch his eye and grin stupidly at him. This seems to go on for hours. Occasionally I think, I should get home, but then Don fills my glass with more rough red wine and the bearded man blasts into song again and I'm having too much fun to leave. I start tapping my foot. I start whooping. And then Don is trying to tug me up. 'Come on,' he is shouting. 'Come on!'

'What are you doing?'

'We're going to dance,' he laughs.

'No!' I shout over the music, sitting firmly in my seat as he pulls at me. 'No way!'

But then the bearded man with the guitar is pointing at us and the restaurant has turned to watch and the diners are stomping their feet on the floor and I have no choice but to surrender to Don's grip, as he pulls me up and loops his arms around my waist and turns me and turns me. The music gets louder and louder and the other diners are clapping, and we are whirling and whirling, drunkenly, giddily, the world as I know it falling away from my delirious dancing feet.

257

Thirty-six

Alexis staggers towards me in scarlet ballet shoes, straining under the load of the enormous cardboard box in her arms. The box appears to be full of files and magazines and personal possessions. A small white orchid pokes out the top and nods as she drops the box on to my desk, scattering my paperwork. 'Oh, haven't you cleared your desk yet? I thought we'd swap, Annie.'

'What?' I gaze at her blankly. My mind is far away, whirling around a Greek restaurant. It strikes me that it's kind of ironic that it wasn't Nick's brilliant Dj-ing that got me on the dance floor again, but the strumming and cheering of Greek folk music, and, Don, of course, chunky, uncool, glorious Don. It also strikes me I have a such a bad hangover it's like a kind of dementia.

'It's just a bit confusing for the rest of the staff, Annie,' Alexis says, speaking to me as if I were retarded. 'If we swap jobs but not desks. I know this is difficult for you. If the desk move is an issue, I can talk to Pippa about it? Sorry. There's no nice way of doing this.'

'Nope. You can't polish a turd.' I smile because, despite all the stuff going down at work, dancing with Don has left me in a light mood – it feels like there is an electric blanket under my skin – and I cannot be bothered to rise to Alexis. I cannot remember the last time I danced like that. I cannot remember having so much fun. What a wonderful, silly, unexpected evening. 'It's all right, I'll move. Give me a moment.'

'In your own time,' says Alexis, tapping her pump against the stainless-steel table leg of my grey kidney-shaped desk and evidently not moving anywhere.

I stand up, scoop up all my papers and magazines in my arms and walk over to the features desk, where I dump them in a chaotic pile on Alexis's recently vacated work area. The features staff smile at me, then quickly look away, embarrassed to witness my demotion.

'I feel your pain,' mouths Lydia from the fashion desk. She points to Alexis and makes a cutthroat action with her hands.

I glance over at Alexis to see her position the orchid territorially at the front of the desk. 'Ugh. What the fuck's this?' she is saying, holding up an old peppermint tea bag. I identify the tea bag as the one that has been festering inside a nest of wires behind my telephone for the last couple of days, the one I've been meaning to extract but haven't. Oh. Now she's studying an old passport-sized photo of me and Nick that used to be stuck to my computer with a blob of Blu-Tack. Alexis throws both the tea bag and the photo unceremoniously in the bin. 'Belle!' she barks – she seems to imagine that Belle is her new personal assistant. 'Could someone come and wipe down this desk for me? Thanks. It's kind of gross.'

I arrange my possessions – an old coffee mug, Rolodex, notebooks, lip salve – on the desk, the desk I left three months ago for the deputy editor's chair. The world looks different from here. Out of the (smaller) window I look down on dirty business offices rather than the London Eye, streams of traffic rather than the majestic Thames. My chair has a squeak and I feel exposed because my back faces the office so I don't know who's peeping at my screen behind me. Which means no pre-warning of Don's appearance. What effect will his presence have on me? Will I be able to keep it together? Or will I give myself away by blushing and stammering and therefore send the entire office into an orgy of speculation and gossip?

As the morning progresses, touchingly, many people make their way over to my desk to try and cheer me up and slag off Pippa and Alexis. I think that they expect me to be sadder than I am, perhaps weeping in the toilets and asking the beauty editor for doses of American red-nuking eye drops. They certainly take my Greek-wine-withered complexion as a sign of suicidal despondency.

It is Melanie on the subs' desk's birthday, so someone buys a cake from Konditor and Cook. It is covered in pale yellow icing and edible glitter. When the subs sing 'Happy Birthday', she looks like she'd rather be anywhere else, probably in a bar with a stiff drink. Hearing the song, Pippa strides over to tell everyone that the issue is running late and can they please just get on with their work? She doesn't accept a slice of birthday cake, obviously. Nor does Alexis, 'Oh, I had such an enormous breakfast.' Yeah, right. Nor do any members of the fashion desk eat any cake. The beauty girls insist on teeny slivers fit for elves and don't eat the icing and will skip lunch later. The features staff do eat the icing and spend the next hour moody with self-loathing. The subs eat as much as they can get their hands on. Uncharacteristically, I have lost my appetite.

It's hard to motivate myself to do any work. The very fact that I am still here at all is horribly undignified. If it weren't for the mortgage . . . So yes, I need to plan my escape, send out emails to contacts gently probing as to whether they know of any vacant posts on other magazines – few of the good jobs are advertised. Yes, this is what I should do. But I don't. Instead, I am flashbacking to last night, fidgety, distracted, glancing at the clock, wondering how long it will be before there is contact from Don. *Give me a sign.* The Britney Spears song, inexplicably, goes round and round my head. *Baby hit me one more time.* The office clears for lunch. I try to eat mine at my desk, an open wheat-free sandwich. But I can't eat. I am full of something. I am full of anticipation. I am full of Don. Will he poke me on Facebook? Or use coded language in a company email?

At two thirty, everyone filters back into the office from lunch, carrying sandwiches and drinks and bags stuffed full of January sale stock. There is a low hum as people pick up where they left off, and then the phones start trilling again. It starts to rain harder and the office, despite the great planes of glass that contain us, becomes almost cosy, for the time being preferable to the cold, wet London waiting for us at street level. I walk over to the colour printer to collect a printout of the Scorching pages. The printer is near my old desk, now Alexis's desk, covered in Alexis's stuff. A young features writer jumps back guilty and grabs something from the printer tray. I glimpse a CV. She knows I know and looks immensely relieved when I smile. As I stab the printer, trying to get it to work, Belle scuttles over to Alexis's desk.

'A Michaela Freemantle. Do you know her?' she says loudly to Alexis. 'She is in reception being arsey and demanding to see Don. He's not around today, I said. I'll see Pippa

261

then, she said. When I said Pippa wasn't here today either, she said she'd see the next in command.' Belle hesitates. 'I guess that means you.'

'It does indeed, Belle!' Alexis says with relish. 'Don't worry. It's probably a crazed reader. I'll deal with her. Go sign her in and bring her.'

The printer is still not working properly, so I am standing there cursing it when the woman walks into the office, escorted by Pippa. She does not look like a crazed reader. Skinny, attractive, about six foot tall, with shiny dark hair swept into a ponytail that pours down her back, she's wearing a sharply tailored voluminous coat with an enormous fur collar. She is very attractive.

'I was hoping to find him here,' she says to Alexis. She talks with an American accent. I notice that her mouth has the upper-lip plumpness of the artificially inflated and doesn't seem to follow the phonics of her speech. 'If you could check his schedule and let me know where I can find him, it would be much appreciated.'

Alexis looks puzzled. 'Do you have an appointment?'

The woman laughs, a small, dismissive laugh, like a hiccup.

Alexis and Belle exchange glances. Alexis flicks her hair off her face and says stagily, as if the woman is already boring her, 'Everyone needs an appointment to see Don.'

'I do not need an appointment,' smiles the woman humourlessly, flashing square paper-white teeth. 'I am Don Wilberforce's wife, honey.'

Thirty-seven

'His wife?' asks Alexis slowly, in disbelief. 'You're sure?'

The woman is irritated. 'Do you need to see the marriage certificate?'

Alexis just stands there, flushed, mute.

The printer is beeping at me, flashing red buttons. I ignore it. Like Alexis, I am frozen too.

Belle steps in to this awkward situation. Follow me and I'll take you up to the top floor.' She leads The Wife out of the office.

I walk back to my desk slowly, hurting all over, unable to process what I've just heard. But I can't sit at my desk. Out of the corner of my eye I spot Lydia lurching towards me on her heels. I don't feel capable of holding down a normal conversation, so I flee to the loos.

The loos are empty apart from one locked loo door. From behind it comes the sound of heavy sobbing, someone making the sounds that I am trying to hold back. I knock on the door. 'Are you OK in there?'

'Fuck off!' shouts Alexis's unmistakable voice. 'Just fuck off and leave me alone.'

I do fuck off. Later that day I book a week's holiday, telling Pippa that I need time to recharge my batteries. It's a quiet time in the production schedule and she approves of this type of emergency holiday, suggesting as it does that I'm working hard and taking time off so I can come back and work even harder. My resort of choice is my messy, empty bed, dressed with a box of tissues, a tea-stained copy of *Grazia* and a packet of Haribos. Georgia sits on the side of the bed, offering me tea and soup, as I did for her all those weeks ago. She asks, What man? Nick? She is confused. Not Nick, I say. When I tell her about Don, Georgia's mouth opens and shuts silently. As I explain the sorry situation, it strikes me how stupid I sound. What a mug I have been. How ridiculous it is that I've kept it to myself all this time.

'Crikey, sis,' she says. 'So he's the reason you let Nick go. You are such a dark horse!'

'Don's not the reason,' I say, and as I say this it becomes true. No, I've realised that Nick and I were slowly working towards the end of our relationship in clear marked steps, like a new couple becoming more committed, only in reverse. Don was the catalyst, the shaft of illumination that briefly made sense of everything, then disappeared. I sniff. My head feels full of cement again because I've been crying and my nose is blocked. I realise that I am far more gutted than I ever thought possible about someone I hardly know, and that I should have felt like this about Nick leaving except I didn't. And this makes the whole sorry mess more sorry somehow. Disaster unfolds later when Georgia decides the most sensible course of action is for us to drink. The lapping sadness is replaced by a deep Rioja-red anger in my belly. I pick up my phone.

Georgia puts a hand out to stop me. 'Don't,' she says. 'If it was me, you'd say don't.'

I nod drunkenly and drop the phone on my lap. Georgia goes to the loo. I drain my glass of wine, pick up the phone, and yes, I text him.

Met yr wife today. Nice. Fuck U 2.

I press send, feeling a satisfying rush of triumph. But this is quickly replaced by an agonising what-have-I-done wretchedness when he doesn't respond in the next five seconds.

'You've texted him, haven't you?' demands Georgia sternly when she comes back into the room. 'Annie!' She shakes her head. 'I just can't believe it. It's all so unlike you somehow. It's the kind of thing that would be much more likely to happen to me. You're usually such a good judge of character.'

I don't want to be a good judge of character. I want to get filthy with a funny, unsuitable man with hairy hands and thighs like beams in a warehouse apartment in Bermondsey.

'Oh shit. You really have got it bad, haven't you?' Georgia stands up, rising to the occasion. 'We can't stay here. You'll be liable to do something you'll regret. You mustn't dignify that man with even a phone call. Right, pack up your stuff. We're getting out of here.'

Waves thunder on to Brighton's pebble beach. Clouds cast Zeppelin-shaped shadows on the sea. The air is cold as a slap. I'm eating chips. I bet Don's wife doesn't eat chips.

'What was wrong with Nick, Annie?' asks Georgia gently, dipping her hand into the cradle of chips warming my lap. ' I just don't get it.'

'It's hard to explain. I guess I'm trying to figure it out myself.' I down a chip with a bracing gulp of ice-cold Diet Coke. 'Sometimes I felt like I was turning into his mother and that he was the errant lazy teenage son. Get a job! Turn the music down! Don't use *Vogue* as a beer mat!' I laugh weakly. 'But that wasn't the reason I didn't marry him.'

'You know, I thought Olly wanted me to mother him. I thought that's what all men wanted.'

'Olly doesn't know what he wants, George,' I say softly.

Georgia presses her hand, cold from the sea wind, on mine. 'Talking of Olly. Will you accept more money for rent? Please. It's Olly's money. I think we should enjoy spending it.'

'It was intended to set you up.'

'You have set me up!' says Georgia appealingly, her flame-red hair buffeting around her face. 'I love living in Kensal Rise. I love your little house. Please accept some rent? You always help everyone else, Annie. You never let anyone help you.' She hugs her knees to her chest, pulling a tent of cashmere cardigan over them. 'This Don guy, he's the one in control this time, isn't he?'

'Don't practise your cod psychology on me, sister,' I say, a little startled at Georgia's hitherto well-camouflaged powers of perception. My hair lashes into my mouth, tasting of sea salt and chips. 'Look, there's the folks.'

My mother walks towards us down the promenade, bundled up against the cold in a bulky woollen beige coat and a knitted hat. My father walks beside her wearing a large moth-nibbled duffle coat that I remember from the coldest winters of my childhood.

'What are you two doing sitting on this bench in such god-forsaken weather?' says Dad, his mouth hidden by a thick navy scarf, only the spiky hedge of his moustache protruding. 'It's bloody freezing. It's like dipping the bones in liquid nitrogen.'

'It is sea air, Arnold,' sighs Mum. 'It's good for the soul.'

'The soul. Pah!' mumbles Dad. 'Girls, your mother is

266

trying to kill me off by forcing me to take bracing walks along the sea front every day.'

'There's a lovely veggie café over the road. Does a super carrot cake,' says Mum, trying to be cheerful. 'I thought we could have a treat there before heading back to the flat.'

'What's a man to do to get a pint around here? If I have to visit one more café that sells sprouting salads, I swear I will have a heart attack right here on the promenade in protest.'

'There's that nice little pub up the way there,' I say, pointing towards a road that rises up from the promenade, lined with pretty Regency houses. 'Shall we?'

The pub is just how I like them, small, cramped, with sinking ceilings and old codgers drinking ale. I immediately think, Don would like this pub.

'Well, you look bloody awful, if you don't me saying, Annie,' says Dad, Guinness foam catching in his moustache.

'Arnold!' exclaims Mum.

'She's all skin and bone. Looks like she hasn't slept for a week.' Hc looks at me sternly and tears open a foil pack of roasted peanuts with his teeth. 'You haven't developed a drug habit, have you?'

'Don't be ridiculous,' I say.

'Well don't. You know I wouldn't be able to afford to send you to rehab now, don't you?' Dad laughs, thinking this very funny indeed.

'Just busy at work, I imagine, aren't you, love?' probes Mum, looking concerned. 'It's not easy being a . . .' she pauses, searching for the right word, 'a high-flyer.'

I nod, and shoot Georgia a look that means, do not say anything. I do not want my parents to worry about my job, as well as everything else. 'It's been manic,' I say.

'Well I hope it's all worth it,' says Dad, slamming his pint glass down hard on the table. 'Is it?'

I shrug. 'Possibly not.'

'Still, needs must.' Dad flicks the Guinness foam from his moustache. A tiny blob lands on the side of my wine glass. He turns to Georgia. 'Anyway, you look better, George. Got a bit of flesh on your bones at last.'

'Oh.' Georgia looks gutted.

'A broken heart needs feeding, I've always said that,' says Mum approvingly. 'And now, well, look at you. You look quite ravishing.'

'Thanks.' Georgia doesn't touch the roasted peanuts again.

I change the subject. 'So tell us about Brighton. You're finally by the sea, Mum. How does it feel?'

'It's not Hedgerows,' Dad interjects.

'Oh . . . it's like being young again,' Mum says wistfully, ignoring Dad. 'When I was a teenager, we'd come down here for the odd sunny Saturday, you know, your grandpa and granny and me.' She looks wistful. 'I can almost see them, you know, huddled against the rain, my mum in her best red coat, my dad holding his trilby to his head in the breeze, walking along the sea front.'

'That's what happens when you get old, girls,' says Dad wryly. 'Everything reminds you of something else. It's impossible to have new experiences.'

My mother looks at Dad crossly now. 'You know what, girls? I will tell you honestly how it has been! Your father has been a right royal pain in the neck. Anyone would think I've forced him to move to the Outer Hebrides. He's still obsessing about Hedgerows. It's in the past, dear! Move on!'

Mum's new tone of voice is surprising. She's always been

so accepting of Dad's foibles. Not for much longer, it seems. Brighton seems to have given her a new blast of life.

'I just can't bear the idea of them neglecting the garden,' says Dad.

Georgia and I laugh. 'Dad, it'll be some apple-cheeked west London family who hire a gardener to tend patches of organic rocket.'

'I hope you're right.'

'Well, you met the man in the end, didn't you, dear?' says Mum. 'He was nice enough, you said.'

Dad nods. 'Yeah, he came for a last recce. I have to admit that he seemed like a decent kind of fellow.'

'There you go, Dad,' I say. 'I'm sure the new family will appreciate the house, and the garden.'

'Hmmm. I still dread to think what that Mr Wilberforce is going to do to my tomato plants,' says Dad, walking unsteadily towards the bar.

'Wilberforce?' I whisper.

Thirty-eight

Sunday evening. Maggie's kitchen. There are four half-drunk glasses of wine on the table. An empty wine bottle. A dangling industrial-style pendant light, like a huge aluminium bowl on a wire, casts a perfect pool of light on my hands, which are drumming the tabletop slowly, like drugged tap-dancers. Maggie, Vicky and Jake sit around the table silently watching my fingers as the news sinks in.

'Blimey. Well the guy's obviously a loon, Annie,' says Jake.

Is he? Is it some kind of sick joke? Is this how stalkers close in on their prey? The idea that I knew Don, that we had a connection, now seems absurd when viewed through the facts of the case. 'Don't, Jake,' I say, slumping my face into my hands.

'Jake, go and check on the boys, will you?' says Maggie sternly. 'Leave us to it.'

Jake pulls a beer out of the fridge and lopes off.

'Got to hand it to you, girl,' says Vicky, brushing her hair with her fingers. 'You've got some soap opera going on. I never would have guessed you had it in you.'

'Excuse me. Has my life been boring you up to this point?'

Maggie laughs and brings a bottle of cool white Chablis to the table. 'I genuinely had no idea he was married, Annie,' she says. 'I only ever met him briefly. I don't remember a wife.'

'She's American,' I say. 'The wife.'

'Ah,' says Maggie.

'You know what?' Vicky pours the wine, filling each glass to the brim, twisting the bottle and pulling it away. 'I think we can forgive him for the wife.'

'We can?' I say doubtfully, reaching for the solace in my glass.

'But we cannot forgive him for being a bunny-boiler and buying Annie's family home,' declares Vicky emphatically. 'Too weird. Delete. Wouldn't you say so, Maggie?'

'One complication,' I say. There are a million complications. 'We work together.' And I have had six missed calls from him in the last forty-eight hours. And I don't know how long I can hold out not answering the phone.

'Yeah, fuck. There is that,' says Vicky, thinking up a new strategy. She sips her wine thoughtfully. 'Aha! I've got it. Report him. Get him sacked. Sexual harassment.'

I fear she is only half joking. That Don has become such a source of casual girlie banter demeans him in a way that makes me feel uncomfortable. Misplaced loyalty, I guess.

My phone starts ringing again. I look at the flashing green interface. 'Fuck! It's him.'

'Don't answer it,' says Vicky, leaning forward as if about to restrain me.

'Step away from the mobile,' says Maggie. 'Annie!'

Ignoring them, I put the phone to my ear and walk out into the garden. Vicky and Maggie hiss at me and shake their heads. I stand beneath the beautiful twisty branches of Maggie's magnolia tree.

'Annie,' says Don, his voice tight and hoarse. 'For fuck's sake. Why haven't you returned my calls?'

'Guess.' I lean against the tree trunk to support myself. I fear if I don't, I might just fall over.

'We need to talk. It's not how it looks.'

'Don't use that line.'

'Hear me out. Meet me now.' He is insistent, cross that I'm not doing as I'm told.

'No.'

'Please, Annie. Don't do this.'

'Will she be there?'

'Of course not.'

Vicky and Maggie are standing next to the open patio doors, straining to hear every word, waggling their arms wildly and mouthing, 'Don't meet him.'

When I arrive at the bar, Don is outside, leaning against a graffiti-tattooed wall and sucking hard on a cigarette. He has dark circles under his eyes and his whole face seems to be in shadow. Seeing me, he throws the cigarette to the ground and grinds it with the heel of his shoe. There is an uncertainty to him that I've never seen before.

'Michaela and I haven't been together for two years,' he says later, as I sip my vodka and tonic and try not to throw up with nerves.

'She calls herself your wife.'

'She still is. Officially. We're divorcing.'

I shake my head. 'Don, I don't know what you want me to say. It's rubbish. It's all rubbish. It's just one thing after another. I don't know what you want from me. I don't know why you bother.'

Don leans across the table and grips my hands. 'Because of

you, Annie. You're wonderful. I've always thought you were wonderful.'

'But not wonderful enough to deserve honesty?' I stand up and grab my coat. Maggie and Vicky were right. 'I can't do this, Don.'

'Sit down, please.' He isn't ordering me this time. He is begging. 'Please, Annie.' His voice is quiet now. 'Ask me anything you like.'

I sit down slowly, reluctantly, knowing that if I leave now, I'll regret it for the rest of my life and will think of a hundred questions I should have asked him but didn't. The problem is, right now, I can't think of one.

'It was a whirlwind,' he says quietly. 'We married at City Hall six months after we met. It was the stupidest thing I've ever done. We hated each other by the end of that first year of marriage.' He puts his hand over his mouth, speaking through his fingers. 'It wasn't my finest hour, to be honest.'

'Are there any children?'

He looks startled. 'No! Thank God, no.'

'Why didn't you tell me?' My voice is nothing but a whisper now. In a way, this is the only question that matters.

'I'm a private person, Annie. New York feels like another life. But of course I would have told you in time. I had no idea that this ... this ... Well, I had no idea how I'd feel about you.' He shakes his head, as if in disbelief. 'It's knocked me sideways.'

'You are a womaniser, Don. A flirt. I'm not stupid.'

'I am a flirt. At first I thought we'd just have fun ...'

'You know what?' My voice is harder, my patience is wearing thin. 'I'm not having too much fun right now.'

He grips my hands tightly. 'I'm so terribly sorry, Annie. If I could turn back the clock ...'

I chew the inside of my cheek. 'You bought Hedgerows, didn't you?'

Don's mouth opens, then shuts silently before he speaks. 'How the hell do you know that?'

'Er, you went round the house when Dad was there?'

'But he doesn't know me ...' Don is smiling, more brazenly now. 'Shit, I really did think I'd get away with it! It was going to be a surprise.'

'It was.'

'I wanted to invest in a country place. Ever since my gazumping débâcle with that house near Bath I've been looking for another property. And you loved Hedgerows so much. You sold it to me.' He smiles softly. 'I had this vision of you writing a book down there or something.' He puts up his hands as if in surrender. 'Oh Christ, I know it sounds freakish. I am a fucking soppy twat at heart, Annie.'

'I'm not sure I believe you.' I pull back in my chair. 'It's weird, Don.'

'Weird?' He looks puzzled, as if I've suggested something completely radical.

'Normal people don't lie about their personal history. Normal people don't buy the family homes of women they've snogged.'

Don is silent for a few moments. 'Nick was normal,' he says eventually.

'That's a low shot.' I pick up my handbag. I've had enough. Enough lies. Enough confusion. 'Don't contact me ever again,' I say. So that he doesn't see me cry, I stand up and run out of the door into the wet, starless night.

Thirty-nine

The office is the same as when I left it. It's hard to believe that I've been away for a week rather than just popped out during a lunch hour. This place shrinks time to nothing, swallowing meetings, mornings, weeks, years ... I sit down on my squeaky chair. I can see Alexis swivelling, feet up, on my old deputy editor's chair. I can hear her talking in a loud, posh TV presenter voice. I say hello to her. She raises her eyebrows rather than bothering with a greeting.

At eleven o'clock, just as I am slicing through a silver KitKat wrapper with my fingernail, Lydia hurries over from the fashion desk wearing an odd fashion-forward outfit constructed from olive felt pleats and strange shoes that make her feet look like hooves. 'You look so skinny! Gosh, you do have good cheekbones,' she marvels. 'What a week, though. Shit's been going down here. Pippa gave this hideous pep talk last Tuesday, you know: "The figures aren't looking as bad as they might at first seem, we need to give it a hundred and ten per cent ..." all the usual bullshit. Then she said we urgently needed six new pages of editorial, which as we all know means stacks of advertising has pulled out. Louise handed her notice in, she's leaving to be beauty ed for an in-house trade glossy – must be desperate, eh? – and Tina's been prowling the floor looking like she's just lost a wardrobe full of Marni and won a Primark handbag. Sweetie, it's ugly.'

'And Alexis?'

'Insufferable, of course. She's been asking fashion assistants to sort her out outfits. Apparently she's also been stalking Jill – you know the freelance who does the travel section? – and hounding her for freebies, demanding Chiva-Som for two weeks for her and a girlfriend. Unbelievable.'

I snap off a KitKat finger and offer it to Lydia.

'No thanks. Look, I should tell you.' Lydia looks a little uncomfortable. 'Alexis has also been stirring a bit, little digs about your work.' She suddenly reverts to a normal non-gossiping face and whispers under her breath, 'Watch out. The storm cloud cometh.'

I look up to see Tina, the publisher, thundering across the office straight towards us, papers fluttering in her wake.

'Hi, Annie.' Tina speaks through a set mouth. She looks like she's aged ten years since I last saw her. 'Can I see you and Alexis in Pippa's office? Five minutes.'

When she's gone, Lydia and I exchange glances.

'D-ram-a,' says Lydia.

Pippa is not in her office, as I expected. Instead Tina is sitting in Pippa's tall leather chair, chewing ferociously on a red biro. In what Lydia calls her 'front-of-house' skirt suit, she looks out of context among the chicness of the black-and-white photos and the floral bouquets. 'Alexis, Annie, sit down,' she says gruffly, turning the biro round and round in her stubby fingers. 'You may notice that Pippa isn't here today.'

276

'I'm happy to chair the ideas meeting if she's ill,' says Alexis brightly. 'I've done it before.'

Tina offers Alexis a small, tight smile. She's never been sold on Alexis. Alexis, I suspect, knows this and makes even more of an effort to schmooze, which makes Tina like her less. 'I'm afraid Pippa is not coming back. She's gone.'

Alexis and I exchange alarmed glances.

'It's very sad,' says Tina, not sounding the least bit sad. She puts the pen down and flicks it with her fingernail so that it rolls across the desk.

Pushed or fired? I want to ask, but don't dare. 'It's very sudden, Tina.'

Tina cradles her hands under her chin and rests on them sanguinely. 'It is, isn't it? But things . . . Well, I'm sure you're aware, things haven't been going that well here for a while. Something needed to change. Pippa recognised that.'

'She fell on her sword?' gasps Alexis.

'Not exactly. It was by mutual agreement. Anyhow . . .' Tina clearly does not want to elaborate. 'I'm going to announce her departure and a few other things at a staff meeting in a minute, but I wanted to put you two senior members of staff in the picture first.'

'Thank you, Tina,' gushes Alexis. 'Thank you very much. Who will be in charge? Does this mean . . .' A wide smile is spreading across Alexis's face.

'It means,' says Tina abruptly, standing up and smoothing down her skirt. 'It means that we need to get a new editor. Fast. We want someone dynamic, young . . . with an understanding of this market.'

Alexis leans forward on her chair, grinning from ear to ear. 'But of course.'

'Preferably somebody with a bit of a profile. We have to

advertise, obviously. But all hats can be thrown in the ring. In the meantime, one of you will be acting editor.'

'One of us?' Alexis flicks her hair back like a taunted prize pony. She is practically snorting with indignation. 'I don't understand, Tina. *I* am deputy.'

Tina fixes her with a steely gaze. 'You have been doing a good job for the last couple of weeks, Alexis. But I thought Annie did an excellent job as deputy too, to be fair. We need to rethink everything if we're going to make this magazine work. I will announce who I think should do what in a couple of days, when the dust has settled a bit.'

I can feel Alexis's fury radiating off her in nuclear waves. She stands up to leave.

'Right, can you get Belle to box up Pippa's stuff for her? Thanks. Oh yes, one other thing. I regret to say that Don Wilberforce is also leaving us.'

'No!' Alexis holds her hands over her mouth. 'Not Don. Why?'

Tina looks grave. A violin-string muscle twitches on her neck. 'He was offered a position he felt he couldn't turn down at another publishing house, Crunch Media. Obviously there's a conflict of interest, so he had to go with immediate effect.' She sighs. 'I won't pretend I'm happy about him leaving. It's a shame, a real damn shame.'

Forty

Reasons why I should not feel as I do.

1. He shagged Alexis
2. He didn't tell me he shagged Alexis
3. He is rude and crude and unreconstructed
4. He is fat
5. He has hairy shoulders
6. He made me think that wearing pink was a good idea. It's not.
7. He bought my parents house to weird me out
8. He has deserted Glo
9. He was married
10. He is married

Forty-one

Georgia wanders in wearing a vintage silk kaftan in peacock blue, glossy red hair spilling over her shoulders. She looks a bit like the model Lily Cole. She looks exactly how I don't feel. 'What up with you, sis?' she asks chirpily, flicking hair from her face.

'Thinking.' The editor's chair could be mine. Yes, it could. It really could. All I need to do is put together some shit-hot ideas and have a dollop of good fortune thrown in my direction. I have waited for this moment all my life. But am I behaving like I've waited for this moment all my life? No I am not. I am watching Kirstie Allsopp on telly and thinking about how much I like her royal-blue coat with its big lapels and buttons as big as cupcakes. What has happened to me?

'You look like you're planning your own funeral.' Georgia sits on the floor, leans against the sofa, extends one leg and starts to paint the toes of her right foot. Doing her own pedicure counts as one of Georgia's new cost-saving activities. It's also a clear sign she's in a vastly improved head space. 'Right, all those clothes are photographed and are up on eBay.'

'Really? You actually did it?'

'Yes, I did it!' She beams. 'Don't sound so astonished. I've kept a few of the old favourites, obviously.' She looks at me coquettishly. 'You wouldn't begrudge me that Joseph shearling coat, would you?'

'Georgia, it was your idea to sell this stuff. I do not want to take responsibility for the separation anxiety that might ensue when Marni is yours no longer.'

'And my Luella. Stop! Actually, I don't want to think about it.' She splodges candy-pink varnish on the toe rather than the nail. 'Bollocks. You know what? I reckon I could drum up a thousand pounds pretty easily.' She wiggles her toes prettily, surveying her handiwork. 'Not bad, considering. Oh, by the way, can I borrow that pink jacket of yours?'

'Nice of you to ask.' I smile at her. 'Of course. Where are you going?'

'An interview,' she says proudly. 'My friend Flossy . . .'

'Flossy? What kind of name is that?' I'd forgotten that Georgia has posh friends with the kind of names you might give a hamster.

'She used to live a couple of doors down from Olly and me? Pretty, blonde, used to model for the Brora catalogue? Do you remember her? Well, I bumped into her in Portobello and she said that her friend Tatiana is an interior designer and she is looking for an assistant, and I said I'd love to be an interior designer and she said how much she loved how I'd done Olly's place and she recommended me to Tatiana,' she says breathlessly. 'Who phoned saying she's seen Olly's place in Livingetc and that we simply must meet as soon as possible so we're meeting at Cecconi's to talk about my new role this afternoon.' Georgia pauses for breath and beams at me. 'I reckon I could get this job.'

'Gosh.' How different life is for the beautiful and well connected. 'Well done, Georgia.'

Although it's cold enough outside to freeze the gloss on my lips, the Tube is improbably hot and the ink from my newspaper sludges the tips of my fingers. Interest rates are up again. There is more talk of a house price crash. I flip the page quickly, skip the article about knife crime and read a nice calming story about the joys of oversized grey cardigans. Every time I think about Don, I make myself read another line. 'Falling to just above the knee, the grey cardigan – the smart money's on double-ply cashmere, girls – is one of the season's . . .' Will he ever contact me again? '. . . best investment pieces, straddling that tricky gap between . . .' How long was he married for? '. . . winter and spring dressing when the winter coat is too cumbersome and a skinny blazer too unsubstantial . . .' He got over me pretty damn quickly. It is my Tube stop. The week starts here. The battle for the editorship must commence!

Alexis, wearing a grey Grecian draped dress and vertiginously high black studded dominatrix-style platforms, strides into the office like a gladiator walking into the arena. Glaring at me through the palisade of her lash extensions, she swaggers towards her desk. It suddenly occurs to me that my understated glam look – black trousers, white shirt, L.K. Bennett black boots – might be a little too underwhelming to look ambitious.

Then the morning meeting is rescheduled for after lunch. Alexis looks cross: adrenalin peaking, she's ready for battle now, not on a full stomach after six rolls of sushi. I am relieved that the meeting's been delayed: it gives me more time . . . time to, well, pick at a tuna mayo sandwich and log on to Facebook. No pokes from Don. Of course not. I feel tears well up again and have to log on to eBay to distract myself. I search for Georgia's stuff, not entirely sure I believe that she will actually sell it. Aha! Bless. There it is. Blimey. She's even put her beige Luella handbag up for grabs, at a reserve price of £200. Some Marni. Reiss. I never thought she had it in her. I become aware of a presence behind me and turn round.

'Alexis, you made me jump,' I say.

Alexis is staring at the computer screen, looking puzzled. 'Are you buying that bag?'

'Oh no. It's Georgia's stuff. She's flogging it. I was just checking it out.'

'Georgia's? Oh, right. Very nice. I might have a bid myself,' she says, walking away.

A few hours later, Belle walks over to my desk, flamingo legs in electric-blue tights and a miniskirt. 'Tina will see you in Pippa's office, Annie.'

The call to arms. I am determined to give it my best shot. I can do this. Picking up my notebook – now, thankfully, crammed with ideas – I calmly stand up and prepare to walk into the most important interview of my life.

Belle continues to hover beside my desk, her mouth half open, as if she has something terribly important to say and is holding her breath until the words come.

'Is there anything else, Belle?'

'Um . . .' She hesitates for a moment. 'No. Um, no, there isn't.'

Tina is standing at the window with her forehead close to the enormous sparkling pane of glass. When I come in, she quickly stands up straight. 'Hi, Annie,' she says, her face betraying nothing, her smile tight.

'Hi.' Do I sit down? I don't want to appear presumptuous. There is a slightly uncomfortable silence. 'Would you like me to start the pitch?'

Tina sighs. 'No. Not right now. Sit down, Annie.'

I sit down, grateful to do something. A funny raw feeling settles in the back of my throat, like a nasty strain of flu brewing.

'Annie, this is awkward.' She rests her chin on her hands and looks at me intently. 'Look, I think you're great.'

'Er, thanks.'

'But, well, something's come up that I can't ignore.' She winces as she speaks. 'It kind of stops things in their tracks.'

'Oh. What's happened?' That funny raw feeling is now a noise inside my head, and it's getting louder and louder.

'It's come to my attention . . .' She clicks her fingernails along her bottom row of teeth. 'Someone has reported that some of the items that were stolen from the fashion cupboard are now on eBay.'

'Really? We guessed they'd turn up there eventually.'

Tina looks uncomfortable. 'That your sister – is it Georgia? That your sister is flogging them, Annie.'

Heat rushes to my cheeks.

'The implication being that . . .'

The walls close in and pulse in and out, like they are breathing. 'You don't think that I . . .'

Tina shakes her head vigorously. 'No, of course not. But this puts me in a slightly awkward position. I'm duty bound to look into it, since the accusation has been made, as I'm sure you appreciate. And right now, well, the magazine is rudderless. I've got ten other magazines that need my attention, and

I'm about to go on holiday. *Glo* desperately needs a captain. To be perfectly frank, I wanted that captain to be you. But until we clear this little matter up, I feel that I have no option but—'

'You're not serious?' Oh. My. God.

'It's the obvious thing to do. Alexis is deputy,' she says apologetically.

I slam the editor's door on the way out. Belle looks up at me sheepishly. Somehow I know she knows. I march over to Alexis's desk.

'Nice work,' I say.

Alexis jumps. 'Hi!' She smiles brightly. 'How did it go?'

How I want to slap that smile from her face. 'Did you tell Tina that that stuff on eBay was actually stuff stolen from the fashion cupboard by me and laundered through Georgia? Are you fucking insane?'

'I don't know what you are talking about.' Alexis's mouth snaps shut with teeth-clicking finality, like the lid on a lipstick. She turns away from me to face her computer. 'Maybe you should ask Don.'

Forty-two

It's one of those clear, sunny winter days that feels like an invitation for lovers to stroll and congratulate themselves on their union, for such skies always feel a bit wasted on the single. Nick and I walk down Villiers Street towards the pockets of gardens near the Embankment, clutching posh seedy-bread sandwiches in brown paper bags and paper cups of steaming coffee. He phoned me out of the blue saying that he'd like to see me, 'so that it doesn't get too weird', and was I around for lunch? Yes, I would like to see him, very much. Little things have made me miss him, little things like the way his shoulders are about a foot above mine, the familiar lazy scuffle of his trainer-shod feet on the pavement and the defiant tufts of his blond hair that don't move in the breeze. I miss his advice and support, too.

We sit down on a wooden bench facing an area of green landscaped lawn, which faces the Thames, the scene of the disastrous proposal. Other benches are taken by office fugitives, grabbing what they can of the outdoors before the incarceration of the afternoon. A few tramps eye us dispassionately, sipping at their beer cans, leaning their heads back, letting the sunshine splash on to their grimy faces.

'It's nice to see you, Annie,' Nick says, fingering his brown paper sandwich bag.

'And you,' I say, too politely. It seems so strange that we once shared a bed. That we inhabited the same domestic universe. 'How's work?'

'Oh, you know, work is work. It's not what I want to do with my life, but hey, I only work at Maggie's office three days a week. And I've been doing this club night in the East End. That's been fun. It's even bringing in a bit.'

'That's great!' I say with more enthusiasm than I ever did when we were together.

'I'm still at Alf's,' he says, talking a bit too fast to fill in any conversational gaps. 'But . . .' He stops.

We are silent for a few almost-comfortable moments and London hums around us. Pigeons peck around our feet. A couple sit down on the bench next to ours and start snogging noisily. It feels vaguely excruciating, like watching a sex scene on telly while my parents sit on the sofa beside me.

'I'm sorry, Nick,' I say gently. 'I'm really sorry about the way things happened. It was my fault.'

He scuffs at a pebble with his trainer and looks down at it, not meeting my eye. 'You did the honourable thing, Annie,' he says generously. 'It was crunch time. We'd drifted for ages. We couldn't go on as we were.'

'No. I guess not.'

He unwraps a pastrami sandwich and takes a bite.

We sit in silence for a few moments. 'I'm sorry that I banged on about jobs and stuff all the time,' I say. 'It wasn't helpful, I realise that now.'

287

Nick laughs mirthlessly. 'Well, useless beta male stoned at home, not such a great look, I guess.'

'Stressed-out control-freak girlfriend not such a good look either.'

'No,' Nick says quietly. 'I tried, you know, Annie. But, fuck, the more you went on, the more useless I felt.'

'Shit, sorry.' I put my hand across my mouth and feel dreadful. 'There was a part of me that understood all too well your craving for something more meaningful . . . Maybe I was a bit jealous of your freedom.'

'Jealous? You?' he says, astonished.

I nod. I guess I was. I was jealous that I'd become the safety net on which Nick could rely. I wanted a safety net too. 'It sounds ridiculous, I know.'

Nick laughs and snorts a bit, hands over his nose, as if this revelation makes it a struggle to breathe. 'Shit, but I was never going to be this perfect boyfriend, you know.'

'I know. I know.'

'It was very much square peg, round hole, wasn't it?'

I pull at a straggle of wool worming its way out of my scarf. 'Why did you propose, then? I don't understand. I don't understand that bit at all.'

'Ah.' Nick winces apologetically, as if I've asked a question he really doesn't want to give an answer to. 'I thought, ulti-mately, that's what you wanted, marriage, babies . . .'

I'm trying really hard not to cry now and have no idea how to respond to this without hurting his feelings horribly. Yes, I do want marriage, babies, the whole thing – more than ever, strangely, now that's it's not really an option – but with the right person, and Nick and I didn't feel totally, future-proof right.

'I thought that perhaps it was my flakiness, my inability

to grow up – I know I behave like a teenager at times, Annie.'

I laugh, teary. 'Big kid.'

He smiles. But he doesn't laugh. Our coupley shorthand, that duty to respond as expected to jokes and confidences, it has gone.

'I thought that by moving our relationship to another, more mature level,' he continues, voice warbling a bit too now, 'we would be able to put all the shit of the last few months behind us.' He stops, collects himself and his voice becomes colder and harder. 'But, it obviously wasn't just my lack of a job that ballsed things up, was it?'

'No.' I swallow hard and fidget with my scarf again. He is right, of course. I realise with clarity that if we were meant to be together, we would have got through that rough patch, job or no job. Because, as I said to him all those months ago, a job doesn't define you as a person. I doubted myself when I said those words back then, but I now know they were absolutely right. His job, or lack of job, didn't define him. *Glo* never defined me. How could I ever have been stupid enough to think it did?

'There was a . . .' He stops, and his brow furrows. 'There was a reason that we didn't fully commit to each other, even before I left the PR agency. I've thought about this a lot, Annie . . .' he sighs, 'and I just think something must have been missing.'

I gulp. Hearing these words, this cold, male analysis is painful. There was a chink in me he didn't fulfil, a need in me he couldn't meet. And there was a need in him that I couldn't meet either. 'I guess there must have been,' I say softly, and realise that the edge of my scarf has completely unravelled and a long worm of blue wool is wrapped around my finger.

Nick smiles at me softly. 'I think we will always love each other in a certain way, though, won't we?'

'We will!' I say, overemotional, swept away by Nick's maturity, his ability to be dumped and re-emerge with such dignity and forgiveness.

'Annie, there's something I wanted to tell you, like, in person,' he says carefully.

'Sadie Zuckerman,' I say, wanting to make it easy for him.

He looks shocked. 'Shit. How did you know?'

'Little bird.'

'Maggie. You women, should have known.' He shakes his head, laughing nervously. He looks at me, checking my reaction. 'Um . . .'

'It's OK. I didn't expect you to be single for long.' I feel very grown up saying this. Grown up, and magnanimous. I am certain now that we will remain friends, that the last three years won't have been a total waste.

'Well . . .' He shifts on the bench. 'It's a bit more than that.' He stops and takes a deep breath. 'Annie, Sadie's pregnant.'

'Pregnant?' I grip my hand so tight around my coffee that it squirts out of the spout and all over my coat. 'But she's forty or something,' I blurt out stupidly, trying to flick the spilled coffee off my coat.

'Yes, she's forty-one.' Nick smiles. He looks at me with his soft hazel eyes.

Ah, so this is why he can afford to be so generous. He's being gentle with me. He's moved on to a totally new life in the space of weeks.

'We're going to keep it, Annie, make a go of things.' He spells it out.

'Wow! Well, that's amazing. Um, congratulations.' The

conversation with Vicky is buzzing in my head now, like emotional background musak. I don't feel too great all of a sudden. I can see me and Nick last year so clearly, curled up on the rug in front of the fire in the cottage in the Black Mountains, rattling off silly baby names. Ickerbod ... Gertrude ...

'It's a bit mad.' Relaxing now he's unburdened himself, Nick stretches his legs out in front of him. 'But sometimes you have to go with what life throws at you, I guess.'

'Yes,' I say, trying hard not to cry, because this is so final, this is the news that means that we have passed the point of no return. 'I guess.'

'I'm going to be Dad, at home, you know, balance it with my DJ-ing so Sadie can carry on working.'

I nod and wrap up my sandwich in its crinkly paper. I've lost my appetite. I want to leave. I don't want to sit here. I don't want Nick to see me upset. And I don't want to spoil his good news.

'And you?' He nudges me with his elbow. 'Have you met anyone?'

I take a deep breath. 'Well, there's ... there's ... this guy.' I am stuttering. 'But ... but he's married, well, he's separated but he didn't tell me ...'

'Oh.' Nick looks doubtful.

'Yes, I know how it sounds.' It is my turn to scuff the ground with my heel.

'You deserve someone really good, Annie.'

My eyes well up. Don't cry. A weepie in front of an ex is never a good idea. I don't want him to think I need his male affirmation because I'm single and can't get it anywhere else. His pity would be the worst thing imaginable right now.

'You like this guy, don't you?'

I smile and roll my eyes skywards. 'Kind of, but, you know, wrong type. Highly unsuitable, as Vicky says.'

'Hmmm. Vicky hasn't had a boyfriend for the last ten years, Annie.'

'So what?'

He leans back on the bench. 'Listen to your heart, not Vicky. Sorry if it sounds corny. But you're overanalytical. You analyse things to death and talk yourself out of them in your quest to do . . .' he makes quote marks with his fingers, 'the right thing.'

'I didn't marry you.'

'My point exactly.'

I take a slurp of coffee. 'So you want me to run off with a married man?'

'No! But life is messy, Annie. That's what I'm learning, it's messy. I say embrace the mess, man!'

We stand up to leave. Nick to go on to a record shop in Soho, me to head back to the office. Neither of us have finished our sandwiches.

'It was nice to see you,' says Nick a little formally, looking somewhat relieved, as if a difficult mission has been successfully dealt with and he can move on.

'You'll make a brilliant dad,' I say, and mean it. 'Good luck.'

'Thanks, Annie. Thanks a lot.' He kisses me on both cheeks like we were never in love. I watch him walk away, his languid boyish gait, his thatch of blond hair, and I realise he is no longer mine. He has gone, like something dropped over a bridge in a thoughtless moment, swept up in a strong current, carried off someplace else. I am startled at how quickly my life has dismantled itself. I didn't plan it this way.

Forty-three

The unimaginable has come to pass. Although Lydia sent an email to Tina pointing out that the Luella bag up on eBay is a different colour to the one that disappeared from the fashion cupboard, the email bounced back with a 'Tina Krum is out of the office . . .' message. Yes, Tina, who promised that she'd clear up the 'faintly absurd accusation' (what's with the 'faintly'?) straight away, has gone on holiday to Cape Town without clearing anything up at all. This means that Alexis is still sitting in Pippa's office. Yesterday she put up on the wall a photograph of herself interviewing Elizabeth Hurley. It is all quite horrible. No one knows who to answer to. Everyone is demoralised, bewildered. Belle looks like a biblical beauty in ungodly torment. She sits at her desk outside the editor's office gnawing her fingernails and waiting for the next order to be barked out imperiously by Alexis. Internal emails are hissing with the news that Alexis has decided that she, as the figurehead, needs an appropriate wardrobe and has demanded that the fashion assistants source one. The fashion cupboard is thus a hive of resentful activity. If they were chefs they'd piss in Alexis's soup. It is, as

Lydia despaired in her last email, *a typical* Glo *scenario epit-omising everything wrong with this no-hope culture of blame, lies, miscommunication and greed*. She signed off excitedly saying she's beside herself because she's managed to get on the shortlist for a dream job at *Marie Claire*.

And me? Well I could just resign now, except there's no one to resign to while Tina's away, and I don't want to give Alexis the satisfaction. I scribble sums on my notebook, trying to work out how much money, now that Georgia is paying full rent, I need to cover the mortgage. Perhaps even a house repossession is preferable to this? After a while, the job thing just exhausts me. I sit in my chair, stare out at the London Eye, wondering what Nick and Sadie Zuckerman's baby will look like and if Don will contact me again.

And then, at 11.07 a.m., it happens.

Morning, Miss Rafferty. Sorry I didn't say goodbye. Things changed so quickly – got a stonking great offer that makes me master of the universe, so obviously I had to take it. You must be v relieved at Pippa's move to the departure lounge. I heard that you are up for the acting ed role. At the risk of offending your moral stance on cronyism, I put a word in for you, not as a favour but because I know best, obviously. I also hear that you are getting married. Con-gratulations. Don x

Married? The world funnels in to the bright white oblong of email with its lines of black text marching across my screen like ants. I read this email about ten times, searching it for any coded hidden meanings. Do I write back and say no, I'm not getting married? Does it actually make any difference whether he thinks I am getting married or not? How do I broach the subject of the eBay débâcle? What did Alexis mean? The email suggests he knows nothing about it. Then the clock says noon and, still paralysed by indecision, I take an early lunch.

Maggie is waiting for me at our favourite café in the wharf. She is drinking citron pressé and has her dark eyes fixed far away on the Thames. We both do the girlie thing of ordering the same low-cal lunch, garlic prawns and salad, and pick guiltily from the bread basket. I persuade her to order some Sancerre – I've already exceeded my alcohol units for the week, so who cares – and even though she's decided to go for a new year-ish purge she gives in easily. We chink glasses.

'What are we celebrating?' I ask.

'I've found a house. It's just outside Oxford. Not far from your parents' old house. And Jake is going part-time.'

'But I thought he was back on the gravy train?'

'Misses the kids.' Maggie smiles and bites the head off her prawn, eating the eyes and everything. 'And he's supercritical of our poor nanny. I mean, I think she does a good job. But he says she's lacking in the imagination department – bad at rustling up rockets out of old washing-up bottles or some such – and makes them funny eastern European food that makes the house smell of cabbage. Honestly, he's like the worst high-maintenance working mum.' She leans back smiling, looking more relaxed than I've seen her for a long time. 'I am over the bloody moon, Annie. Seriously, since Jake has gone back to work the house has fallen apart. The nanny is almost as bad as me. And you know me, I wouldn't be able to identify window cleaner in a line-up of domestic products. I'll be scaling down a bit when we move, too. I'm so excited that me and Jake are actually going to see each other during waking hours again. Suddenly, all the hard work feels worth it. Country, Crocs, mud! Bring it on!'

'Can't you adopt me? You know what, I never thought I'd say this, but I'm with you, Maggie. If I were you, I'd do exactly the same, get out of this dirty old city.'

'I never thought I'd hear you say that.' Maggie holds up her glass. 'You, Annie, have changed!'

'I guess I'm feeling a tad jaded. The idea of working from home, or not working at all, is suddenly rather appealing.' I explain about eBay-gate, about the fact that everything I worked towards in my twenties is seeping between my fingers like a fistful of sand and I'm not sure how much I care and this is the most worrying thing of all.

'Well, this house has got six bedrooms, and I will insist that one of them is yours whenever you want it.'

'Bless you. You'll have to evict me.' I look at her intently for a few moments. 'Did you know about Sadie being pregnant, Maggie?'

Maggie stops mid-munch. 'Only as of yesterday. I was going to tell you,' she says apologetically. 'I was waiting for the right moment.'

'Nick told me yesterday.'

'Listen, you'll meet someone else, Annie.' Maggie leans forward and presses her hand on mine. 'It's so important to have kids with the right person. It's hard enough as it is, honestly. You've done the right thing. Please don't look so sad.'

'Suppose.' The idea of meeting someone new is very unappealing. I met someone. It didn't work out.

Maggie smiles. 'You'll be hitched by the end of the year if Vicky's got anything to do with it. She's already got you slated for a whole social season of singledom.' She checks her watch. 'I should be getting back to the office. But you know what I really want to do? I want to see that new exhibition at the Tate Modern. I live in London but I never see any exhibitions, bloody ridiculous. It's work or kids. I may as well be living in Milton Keynes.'

'Why don't you go? It's only a fifteen-minute walk from here.'

Maggie smiles slowly. 'Only if you come with me.'

'I've got to go back to the office.'

'Come on! What's the worst that can happen? Who cares about your stupid office? They've just accused you of nicking handbags, for God's sake. Fuck 'em. Be my partner in crime instead.'

I've worked in the office for three years and not once have I ever gone to the Tate Modern in my lunch hour. I've often wanted to, but always put work first. And for what, exactly? 'Let's do it!'

As we march down the path beside the Thames, wind in our hair, our feet create a new rhythm, energising us both. Maggie links her arm in mine and we become as one, taking up more of the path, so that the tourists have to scoot around us.

'Annie!' Maggie starts laughing. 'That look. I know that look! You are thinking about Don, aren't you?'

'Am I really that obvious?'

'It's the kind of windswept longing thing going on that does it.'

We pass a busker violinist, his music spiralling up off the pavement, over the river. I stop and throw a one-pound coin into the upturned hat. Then we walk on again, the blocky silhouette of the Tate Modern visible. Opposite the Tate is the Millennium Bridge, all leggy and silver.

'Don is married, Annie,' says Maggie as we walk. 'He lied to you and he has acted, well, a bit freakishly.' She squeezes my arm tighter in hers. 'And all this stuff at work? It strikes me as a bit fishy that it all kicks off when he leaves. Do you think he had anything to do with it?'

Could Don? Would Don? In my gut . . . No. I shake my head.

'And there's the fact that he bought your parents' house.'

'Isn't that kind of sweet?' I say hopefully, ducking as a low-flying pigeon flaps past my shoulder.

'It's a bit bloody Freudian, Annie, isn't it? Buying the house of your father? Still, no, let's give him the benefit of the doubt, maybe it's not stalkery. Mind the dog poo. Maybe we shouldn't read that much into it. He was looking for a second home, right? And unwittingly you did a great job selling him your parents' house? Then, my dear, he's just a cynical opportunist.'

'Maybe . . .' Oh, I don't know what rings true now. 'I just really thought we had a connection, that's all.'

'Annie, I remember those connections. They always turn out to be with guys who hold something back, a lack of emotional commitment that is so bloody easy to misinterpret as depth. Yes, he's charming, if you like that kind of thing, and he's colourful, but being colourful is no excuse for being a crap human being. It just papers over the cracks.'

Everything Maggie says makes a horrible clunking sense. And yet . . . 'Argh! Give me some good news, Maggie, or I'll have to throw myself from the upper floors of the Tate Modern.'

'Oh my God!' Maggie stops and looks at me excitedly. 'I do indeed have some good news. Have I not told you? Our Vicky Vick Vicks is in love! I jest not. She has been locked in all weekend with this new stallion. They've barely left each other's side.' She sighs. 'Remember that feeling, when you can't be separated even to go to the toilet? Well, that's what it's like, apparently. True love. And—'

'She's not been picking up crumbly old pervs at the Groucho again, has she?'

'No. He's twenty-seven years old! Look, we're at the Tate already. Isn't this great? I feel like I'm skiving. No work! No kids!' She breaks into a trot, tugging me with her. 'Come on!' she says. 'School's out! We're free.' And we run, laughing, into the Tate Modern's vast sloping entrance, which yawns open like the lower jaw of a giant whale.

Forty-four

Georgia is employed: three words that haven't inhabited the same sentence for two years. She's assistant interior designer of Bello Interiors and her spirits are rising slowly from post-Olly misery like a cupcake cooking in a tin. Even though she doesn't need to be in the Kensal Road office, a short walk away, until ten, she is struggling to get up in time. I wake her when I get up and she is still a blear of freckles and sleep. But she is learning not to spend an hour choosing her outfit. She is learning the advantage of no-brainer black and is starting to eat breakfast, for the first time in her life. She comes back late in the evening, not because she is working late, but because her and Tatiana like to go out for supper at the Electric. She's been phoning me, excitable and tipsy, asking if I'm OK, if I'm lonely, and whether work has sorted 'the misunderstanding' out yet. I tell her that it's fine – which is not true – and that most people know it's a stupid misunderstanding – I really hope this is true – and we're all just waiting for Tina to get back from Cape Town next week and when this happens it'll all be done and dusted and Alexis, hopefully, will be smartly booted out of the role of acting editor.

At nine o'clock I am settling down to a night of solitary telly and pore strips when Olly appears on the doorstep. Drops of rain are splashing from his fringe into his eyes. He looks tired and crumpled.

'She's not here, Olly,' I say, satisfied by the froideur in my own voice.

'I know you want to protect her, Annie, but . . .' He puts a hand out to stop me shutting the door.

'No, seriously. She's not here. She's out on the town.'

'Out on the town?' He looks put out, as if he expected to find her in a darkened bedroom, cutting his name on to her arm with tweezers. 'Oh. Right.' He hovers uncomfortably for a few moments and begins to move away.

I take pity on him, recognising the greyness of his skin, the look in his eyes, the stoop of his shoulders. I recognise them as mine. 'Are you OK, Olly?'

He smiles. 'Yeah, sure. I'm busy at work. Might be moving to Hong Kong . . . Things are . . . yeah, I'm really busy.'

Why do men answer questions about their emotional state with a statement about their career? 'Hong Kong?'

'I wanted to see George. I wanted to tell her,' he says plaintively.

'I've just made some coffee. You better come in.'

He hesitates, then smiles gratefully. 'Thanks. I'd like that.'

Olly sits on my new beige sofa, a little uneasy. He's no future brother-in-law now. He won't be stretching out his legs or pulling a beer from the fridge as he used to. 'Where's Nick?'

'We split up. Do you take sugar? I can't remember.'

Olly looks shocked. 'Really? Fuck. I'm really sorry to hear that, Annie. I never . . .'

'It's OK.' I wave a let's-not-go-there hand and he lets the subject drop.

301

'One sugar, please.'

I hand him his mug of coffee. 'Nice sofa.' He puts his mug on the coffee table. 'Does Georgia talk about me?'

'You big girl.' I laugh.

Olly blushes. 'Yeah, well.'

'She mentions you occasionally.' I shrug. 'She's OK. She's survived being dumped on the eve of her wedding, believe it or not.'

'Right.' He fiddles with the cuffs of his shirt and looks up at me. 'I know I've been a twat.'

'Stronger words come to mind, actually.'

'I was trying to do the right thing.' He drops his head into his hands. 'Oh, I don't know. I'm a mess. I'm exhausted, Annie. I'm exhausted by work, by everything. It's been mental. Non-stop mental. I go to work. I go out in the evenings. I try not to have a nose bleed in a meeting the next day.'

'Well, the rehab worked well then.'

'I was in for depression,' he corrects, sipping his coffee.

'And the coke helps, right?'

Olly shakes his head, looking as shamed as his goliath ego will allow. 'No. It's just the whole culture.'

'Well, get out. Or do you like the dough too much?'

He smiles. 'I like the dough too much. And it's not a bad life,' he says. 'I meet lots of women. You know, lovely young women.' He scratches his head. 'And not so young. In fact I think I met a friend of yours – it was only afterwards that it all started to fall into place and I thought I bet you know her because she knew your mate Maggie, is it Maggie?'

'Who?'

'Vicky. Vicky Vickerson Lawyer? Do you know her?'

'Oh God. Yes! I know Vicky. You were the City date?' I

start to laugh. Olly! The one who couldn't get it up! 'Of course you were. I'm surprised she didn't eat you for breakfast.'

Olly grins. 'She tried. Annie, there have been so many . . .' He manages to stop himself before he starts sounding like a total tosser. 'But they're not George. They're just not Georgia.'

'Well, they wouldn't be, would they? For fuck's sake, Olly. Please don't tell me you've changed your mind? You have, haven't you? Jesus.'

'I miss her, Annie.' He sinks his face into his hands, as if this realisation is a terrible inconvenient truth he just can't get around. 'I can't get excited about anyone else.'

'You can't miss her! She's finally sorted herself out. She's been to hell and back. You can't do it to her. You can't mess her around.'

'I'm not going to mess her around. Please, Annie. Please try to understand. It was the pressure of the wedding . . . I'm not good at the wedding thing. I don't think I am the marrying type.'

'Oh, please.' I stand up, hoping he'll go. I don't want him in the house now, suddenly fearful that Georgia will come home. I'm not sure she has the strength to resist him. The thought of her unravelling again is just too awful.

'I want to start again, Annie.' Olly speaks intensely and quietly. 'I want Georgia back. I want her to come to Hong Kong with me.'

The front door slams. 'Bloody hell, these heels are killing me,' shouts Georgia cheerily from the hall.

Forty-five

My parents' new flat in Hove is a nice place to grow old. It's in an old deco block, not far from the sea. In the living room, a curving grid of windows frame a panoramic sweep of sea, pier and marled grey sky. The window itself opens up to a shallow balcony big enough for two white iron chairs and a small table. My mother has taken to sitting on the balcony in all weathers, sighing happily and gazing. Here she is in her element: most of the neighbours have already dropped round with biscuits and details about where to buy the best bread in Hove. After the increasingly decrepit isolation of Hedgerows, here she feels part of a community and has, in fact, just popped out with the fiftysomething divorcee potter who lives on the floor above to discover a new deli. She's also buying new clothes, figure-hugging, almost glamorous clothes. I don't think I've ever seen her happier. My father, however, is a different story. He sits in his favourite armchair and gazes out of the window at the brown-green sea, stirred by a strong wind, like stewed tea in a cup.

'I'm dying,' Dad says, not sounding entirely displeased about it.

'Is this a new development?'

'There are clues to an imminent demise, Annie.' He rubs his thigh, as if trying to pummel life back into it. 'I've developed aches and pains that I never used to have, in my arms, my legs. I've got this . . . what I can only describe as a ghastly prickle in my left knee, like I've fallen into a patch of killer nettles. My eyesight is off. I can't read the newspaper.'

'You need new glasses, Dad. Or large print.'

'Large print? Never!'

'You're just getting old.'

'Pah!' He stretches out his legs and twirls his feet in the knitted Peruvian slippers that Mum bought from a hippy shop in Brighton which are so not my father but which he's wearing anyway to prevent chilblains. 'Death's waiting around the corner like a dog turd on the pavement.'

I sip my raspberry smoothie, an entirely uncharacteristic contemporary foodstuff that has found its way into my mother's shopping. 'I do believe that we're all going to die, Dad.'

'Let's drink to that. Before your mother gets home.' Dad rubs his beard. 'I'll have a sherry, please. In one of my nice old glasses, not those ridiculous multicoloured things your mother has just bought.'

I rummage through the cupboard. Dad's small old utilitarian glasses are at the back, behind Mum's new purchases. I pour some sherry and tip some peanuts into a bowl and pull up a chair next to Dad. I notice how old he looks, his skin parchment-thin in places, bubbling with hairy lumps and bumps and new colourless moles. What if he is about to die? What if he's right?

Dad takes a noisy swig of his sherry. I smell his alcoholic

exhalation. And I wonder whether I will ever have a daughter who will watch me getting old and drinking sherry and downsizing at the seaside.

'The problem with you always being about to die, Dad, is that nothing I say seems significant enough.'

Dad starts to laugh. 'I've been waiting all my life for sensible significant conversation from you lot. It doesn't happen, Annie. It doesn't happen in a household of females. I've learned to live with it. Maybe it'll happen in the big black beyond.'

I roll my eyes. 'OK. Spill your pearls of wisdom. Go on. Try and say something meaningful.'

Dad's face freezes with concentration. He likes any game that is even vaguely competitive. 'Hmmm. Pearls. Blimey, Annie. Let me think.' He swigs his sherry. 'What have I learned? Not much, actually. Time just runs away from you. A-ha! That's one! Time definitely gets faster as you get older. It's not a myth. One day they'll find out some new rule of the universe that proves my point.'

'Not wholly original, but instructive.'

Dad pulls at his beard. 'Nothing's bloody original, Annie. It's all been said before. You just have to find new ways of saying it.' He stops, and his face lights up. 'There! There you go, another bloody pearl! You see, give me a sherry and I'm like a bleeding guru.'

I laugh, enjoying seeing him like this, engaged and riled. 'More, please, Papa.'

'Oh, I don't know, girl. I don't know.'

'When and where were you happiest?'

'I'm not one of your stupid celebrity interviewees,' Dad says. 'Don't go all journalese on me. But as you ask, well, I was pretty happy the day you were born, same with Georgia, of course, but you were the first. That was special.'

306

This fells me. Eyes welling up, a bit embarrassed, I fix my gaze on the sea. 'Ah,' I say.

'The midwife said, "You can come in now, Arnold." I didn't want to see the business, obviously. And there you were, an ugly little thing, knotted red face, furious fists, a nose that you had to grow into. I thought, here's an ally, a chip off the old block.' He sighs, gazes thoughtfully out of the window. 'I was also really very happy tending to my tomatoes at Hedgerows. Sun beating down on my back, tinny by my side, fingers muddy, the tomatoes plump and red and almost splitting with ripeness.' He shudders. 'I hate to think of those poor plants now. Next?'

'What?' I'm trying to disconnect from a thought route which trails like a row of seeds from tomatoes to Hedgerows to Don.

'Next question. Go on, I'm getting into my stride now.'

'Um . . .'

'I pity your interviewees. Do they take a tea break at this point?'

'Very funny.' Rain starts to patter against the window. The sea is whipping up, foam breaking on the shingle. A crowd of teenagers run screaming and laughing from the beach, holding their bags over their heads, kicking up pebbles and rain as they run. 'What's the most important lesson life's taught you?'

'Gordon Bennett. I'm not sure. I think I know less now than I did at twenty. Life has a lot of grey areas. If anything, that's it. That very few things are totally right or totally wrong. That's pretty boring, isn't it? Sorry.' Then he grins. 'A-ha, yes, wait a minute, I've got a proper one! A warm beer is a wasted beer.'

'I'll have that inscribed on your gravestone, then. Clear as mud, Dad.'

'You get your lucidity from me, then, don't you? What I mean is that there's no point compromising in life, that's what. If you want one thing, don't settle for something else. Because that kills you slowly.' He shakes his head, lost in thought. 'The most important thing in life is to feel alive. Yes, that's it! Scrub that beer line and quote me on that instead.'

The door slams open. 'Arnold!' shouts Mum in a singsong voice, and she comes into the room bright-eyed, carrying something tall and cone-shaped covered in brown paper. 'Are you OK?' She kisses me and drops the package at Dad's Peruvian-slippered feet. 'For the windowsill,' she says, as he begins to carefully tear the paper away. A leaf pops out, another, then another, until the plant is revealed, ruby-red tomatoes hanging from it like baubles on a Christmas tree. Dad's face lights up like a child's.

Forty-six

The waiter sets down eggs Benedict and minces off. I am struck by the overwhelming sense that my London life hasn't changed in ten years. My shoes get better. My thighs get a little bit rounder. But I am still ordering cappuccinos, still sizing up calories and then eating the food anyway. It seems I am still in motion, blown from one relationship to another like a bit of litter down a street. Gosh, it would be nice to have a full stop, an end to speculation, the freedom to put on weight without thinking that it might tip romantic fate one way or the other, the extra few pounds the reason that a potential 'The One' doesn't keep eye contact and slips back into that soup of strangers you'll never meet. I teaspoon the cappuccino's frothy, chocolatey bits into my mouth. 'You were saying?'

'Sorry about all the shit that fell on your head about the TV stuff.' Dave smiles, readjusts his caricature black media glasses. 'Georgia told me.'

'It's OK,' I say, wondering when Georgia and Dave have been speaking. I can't keep up with her at the moment. She's been working on a project with Tatiana – New Best Friend –

in Brittany for the last week, leaving me alone in Kensal Rise. 'It's kind of been one thing after another at the magazine, actually. But I've just about survived it.'

'I can't believe this is the Annie I know,' says David, looking at me intently.

'What do you mean?'

'I can't believe you're being so bloody stoic. I thought you'd go mental. You're quite within your rights to go mental, Annie. I can take it.'

'Well, you're a cheeky media monkey. I should blame you. But it's more complicated than that.' I check my watch, wondering how late I can leave it before I'm definitely late for my morning meeting, part of me rather relishing the idea of being late for one of Alexis's endless, pointless meetings. In fact maybe I won't even bother going at all. I will wait for Tina, who is due back in the office today, finally, after what feels like the world's longest holiday.

'I'll get to the point, Annie. The magazine spoof idea, it's kind of got bigger . . . maybe not a one-off?' David has developed an irritating habit of ending his sentences with a question mark. 'And I was wondering if you'd like to play a part, you know, in a consultancy role?'

'Are you trying to get me fired?'

'Not my business how you play it, Annie.' He laughs, puncturing his bright yellow yolk. 'I'll give you a fancy title if you like.'

'Money?'

'But of course, my dear. Not a huge amount, it being the crappy old tube and all that.' There are crashes outside as the wind whips up, the sky darkens and the awning flaps like a sail outside the café window.

I feel excitement bubbling up inside, an excitement I

haven't felt for months. I chance it. 'Would you let me have a go at writing something?'

Dave looks taken aback. 'You? Well, I guess . . .' He looks thoughtful. 'I guess we could come to some arrangement,' he adds tentatively.

Walking back to the office, wind tunnelling through my ears, my brain whirrs with possibilities. I could resign now. I could work with Dave. I could . . . I could . . .

Come on, Tina. I'm staring at my phone, willing it to ring, willing it to be Tina. I'm desperate to see her after her holiday, to finally lay the eBay nonsense to rest and have the satisfaction of watching Tina boot Alexis off the editor's chair. Enough is enough. I glance over at the editor's office. Alexis has opened her door just wide enough to give the rest of us a seat at the best show in town, starring and directed by herself, of course. She has her shoeless bare feet up on the desk and is throwing her glossy head back, laughing, as if in campy self-parody. Belle is walking towards Alexis's office door, looking even more nervous than usual. Then just as she gets to threshold, for no apparent reason she stops and scampers back to her own desk.

'Belle!' I shout from the features desk. 'I've got some proofs for Alexis. Can you chuck them over to her?'

Belle comes over and puts her hand out to collect the proofs. I notice her eyes are red-rimmed, kind of wounded.

'Hey,' I reach out and touch her on the arm. 'Are you OK, sweetheart?'

Obviously not OK, she nods and sniffs. 'I'm fine, thanks. Just a horrid cold.'

'It's not Alexis?'

Belle says nothing.

'Do you want to go for coffee and talk about it?'

'No, no, I'm fine,' she says unconvincingly before sloping off to her vulnerable little perch outside the dragon's office. There are more comings and goings. Then I spot a very tanned Tina striding through the door. At last!

I leap up from my chair. 'Tina!' I shout.

Tina puts a hand up. 'Not now, Annie. Later.'

Oh. I deflate. I've been waiting for her to get back for so long. And now I can't even get her bloody attention. This does not bode well.

Tina is straight into the editor's office, fast, cross, almost kicking up dust as she walks. A few minutes later the blanket of office hubbub is pierced by a loud jungle squawk. Everyone glances up from their desks to clock the drama. Through the half-open office door we can all see Alexis, standing up now, hands fisted on her desk. Tina is talking to her in hushed tones, leaning against the wall, in control, severely unamused. Belle is called into the office. Then two terrified fashion assistants are called in too. By now everyone knows that something is going down. Work stops. Staff begin to cluster around the colour printer that is stationed close to the action. Trilling phones are left to go straight to voicemail. Alexis flings open the door of her office. 'You bitch, Belle,' she hisses. Then she looks up at the rest of the staff, who are watching her open-mouthed. 'What the fuck are you all staring at?'

Forty-seven

I ring the bell of my parents' flat, once, twice. No one answers. I turn the handle, suspecting they're still in the habit of leaving everything unlocked, and the door opens. I can hear the radio.

'Hullo!'

No answer. The sitting room is cold, empty, and a breeze fingers an open newspaper on the coffee table; the balcony doors are open. And then I see him. Dad is slumped asleep on one of the white wrought-iron chairs on the balcony, his head resting on the table. He is wearing a big Fair Isle jumper. Beneath the chair legs a coffee cup is smashed on the floor, its pool of spilled coffee spread into the shape of a star. The big boozy chump.

'Wake up, Dad!' I say breezily, giving him a nudge. 'The party's over.'

He doesn't wake up.

'Dad! It's Annie,' I shout, poking him harder. 'Dad!'

Still no response. A cold panic sweeps over me.

'Dad! Please! Fucking wake up!' I poke him harder. I put my arms around him and try to make him sit straight. I shake

313

him. But he doesn't wake. I lift his head up. It is so heavy I can barely move it. Oh my God. I touch his neck. He is strangely cool. He does not look or feel like a man asleep. 'Help! Someone help!' I shout, over his head, but there is no one in the street below, or on the balconies either side, and an angry sea wind whips my words away. What do I do? What the fuck can I do? Why did Mum go shopping this morning? Why? Oh God.

Still holding his body in my arms, so that his head is lolling back on my chest, I manage to twist around, dig my hand into my bag and call an ambulance. They ask me if I can move Dad and lay him on the floor in the recovery position. I try but he is too heavy to lift and I don't want him to drop on to the floor. The wait for the ambulance seems to take for ever. 'Come on, come on,' I mutter, my tears blinding me, streaming down my cheeks, soaking on to Dad's jumper. I hear the ambulance before I see it. It's not racing to some anonymous person, somewhere where it doesn't matter, as ambulances usually do. It is coming for Dad. When the para-medics clatter on to the balcony there is a flurry of activity, tubes, machines and pushing. They stick a tube in his mouth attached to a bag that inflates, deflates, inflates, deflates. Come on, Dad! They push down on his chest harder and harder. They keep going. They get a paddle thing and put it on his chest and order me to stand back. Come on. Come on, Dad! You can do it! A few minutes later the activity ceases.

'Why have you stopped?' I shout at one of the paramedics. 'You've got to keep going. Please. Don't stop!'

The paramedic puts a hand on my arm. 'He's gone, love,' he says gently.

Later, in the ambulance, as we head to the hospital, I phone Mum. She doesn't pick up her phone. I leave her a message to call me back. I don't say why I've phoned. I say it's important. When she finally calls back, I am at the hospital. She doesn't react when I tell her. There is a deadly abyss of silence and I can sense her slithering away from me downwards into a deep, dark place. When she gets to the hospital, she is ashen-faced and still carrying her shopping, the ingredients for their supper – mince, garlic, tomatoes, red kidney beans, Tunnock's tea cakes – are visible through the thin white plastic of her carrier bag. She spends some time with his body, alone. When she comes out, I squeeze her hand. She isn't crying yet.

'He would have approved,' I say, voice cracking, tears streaming down my face. 'No hospitalisation. No slow decline.' But inside I am thinking, is there anything I could have done? Could I have saved him? Dad will hate being dead.

Mum smiles weakly at me, her eyes someplace else. After she finishes the paperwork, we look at each other helplessly, unsure what to do next.

'What now?' I ask the nurse, a pretty dark Chinese lady with neat fuchsia-pink fingernails. I know that I will always remember her pink fingernails.

'You can go home,' the nurse says softly.

'Home?' says Mum. It hits her now. 'I can't go home without him.' The tears gush suddenly, powerfully, a flash flood. I put my arms around her and she seems to fall apart, piece by piece. I know that right now I can't put her back together again. As I guide her to a taxi, I'm not sure she's aware of where she is or what's happened. I try to be strong for her, but going home without Dad is the hardest bit – it feels so horribly disloyal, neglectful. The taxi driver turns up the radio so he can't hear Mum sobbing.

*

315

Later that afternoon, Georgia comes out of the kitchen holding a tray full of tea and digestive biscuits. She wraps her
fawn pashmina around Mum's shoulders. I can see that
Georgia is sniffing back her own tears and I am impressed by
the way she is handling it. I feel like I should be taking
charge, that this is what Dad would have wanted and
expected. But I am not sure what to do next. Now we're
home, it's almost anticlimatic. I can't believe he's actually
gone, that he's been permanently erased, that his empty shell
is lying on a gurney in a morgue. His slippers are still beside
his armchair. There's an unwashed-up whisky tumbler by the
sink. It feels like any moment he will walk back in. Neither
Georgia or I want to sit on his chair, because it is his and he
will want it. We squeeze next to Mum on the sofa.

'I must get on with the arrangements,' says Mum, as if
talking about organising Sunday lunch.

'We can do that,' says Georgia firmly. 'Don't worry about
it now.'

'Oh, I know what to do, Arnold made sure of that,' says
Mum, her voice unsteady. 'There's a file in the dresser called
"When I Expire". He wrote it six months ago. I never
thought we'd use it. I thought he'd outlive me, you know, that
his belligerence would keep him going.'

I smile, imagining my father painstakingly working out
funeral costs and details. He always did want to shield Mum
from everything. And he always wanted the last word. But
Georgia finds the idea of the file unbearable. She opens the
glass door of the balcony and a gust of cold, salty air whips
into the apartment. Tears streaming down her face, she stands
on the balcony, gripping the iron railing, gazing out at the
sea. Me and Mum watch her because it takes our focus outwards and there's too much of Dad inside.

316

Mum sleeps in the spare bedroom that first night. She can't face the big empty bed that she shared with my father for over thirty years. Georgia and I can't face it either. I sleep in the armchair, finding the smell of Dad caught in its tobacco-coloured velour comforting. Georgia curls into a foetal position on the sofa. At dawn I awake after a fitful night of sleep pierced with dreams of childhood summers: afternoon light dappling through the apple tree in the back garden at Hedgerows, my dad climbing up on an old painted green stool, picking apples and lobbing them down to Georgia, who is about eight years old and standing there skirt hitched up to create a basket. I rub my eyes. Georgia is awake too, pale and shivery beneath a thin duvet on the sofa. We don't speak. I grab the herringbone blanket from the armchair and snuggle up next to her. In my arms she feels as small and fragile as the child in my dream.

The following days pass in a strange mix of pragmatism and numbness. We pack away the most obvious bits of Dad – his slippers, glasses, coat – into a suitcase, and it feels like I'm sending him off away somewhere for a long holiday. There is lots of paperwork, all held, as my mother said, in a clear plastic file, annotated by Dad: 'Marj darling, I'm more than happy to be cremated in Brighton. You may keep my ashes if you like, but if they start to spook you, I'm quite content with being tossed into the sea, as they can no longer be scattered under the pear tree at Hedgerows. I'd like Annie to do the tossing, as the eldest. Tell her to give it some welly. I don't want to end up on the beach.'

My mother's best friend Hilary from Lower Dalton comes to help and stays in the guesthouse down the road. This takes the pressure off me and George for a bit. Wrapped in scarves and jumpers, we wander to the beach and throw pebbles into the sea. Sometimes it feels like we're in a film and we're struggling to act in an appropriate way. It's really hard to believe Dad's not going to stroll along the promenade with a bag of hot greasy chips. I realise that despite all the preparation – my father's previous heart attack, his warnings, and the inevitability of one's parents eventually dying – I am still totally unready for the fact that my life has changed irreversibly in the space of one cold afternoon. I really need to discuss it all with him.

Georgia's pebble hits the water with a splosh. The sea takes a good noisy suck at the shingle, raking it away from our feet.

'I'm not taking Olly back,' says Georgia suddenly. 'I've decided. I can't go there again. Not now. Not without Dad. It would finish me off.'

'Really?' I thought that Dad's death would be the clincher that sent her back into Olly's arms. I'm not even certain any more that Georgia going back to Olly would be such a bad thing. I worry that I've tried to make her into someone she's not and that she would be happiest living an easy, wealthy life in Hong Kong. I don't know what to think about anything any more. For once, I resist the urge to advise her. She needs to find her own way. We hold hands and stare silently out to sea. A few people passing stare at us, more at my pretty little sister. It strikes me that they might think we're lesbians in love. It feels wrong that my dad is dead and I can still think such flippant thoughts.

'Dad always thought I was a bit stupid, didn't he? Thick and pretty.' Georgia kicks pebbles angrily. 'It's been hard to think of myself as anything else.' She sits down on the cold shingle, hugging her knees to her chest. 'I can't even get married properly.' She starts to laugh, a hysterical weep-laugh hybrid. 'Fuck. I was so nearly there.' Then she suddenly stops laughing. 'Maybe now Dad's dead, we'll reverse. I'll be free to be clever and successful. You can be flighty and find yourself a gloriously rich husband.'

'Unlikely.'

'I wanted a chance to show Dad that I could be independent,' says Georgia suddenly.

It strikes me that she is no longer calling him Daddy, as if his death has reverted her to her roots.

'You are independent. You're working. You're paying rent. Don't be so hard on yourself.'

Georgia looks at me, her eyes brimming with tears. 'You've always looked after me, Annie.'

'I haven't,' I say. It just shoots out. 'Not always.'

'You have.'

'That time . . .' I stop, reluctant to bring it up. We haven't talked about it for many years. The man in the cornfield, the one that jumped out at her with his dick hanging out and nearly managed to pull her off her bike. That hot summer's day on her cycle ride back from school, that hot summer's day when I should have met her to accompany her home but didn't. It suddenly feels incredibly important that I have a chance to say sorry. I realise now that you can't always wait for the right moment. Not everything always has to be right. There isn't time.

'What, Annie? Why do you look all weird?'

'That man in the cornfield . . .'

Georgia flinches. She knows exactly what I am talking about.

'I'm sorry. I should have met you outside the school gates. I let you down. I'm so sorry. I just wanted to say sorry, that's all.'

319

Georgia is silent for a few moments. Then she squeezes my hand. 'You know what I always thought? I've run through it hundreds of times in my head and I always thought, ultimately, that if he had managed to pull me off my bike, it would have been OK, because you were only a few minutes behind me, I just didn't know it at the time. And you would have fought him off.'

'Yeah, of course I would have fought him off,' I say, relieved of a lifetime of guilt in one golden moment.

'But Annie,' says Georgia softly, 'you don't need to fight anyone else off. I'm a big girl now.'

'Hey, you're saying smothering is no longer necessary?'

Georgia laughs. We stand up and walk along the promenade in silence, letting the sea breeze lick the hair from our sad smiling faces.

The funeral is a quiet affair with just close friends and family, held at crematorium on Lewes Road. The chapel has a red carpet and a steep gothic window. At first it feels like a wedding – the hushed pomp, the guests, the flowers – and then I see the coffin, the cold, hard oak box. And I think how Dad never got to attend either of his daughters' weddings. And I think of the possible grandchildren he will never get to know, the Christmases he'll be absent from, the whisky tumblers doomed to gather dust at the back of Mum's shelves, as she replaces them with brightly coloured modern glass. I think how much he'd enjoy being present at his own funeral, witnessing the loud, competitive sobbing of Aunt Bessie, Georgia's hat, which looks like a raven in midflight, the bulbous purple nose of the funeral director. It hits me hard. He isn't coming back. And I miss him so much.

a good girl comes undone

The funeral feels like it lasts five minutes. There are a few words said about a man I don't really recognise – he is sanitised of all the bits I love – the coffin disappears behind red curtains like something from a provincial magician's show, and it's all over. Dad comes home in an urn, reduced to fine gravy granules.

Forty-eight

I could have stretched out my compassionate leave longer, until after the weekend, but I felt strangely compelled to come back, to leave the house, get away from all the stillness and the sadness, if only temporarily. Now, outside the tall stone offices, I hesitate for a few moments on the pavement, looking up, squinting into the sunlight that flashes on the building's numerous vast, blank windows. Walking into reception, swiping through, I am strangely reassured by the people and the bustle, the proof that life goes on regardless, that there is still a place for the right handbag in the grand scheme of things. But the routine familiarity of standing in the lift, pressing the eighth-floor button, brings home to me how different I feel since I was last here, kind of hollowed out, older, wiser, sadder, but less scared somehow. The dramas that have gone down in the office in the last few months shrink to insignificance next to Dad's death. They just don't touch me as they once did. I don't think they ever will again. The lift door opens. As I step across the stained carpet tiles, Lydia rushes over and gives me an enormous hug, crushing my solar plexus against a robust

322

necklace. 'I'm so sorry about your dad,' she says. 'Are you OK?'

'Thanks, Lydia,' I say. 'I'm OK.'

'I've got you a present, something to cheer you up.' And she hands me a package roughly wrapped in black tissue paper.

I unwrap it slowly. Emerging from its crinkly nest is a beautiful pair of black Christian Louboutins, platform-heeled, ankle straps, red-soled. 'Oh. My. God. You can't possibly give me these. They must have cost a fortune!'

Lydia beams at me. 'Sample sale. You're a size six, aren't you?'

'I am!' I say, bending down and prising off my Kurt Geigers and slipping one foot, then the other, into the black heels. 'They are a perfect fit! Stunning!' I hug Lydia tightly, thinking that shoes don't take away the sadness but they still give a shot of something rather nice and life-affirming. 'Thank you, Lydia. Thank you so much!'

'A huge improvement,' she says, studying me, hand on her hip. 'Promise me you'll throw away those clumpy old shoes?'

I smile, glancing down. 'Promise.'

'Listen, I'm sure this must all seem really trivial now, Annie. But do you want a dollop of serious gossip?'

'Of course.' I flex my feet in my lovely new heels, marvelling at how much taller and sexier I feel in them already.

'Take a look around you, hon. Spot the difference.'

I look around the office. 'What?'

'Alexis has gone!'

'For good? I knew that there was something going down, but surely not . . . Tell me!'

'Belle risked life and long limb to report two sightings of Alexis stealing out of the cupboard out of hours with her designer booty, sightings which have been corroborated by my fashion assistants,' says Lydia breathlessly.

'Oh, OK. So that was what all the shouting from the ed's office was about that Friday afternoon?'

'*Exactly*. Then Monday – you weren't here – it all kicked off massively, HR involved, the whole shebang. I got called in too. Turns out that Alexis couldn't understand what the problem was – she was planning to return them, she said, which is bollocks obviously and I said as much. Why didn't she wear the clobber to the office if it was all above board? Thankfully, Tina wasn't interested in Alexis's piss-poor excuses.'

'Fuck.'

'And guess who spread that ridiculous rumour about Georgia's eBay stuff?'

'She admitted to it?'

'Tina told me.'

So it wasn't Don. Thank God it wasn't Don.

Lydia kisses me on the cheek again and claps her hands. The witch is dead!'

I settle down to work (struggling very hard to care about the top ten moisturisers under £20) and soak up the carnival feeling in the office. It is different here, Lydia is right. I slowly notice that everyone is joyfully accessorised and wearing colour – splashes of neon, pink, star-print shirts – and more work seems to be getting done.

After lunch – an emotional, huggy affair with Lydia and Louise at the Oxo – a huge bunch of pink peonies arrives at my desk. The little white notecard reads: *Very sorry. Tina x P.S You're sitting in the wrong chair.*

Wrong chair? I look down at my chair, confused. What's wrong with it?

Belle taps me on the shoulder, smiling. 'Shall I take you through to your office now?'

Clicking into an automaton daze, I pick up my handbag and, teetering on my new black heels, obediently follow Belle, not sure what is going on. As she opens the door to the editor's office, I hear the sound of clapping. I turn around to look back. Lydia is standing up. 'Go, Annie!' she shouts.

'Woo woo woo!' shout the rest of the girls on the fashion desk, then the features desk start clapping too. 'Woo woo woo!'

I blush furiously and laugh and step inside the editor's office. Belle closes the door softly behind her. I take a deep breath.

I am here!

I am where I always wanted to be! I am throned in the editor's high-backed leather chair. There are flowers, fresh antique roses, sitting in a square vase to my left on the enormous glacier-white desk. My email inbox pings continually with congratulations from well-wishers. I can't believe it, not at all, and spend the next hour spinning in my leather chair, feet up, admiring my posh heels, wondering, marvelling at it all. Tina calls me and says that I am holding the fort before the first round of editor interviews commence. She hints that there are some major players applying for the job but that I've got a reasonable chance if I want to throw my hat in the ring. Lydia and Louise are agreed that this is the opportunity of my career and that I must just go for it. They will support me. How lucky am I?

It's 5.30 p.m. now. I've been sitting at this desk, flexing my feet in my heels, all day, waiting for it to sink in. Outside it's already dark. Because it is Friday, people are leaving early, excitable, light-footed for the weekend. Lydia, Louise, Isla,

Pam . . . more and more heads poke around my door to say goodbye and wish me luck, their smiles wide and genuine. I continue to sit at this desk – not my desk, it just doesn't feel like my desk somehow – and stare out of the vast plane of window, feeling shaken, happy, sad, numb all at the same time. This is what I always wanted. This is the end point on the trajectory of Annie Rafferty of Lower Dalton's long journey. This is where rainbows end. I made it.

It just doesn't feel like it.

It begins to dawn slowly but unshakeably: I don't belong here. It feels like the person who did belong here might have died with my father. As this realisation sinks in, I sniff back tears, lean back in the chair and wonder: is this what Dad wanted for me? And it hits me, painfully, that although he would be proud, of course he'd be bloody proud, there would be a part of him that might wish simpler things for his daughter: a future involving a big love, a big nourishing love, bigger than this, bigger than me, like he and Mum had all those years. What did he say again? 'The most important thing in life is to feel alive.' That's what he said. Yes, that was it.

There is a knock on the door.

'Come in, Belle,' I say. Bless Belle, loyal, brave Belle.

'Miss Rafferty,' says Don, striding into my office with an enormous wolfish grin, shutting the door and leaning back, as if to seal it shut.

It feels like the floor has just tilted forty-five degrees and I'm sliding off. I grab the desk for support. Don looks stockier and darker than I remember him, his features sharply cut, his mouth set in that familiar feral smile. There is that old confrontational glint in his eye. He suddenly reminds me of my father. Shit. How could I not have seen this before?

'You got here, then,' he says, striding over to my desk,

pulling up the orange chair and sitting down on it, legs stretched out, claiming my space, nonchalant as ever. He looks down at my feet. 'Nice shoes.'

I smile, speechless, fearing that if I open my mouth I'll start bawling like a baby and clinging to his trouser legs. My body is surging towards him, like filings to a magnet. He is the opposite of death, I think. The complete opposite in all its messy, confusing vitality.

'Feel good?'

'Yes,' I say, wishing my heart wouldn't slam so loudly in my chest, sure that he can hear it.

'You haven't called me,' he says.

'You're married.'

'Are you?' He looks at my hands.

'No!' I hold up my ringless left hand. 'I don't know who told you that. I'm about as far from getting married as it's possible to be.'

'Oh. Alexis said . . .' He stops, looks at me and a smile spreads slowly across his face. 'Right.' He rolls his eyes. 'Bloody Alexis.'

'She warned me off you, you know. At the Christmas party.'

Don laughs. 'Did she indeed? It doesn't surprise me. She's horribly jealous of you.'

'Jealous?' I laugh. 'Why would Alexis be jealous of me?' I sweep my hands along the white desk. 'Apart from the fact that I am sitting in the ed's chair, of course. And she isn't.'

Don shrugs. 'Alexis is the ultimate lost little rich girl, Annie.'

'She's a thief, the fashion cupboard thief, who was happy to let someone else take the blame.'

Don winces. 'Yeah, I heard. What a shame. But, oh, I don't

know. Part of me feels for her. She's a mess. Parents in Dubai. Junkie brother. Bulimic sister. Men who just want to fuck her and leave before she wakes up. I think she saw you as someone with a boyfriend and a nice normal family, someone valued for their brains, their individuality.'

Am I? The idea that I am valued for my brains and my individuality gives me a wonderful warm feeling inside.

'That's all she wanted really,' Don continues. 'That's all anyone wants really, isn't it?'

'I guess.' I feel a real pang for Alexis, and for the first time, I realise that in a strange, perverse way I'll miss her around the office. 'I just thought she was rich, beautiful and connected, and a right royal pain in the backside, to be honest.'

'Well, that as well, of course. Anyway, let's not talk about Alexis.'

The leather of my chair feels hot against my back. I already feel like a different person to the person I was ten minutes ago, before he opened the office door. In Don's presence the world suddenly becomes luminescent, the greys fairground-pink.

'Annie, I know you think that I am a sleazy misogynist halfwit, but I am trying to get my house in order . . .'

'Where's the wife?' I ask quickly.

'With her divorce lawyer, counting the spoils of war.'

'Oh dear,' I say, sounding far calmer than I actually am. 'That sounds expensive.'

'I'm not sure how much I care any more, Annie.' He rubs his eyes, as if the subject just tires him. 'We've both got enough. She's got our old place in Tribeca. But I've got my flat in Bermondsey and she can't get her hands on Hedgerows.'

'Shit, I'd never thought of that!' I lean forward on my

chair, alarmed. The thought of . . . God, it's too horrific. 'You sure?'

'Sure.' Don looks down at the desk, sheepish. 'Sorry about . . . about . . . buying your Hedgerows.' The words tumble out of his mouth clumsily. I guess he's not a man who says sorry very often. 'Sorry if it freaked you out. It's since been pointed out to me by exasperated friends that such an act makes me look like, well, a total bunny-boiler.'

'Yup!' I grin. I can't stop grinning.

'It's just me being my stupid, impulsive, romantic self, nothing more sinister. I hope you know that.'

'It's OK.' Suddenly it is OK. Suddenly I don't mind stupid, impulsive, romantic. And I realise that Don is the first man I've ever met who makes me feel these things too.

'I've got a few days off. I'm going down to the country next week,' he says. 'And . . .'

The country? Hedgerows. I see it clearly, brilliantly, its warped roof tiles against a perfect blue Cotswold sky, the curl of the pink hollyhocks on the stone garden wall, wet ivy leaves like hearts, stuck to the window pane . . . It is all too much. I am overwhelmed by tears, which I sniff back noisily.

'Hey, darling. Sorry. You OK?'

I shake my head, eyes filling. 'My dad died.'

Don stands up and I'm tight in his arms. He is stroking my hair and saying, 'Baby.' And the tears start to fall, hot and wet against his neck, sticking my cheek to his skin. I can't make them stop. He holds me bandage-tight. I don't want to let him go. He is holding the back of my neck now, firmly, his fingers pressed into the base of my skull. And it feels like the most natural thing in the world for me to turn my head and for my lips to meet his. I am clinging to him passionately, hitching my skirt up, undoing his trousers. We are leaning against the vast window, my legs trembling on my new heels. He is behind me. I am facing forward, hands pressed against the window like Spiderman suckers, framed by blue sky, the London Eye shaking as I stare at it, then I close my eyes, blocking it all out. I am no longer aware where I am, what I am doing. It is all heat, light, a burn of joy. When it is over, I lean forward towards the window and I start to laugh, a free-flowing river of laughter, as if a damn has burst. I open my eyes slowly and only then do I see that there is a huddle of people staring up at us from the pavement eight floors below.

Forty-nine

When I surface from a rioja-induced coma the next morning, everything feels OK at first. Then it doesn't. It comes back to me in thuds. Thud, thud, thud, like I'm falling down the stairs. The first realisation is that Dad, my wonderful, cantankerous dad, is dead. The second is that I fucked Don in the editor's office. The third is that a crowd appeared to be watching.

Who saw us? What did they see? I know two things with terrible certainty. First, that anyone outside the building is likely to be an employee, probably a smoker, for that's where they huddle. And it only takes one person and the gossip will spread like a virulent flu throughout the building within minutes. It is surely the best gossip to have hit the office for years, easily trumping the exposure of Alexis as a kleptomaniac. Second, looking up from below, they are likely to have seen everything. Oh. My. God.

I force myself out of bed, wincing at my fretful reflection in the mirror, and pull open the curtains. It is snowing. Large, soft flakes drift down. When they meet the warm air from the extractor fan beside my window, they dissolve mid-flight.

The roofs are powdered tissue-white. London is muted, dreamlike.

'Isn't it lovely?' says Georgia, peeking into my bedroom. 'Fancy a bit of breakfast? Then I thought we should head over to Maggie's. It's pretty late. Lunch at Maggie's, remember? The last big lunch before they hightail to the country.'

'Yes, shit, Maggie's. I almost forgot.' I have no idea how I will operate on a social level today.

I play with a bowl of Cheerios, watching Mum tidy up the kitchen. Considering it's only been two weeks since my father died, she is doing reasonably well. She's been staying with us since it happened, but I'm getting the feeling that she's ready to go back to Brighton now. Me and George protest and tell her to relax and sit down. She doesn't. 'Annie,' she says, smiling, as she dries up the mugs and stacks them so all their handles line up. 'What on earth has happened to your standards?'

'My standards?' I blush instantly. How does she know?

'You used to be the tidiest, most orderly girl in the world.'

I sigh, relieved. For a moment there . . .

Georgia starts to laugh. 'Anal is the word, Mum.'

I flick Georgia with a tea towel. 'Shut up, George. You sloven.'

'I mean, look at all this,' says Mum, opening the cupboard door. 'Bowls on top of plates. Opened packets of pasta in the tins cupboard.' She looks at Georgia faux-sternly. 'Have you been enraging your sister, Georgia? Have you been messing up Annie's household?'

'Yes,' I tease. 'Georgia's dragged me down to her disgusting reprobate level.'

'Rubbish!' squeals Georgia. 'Admit it, you're as bad as me now.'

'Never!'

'Admit it!'

'Oh . . .' I start to laugh. 'Maybe just a little bit. It doesn't seem that important any more,' I say, realising as I say it that there is a certain liberation in letting things hang a little looser. Is the world really going to end because I haven't lined up the tins of chickpeas in the cupboard according to their descending sell-by dates?

The door to Maggie's detached thirties house in Brondesbury is wide open, and children race in and out screaming with laughter. Maggie does good weekend lunches. They usually involve a random selection of people – she never knows who is going to turn up until they do – and their broods of children, and copious amounts of alcohol. Georgia thinks it will be just the thing to take our minds off things. If only. I need to pretend it never happened. I need to savour the time between now and Monday morning while my life retains some of its old order. Disaster awaits. Still, I do not understand why I don't feel more wretched about the whole episode. Most peculiar. I guess I'm in denial.

We walk into a wall of chatter at Maggie's. About twenty people in various states of Saturday disrepair are eating and drinking and flirting. Food is piled in a haphazard heap on the dining table: pasta, olives, bread, pizza, cold sausages, nuts and big bowls of green leafy salad. Gangs of children slyly swipe bowls of crisps off the table and squirrel them to the treehouse, then start racing back and forth with handfuls of cocktail sausages. Half-drunk glasses of wine litter horizontal surfaces as guests lose track of which glass is theirs and grab and fill another. There are some faces I do recognise and many I do not. But I do recognise Danielle Brown: the neighbour who ran off with her male au pair is back with her husband and lurking in the shadows, nibbling nervously on a cocktail sausage. I identify Vicky by her glossy mound of hair, because her face is permanently stuck to that of her handsome blond twentysomething boyfriend.

'Get a room!' someone shouts.

Mum looks bemused by the lunch party at first but quickly finds her stride. Unusually for her, she doesn't protest when Jake fills up her glass, once, twice. Jake, I notice, is on form, buoyed by a new dad column he's managed to secure in a free London paper, and frequently and endearingly planting kisses behind Maggie's ear.

I am not functioning terribly well as a social animal. I try to make conversation but the words fall out fuzzy and wrong. Drinking isn't blocking anything out either. I did what I did stone-cold sober, so it's etched in my brain in excruciating, delicious detail. I can't sit still. I can't be still. I need to talk to someone. But obviously not just anyone, it being a bit of a conversation-killer, especially if it follows 'My father died.' I am desperate to tell Maggie. But Maggie is being hostess and bombarded with people who want to know how much houses in the country cost and what the schools are like. I can't grab even the smallest private moment.

I perch on a tall breakfast stool next to an enormous bowl of nachos and start to eat, thoughtlessly devouring nacho after nacho, my fingers returning again and again for the salt and the crackle. Dave arrives. He kisses me, Maggie and Mum and then almost runs straight to Georgia, who is chatting with a boxy-faced man in a corduroy suit in the corner of the kitchen. Her face lights up when she sees Dave. The boxy-faced man quickly realises he's surplus to requirements and makes his excuses. I watch them, Georgia's hand touching

Dave's arm, her delighted smile. Interestingly, it's not the flirting I used to witness round Olly, which was, at times, painful to watch, self-conscious, needy and a little false, as if Georgia were flirting for the camera. And endearingly, in her company Dave's cockiness is replaced by something rather more gallant. He attends to her like an assistant, bringing her fizzy water, wine and a selection of food on a white china plate. When they step out into the garden to admire the long lawn and the enormous willow tree, he spreads his jacket over her shoulders.

Mum sidles up to me as I watch them.

'Are you thinking what I'm thinking?' I ask her.

Mum smiles. 'He's a nice boy.' She gazes wistfully at the garden, smiling at the whooping children.

'Are you OK, Mum?' I squeeze her hand. It is cold. It has been cold ever since Dad died, as if his death has caused her basal body temperature to plummet.

She sighs, not unhappily. 'It's funny the things you miss about someone, love,' she says. 'I was just thinking how your dad would have had something to say about those children running so wild and free with those sausages. He'd say it was bloody bad manners, wouldn't he?'

'And you'd tell him he was Victorian.'

'And he'd roll his eyes and look for a drink,' laughs Mum. 'He was always looking for a drink.' She picks up a nacho, nibbling its edges as if it were a cucumber sandwich. 'He wasn't like other men, your father. Your grandfather thought he was trouble, you know, at first. It took years to win him round.'

I laugh. How Dad Won Over Your Grandad: this is part of our family's folklore, one of those stories that reappears every couple of years, makes the Raffertys what they are. Or were.

'Grandad wanted you to marry Derek the clerk,' I say, filling in the blanks.

'He did. God, Derek was a bore.' Mum shakes her head. 'I wanted your dad, I'm afraid, always.'

'He didn't turn out so bad after all, did he?'

'No. He didn't turn out bad. Far from it, love.' She shivers, rubs her arms. 'Annie, would it be terribly old-fashioned of me to ask for a small cup of tea?'

I make Mum tea and, feeling very protective, stick close beside her for the rest of the lunch. At about four o'clock we start saying our goodbyes. Jake hugs us both warmly. Maggie parcels up gooey chocolate cake – made by Jake – in paper napkins for us to take home. As she hands it over to me, she pulls me aside and whispers, 'I keep trying to talk to you, but you know how it is, all these people. Anyhow, the thing is, I bumped into an old friend, Holly Hastings, at a party in Crouch End last night. She was the friend who introduced me to Don all those years ago, and she still knows him. So, obviously, I did some digging.'

'Go on!' I say, practically hopping from leg to leg. 'What?'

'She said that yes, Don was married, to an advertising executive, beautiful, rather fearsome according to Holly, and that it was over within months. They were terribly badly suited, apparently. All his friends are desperately hoping he'll meet a nice English girl.'

I feel myself lighten, weightless, everything locked in my throat.

'Oh yes, and she *swears* he's lovely and not a psycho by the way, just mildly eccentric and a bit full of himself at times.' She winces apologetically. 'Maybe I've been a bit hard on him?'

I smile stupidly and clutch the chocolate cake so hard it

oozes out of my fingers. Mum looks at me, puzzled. I don't have a chance to relay this gossip to Georgia because Georgia is preoccupied. She wants to stay – just a little bit longer – with Dave. She doesn't return until seven that night, looking happier than she has in ages.

Don calls three times over the weekend. I don't return the calls because I don't know what to say yet. He doesn't leave messages. I guess he doesn't know what to say yet either. On Monday morning I slowly, reluctantly, swipe in to the building and stride as fast as I can across the office, feeling eyes burning holes into my black tailored jacket – I'm wearing very serious cover-up clothes today. I feel even a heel would damn me. The walk from door to desk must take thirty seconds, but it feels like it takes years.

Belle bows her head and grins when I say hello. She cannot meet my eyes. And I know that she knows. And if she knows, everyone knows. I half expect to find the editor's office door locked. It is not. I close it behind me and lean against it with a heave of relief. I look around. There is no immediate sign that anything happened in here. No comedy knickers strewn about or furniture on its side. But to my horror, I can see that there are two greasy hand-shaped patches on the window. Fuck. It happened. As soon as I sit down, the phone rings. My company is requested in the publisher's office.

I take the lift up to the fifteenth floor, where the carpet is blue and the fittings are brass and piped musak drips from speakers in the corridor's ceilings. Part of me shuts down in order to cope with what is about to happen. I walk the long dark corridor that leads to Tina's office. It's the walk of shame. But with every small step it begins to feel more and more like the walk to freedom too.

Tina sits at her long mahogany desk, fists clenched like clubs in front of her. Her tanned face is contorted with a strange mix of embarrassment and fury. I cannot meet her eye. 'There are rumours, Annie,' Tina says slowly, delivering every word with needle-sharp precision. She doesn't ask me to sit down.

'Rumours?' I shut my eyes, willing myself out of the office, imagining I am a starling, dropping off the windowledge, plunging downwards, wind skating across my wings.

'Your name has been mentioned. The man has not been identified . . .' She coughs, and it strikes me that she'd probably rather be anyplace else but here, just like me. Then she looks at me sharply, as if she knows exactly who 'the man' is. 'We can take some refuge in that.'

'I'm sorry, Tina. I am so very sorry for any embarrassment I've brought to this company.'

She puts her head in her hands. 'So it's true?'

'It's true.'

'Fuck.' Tina stands up, shaking her head. 'What the fuck were you thinking, Annie?'

I wince. Nothing I can say should be said at this point. I wasn't thinking at all.

'It's so out of character! I can't fucking believe it.' She walks across the office, then back again. Her anger seems to dissipate quickly, hissing out of her like air from a balloon, far faster than I expected. 'I don't know why I am saying this, but . . .' She looks at me intensely, as if a million thoughts are whizzing behind her eyes, judgements made, solutions grasped, blink-fast. 'I lost my mum a few years back, Annie.' She pauses. 'It caused a kind of temporary insanity in me too.'

It's hard to know how to respond. Was it an act of insanity? It was certainly an act of foolhardy passion. Yes, it was

338

probably the stupidest, most passionate thing I've ever done. I never knew I could behave like that.

'Listen, I hope I won't regret saying this,' she says cautiously, 'but if you want to ride this one out, deny everything, well, I'll support you. We'll just have to find a way of fudging it.' She pauses, staring at me for a moment. 'Pippa clipped your wings. I'd like to see you reach your potential.'

'Sorry?' I wasn't expecting that. I stand rooted to the spot for a few moments.

'I'm offering you another chance.'

Think about this. Think. Think. And I do think fast, blink-fast. And suddenly everything makes sense. 'Thank you, Tina.' I know what I have to do. 'Thank you so much. But . . . I want to resign.'

Tina's mouth drops open. 'It's such a fucking waste, Annie,' she says eventually.

And it is a waste, I know this rationally. But I am not, I realise with some surprise, poleaxed with regret. I wonder if this is because Dad dying has given me some strange kind of emotional armour, or because I no longer care as much as I did. At least, for a few minutes, I got to feel total aliveness. I never knew I could feel like that.

'You'll go on to good things, I'm sure. Different things,' says Tina brisk now, offering a firm handshake. 'Stay in touch, Annie.'

Good things. Different things. As I walk slowly out of Tina's office, along the blue-carpeted corridor for the last time, I think of all my notebooks, all my sketched ideas for books and screenplays and freelance features, all those things I thought I'd do when I was sixty-five. Well, I will do them now! I am exhilarated and hungry for the future for the first time in a very, very long time.

Back at my desk, excitable – 'Is it true?' – emails shower into my inbox. My phone starts to ring. Lydia's voice shrieks out of my answerphone, ordering me to phone her back and 'Tell me what you've done, you hussy!' I have left by lunchtime. I take with me only my diary, my spare heels and a few issues of *Glo* that I am particularly proud of. I tidy the editor's desk, realising it never felt rightfully mine. I rub the hand marks off the window carefully with a white tissue and delete all my more personal files from the computer. I don't tell the rest of the staff I am not just popping out for a sandwich but popping out and not coming back. I don't want fuss. I will write to the ones that matter to me later. I will also write to Alexis, poor Alexis, who, I now realise, possibly did deserve, in her own fucked-up kind of way, to be in this editor's office, deserved it more than me anyway. It's strange leaving without the usual rituals – the goodbye cake, the card signed by everyone in the office, the present, and the magazine cover customised by the art desk with a photograph of the leaving lady. No, I get none of this. It's just me, undone, ruined but strangely relieved, my stomach unknotting as I head through the wet London streets towards home.

As I walk along the South Bank I hear my phone beeping. I rummage in my pillow-sized apple-green handbag. It is a text from Don. My heart slams.

Am @ Hedgerows call me on landline.

I realise that the landline is my parents' old telephone number, which is very weird. There is a sudden rushing sound, the sound of hail. I look up, mouth open. As each hailstone hits, it wakes something deep inside. It's like showering under frozen peas. Newly energised, I jump on a bus and sit at the top as the hail pings against the windows and rattles its metal roof. I watch as Londoners scuttle into shop doorways, mouths open, the hail rousing them from the sludge of the working week. I draw smiley faces in the condensation on the window, enjoying, like a child, the tip of my finger getting cold and wet as a dog's nose.

Tina's words go round and round my head: 'out of character'.

Am I out of character? Have I become someone else? The odd thing is that I feel more like myself than ever. I have fallen as far as it is possible for me to fall. I've landed with a bump. I am jobless, bereaved, and shamed. But I feel that part of me has been unleashed. There's nothing left to prove. I am free.

When I get back home to Kensal Rise, for once I know with absolute certainty what I want to do next. I pick up Dad's urn from the mantelpiece. 'Let's get you home,' I whisper. I wrap the urn in a white towel and put it in the boot of the car, carefully nestled in an old tartan picnic blanket. I put my favourite pen and a blank notebook in my handbag, so that it is there, ready to soak up the storm of ideas I can already feel stirring in my head, the ideas that will be the bedrock of a new kind of career, self-sufficient, free, boss-less. Before I leave, I apply some make-up, a little bit of foundation and a streak of pretty pink lipstick. It is the first time I've worn lipstick since Dad died. I rummage around the bottom of my wardrobe and dig out the fondant-pink jacket, stick on a red corsage, and wrap my leopard-print scarf around my neck.

I turn the key in the ignition and begin to drive, feeling brave and pioneering. The traffic is terrible. The hail has left a deadly slimy slush on the roads. The hail gives way to snow. Big thick drifts of snow bulge at the sides of the A roads like

341

piped cream. It begins to collect around my windscreen wipers. Will Dad freeze in the boot? He'd be really pissed off if I let him freeze in the boot.

Eventually, after three hours, I am there, like a homing pigeon. The house is as I remember it, the ivy draping out like a skirt, the painted door peeling, the front garden overgrown. It hasn't been repainted or spruced up as I feared. There is a safe warm glow at the windows. The path to the door looks like unmarked white carpet. Improbably, at the edges of the path, I can just see the heads of Dad's spring bulbs, yellow and red balls of premature colour breaking through the virgin snow. I leave the urn inside the car for the time being and walk up the path slowly, my feet squeaking on the ice crystals, leaving a trail of unfaltering footprints. On the front step I brush against the overhanging ivy and a shower of snow falls on my hot cheeks, instantly melting. I take a deep breath and ring the bell.